> *"I love you. I want you.
> I'm waiting for your answer."*

Only he wasn't waiting. Now that Donal had her alone, her perplexed, shocked face turned up to his in the starlight, his arms went around her and his mouth came down over hers in a kiss that threatened to make Cordelia's body explode.

She'd had no idea, she'd never dreamed that a kiss could be like this. It was as if heaven's gates had opened and let her pass through. Or were they the gates to that other place, enticing her into the depth of the inferno? The devil is a tricky one, nearly every sermon she had ever heard had assured her of that. But if this were the gateway to Hades, how could anyone in the world resist stepping through?

Books by
Lydia Lancaster

Desire and Dreams of Glory
Love's Hidden Glory
Passion and Proud Hearts
Stolen Rapture
The Temptation
To Those Who Dare
Heaven's Horizon

Published by
WARNER BOOKS

ATTENTION: SCHOOLS AND CORPORATIONS

WARNER books are available at quantity discounts with bulk purchase for educational, business, or sales promotional use. For information, please write to: SPECIAL SALES DEPARTMENT, WARNER BOOKS, 666 FIFTH AVENUE, NEW YORK, N.Y. 10103.

**ARE THERE WARNER BOOKS
YOU WANT BUT CANNOT FIND IN YOUR LOCAL STORES?**

You can get any WARNER BOOKS title in print. Simply send title and retail price, plus 50¢ per order and 20¢ per copy to cover mailing and handling costs for each book desired. New York State and California residents add applicable sales tax. Enclose check or money order only, no cash please, to: WARNER BOOKS, P.O. BOX 690, NEW YORK, N.Y. 10019

Heaven's Horizon

Lydia Lancaster

WARNER BOOKS

A Warner Communications Company

WARNER BOOKS EDITION

Copyright © 1983 by Lydia Lancaster
All rights reserved.

Cover art by Dennis Luzak

Warner Books, Inc.,
666 Fifth Avenue,
New York, N.Y. 10103

 A Warner Communications Company

Printed in the United States of America

First Warner Printing: June, 1983

10 9 8 7 6 5 4 3 2 1

Heaven's Horizon

Chapter One

The March wind ballooned Cordelia's skirts as she walked along the quiet Boston street, and the nip in the air brought color to her cheeks and made her eyes smart. Altogether, it wasn't the most salubrious of days for a constitutional, but she'd felt stifled in the Reynards' house, and the way Nadine had been primping and fussing, in preparation for Mr. Donal MacKenzie's impending visit, had made her feel as though the walls were suffocating her.

It wasn't that she didn't love Nadine. In all the four years Cordelia had spent at Miss Virginia Baker's Academy for Young Ladies, hundreds of miles from her Georgia home, Nadine had been her dearest friend. Nadine had taken the bewildered and heartbroken girl who had so recently lost her mother under her wing; her affection had alleviated the aching in Cordelia's heart. And all through those four years, broken only by one month-long visit a year to her plantation home, the Reynards had taken the orphaned girl into their hearts, welcoming her into their family as a second daughter.

It was hard for Cordelia to think what she would have done without Nadine and her parents. Without their friendship she would have been so miserable that it didn't bear thinking about. Boston, and Massachusetts, were alien country to the southern girl who had barely passed her fourteenth birthday when her father had packed her off without as much as a smile or a good-bye kiss. Aunt Zoe, the house slave who had been her mother's nurse from childhood, and later her beloved personal maid, had been allowed to accompany her on the packet, both of them watched over by a business acquaintance of Cordelia's father who had also been making the journey, but Aunt Zoe had not been allowed to stay in Boston with her.

Cordelia's pace was brisk, and the stinging in her eyes wasn't entirely due to the wind. So soon now, only a few more weeks, her school days would be over and she would have to return to Leyland's Landing, and she didn't think that she could bear it. To be forever separated from Nadine and the Reynards, to leave behind the Boston she had grown to think of as her real home, filled her with dread.

There was nothing for her at Leyland's Landing. She'd had no close friends even during her mother's lifetime, before she had been sent away. Andrew Leyland was not a man who encouraged friendships, and of all the nearby plantations, Leyland's Landing was the only one that never entertained and that almost never accepted invitations. A law unto himself, Andrew was an unbending, stern man, showing affection neither for his wife nor for his daughter. Why Cordelia's mother, Lorelei, had loved him, why she'd continued to accept living in what amounted to virtual exile from society, was something that Cordelia had never been able to understand.

If she had had brothers or sisters, Cordelia's life might have been different, free of the aching loneliness that only her mother and Zoe had made bearable. Sweet and gentle, Lorelei had loved Cordelia with her whole heart and contrived to keep her amused and happy even in the shadow of her husband. And Cordelia had tried to understand that her father hadn't always been so unbending, so cold, that the tragedy of his crippling when he'd been a young man had embittered him and that the almost constant pain from his twisted and shattered hip made his lack of human kindness excusable.

Crippled and bitter as he was, Cordelia could see that her father had been a handsome man in his younger years. His black hair still showed only a trace of gray, his body, except for the twisted hip that made him lurch when he walked, still hinted at the litheness that had once been his, and his brooding eyes under his raven brows must have set female hearts fluttering. Certainly her mother had loved him then, loved him so much that her love had endured even through all the dark and comfortless years that had followed.

Cordelia didn't know what had crippled her father. The accident had happened before she was born, before Lorelei had married him and come with him from Virginia to carve out a new home in what had then been still a virtual wilderness. Her mother had told her that it was something that was never to be talked about, and impressed on her that she must never, under any circumstances, ask her father about it. Aunt Zoe knew, but she wouldn't talk about it either. Whatever it was, it must have been so dreadful that the very mention of it would bring the sky crashing down around their heads.

How can I bear it, to go back to Leyland's Landing, back to Father, Cordelia thought. Her pace quickened, and her dark eyes, her heritage from Andrew Leyland as was the dark hair that framed her oval face, were filled with grief. Her summer visits to Georgia had been like deserts between oases, something to be struggled through until she could reach the sweet living waters of life again. Her father hadn't changed, and Cordelia had no illusions that he would ever change. Her only escape, now that her schooling was drawing to a close, would be through marriage.

The word *marriage* made her wince. It wasn't she who was to be married, but Nadine. Nadine, who already had everything, who would make the transition from happy, carefree schoolgirl to blissfully happy young wife as effortlessly as breathing. Donal MacKenzie! Although Cordelia had never seen Mr. Donal MacKenzie, Nadine's descriptions of him were so vivid that she felt that she'd recognize him if she were to meet him in passing on any street.

Tall, Nadine had told her. And with lightish brown hair that had a tendency to curl around his collar, with eyes so hazel that sometimes they were brown and sometimes they were green, depending on his mood and the light. And a smile that could melt your heart, although he was inclined to be formal and even stubborn, but Nadine had no qualms about that because Nadine could make a marble statue laugh with her teasing and cajoling, with her supreme confidence that every good thing in life would come her way as a matter of course, ordained by fate.

Nadine had met Donal MacKenzie last summer, when the Reynards had gone to England. While Nadine had been enjoying London society, Cordelia had been in Georgia at Leyland's Landing, with nothing to do, nothing to break the monotony, except needlework and reading and reminiscing with Aunt Zoe about her mother. There had been no invitations, no parties, only one endless day after another, culminated by a silent evening meal with her father, so far away from each other at opposite ends of the table that conversation would have been impossible even if they had had anything to say to each other. And when her visit had come to an end, she had had to stay at the academy after her return to Boston, with only Miss Baker and the two other ladies who assisted her, until the Reynards had returned.

Cordelia wouldn't say, even to herself, that she hated her father. Her mother had loved him, and she was loyal to her mother. But all the same, Andrew Leyland had killed Lorelei, killed her because of his driving desire for a son.

Cordelia had been a full-term baby, healthy, perfect in every way. There had been only one trouble. She was a girl, not the boy that Andrew wanted.

She couldn't remember her mother's first miscarriage, the birth that had taken place four months before term. It had been a boy, stillborn. She'd been only two then.

But she remembered the second stillbirth, again months premature, again a boy who had never drawn a breath of life. And she remembered the third. She'd been nine years old the third time, and she'd eluded the maid who was supposed to keep her out of earshot. In the hallway near her mother's room, she had cowered, terrified and bewildered by the moans of agony. That one had also been a boy, born three months too soon, born dead like the other two, and Andrew Leyland had retreated still further inside himself and treated his heartbroken, suffering wife with such correct and formal courtesy that he might better have beaten her.

The last stillbirth had been only a few days before Cordelia's fourteenth birthday, and she had been old enough by then to have overheard the house slaves whispering among themselves that the doctor had warned Andrew that another pregnancy might kill his wife.

Lorelei had found Cordelia weeping, and told her that she loved Andrew and wanted him to have a son, that such matters were in the hands of God and that they must have faith that everything would be all right.

"Ain't all right," Aunt Zoe had muttered. "Somethin's wrong, ain't no way Miss Lorelei's ever goin' have another live baby. I seen it before, one live baby, one good, perfect baby, an' then all the others stillborn afore their time. Ain't no amount of tryin' goin' get Miss Lorelei and Master Andrew a live baby, an' he'd ought to know it by now and leave Miss Lorelei alone afore he kills her!"

Lorelei had died in this last attempt to give her husband the only thing he wanted from her.

Wild with grief, Cordelia had raced down the stairs to where her father was closeted in his study, a glass of brandy in his hand, staring at nothing as he digested this last bitter knowledge that he would never have the son he wanted.

"You killed her!" Cordelia screamed, barely pausing in the doorway before she was across the room, pounding and pummeling her father with her fists, raking his face with her fingernails while her voice rose in demented fury. "You killed my mother! Damn you, damn you to hell, I hate you, I'll hate you as long as I live!"

Aunt Zoe had rushed into the room, breathless and quaking with terror, just as Andrew had pinned Cordelia's arms behind her. He thrust his daughter at the old slave with the terse command, "Remove her, and keep her confined until she's come to herself."

Weeping, sick from shock and grief, Cordelia lay in her bed while Aunt Zoe, her own face streaming tears, tried to comfort her, only to be rebuffed.

Lorelei had died in the late summer. The weather had been hot and humid, muggy and enervating. Because of the season, the funeral had taken place as soon as it could be decently arranged. The closed casket, holding both Lorelei and the boychild who had never lived at all, had been covered with roses, their drooping petals sending a suffocating miasma throughout the parlor. Cordelia had stood rigid beside it, unable to cry, unable to respond to the kind glances and murmurs of consolation from the neighbors who, many for the first time, had come to Leyland's Landing as a gesture of the respect that death deserves.

Among those who had come in spite of the fact that Andrew Leyland was no friend of theirs, only those who stood closest to the open grave as the casket was lowered into the ground heard Cordelia speak for the first time.

"At least I made him bleed, Mama. I made his face bleed!"

And then she had fainted, crumpling into the arms of the man who was standing nearest her.

Six weeks later, Cordelia had been sent to Boston, to Miss Virginia Baker's Academy for Young Ladies. She had scarcely seen her father during the weeks before her departure. Andrew had spent all of his daylight hours inspecting the work in the fields, or behind the closed door of his study. The few times when Cordelia had chanced to pass him in one of the downstairs rooms or hallways, they had ignored each other, Andrew's face expressionless as he had stood aside, Cordelia's contorted as she ran up the stairs to her room, trembling with nausea, to throw herself on her bed in still another paroxysm of grief and hate.

"Ain't goin' do no good to take on like this," Aunt Zoe had told her. "You gotta start livin' again sometime, and your mama wouldn't like the way you're carryin' on. You can at least be polite to your papa. I ain't tellin' you you gotta love him, but you kin be polite like a lady should."

"Polite," Cordelia said witheringly. "He was always polite to Mama, but he killed her anyway."

"She wanted to try again. It was what she wanted. It was God's will that she died."

Heaven's Horizon

"But God couldn't have done it if Papa hadn't cooperated!" Cordelia had stormed, her face set and her eyes hard and hot.

Boston, however, had been a blessing. It had taken time, and untold tears and despair, but Cordelia had adjusted to her new life, a life so different from her old life under her father's shadow that she couldn't have failed to respond to it.

In Boston, there had been no dearth of parties and social gatherings and beaus, even though Miss Virginia Baker's Academy for Young Ladies was administered as strictly as most such institutions were in these days of the mid-1820s. Miss Baker had granted Cordelia permission to visit Nadine's home as often as the Reynards had been willing to have her, and that had been virtually every weekend and sometimes even overnight visits during the school week. There had been hayrides in the autumn, ice skating parties in the winter, excursions into the countryside in the spring and picnics in the summer.

At fourteen, Cordelia had been introduced to hide-and-seek and tag by Nadine's four younger brothers, the first time she had ever romped and played with other children. Nadine seldom allowed herself to be coaxed into joining in the games. A Dresden doll dimples and preens and keeps her skirts clean, she doesn't run and jump with little boys. But for Cordelia, such romping was a revelation, something she had been starved for all her life.

The Reynards were a moderately wealthy and very social family, and Lucy Reynard, with her fair hair and blue eyes, was one of the most popular hostesses in Boston. Nadine took after her mother. The boys were dark like their father, and filled with devilry, aided and abetted by Lucy and regarded with sometimes exasperated but always tolerant amusement by their father, who after all these years could hardly believe his good fortune in winning his wife away from scores of other suitors.

Cordelia and Nadine were perfect foils for each other. Delighted at having another "daughter" to supplement her one girl, Lucy took as many pains in overseeing Cordelia's wardrobe as she did Nadine's. Andrew Leyland provided Cordelia with generous pocket money and an even more generous clothing allowance, and Lucy made the best of it, dressing each girl with a genius for playing up her own coloring and personality.

Nadine was tiny, delicate, breathtakingly beautiful, her disposition sunny. Cordelia was taller, her legs longer, her face oval rather than heart-shaped, her eyes dark brown. Where Nadine bubbled, Cordelia smiled, her eyes warm with friendship or amusement or compassion as the occasion demanded. Nadine was quick to anger, and got over her anger as soon as she got her own way. Cordelia's anger, seldom aroused, lasted longer although she showed no outward signs of it, but worked with dogged determination to set right whatever it was that had offended her sense of fairness or justice.

These last four years had been the happiest of Cordelia's life. And now, walking faster than ever to keep up with her roiling thoughts, she couldn't help but wonder if they would be the only happy years she would ever know. A few more weeks, and they would be over. She didn't know and hardly dared to wonder if her father would allow her to visit the Reynards in Boston, once she had returned to Leyland's Landing. Asking Nadine and the Reynards to visit Leyland's Landing was out of the question. Andrew Leyland did not welcome guests, and even if he could be persuaded to make an exception in the Reynards' case, such a visit could be nothing but a disaster.

If only she'd found someone of her own! But although there had been a dozen or more young men who had been taken with her, who had made attempts to court her, there had been no one among them with whom she could honestly fall in love. Emery Haskwell had come the closest. The son of a substantial Boston citizen who had shipping interests, Emery was darkly handsome, completely attentive, and wildly in love with her. But he was also conceited, overbearing and supercilious, and she couldn't see spending the rest of her life with him, not even to escape having to return to her father.

The tears in her eyes were definitely not from the wind, now. She wanted a husband, a home, she wanted a houseful of romping, laughing, mischievous children. But there was no way, not ever, that she would settle for anything less than the all-consuming love that existed between Lucy and Frederick Reynard, a love that was so

Heaven's Horizon

abiding that even after twenty years they couldn't look at each other without it shining through.

I'll be a schoolmistress first, Cordelia thought, her chin thrusting out with determination. I'll be a governess to a big family of children, a happy family because I cannot and I will not, will *not*, spend the rest of my life at Leyland's Landing, buried alive!

"Cordie, Cordie!" The angry, indignant shout broke into her thoughts as she realized that her name had been called two or three times before she had heard it. "Dang it all, it's up there in the tree all stuck, and I can't get it loose 'cause I can't reach the consarned limb to climb up, so gimmie a hand, will you? I gotta get it down, it's the onliest one I have and it takes a long time to make one and 'sides it's the best one I ever had! Common, will you? Gimmie a boost!"

"Mark!" Cordelia stopped so suddenly that she skidded a little on the cobblestones. "What in the world are you caterwauling about?"

"My kite, dang it! Can't you see it's my kite?" Six-year-old Mark, the youngest of Nadine's brothers and Cordelia's favorite, stood with his legs spread apart and his fists on his hips, glaring at her as though she were a half-wit. "It's right there, anybody could see it iffen they wasn't blind!"

"Your mother'll wash your mouth out with soap if she hears you talking like that!"

"I don't care. I want my kite. Common, gimmie a leg up!"

Squinting up into the newly budding branches of the huge elm tree, Cordelia saw that it had indeed taken Mark's kite prisoner.

"Mark, stop that shouting before someone hears you and you're read out of church, and your mother and father along with you for not seeing that you behave!"

"Gimmie a boost! I can't reach the consarned limb lessen you give me a boost!"

"You aren't allowed to climb the tree. Don't you remember that you aren't allowed to climb a tree for three whole weeks yet?" Last month, after Mark had ripped two pairs of breeches and one shirt beyond repair with his tree climbing, his father had laid down the law. If Mark wasn't allowed to climb a tree for a month, it was

15

Lydia Lancaster

barely possible that he might learn to be more careful with his clothing and his father's suffering pocketbook. His clothing had suffered enough today already without risking rips and tears. It had rained last night, and his shoes were muddy, and there were dirty splashes halfway up his legs.

"Gotta."

"You can't. You'll be punished."

"I'll get me an ax, then! I'll chop that pesky ole tree right down!"

Cordelia couldn't help laughing, in spite of her dark mood. The elm was so large that a lad of Mark's size could hack at it all day and hardly make a dent. Besides, it wasn't proper for small boys to go around murdering trees, even kite-stealing trees.

"All right. I'll see if I can reach the branch." If Mark had been forbidden to climb trees, she had not, because the occasion had never come up.

Mark looked at her with scorn. "You're a girl! Grown-up girls can't climb trees."

Stung to the core, Cordelia glared back at him. "We'll just see about that!" Measuring the distance of the lowest branch from the ground, she walked back a good distance and then gathered up her skirts and ran full tilt, to leap for the branch as she came underneath it. Her groping hands missed by inches.

"Ha! I knew you couldn't do it. Ain't no grown-up girl can climb a tree."

"I need something to stand on," Cordelia said. "If I had something to stand on, I could reach it."

"All right. You wait right here and don't you dast go away!" Mark was already running back toward home as he flung the words over his shoulder.

Cordelia waited. She had nothing else to do. In a few minutes Mark came puffing and huffing back, carrying, of all things, one of the two ladderback chairs, Lucy Reynard's prize possessions, that stood in the entrance hall with a console table between them.

"Oh, Mark, you shouldn't have!"

"C'mon. It won't hurt the ole chair for you to stand on it!"

Heaven's Horizon

Cordelia wasn't so sure of that. Her own slippers were muddied, although she'd been a deal more careful about puddles than Mark had. But a challenge had been laid down and she wasn't about to walk away from it. She'd said she'd retrieve the kite and she meant to retrieve it. After only an instant's hesitation, she removed her slippers and climbed up on the chair.

Just as she had thought, she could now reach the limb by stretching to her tiptoes. She had to jump a little again, from her precarious perch on the chair, before she could get her hands around it. The chair teetered but Mark caught it before it fell over. Cordelia swallowed. If that chair had been dirtied or scratched, she'd be in as deep disgrace as Mark.

Her skirts were a problem, but she did the best she could. Clinging to the branch, and because her arms lacked the strength to pull her up, she literally walked up the trunk until she could first sit on the branch, and then stand on it.

Still bracing herself with one arm against the trunk, she reached with her other arm and her fingers met the tangled mass of string. She stretched to the very limit of her ability, and finally managed to latch on to the tail of the kite itself. Heaven have mercy, that was one of Nadine's best hair ribbons! Nadine would skin Mark alive. Cautiously, she worked at the tail, trying to wriggle the kite free. If she ripped it getting it loose Mark would never let her forget it.

"You up there! Young lady, have you taken leave of your senses? Come down out of that tree immediately!"

The voice was masculine, young, and filled with outraged sensibilities. Cordelia, her bonnet hanging by its ribbons, squirmed and twisted to look down over her shoulder to see who had dared to address her in such a boorish manner.

"I can't come down. I don't have the kite loose yet."

"Come down, I say! Do you want to break your neck?"

Exasperated, all the more exasperated because of her embarrassment at being caught in such a predicament, Cordelia gave a final jerk to the kite and had the satisfaction of feeling it come loose. But the jerk made her lose her footing and in spite of wildly flailing arms and legs, she tumbled down off the branch, to land squarely on top

17

of the young man who was so indignant at finding her in a tree, bearing him to the ground, in all the mud, with herself sprawled on top of him.

"Oh, my lands! Oh, my goodness! I'm sorry, are you injured?"

"Only my dignity." The voice had an unfamiliar accent, and the tone was dour. "If you will be so kind as to remove your person from my body, I will attempt to regain my feet."

Cordelia stood up. Beside her, his face outraged, Mark glared at her as though she were the cause of all the misfortunes in the world. "You ripped it!" he accused her. "Gol dang it, you ripped it!" He shook the kite in her face, still glaring. "You ought to of been more careful!"

"Young man, you need a good caning!" the man said, his voice impersonal. "You are being impertinent to a lady."

Mark's answer was insultingly derisive, a noise made with his tongue thrust between his pursed lips as he turned and ran off with his tattered kite.

"I'm sorry. I apologize for Mark. He isn't always so impolite, he's just upset about his kite. Oh, my lands, look at you! You're all over mud! What on earth are we to do?" Cordelia, unmindful of her own appearance in her horror at what she had wreaked on this young gentleman, knit her brows and then exclaimed, "You must come to the Reynards' with me, it's only just there, down the street, and we'll see what we can do about cleaning you up."

"Young lady, I am scarcely in a proper condition to make a social call! I bid you good day." The young man, his eyes frosty, bent to retrieve his hat, and clapped it on his head, and then, like Mark, he turned his back and went away, not running as Mark had but walking with a purposeful stride that conveyed his outrage with every step.

Cordelia stood staring after him, nonplussed by his anger. Actually, it had been his own fault. If he hadn't startled her by shouting at her, she wouldn't have fallen at all. And he hadn't as much as asked if she were hurt!

She gave an exclamation of annoyance, and another, sharper one when she realized that Mark had run off without taking the chair. There was nothing for it except for her to carry it back, and she realized what a spectacle she must be making of herself as she put her slippers on and marched the few doors down the street with the chair. She was thankful that it was such a raw day that none of the neighbors were abroad, and although she watched out of the corners of her eyes, she could see no telltale twitching of window curtains that would have betrayed an observer.

She removed her slippers again before she entered the house to set the chair back in its proper place in the hallway. Retrieving her slippers, she sped up the stairs to Nadine's room, to close the door behind her and lean against it, her face flushed with humiliation as much as from her exertions.

Nadine was still primping in front of the mirror on her dressing table. She looked up as Cordelia entered and her eyes widened.

"Good gracious, Cordie, what happened? You look as though you'd fallen into a mud puddle!"

"I did. Out of a tree. On top of a young man I'd never seen before."

"Bother! Cordie, do you think I'd look better with my hair curled just a little more around my face? And shall I wear the blue satin when Mr. MacKenzie calls tomorrow, or the lavender shot silk, or the pink taffeta? Out of a tree, you say? How very extraordinary! What on earth were you doing in a tree?"

"I was trying to get Mark's kite. It got caught in the branches."

"Oh." Nadine turned back to the mirror. "More curls, I think. Mama will know. And the blue, because it's exactly the color of my eyes. Cordie, do be careful and don't get mud on the door, what if I were to brush against it and soil my gown?"

"He was very indignant. He looked as if he wanted to hit me."

"Don't be ridiculous. Young gentlemen do not strike young ladies. Mark really should be more careful. I think I'll wear the lavender, after all. It's newer, and the neckline is more becoming."

"I broke my leg, falling," Cordelia said.

"Did you really? That's too bad . . ."

The hairbrush clattered to the dressing table top, as Nadine came to her feet, her face filled with alarm. "Oh, Cordie, are you hurt? Are you really hurt? Your poor leg, let me see!"

Lydia Lancaster

Cordelia burst out laughing. "It isn't broken, you goose. How could I have walked home and climbed the stairs if it were? Wear the lavender, by all means. You're right, the neckline is more becoming. I have to wash, and get out of these muddied clothes before your mother sees me and Mark gets into trouble."

Stripping off her dress, pouring water from the pitcher into the washbasin and reaching for the cake of scented soap, Cordelia wondered if she'd been seen carrying the chair down the street, herself muddy and disheveled, and if repercussions would come down around Mark's head and her own.

The water was cold and goose bumps popped up on her arms and shoulders. She scrubbed herself vigorously. If the young man was visiting in the neighborhood, and why else would he have been here, he'd be certain to mention the incident to someone who knew her host and hostess. But right now she was trying to remember what color his eyes were, flashing with such anger. Green, or were they brown?

It didn't really matter, because there was every chance that she would never see him again. Tomorrow was Sunday, and this being Boston, the family would remain at home except for church services, and the next day she would be back in school, where no strange young man had ever been known to set foot and probably never would.

Looking at Nadine, busy again at her hair, Cordelia thought that if she didn't love her friend so much she'd hate her. Lucky Nadine!

And then her chin firmed, as it always did when she was faced with a problem. If she hadn't been born with Nadine's luck, then she would have to make her own. But she would not, she would *not* settle for being buried alive at Leyland's Landing!

Lucy Reynard chose that moment to come, with her quick, light step, into Nadine's room, her eyes sparking with excitement.

"Nadine, Cordelia! I have the most extraordinary news! A messenger left a note for me while I was taking tea with Mrs. Gladstone. Mr. MacKenzie is already in Boston, stopping at the Liberty Arms, and he said that he would pay a brief visit this afternoon. Nadine, do hurry and make yourself presentable, and you as well, Cordelia.

Heaven's Horizon

Although it's rather late for an afternoon call, don't you think? He should have been here by now if he were coming. I wonder if he could have meant tomorrow? Get dressed anyway, just in case. I must hurry and tidy my hair."

With that she was gone, murmuring that she hoped that her husband would come home from his law office a little early for a change.

Nadine screamed, a high squeal of excitement. "Oh, my goodness! Mr. MacKenzie, here! Cordelia, what shall I wear? Do help me, I'm all of a twitter! Cordie, what on earth is the matter with you? You look as if a goose had just walked across your grave!"

His eyes had been hazel. The personable young gentleman she'd tumbled into the mud had been Mr. Donal MacKenzie!

I won't go down when he calls, Cordelia vowed. Nothing on earth could make her go down and face him.

"Cordie, help me get into this gown!" Nadine demanded. "Do hurry, why are you just standing there? Oh, Cordie, wait until you see him! You'll know then why I'm so excited. I can't believe that he's actually here in Boston!"

And I wish that he weren't, was all that Cordelia could think as she moved at last to help Nadine.

Chapter Two

There was a respite, after all. The lad from the Liberty Arms returned with a second message, apologizing for the delay and asking if it would be convenient for Mr. MacKenzie to call that evening. It wasn't much of a reprieve, but it gave Cordelia time to pull her ruffled dignity together.

She was torn between wanting to tell Nadine what had happened, and hoping that Mr. MacKenzie would be gentleman enough not to mention the incident. In the end, she decided that she'd say nothing just in case Mr. MacKenzie also held his tongue. There was no use in causing the elder Reynards embarrassment and Nadine pain if it could be avoided.

There was no way she could avoid seeing Mr. MacKenzie altogether. All she could do was hope that Mark, at least, of the four boys, would be packed off to bed before he called. Caleb, who was twelve and the best behaved of the lot, would almost certainly be allowed to stay up, and it was possible that Matthew, who was nine, would be allowed the privilege. But Caleb and Matthew, and David, who was eight, posed no danger, it was Mark who had been

Lydia Lancaster

involved in the afternoon's escapade, and Mark wasn't noted for his tact.

Cordelia watched for an opportunity to get Mark alone, and threaten to shake his teeth right out of his head if he opened his mouth. But as it was already late in the afternoon, and Mark had run off somewhere, there was no such opportunity. Mark appeared for the evening meal, his hair slicked back with water, the picture of innocence. Frederick Reynard debated, musingly, whether or not to send him from the table to do a more thorough job of washing his hands and face, and then decided that growing boys needed immediate nourishment more than they needed to be clean. Lucy winked at her youngest son and heaped more boiled beef on his plate, and the conversation turned immediately to the impending visit that evening.

"I wonder if he's changed?" Nadine asked. "It's been almost a year, Mama. Do you think he will have changed? Do you think that he'll think that I have changed?"

"Certainly you've changed, Nadine. You're nearly a year older and a year more beautiful," Lucy told her daughter indulgently.

"And a year sillier!" David said, making a face at his sister. "Nearly a whole year sillier! He isn't coming to see you anyway, he's coming to see Mother and Father."

"That's all you know! Do be quiet, children should be seen but not heard," Nadine snapped.

David's answer was to stick out his tongue at her.

"That's once," Frederick warned. "Once more, and you'll go to bed without your pie." Why couldn't it have been Mark who had stuck out his tongue, Cordelia fumed to herself. Mark would never have been able to resist doing it again.

"Mama, do the boys have to stay up?" Nadine demanded. "This first evening, don't you think they could be sent to bed so as not to be a nuisance?"

Cordelia held her breath, but Lucy Reynard smiled at her male offspring, and shook her head reprovingly.

"Now, Nadine, they're as anxious to see Mr. MacKenzie as you are," she said. That wasn't exactly true, no one could be more anxious to see Donal MacKenzie than Nadine was, but the boys had

Heaven's Horizon

liked him when they'd known him in England, and they were almost as excited as their sister over the prospect of seeing him again.

It was exactly eight o'clock when Donal MacKenzie presented himself at the Reynards' front door and was ushered into the parlor by Gertie, the Reynards' maid of all work. The Reynards had only two indoor servants, Gertie and Mrs. Johnson, who presided over the kitchen, and one man, Isadore Simpson, who took care of the outside work. Although well-off by Boston standards, Lucy and Frederick Reynard did not live pretentiously. Their house was red brick, built of that material because of the disastrous fires that Boston had suffered in years gone by. It was a conventional house, with only four bedrooms, and not even on Beacon Hill although it was close to it. With a daughter and four sons to provide for, Frederick was less interested in a grander house than in giving his children a decent start in life.

Cordelia made herself as inconspicuous as possible in the darkest corner of the parlor, where the light of the whale-oil lamps scarcely penetrated. If she were lucky, Mr. MacKenzie wouldn't recognize her. She had an idea that he'd been so angry that afternoon that he hadn't been able to see straight, anyway. And Nadine was so radiantly beautiful, in the lavender she'd decided on after several agonized changes of mind, that it would be a miracle if Mr. MacKenzie had eyes for anyone else. Nadine's cheeks were pink with excitement, her eyes sparkled. It was no wonder that Donal MacKenzie had been so impressed by her last summer that he had come all the way from England to see her again.

"Mr. MacKenzie! How delightful it is to see you after all these months!" Lucy rose to greet him, holding out her hand.

Donal MacKenzie bowed over her hand, and for a precarious instant Cordelia almost giggled, wondering if he was going to kiss it. But that was ridiculous, it was the French who kissed ladies' hands, not Englishmen, at least as far as she knew.

"It was kind of you to allow me to call on such short notice. I have been looking forward to renewing my acquaintance with you for the past several months. My mother and father asked me particularly to convey their fondest greetings."

Now Frederick Reynard was shaking Donal's hand, his face beaming welcome. "I can't tell you how pleased we are that you have come to Boston! I only hope that we will be able to entertain you as well as you and your family entertained us when we were in England. I'll make sure that you see every point of interest, starting on Monday, of course, as tomorrow is Sunday."

"Perhaps Mr. MacKenzie would like to attend services with us? We can at least introduce him to several people even if it is Sunday. And you'll come to supper tomorrow night, of course. Mr. MacKenzie, you remember our daughter Nadine, do you not? Nadine, come and say hello to our guest."

Nadine glided, rather than walked, the short distance between them. Her hair was a golden halo in the lamplight, her smile enough to strike any male both numb and dumb.

"I'm pleased to see you again, Mr. MacKenzie. I've never forgotten the wonderful time we had in London."

Lucy, always the perfect hostess, beckoned to Cordelia. Why couldn't she have forgotten her in the excitement of the occasion?

"And this is Miss Cordelia Leyland, Nadine's dearest friend, and as dear to us as she is to our daughter. Cordelia?"

It was a command that had to be obeyed. Cordelia rose from her chair and left the safety of the shadows, and gathering every ounce of her dignity, went forward to greet the Reynards' guest.

"How do you do? I'm very pleased to meet you. The Reynards have talked about you so much that I almost feel as though I already know you."

She held her breath, her heart thudding against the bodice of her gown. Drat these styles, the necklines were so low that he could probably see her heart pounding! These Empire gowns left nothing to the imagination, they were scarcely decent with their snug bodices and their straight, round skirts, even though no lady in Boston would dream of going without a shift underneath them, or, scandalous thought, sprinkling them with water the way it was said French ladies did to make them cling to their limbs and outline them almost as though they were naked!

He recognized her! The recognition flashed in his hazel eyes, and then, to her relief, Donal MacKenzie bowed and returned her greeting as though he had never seen her before in his life. So he was a gentleman after all, even if he did have a temper that could use some checking, and a disposition that could use improvement.

And then Mark had to go and spoil it all. The four boys had been waiting to be noticed by their elders, waiting quietly as became children in company. But now Mark dashed forward, to stand in front of Donal, looking up at him with a recognition that was mixed with a liberal dash of antagonism.

"Hey, it's you! I didn't know you this afternoon when you went and made Cordie fall out of the tree! An' you didn't know me either, else you would have said so. I guess it's because I'm so much bigger now. I'm growing like a weed."

"You are indeed. That's undoubtedly why I didn't recognize you this afternoon. And you were so young when you met me last summer that you didn't remember me."

"Naw. I'd of known you only I was lookin' at my kite that Cordie went and ripped! But it was your fault she fell outa the tree, you shouldn't have gone and yelled at her."

"Tree? Cordelia fell out of a tree?" Lucy exclaimed, while Nadine's face filled with dismay. "However could that have happened?"

"She was gettin' my kite. That stupid tree caught it, an' I couldn't reach it, and Cordie climbed up on a chair so she could get in the tree and get it, and Mr. MacKenzie went and shouted at her and she fell. Got him all muddy when she landed on him an' they went down in a puddle, you shoulda seen his clothes! Wow, was he mad!"

"Angry," Frederick corrected him. "Mad means demented, and Mr. MacKenzie is hardly that. Cordelia, whatever possessed you to climb a tree? You should have fetched Isadore to retrieve the kite."

"I never thought of it. I was afraid that Mark would have managed to get up in the tree himself, after he'd been forbidden. So I just went up after the kite to keep him from doing it."

"And fell on Mr. MacKenzie!" Nadine's voice showed her horror. "It was a mercy that he wasn't injured!"

Nobody has thought to ask me if I was hurt, Cordelia thought sourly. Certainly Mr. Donal MacKenzie wasn't kind enough to ask when he picked himself up raging *mad* and went marching off!

As though to refute her rebellious thoughts, Lucy exclaimed, "Cordelia, are you sure you weren't hurt? Do you ache anywhere, are you scraped or bruised? You should have told me; a fall like that could have had the most serious consequences!"

"She wasn't hurt, she fell on him!" Mark said, scornful of adults' logic. "An' he wasn't hurt neither, he was only dirty an' mad." A sideways look at his father, and he amended, "Angry."

"So that's why you didn't arrive this afternoon, as your first message indicated," Frederick said. "You had to return to the inn and repair the damage. Quite a contretemps all around, I see. Come and sit down, Mr. MacKenzie. Would you prefer brandy or rum, or Madeira?"

What Donal would prefer was a stiff portion of good Scotch whiskey, but as a guest in the house he could scarcely voice a preference for something that his host might not be able to provide.

"Brandy, if you please." He sat down, and his disapproving gaze, which made him look so stern, left Cordelia's face and returned to Nadine's, where it immediately softened as he took in all her beauty. She was every bit as lovely as he'd remembered her, even more lovely, although he would have sworn that that couldn't have been possible. During all the months since the Reynards had visited London, Donal hadn't been able to get her out of his mind. Of all the young ladies he had ever met, Nadine was by far the most beautiful, the most graceful, the most charming, the most desirable. That was why he was here, and now that he was actually seeing her again in the flesh rather than in his dreams, he wondered how he had managed to live until he could be with her again.

He had no compunctions about taking an American bride back to England with him. Nadine would fit in anywhere. She was a lady, she was from a substantial and respected family, she would win every heart she came into contact with. He only wished that he were a wealthy man, real wealth, not merely the moderate fortune his family possessed. He even had a moment's regret, for the first time in his life, that he wasn't titled, because laying a title at Nadine's feet would be small tribute to pay for the privilege of making her his wife.

Donal had always been a conventional young man, but right at the moment he damned convention to the lower regions. How short could the conventional engagement be cut without breaking the bounds of propriety? Would the Reynards consider a shorter engagement, or would he have to cool his heels here in America for the full year? It was a good thing that he was no stranger to discipline. He'd need every ounce of it that he possessed to get through the eons of time before he could take Nadine back to England as his bride.

But although his thoughts were dark with impatience, he counted his blessings as well. He was fortunate indeed that his mother and father approved of the Reynards, who had called on them with a written introduction from a mutual friend, their interests similar because both Frederick Reynard and Donal and his father were lawyers. Donal's father had made him a generous allowance to defray his expenses while he'd be obliged to remain in America. He wouldn't be able to live like a nabob, by any means, but he could maintain the dignity of his name and position in society. He wasn't given to extravagance or riotous living at any rate. His Scot-descended father had seen to that. Live well, live with dignity, but moderation in all things.

"I'll be pleased to attend services with you in the morning," he said now, in response to Lucy's question. It took an effort to tear his gaze from Nadine and turn it to his hostess, as courtesy demanded.

"We'll find means to make your stay in Boston interesting and enjoyable," Frederick promised. "I can take as much time away from my practice as may be necessary, and Mrs. Reynard and my daughter will be pleased to show you around the town and the surrounding countryside."

"There will be invitations, as well. Our friends will be eager to entertain you," Lucy informed him. "Many of them still have connections in England, and now that all of the unpleasantness is in the past they'll want to catch up on all the news you can give them."

Unpleasantness! Cordelia snorted to herself, although she took care to make sure that it was silently. The revolutionary war a mere unpleasantness, and the more recent, although to her far in the past, War of 1812?

"Just don't make the mistake of referring to us as colonists!" Frederick laughed. "I'm afraid that would not be forgiven even a guest of mine!"

Bored with the grown-up talk, Mark went to tug at Cordelia's hand where she had resumed her chair at the far end of the parlor, well out of the light. "Cordie, come play hide-and-seek! I'll have to go to bed pretty soon, an' you always play hide-and-seek with us before we go to bed! David wants to play too, an' Matt an' Caleb."

"I do not!" Caleb said, his face flaming with the indignity of being included in a children's game, right in front of Donal MacKenzie. "You and the others go ahead, I want to stay here."

From across the room, Cordelia could see Donal looking at her as though he were trying to determine what species of humanity she might belong to, if any. A seventeen-year-old young lady, playing hide-and-seek! For a moment she felt like choking Mark. And then her chin went up, and she rose to her feet and took Mark's hand.

"Come along, then. We'll play upstairs, so as not to disturb the grown-ups."

"And quietly, please," Lucy laughed. "No stomping around over our heads! Half an hour, Cordelia, and then Mark must go to bed and David as well. Matt and Caleb may stay up a little longer if they wish, in honor of the occasion."

"You'll excuse me?" Cordelia met Donal's eyes squarely, without apology.

Donal rose to his feet. "Certainly. Have an enjoyable... game."

"We always do," Cordelia told him, unruffled. He was insufferable!

"Me first!" Mark yelped, his face alight with excitement. "I get to hide first!"

"Oh, no, you don't! You got to hide first last night. It's my turn to hide first." Cordelia's voice was firm. "And no sass, Mark Reynard! If you want to play, you have to play fair."

"But that takes all the fun out of it!" Mark protested, glaring at her. "If you always play fair, then you hardly ever get to win!"

"If he cheats, I'll tell Father," David said self-righteously. "It's wrong to cheat."

"No, you won't." Where had David come by that self-righteousness? Certainly not from either his mother or his father. "It's just as bad to be a tattletale as it is to cheat. If he cheats, we'll hold him down and tickle him!"

The weeks that followed were the most confusing and frustrating of Cordelia's life. Nadine's incessant chatter about Donal, when they were alone, was enough to drive her to distraction. She was sick and tired of hearing about that insufferable young man, who still looked at her as though she were some urchin who had wandered in off the streets, when he bothered to look at her at all.

It wasn't so bad while they attended their classes at Miss Virginia Baker's Academy for Young Ladies. Even Nadine had to be quiet there, and attend to her lessons, although in her present state of excitement Cordelia didn't see how Nadine would ever manage to get through her final weeks. All Nadine could think about was Donal and how much in love with him she was, and of how wonderful, how fabulously, miraculously wonderful it would be when she married him and went with him to live in England.

"Cordie, I might get to see the royal family! I'll almost certainly get to see them, sometime or other! And London is so gay, it's nothing at all like staid old Boston!"

"I expect you'll be too busy raising babies to chase around trying to get a glimpse of royalty," Cordelia told her ungraciously.

"Oh, that! But there'll be a nursemaid, of course. They call them nannies in England. I'll only have to have them, I won't have to spend all my time taking care of them."

"If I ever have children, I'd want to take care of them myself." Cordelia's tone was decisive. "I wouldn't want a nanny raising my children."

But she probably would never have children, because the chances were a hundred to one that she would never have a husband. Once she had to return to Leyland's Landing, there would be no opportunity to meet any man who would want her to become his wife even if she might wish to become his wife.

"The parties, the balls!" Nadine enthused. "Garden parties, Cordie. In England, they have garden parties. All of the ladies are lovely in their light gowns and wide-brimmed hats, and the gentlemen are handsome and attentive. Maybe I'll have a turban, some of the ladies there wear turbans, with ostrich feathers in them! Nobody would dare wear one of those in Boston! What clothes I'll have! Mother is already making plans, Donal won't have to buy me a thing for at least a year!"

Cordelia was sure of that. There was no doubt that Nadine would be one of the best-turned-out brides in the history of Boston. And I won't even get to attend her wedding, Cordelia thought bleakly. For a moment, tears stung her eyes until she blinked them away. She'd be at Leyland's Landing while the engagement parties and the wedding took place, or established as a governess in some family where there'd be no possibility of being allowed to journey to Boston to attend Nadine's wedding.

She wished that Nadine would hush, but her inborn kindness made her forbear telling her. Nadine had no way of knowing how much her chatter about her coming happiness hurt Cordelia, how it cut her to the quick. She wanted Nadine to be happy, she wanted it very much, only it didn't seem fair that just a little of the happiness that Nadine had been born to enjoy couldn't be spared for her.

There wasn't any use in thinking about it. The best thing to do was to enjoy every moment that she had left in Boston as much as she could. She set herself to enjoy it, to savor every moment, every day, when Donal was being entertained, affairs in which she, as Nadine's friend and the Reynards' protégée, was naturally included.

There was one major drawback to her enjoyment, the enjoyment she was determined to have so that she could remember it for all the rest of her life. Donal MacKenzie was always there, very much there. There was no way she could escape proximity with him, no way she could blind herself to the impact he had on her in spite of her dislike of him, no way she could escape seeing the adoration in his eyes every time he looked at Nadine. When he spoke to her,

Heaven's Horizon

Cordelia, when he was required by common courtesy to dance with her, his face was remote and his eyes were cool, and his conversation was mundane.

"Georgia is a state that has a good many slaves, I understand."

"Of course there are slaves. How else could the plantations manage?"

"I expect they couldn't. All the same, it doesn't seem right."

"Is there no slavery in England, then?"

"England abolished the slave trade several years ago." Donal's voice was maddeningly self-righteous.

"And so did the United States!" There was triumph in Cordelia's voice, a triumph that Donal quickly put down.

"All the same, your southern plantations still keep great numbers of human beings under bondage. And in spite of it being illegal, slaves are still being brought in. There are always scoundrels who will risk anything for profit."

"I'm afraid that I know little about such matters. I've lived here in Boston for the past several years."

"But your father does own slaves, does he not?" Donal's eyes were as cool and unfriendly as ever. "How many does he own?"

Furious, both at him and herself, Cordelia had to admit that she had no idea. "My mother and I had nothing to do with the management of the plantation. Such things are strictly gentlemen's province."

"While the plantation ladies sit on cushions and sew fine seams, and dine upon strawberries and cream." Donal's tone expressed his disapproval.

"We do not! Plantation ladies work very hard, managing the house and the house slaves, and nursing the sick, and entertaining." She'd be hanged if she'd admit to this insufferable man that her own mother had never had the burden of entertaining. "And a great many other tasks that only the lady of the plantation can do."

"Of course they do. Running a large establishment of any kind is a good deal of work. I apologize, Miss Leyland. I shouldn't have spoken as I did."

"No, you shouldn't have!" Cordelia wanted to shout at him. Instead, she bit her tongue, hard enough to make her wince.

Donal, who never seemed to miss anything, no matter how trivial, noticed her expression of pain. "Miss Leyland, did I step on your foot? I wasn't aware..."

"You didn't step on my foot. I'm sure that you would never do such a thing. It wouldn't be entirely correct, would it?" That much, at least, she dared to say.

"Is your temper always this bad, Miss Leyland? Or is there something about me that you find objectionable?"

Oh! Cordelia wanted to slap him, but that would be even more of a scandal than shouting at him. She was rescued at the last possible moment by the music's coming to an end, but she was still fuming as he led her from the floor and returned her to Lucy Reynard. His bow was so formal, so coldly correct, that she wished she could stick her foot out and trip him. How she'd like to see his face if he went down in an awkward heap on the floor!

And then he went to seek out Nadine, and here was Emery Haskwell, bearing down on her, his face filled with determination, and Cordelia found herself struggling against a sense of loss and desolation that almost overcame her. All this, and now she would have to put up with Emery's attentions! It was too much, the world wasn't fair!

March had passed, and April, so swiftly that Cordelia couldn't conceive of where the days had gone. She wanted to hold them back, to make them pass so slowly that every day would have forty-eight hours in it instead of only twenty-four. When one was looking forward to some special event, how slowly time passed, but when a dreaded day loomed ever closer, the hours flew to bring it nearer still! So soon now, she would have to say good-bye to Nadine, to Lucy and Frederick and Caleb and Mark and David and Matt, and with every day that passed she was less sure that she could bear it.

And now it was May, the weather warm and sunny, so perfect that the very beauty of the days seemed a mockery, proclaiming that the world was filled with happiness while Cordelia's spirits sank lower and lower.

They drove out past The Neck on a fine Saturday morning, three carriages of high-spirited people seeking enjoyment in a country picnic. Overflowing hampers were stashed in the cart that brought up the rear of the cavalcade, along with the children, the young Reynards included.

At least on this occasion, Cordelia wasn't thrown into too close proximity with Donal, because Emery was her partner for the day. She couldn't conceive why his company should irk her so much more on this occasion than it ever had before. Emery was Emery, and he wasn't that bad even if she did have to keep telling him that she wasn't going to marry him.

"It's a glorious day. Even more glorious because I'm privileged to spend it with you," Emery said, his eyes, almost as dark as hers, looking into hers ardently. Many other girls would be delighted to have Emery as a swain. Emery was undeniably handsome, and undeniably what the young ladies who attended Miss Virginia Baker's Academy for Young Ladies called good husband material. "I've seen far too little of you lately, Miss Leyland. Even at the functions we've both attended, I've scarcely been able to find a moment alone with you."

You aren't alone with me now, either, you ass, Cordelia wanted to tell him. Instead, she smiled, a smile that held no meaning at all. It was a pity that she couldn't love him. If she were to marry him, all of her troubles would be over.

"You look radiant! Miss Reynard's radiance must be rubbing off on you. I've heard that that is often the case. Nothing breeds love like being in contact with others who are in love."

All that's rubbing off on me is discontent, Cordelia thought, as she went on smiling. Sometimes it seemed to her that men were so obtuse that there was no use in trying to communicate with them at all.

But Emery was right about it being a glorious day. The sun beamed down from a sky washed by a gentle rain the night before. Only a few fluffy white clouds provided contrast against the brilliant blue. The trees had leafed out, their new green so light and delicate that no artist's palette could match it. Wild flowers peeped at them from the meadows, and birds were making a noisy to-do about this invasion of humans on their private domain.

The carriage that Nadine and Donal were riding in was ahead of their own, and when they reached the picnic spot, a grove of trees at the edge of a lush meadow, Nadine and Donal were already on foot, with Donal making a great effort to spread a blanket in the exact spot where Nadine would be the most comfortable. As if, in Nadine's state of blind love, she would have noticed if she sat down on a jagged rock!

Alighted from their own carriage, Emery immediately began his own search for the most suitable spot to spread another blanket.

"Right here," he said, his voice assured.

"Don't you think it's a little too much in the shade? The sun feels so good, I'd like to reap the benefit of it," Cordelia protested.

"Not at all. The sun will be much too warm in another hour, and then we'd have all the bother of moving." Emery's tone was decisive. He had decided, as was a man's prerogative. Exasperated, Cordelia let him have his way. Arguing any question with Emery was an exercise in frustration. "And besides, ladies must protect their delicate complexions," Emery added, filled with self-appreciation. As if their bonnets didn't provide protection enough!

Cordelia detested bonnets. They were confining, like skirts. What she would like more than almost anything in the world would be to be out-of-doors bonnetless, with her hair down, at that, letting it blow in the wind.

After the carriage ride, they must all walk, to stretch their limbs and get their circulation going and work up an appetite for the fried chicken and the crusty bread and butter, for the cakes and pies that had been packed in such profusion. Laughing, her face filled with such happiness that Cordelia's heart caught, Nadine drew Donal with her so that she could link arms with Cordelia and the four of them could walk together. And the way Donal was looking at Nadine! Why under the sun hadn't he asked Nadine to marry him? Why all this delay? Everyone in Boston knew that that was why he'd

Heaven's Horizon

come all the way from England, for no other purpose than to ask her to be his wife. What ailed him, why didn't he get it over with so that the official engagement could begin, and there'd be at least a party or two in honor of the betrothed couple before Cordelia had to return to Leyland's Landing?

"I want to pick some flowers," Nadine said. "Wild flowers are so lovely, so much more delicate than the garden variety."

"Not until immediately before we leave," Cordelia reminded her. "Otherwise they'd be withered before we got them home."

"But I want to look at that clump over there, to stake my claim to it!" Nadine laughed. "Hurry, Mr. MacKenzie, before some other lady sees it and lays claim to it!"

Indulgently, Donal quickened his step, but Emery held back and maneuvered Cordelia in another direction. "We'll find you a clump too, better than Miss Reynard's."

"It doesn't have to be better. As a matter of fact, I don't have to have any at all, because Nadine will pick all we'll need."

"But you should have your own." The tone was decisive. Really, now! Why should she have her own, when she had no house of her own, no room of her own, to place them in? "Over there, in the trees, they look to be exactly what you want."

Too late, Cordelia realized that Emery had no interest in wild flowers at all, that he was deliberately taking her deeper into the trees and away from the rest of the party so that he could get her alone. She stiffened, her resistance automatic. "No, really. I don't care for any wild flowers. Nadine will share hers with me. And besides, as I told Nadine, it's much too early to pick them, in any case."

But they had already penetrated the grove of trees more deeply than she had realized, so that they were well out of sight of most of the rest of the party.

"Miss Leyland, Cordelia, I don't give a hang about the flowers! I'm never able to get you alone, there are always other people around even when we happen to attend the same affairs, and sometimes I'm convinced that you're deliberately avoiding me! I've had enough of it. It's time that things were settled between us. I have no desire to go chasing off all the way to Georgia to court you, and besides, my father can't spare me. Cordie, you know that I love you, you know how much I want you to be my wife!"

"Mr. Haskwell, this is neither the time nor the place..." Horrified at the tack Emery was taking, Cordelia backed up a few steps and then turned to go back into the open and the safety of the rest of the company.

Emery would have none of it. He was beside her again in an instant, his hand on her arm, jerking her to a stop as he forced her to turn and face him.

"I want an answer now!" Emery said angrily. "You know you're going to accept me eventually. I've gone along with your putting me off, because it's natural for a schoolgirl to want to be free to flirt a little, but your school days are almost over and it's time that you grew up and settled down. Father is ready to write to your father stating my qualifications and asking permission for me to make a brief visit to Georgia so that he can satisfy himself in person. There's no point in delaying it any longer. I want it settled between us, and settled today!"

"Emery, please let me go. I do not wish to marry you. I do not wish to marry anyone. I'm sorry if you have received the wrong impression. I didn't lead you on intentionally, I thought I'd made it clear that I didn't intend to accept you, today or any other day."

"Don't toy with me! It doesn't become you. Besides, there isn't time. I'll ask Father to write tonight."

"Let me go!" Cordelia demanded. She tried to free her arm from his grip but instead of turning her loose, he pulled her closer, both of his arms going around her until she was crushed against him as his mouth came down over hers in a kiss that was so demanding that her blood flamed with fury.

She struggled, and she was by no means a weak and fragile girl. But Emery was stronger, the contest so unequal that Cordelia's anger grew until she thought she would burst with it. How dared he treat her so!

Returning to the spot where the picnic hampers were being unpacked, Donal stiffened as he saw two figures, a male and a

Heaven's Horizon

female, struggling just at the edge of the grove of trees. No one else had noticed, but Donal's eyes were keen, and it took him no more than an instant to recognize who they were and that Cordelia was being held and kissed, mauled was a more accurate description, against her will.

His long legs covered the intervening distance in record time, and Emery felt a grip of iron descend on his shoulder as he was spun around to face a pair of blazing eyes in a face gone white with anger.

"I believe that the lady does not welcome your attentions, Mr. Haskwell. I think an apology is in order," Donal said, his voice filled with icy control.

"Look, Mr. MacKenzie, this is none of your affair. I've asked Miss Leyland to marry me—"

"It doesn't look to me as if she's accepted!" Donal cut him off. "Miss Leyland, am I mistaken?"

"No, you are not. I have no intention of accepting." Cordelia's face was flaming, she had never been so embarrassed in her life. Why, of all people, had it had to be Donal MacKenzie who had come to her rescue? Behind Donal's shoulder, she saw Nadine hurry toward them, her eyes wide with alarm. "I'll go back to the picnic with Nadine now."

"Don't you move!" Emery barked at her, his furious eyes still on Donal. "Mr. MacKenzie, we have no desire for your company. If you and Miss Reynard will be so kind as to leave Miss Leyland and me, it will be very much appreciated."

"Miss Leyland does not wish to remain with you," Donal told him, his own voice as furious as Emery's.

Emery's temper, never dependable, had reached the breaking point. Regardless of the fact that what he was doing would cause a scandal that would take months to die down, he struck out at Donal.

The next instant, Emery was stretched full length on the ground, as Donal's fist crashed into his jaw. Behind them, out in the open, ladies were screaming and gentlemen came running to put a stop to this unheard-of disgrace, two gentlemen fighting on a social occasion, in the presence of ladies!

But the fight, if it could have been called a fight, was over.

Donal, himself slow to actual anger, had learned the art of fisticuffs on forbidden occasions when he and other boys from the school he had attended as a lad had roamed the sleazier parts of London in search of adventure. Young toffs not being welcome in such neighborhoods, more than one fracas had ensued, and it hadn't taken Donal long to learn the finer points of self-defense as well as aggressive offense, and the most vulnerable parts of the human body. He had been, he admitted with modesty, the champion of his school, even though he would never have dreamed of and would never have used on this occasion, the finer points of mayhem.

"Mr. MacKenzie! What have you done?" Nadine's voice was agonized. "Oh, dear, the disgrace of it! Cordelia, whatever happened, what brought this on? Is Mr. Haskwell badly hurt? You don't think that Mr. MacKenzie has killed him, do you?"

Cordelia looked down at the inert form that had been causing her such distress only seconds ago. "Of course he hasn't killed him. He'll be all right. Mr. MacKenzie, thank you for your assistance, although I hardly believe that such drastic means were necessary. I'm quite capable of taking care of myself."

With that she picked up her skirts and, her eyes smarting with tears of humiliation, hurried to the shelter of Lucy Renard's company. But the day was ruined, and probably all the rest of the short time she had left in Boston. No matter how innocent she might be, when two young men fought publicly over a young lady, her reputation suffered. Drat Donal MacKenzie, anyway! Why had he had to go and spoil the little time she had left?

Chapter Three

Just as Cordelia had feared, the rest of the day was an agony. On recovering consciousness and realizing what a sorry picture he had presented, Emery had to be forcibly restrained from taking up the fight again, and as forcibly removed from the picnic spot and driven back to Boston and turned over to his father. And although Emery had clearly been in the wrong, Donal was looked upon with less friendly eyes than he had been before this unsavory incident.

Cordelia, as well, although she had done nothing to provoke Emery's behavior, received her share of cool and less than friendly glances even though Lucy and Frederick Reynard and Nadine rallied around her giving her moral support and comfort. A well-bred young lady should never have allowed herself to be maneuvered into a position where such a thing could have happened. By nightfall all of Boston would be abuzz with it, and the story would grow out of all proportion as it was passed from mouth to mouth. If Cordelia hadn't been so close to returning to Georgia, her social life would have been all but ruined anyway. Now, she thought bleakly, it hardly mattered.

Lydia Lancaster

Nadine didn't make it any easier for her. Her face alight with adoring admiration, she couldn't stop running on about how strong Donal was, how brave, how gallant, coming to the rescue of a damsel in distress. Cordelia hadn't been a damsel in distress! She'd already worked one arm free when Donal had appeared, and in another instant Emery's ears would have rung and gone on ringing for a week as she'd poised it to give him a cuff on the side of his head that would have set his brain to reeling.

It was even worse that night after the two girls were in bed, because there was no stopping Nadine's tongue. Her chatter drove Cordelia to distraction, until she wanted to scream "Shut up!" Instead, she bit her tongue until it smarted. She wanted to go to sleep and forget about it. She wanted to go to sleep and forget that she had only a few more weeks of school until she must return to Georgia. She wanted to go to sleep and forget about Donal MacKenzie, and wake up forgetting that she had ever known him.

But when Nadine finally wound down from sheer exhaustion and Cordelia was able to get to sleep at last, her dreams were filled with Donal. In her dreams, it wasn't Emery who held her in his arms kissing her against her will, it was Donal and it wasn't against her will, it was very much to her will, and when Emery intervened and sent Donal sprawling in the grass, she'd turned on Emery with clawing fingers, screaming at him that he was an ass, that she loved Donal and she was going to marry him and nothing or nobody on the face of the earth was going to come between them.

She woke up more exhausted than she had been when she had gone to sleep, her dreams still haunting her. Crazy, insane dreams! She didn't love Donal MacKenzie, she wouldn't allow herself to love him even if she'd wanted to; Donal belonged to Nadine and she'd rather cut off her arm than hurt Nadine.

In any case, she disliked Donal MacKenzie. She'd disliked him on sight and her dislike had deepened the longer she'd known him. She did dislike him, she did! So why did the blood rush to her face, why did her eyes feel hot and shining, when she thought of Donal's angry face, when she relived that moment when one blow from Donal's fist had sent Emery sprawling? Donal MacKenzie wasn't a

Heaven's Horizon

knight in shining armor, he was a dour-dispositioned Scotsman she could scarcely abide!

But that one blow had been something else again, and the look on his face, the fury in his eyes, just as if he might really have cared, cared personally, that another man was kissing her! Why couldn't she forget that dream, why did her mouth feel warm and bruised, as if she had just been kissed?

Mark didn't make it any easier at breakfast. "Bam!" Mark said, making a striking motion with his fist. "Pow, bam! And down he went, down stupid old Emery went!" Mark had a new hero, complete with both shining armor and white horse. "Bam!"

This time his fist struck his bowl of oatmeal, and sent porridge and milk spattering over the table.

"Mark, stop that! That's no way to behave at the table!" Lucy reprimanded her son.

"Besides, it's wasteful. Oatmeal porridge doesn't grow on trees," Frederick added. But Frederick was trying to control the smile that twitched at the corners of his mouth. Bam! Just one Bam, that was all it had taken. Frederick was glad that Donal MacKenzie would probably never have occasion to perpetrate a Bam on him!

"It was so exciting!" Nadine enthused. "I never saw anything so exciting! Of course I'm sorry it happened, but all the same..."

"Nadine, it's over. Could we please change the subject?" Cordelia asked, her face flaming. Her own porridge stuck in her throat.

"But it isn't over. I'll wager that every girl in school will know about it tomorrow. Miss Baker, too. I wonder what Miss Baker will think! It'll shake her right down to the toes of her black kid boots!"

"Nadine, that is quite enough. We must hurry or we'll be late for services. Mark, run up and change your shirt, it's all over porridge. And wash your face and hands again. How you manage to come to the table grimy after washing when you rise from your bed is more than I can understand."

"He's a boy," Frederick said mildly. "He'll outgrow the talent in time."

"Cordelia, you have scarcely touched your breakfast. Aren't you feeling well?"

Lydia Lancaster

"I'm perfectly well, thank you." But she wasn't perfectly well. That dream wouldn't go away. How could she eat oatmeal porridge with the same mouth that had just been kissed within an inch of its life?

The Reynards always walked to Sunday services, and the walk itself was uncomfortable as people they knew nodded and greeted them on the street. They attended North Church, long since restored after the depredations that had been inflicted on it by the British troops during the War for Independence. Ever since she had first stepped through its doors, Cordelia had been moved by its beauty, by the simple, graceful lines that made it such a place of distinction.

The Reynards had their own pew, entered through a gate that bore their nameplate. If she were to find any measure of peace of mind, this would be the place, except that Donal entered shortly after their own arrival and took his place in the Reynard pew just as he had ever since his arrival in Boston. Although he sat at the outside of the pew, Cordelia was all too conscious of his presence. Those disconcerting hazel eyes of his had seemed to look right inside her when he had nodded his greeting to all of them, and to see the dream, step by shameful step, that she had dreamed last night.

After the services, which Cordelia was hard put to follow because of her unsettled state of mind, Donal left them and returned to the Liberty Arms. But all the rest of the day Cordelia was forced to listen to Nadine extol every virtue that he possessed and a good many that Cordelia was convinced that he did not possess at all.

"Did you see how everyone looked at him? The men with such respect, and the ladies with such admiration! And all of them jealous of me, Cordie, how could they help but be jealous?"

"Not the married ladies, surely?"

"They don't count, you goose! All of the single ladies, I mean, why do you have to distract me? Emery wasn't there, did you notice?"

As a matter of fact, Cordelia hadn't noticed. She hadn't been thinking of Emery.

"I expect that he was ashamed to come," Nadine continued, "but he'll have to show his face again eventually. I can hardly wait until next Sunday, to see how he and Donal will react when they see each other."

"They won't react at all. They're both gentlemen, I should hope. They certainly wouldn't react in church."

"Well, I suppose you're right. All the same, it will be amusing. Everyone will be holding their breaths! Cordie, I'm the luckiest girl in the world! If I were any happier, I'd burst!"

How sure she was of herself, Cordelia thought. She knew that Donal hadn't spoken for Nadine yet, and still Nadine took their engagement and marriage as much for granted as if the engagement were already official. But that was what came of being Nadine Reynard, born to have everything she wanted. It was wrong to envy anyone, it was a sin.

The Leylands had never set foot in a church in all the years Cordelia had lived at Leyland's Landing. Andrew Leyland believed in nothing except the strength of his will. But Lorelei, and almost to as great an extent Aunt Zoe, had taught Cordelia the Bible stories and instilled in her a sense of what was right and wrong. Lorelei had heard Cordelia's prayers every night, and Aunt Zoe would remind her, whenever she had an inclination to be fractious, that Jesus was watching her.

So Cordelia knew, she felt in her deepest heart, that it was wrong to be envious of anyone, much less of your dearest friend. All the same, she did envy Nadine, and she wished that Donal would hurry up and end her own suspense, even if Nadine felt none, and get it over with, so that she could thrust her envy behind her and go on from there to make whatever of her own life that she could make of it.

Donal appeared for Sunday supper. Cordelia was unnaturally quiet during the meal, but Nadine chattered enough so that no one noticed. Or did Donal notice? He looked at her once or twice, his eyes probing, and she felt herself flush before she averted her own glance. Immediately the meal was finished she excused herself and went up to Nadine's room, the room she had shared so often that it was almost like her own.

She was already in bed when Nadine came up after Donal had

left, feigning sleep. Tonight she couldn't bear Nadine's chatter, and if it was wrong to pretend to be asleep when she wasn't, so be it. And Nadine, who was naturally kind and considerate when she remembered to be, forbore to wake her even though she was bursting to talk about Donal for at least another hour before she too went to sleep.

Monday was as bad as Nadine had predicted it would be. The excited twitterings and sly looks of the other young ladies who attended the academy were almost more than Cordelia could bear. Some of the glances were speculative, as though girls who had been her friends were wondering now if she wasn't quite nice, wasn't quite a lady. Some of them were openly envious, and all of them were filled with curiosity. Imagine being fought over by two handsome young gentlemen! Miss Baker, her mouth a stern line, strove to maintain order, choosing to ignore the distasteful rumors that had also reached her own ears.

Such unpleasantness was better ignored. The spinster was glad that the academic year was drawing to a close. Next semester, Miss Leyland would not be among her pupils, and it was more than probable that such an incident would never again find one of her young ladies involved.

If Cordelia had a hard time in the aftermath of the battle of the picnic grounds, Donal found himself in even worse case. He kept to his room at the Liberty Arms, in a brown study. He had no censure for himself for having laid Emery out. The young man had had it coming, he'd thoroughly deserved it, forcing himself on an unwilling young lady as he had. It was the anger, the pure fury, that Donal had felt when he'd seen Cordelia struggling in Emery's arms that set Donal back on his heels.

Pacing the floor, he wondered what ailed him. He'd been in Boston for weeks, and he still hadn't spoken for Nadine although that was the reason he had come to America. He'd had every intention of asking Frederick Reynard for Nadine's hand within a week of his arrival, as soon as it would be barely decent. And every day since his arrival, he'd found Nadine more beautiful, more charming, more the girl he wanted more than any other girl in the world. But still he had put it off.

Nadine hadn't changed. She was every bit as desirable as she had been when she had stolen his heart back in England. He must be out of his mind not to have settled the matter by now.

But it wasn't Nadine who crept unbidden into his thoughts every night just as he was falling asleep. It was a girl with dark brown hair and brown eyes, a girl he'd first seen teetering precariously on the branch of a tree, a girl who had had the temerity to come tumbling down on top of him to the destruction of his dignity and his apparel. A girl who lifted her chin and looked at him mockingly as she ran off to play children's games, to play hide-and-seek with six-year-old Mark and eight-year-old David and nine-year-old Matt. A young lady who didn't behave as a young lady should, whose home was in Georgia, whose father was a slave owner! There was nothing about Cordelia that would recommend her as a wife for any proper Englishman, much less Donal MacKenzie.

All the same, he'd found himself thinking about her so often that it disconcerted him. Her image seemed to creep into his mind's eye, whether he wanted it there or not. Once he'd even dreamed that he was introducing Nadine to friends at a garden party, and Nadine's blond curls and blue eyes had dissolved and brown hair and dark eyes had taken their place, and then the brown-haired girl had laughed and taken off her slippers and climbed a tree before the shocked eyes of the entire assembly, laughing down at them, mocking them, mocking Donal.

"You," Donal told himself on that Monday after the incident at the picnic grounds, "are a fool. You are an unmitigated ass. You aren't in love with Miss Nadine Reynard, no matter how moon-eyed you were when you boarded ship to cross an ocean to get to her. You are in love with Miss Cordelia Leyland, and if you haven't the guts to face it, then you'd better get on another ship and go back home without either of them."

If he were any kind of a gentleman, he would get on a ship and leave. He was acutely aware that Nadine, that the Reynards, that everyone in Boston, expected him to ask for Nadine's hand. To ask for her friend instead would brand him as the bounder he felt himself to be. Nadine would be hurt, humiliated, it might scar her for life, although now that he knew her better he had to admit that he didn't believe that. She'd be wounded, certainly, but with her inborn bounce and gaiety and her breathtaking loveliness, there would be another suitor immediately, one who would make her a great deal happier than he could make her.

His thoughts turned to his mother and father. What would they think, if he were to show up back in England with an entirely different wife from the one they expected, a girl of whom they had never heard? His mother would be shocked, his father scarcely less so—a gentleman does not jilt his sweetheart for his sweetheart's best friend.

Ass and double ass! As if Miss Cordelia Leyland would have him, even if he could bring himself to be such a cad as to ask her! She'd never given the least indication that she even liked him.

So if he had an ounce of sense, he'd book passage and put an ocean between himself and both Miss Nadine Reynard and Miss Cordelia Leyland before he not only disgraced himself, but made a fool of himself. Thank Providence that he hadn't asked Nadine as soon as he'd arrived!

I'll do it, he told himself. I'll go home, and that way, as little harm as possible will be done. People will wonder and speculate, but they'll be too polite to let Nadine and the Reynards know that they're wondering and speculating. And Nadine will get over it. She's still a child, what could have possessed me to contemplate marrying a child in the first place? Perhaps he'd never marry at all.

A premonition of what it would be like to spend the rest of his life without a wife, without a home and children of his own, loomed in front of him like a bugbear. Hang it all, what was to be done?

He remembered a day when he had been eleven years old and he'd broken his finger playing some boys' game. It had hurt. The physician had been called. Donal had put his hand behind his back, refusing to let the physician look at it. But his father, Duncan MacKenzie, had spoken to him man to man.

"Let him set your finger, Donald. It will hurt for a moment, one quick jerk to put the bone back in place and then it will be over with and start to heal. Otherwise it will trouble you all the rest of your life.''

Donal had held out his hand, and his father had been right. He'd bitten his lower lip almost in half at that one quick jerk, but he hadn't cried out, and then it had been over with and his finger had healed and he hadn't been faced with its bothering him all his life. A broken finger, a broken life. Duncan MacKenzie was a wise man. Sometimes, in fact almost always, Donal forgot that Duncan MacKenzie wasn't his real father, but his stepfather. Donal's name wasn't actually Donal, it had been Donald, but Duncan had wanted it changed and his mother had agreed.

He couldn't even remember that other man, the shadowy figure who had been his real father. His real father had died in an attempt to rescue a lad who had fallen out of a ferry crossing the Thames. The ferryman, in an attempt to help, had maneuvered his craft too close to the spot where Donal's father had dived after the boy, and Donal's father had struck his head against the bottom of the craft when he'd come up, and drowned, while the lad he had rescued had managed to grasp the oar the ferryman had held out and was hauled to safety.

"He was a hero, Donal. Your father was a hero. I loved him very much and I want you to respect his memory for as long as you live," Donal's mother had told him.

"But I love the father I have now."

"Of course you do. There is more than one man in the world who is worthy of being loved. I love your stepfather too. Loving him has eased my grief and made my life worth living again. But we must still remember your father, and love him, knowing that it's all right for us to love your stepfather because that is what your real father would have wanted." And, somehow, the small boy had understood.

Donal loved Duncan MacKenzie. He so seldom thought of his real father that it never failed to startle him when he remembered that he had once had another father. His mother had borne Duncan MacKenzie two children, both of them girls, little sisters of whom Donal was extraordinarily fond. But after the two girls, there had been no more children, and Duncan MacKenzie had adopted his stepson and made him his own. The last birth had been a difficult one, and Duncan had known that there would never be a chance for a boy.

So Donal thought of Duncan MacKenzie now, and of how wise he was. He hadn't recommended chopping the finger off and doing without it all the rest of his life. He'd recommended the only sensible course.

Donal made up his mind. But having made it up, finding an opportunity to put it into action was a good deal more difficult. There was never an opportunity for him to see Cordelia alone. It was almost as if Cordelia herself contrived to avoid him. Didn't she excuse herself every evening he visited the Reynards, and go upstairs to play hide-and-seek with the younger boys? No seventeen-year-old girl could be that fond of playing hide-and-seek!

And now he couldn't go on calling at the Reynard home almost every evening, he couldn't go on escorting Nadine to affairs to which they were both invited. That would be a continuation of a courtship that was no longer a courtship at all. It would be beyond decency.

Consumed with frustration, Donal set himself to be patient. What must the Reynards be thinking, now that he no longer called? Should he, after all, go and explain himself and ask to see Cordelia, or should he go on waiting in hope that some other opportunity would present itself?

He had almost given up hope and steeled himself to beard the lion in its den when a message arrived that the Schynders were giving a party in honor of their daughter Frances's engagement. Donal had been at several affairs the Schynders had attended, and Frances was a sweet, shy girl who fell just short of being pretty, and he recalled the young man she was engaged to even more vaguely as being as shy as Frances. They would make a nice couple, they were suited to each other, but the important thing was that the Reynards would also have received an invitation.

The Reynards had indeed received their invitation, which Nadine regarded with mixed emotions. It was lovely that Frances and Nathan had decided to take the plunge, and she was happy for her friend,

Heaven's Horizon

who had graduated from Miss Virginia Baker's Academy for Young Ladies last year. On the other hand, she'd been so certain that her own engagement to Donal would be announced and celebrated before Frances's that it was a shock to be forced to realize that Donal had thus far given no indication that he was going to ask her at all.

For the past several days, after Donal's continued absence, Nadine had fretted and worried until she was almost sick. Sick, that was it! Donal must be ill, or why hadn't he come to call? But when Caleb offered to go to the inn and inquire, she boxed his ears so hard that it made him yelp.

"You'll do no such thing! Do you want him to think that I'm chasing him? I'd be humiliated!"

"Well, you said you wanted to know! You didn't have to go and hit me!" Caleb's voice was filled with disgust as he stalked away nursing his ear.

"Cordie, what on earth can be the matter? I don't understand it! It would be dreadful if he's really ill, and we haven't even inquired!"

"He can't be ill, at least not seriously, or word would have got around. Nobody can keep a secret in Boston; someone would have told your father and he could have told us."

"Perhaps he's been out of Boston, perhaps he'd made some side trip, and forgot to tell us." Nadine was ready to grasp at any straw.

"Yes, that's undoubtedly it." Cordelia didn't really believe that. Donal was much too correct to be so impolite. She was as confused at the young Englishman's continued absence from the Reynards' home as Nadine, but she had no intention of telling her friend that and adding to her misery.

When the invitation arrived, she was able to say something positive. "Well, now we'll find out. If Mr. MacKenzie is in town, he'll be sure to be there."

"Maybe I won't go." Nadine's eyes were stormy. "If he doesn't care to call on me, why should I put myself out to go where he might be?" It was just talk, of course. Wild horses couldn't have kept Nadine away. But if she arrived at the party to find that Donal had escorted some other young lady, she'd die. Only that, she had to admit, was highly unlikely, because if Donal were seeing some other

51

girl the news would have got back to the Reynards even faster than news of his illness.

"Cordie, what shall I wear? Help me choose!"

"The blue. I've always been told that gentlemen prefer blue."

"Maybe Mama will let me have a new gown. I really need one, Donal has already seen me in everything I own."

"There isn't time for a new gown to be made. Wear the blue."

Nadine wore the blue, and she was beautiful. Her excitement made her eyes sparkle and her cheeks glow. Looking at her, Cordelia told herself that Donal MacKenzie was a fool. If he weren't a fool, he'd have asked Nadine to marry him weeks since. Was it possible, she wondered, that his parents had chosen some British heiress for him in his absence, and directed him not to ask Nadine? But she couldn't imagine him obeying such instructions.

The Schynder house was crowded almost to its doors when they arrived, late because Nadine had spent an extra half-hour having to be persuaded not to take off the blue and put on the pink. But Donal was there. Cordelia saw him almost as soon as they had been ushered in. He saw them at the same time, and came to greet them, not looking at Cordelia at all, but his eyes lingering on Nadine. Ass! Cordelia fumed to herself. If you're so much in love with her, where the devil have you been all this time?

Donal was not looking at Nadine because he was so much in love with her. He was thinking how delicate she was, how lovely, and how much it was going to hurt him to hurt her. As the Reynards were still, in a manner of speaking, his sponsors here in Boston, he was obliged to ask Nadine to dance, and when he felt her tremble under his touch he felt like stepping outside and shooting himself.

He must also dance with his hostess, and Frances, and Frances's older sister and Frances's Cousin Bessie and Frances's Aunt Matilda and her Aunt Cora. His name was already on their cards, and he hadn't yet had a chance to get to Cordelia to see if there was any room left on hers.

Damn it all, she was dancing with Emery Haskwell! He should have realized that Emery would be here. With the Haskwells' position in Boston, there was no way that he could have been passed

Heaven's Horizon

over. Cordelia was not only dancing with Emery, but she was smiling at him!

Cordelia was smiling because this was a party and not to smile would have been a breach of etiquette. She wanted nothing more than to step on Emery's foot and send him limping from the floor. But that was impractical as well as socially unacceptable. Her satin slippers wouldn't make a dent in Emery's polished boots, he probably wouldn't even realize that she had stepped on him. Women were always at the disadvantage!

"Miss Leyland, you've never been more beautiful! That color becomes you. It's ravishing with your hair and eyes." So Emery hadn't given up trying to win her, even after that disgraceful episode at the picnic. But she supposed that he was right about the gown. Cream was her color, a light, rich cream that set off her complexion and brought out the darkness of her eyes. And Lucy Reynard had insisted that she wear it tonight.

"Thank you, Mr. Haskwell." The smile was plastered on her face, she must look like a silly fashion doll. How was she ever to get through the evening? Her last party in Boston, and Emery had to spoil it by writing his name on her card in half a dozen places before anyone else had a chance! He must have been lying in wait for her, not to have contracted to dance with other ladies until after he could get at her card.

Thank heaven the number had ended, but her respite was brief. Mr. Schynder was the next name on her card, and then one of Frances's younger cousins, a lanky, callow young student. Where was her Prince Charming, why couldn't some fabulous young stranger have been invited to this celebration, and taken one look at her and fallen in love with her and swept her off her feet, to carry her off to some enchanted land so far away from Georgia that for the rest of her life she would never have to remember that Leyland's Landing existed?

Where were Nadine and Donal? She strained over Emery's shoulder to try to locate them. But Nadine wasn't dancing with Donal, Donal was dancing with one of Frances's aunts, and looking as though he thought the matron was the most charming dancing

53

partner in the world for all of her one hundred and fifty perspiring pounds. And poor Nadine, she was stuck with Frances's cousin now, and things weren't going at all the way they were supposed to. Nadine still looked radiant but Cordelia, who knew her so well, knew that she was miserable.

The music came to a stop, and Emery was escorting her from the floor. And, then, she hadn't even seen him approaching, how had he disposed of Francis's aunt so quickly, Donal was bearing down on her.

"Miss Leyland, may I have the pleasure of the next dance?"

"Mr. MacKenzie, I believe that your name is not on Miss Leyland's card," Emery said, his tone far from friendly. "As a matter of fact, my name is down for the next dance."

"Then it will be kind of you to relinquish your partner to me. It isn't right that you should monopolize her," Donal said, not in the least ruffled. "Miss Leyland, the music has started. May I?"

He held out his arm. Cordelia put her fingertips on it. Emery's hand came down on Donal's shoulder, his face livid, but Donal looked at him with steel in his eyes.

"I wouldn't, Mr. Haskwell."

Emery, aware of where he was, didn't. He stalked off, and Cordelia breathed a sigh of relief. If there'd been another fight, here at this party, she would have died of mortification!

"You can breathe again now," Donal told her as he whirled her into a waltz. Why did it have to be a waltz, where his arm had to be around her? She could feel the warmth of his hand against the small of her back and she thought she was going to die of it. Why had he even asked her to dance, he should be dancing with Nadine, this was disgraceful.

It was more than disgraceful, because Donal, with a skill that came from desperation, had danced her across the room to the door nearest the entrance hall, and now he maneuvered her through the door, and through the entrance hall and right out through the front door, and his hand under her arm was propelling her around the side of the house into Mrs. Schynder's rose garden.

"Mr. MacKenzie! What in thunder do you think you're doing?"

Heaven's Horizon

"I'm proposing to you. Or I'm about to propose to you. Miss Leyland, will you marry me?"

"You're insane!" Cordelia gasped. She felt as if she might faint—no, she'd be hanged if she'd give Donal MacKenzie the satisfaction. "You're either mad, or you're intoxicated!"

"I'm not intoxicated, Miss Leyland. I haven't as much as sampled the punch. And if I'm mad, it's because you've driven me mad through no choice of my own. I love you. I want you to marry me. I'm waiting for your answer."

Only he wasn't waiting. Now that he had her alone, her perplexed, shocked face turned up to his in the starlight, his arms went around her and his mouth came down over hers in a kiss that threatened to make Cordelia's body explode.

She'd had no idea, she'd never dreamed, that a kiss could be like this. It was as if heaven's gates had opened and let her pass through.

A roar of rage shattered her ecstasy as Emery, whose eyes had never left them after Donal had virtually abducted her, came charging straight through an obstructing rose bush, never feeling its thorns, to throw himself at Donal.

Cordelia didn't scream, although her hand at her wildly pulsing throat had to squeeze the scream back. She dasn't scream, or everyone in the house would be out here. Drat Emery Haskwell, drat him!

But if Cordelia was silent, and if Donal was silent, fighting back like a panther, Emery was not. His rage came bellowing forth with every blow he landed.

There was a rush of people from the house as the noise of the conflict reached them. Cordelia closed her eyes. This had to be a nightmare, she must wake up!

It was over almost before it had started. Donal's left eye was swelling shut, there was a gash on his right cheek, and he was breathing hard. But Emery lay sprawled on top of one of Mrs. Schynder's rose bushes, its branches broken under his weight. Poor rose bush, it would take a good pruning and weeks of time for it to recover.

Lifting her eyes from Emery's inert body, Cordelia looked directly at Nadine. Even in the dim light from the stars, Nadine's face was so white that she looked like wax.

But Nadine had been born and raised a lady. "Cordelia, I believe that we should be leaving."

Her head high, although she felt like crawling under Emery's still unconscious body to hide, Cordelia moved to join the Reynards. The other guests parted to let them through. She was ruined, but that didn't matter. It was Nadine who would have to stay and bear the humiliation and disgrace.

"I'll call on you tomorrow, Miss Leyland." Holding a handkerchief to his gashed cheek, Donal's eyes met Cordelia's across the intervening distance.

"Don't you dare!" Cordelia said. And then she left with the Reynards, with as much dignity as she could muster, leaving Donal to make apologies to his hostess while he mentally cursed Emery Haskwell and his own lack of the common. He wouldn't blame Cordelia if she never spoke to him again. Her reputation was in shreds, and he had only himself to blame, and the scandal of this evening would be years in the forgetting.

Chapter Four

Donal woke reluctantly the next morning, his subconscious aware that he had no desire to face a new day even before his conscious mind remembered what had happened the night before.

There was no use in lying in bed. What had happened had to be faced, and the sooner he got to it the better. While he shaved and dressed he determined that the first step would be to call on Frederick Reynard at his office, where he could try to explain himself. The chances were that Frederick, as even-tempered as he was, would throw him out, but he owed it to him to try. And after that, he would have to face Lucy and Nadine Reynard at their home, and Cordelia as well, unless Frederick Reynard forbade him. In that case, his predicament would be a good deal worse than it had been to begin with.

Frances Schynder's engagement party had been held on Friday evening, and Donal knew that Frederick would be at his office as usual on this Saturday morning.

All eyes turned toward him when he went downstairs in search of his breakfast. His landlord, Silas Cristy, looked at him with sour disapproval before he sent his eldest daughter to serve him. Betty Cristy's ample posterior waggled as she crossed the room to where Donal had found a place at one of the tables, her overflowing bosom strained against her bodice, her broad face and small eyes were filled with spiteful curiosity.

Donal winced when he saw her coming. The landlord's daughter had made overtures toward him when he had first arrived in Boston, and she hadn't taken it kindly when he had pretended not to understand her meaning. Well over thirty, overripe now and her chances for getting a husband long fled, Betty's main object in life was to form fleeting alliances with her father's patrons, without her father becoming aware of it or of the small hoard of coins with which she was paid for her favors.

Donal kept the distaste he felt for the woman from his face, even as he was all too uncomfortably aware that his landlord's eyes and the eyes of every other man in the room were filled with antagonism as they looked at him. A foreigner, an alien, and an Englishman at that, and he had had the termerity to toy with the affections of the daughter of one of Boston's most respected citizens, while at the same time he lusted after the daughter's friend and ended up in a disgraceful brawl at one of Boston's most elite affairs. Donal MacKenzie was no longer welcome at the Liberty Arms and it followed that he was no longer welcome in Boston itself.

"I trust you slept well, Mr. MacKenzie?" Betty Cristy's sly dig was accompanied by a slyer smirk. "Will you have ham or bacon, or both, with your porridge? Eggs? I expect you'll want tea instead of coffee."

"Coffee will be fine. And ham and eggs with the porridge." The thought of that much food left him queasy, but he'd eat it, all of it, and give every appearance of enjoying it as if nothing at all was on his mind.

The service at the Liberty Arms was usually good, but this morning Donal's breakfast was a long time in coming. The food was usually good, but the ham on the plate that Betty slapped down in front of him was burned, the eggs were undercooked and oversalted. Betty hadn't been able to do anything to spoil the coffee. Since his

Heaven's Horizon

arrival in America, Donal had developed a taste for coffee, preferring it to the tea that was always served in his parents' home in London.

Thinking of his parents made him wish, shamefully, that Duncan MacKenzie were here with him now, that he could have the benefit of the older man's advice. He pushed the thought away. He was a grown man who had got himself into a predicament, and it was up to him to get himself out of it if he could, or face the consequences if he couldn't.

He was struggling to force down a mouthful of the runny, unpalatable eggs when the outer door opened to admit a young man whose face showed that he was carrying out an errand that he'd rather not have had thrust on him. His face was vaguely familiar, and even as the young man crossed the room directly to where he was sitting, Donal placed him. Rupert, no, Robert, Babcock. He'd been at the engagement party last night, and he was a friend of Emery Haskwell.

"Mr. MacKenzie, Mr. Haskwell wishes to meet you at dawn tomorrow morning, past The Neck at the place where we picnicked this spring. I trust that you recall the location and can find your way there?"

Donal swallowed the eggs, nearly choking in the process. "Am I to understand that I'm being invited to participate in a duel? And on Sunday! For shame!"

"Pistols will be provided. If you object to tomorrow morning, Mr. Haskwell will no doubt agree to wait another day."

Donal helped himself to an ample bite of the burned ham. It was hard and tough. He washed it down with coffee before he answered.

"You may tell Mr. Haskwell that I have no intention of meeting him at the picnic grounds or any other place at any other time."

Robert Babcock's face flamed. "Sir, do I understand that you refuse to meet him?"

"You do."

"And may I be given a reason to convey to him?"

"You may not. Simply tell him that I will not fight him, and that's an end to the matter." A duel! Donal shook his head as though he couldn't believe it, and went on eating, ignoring Emery's messenger until he looked up as if he had just recollected himself and asked, "Would you care to join me at breakfast, Mr. Babcock? I can recommend the ham and eggs."

"Good day to you, sir!" Robert said. His back conveyed his outrage as he left the inn.

He left silence behind him, so silent that if a pin had been dropped it would have been audible from one end of the room to the other. The other gentlemen breakfasters looked at Donal as if they weren't sure that they were looking at a flesh and blood man. In the corner by the kitchen door, Betty tittered and spoke to her father, "Not only a lecher, but a coward!"

"Get to your work," her father ordered her, but his own measured look at Donal made it plain that he agreed with his daughter.

Donal polished off every scrap on his plate, drained his coffee cup and motioned to Betty that he wanted it to be refilled. For good measure, he asked her to bring him a piece of pie.

It was a good half-hour after Robert Babcock had left before Donal rose from the table. Every pair of eyes in the room followed him as he left to return to his room to make sure that he was presentable before he walked to Frederick Reynard's office. There wasn't any use in trying to rehearse what he would say. He'd simply have to make a clean breast of it and hope that Frederick's wrath would be tempered with mercy.

Frederick's office was unpretentious. A desk, two chairs, a bookcase filled with legal tomes to which he seldom had to refer. He regarded Donal with level eyes, waiting.

"I thought it would be best to speak to you first," Donal said. The words seemed to find an obstacle in his throat, and he cleared it and started again. "I feel that some kind of explanation is in order."

Frederick nodded. He wasn't being much help. Desperately, Donal searched for the right words, but the trouble was that there weren't any.

"I find myself in a most difficult position. As you must have surmised, I came to Boston for the primary reason of renewing my acquaintance with your daughter."

Frederick nodded again.

Heaven's Horizon

Donal plunged on. "I found her every bit as lovely as I had remembered her. The trouble is, I also met your protégée, Miss Leyland. And through no fault of anyone, I found myself falling in love with Miss Leyland, and it put me in a predicament that I didn't know how to get out of. I didn't fall in love with Miss Leyland intentionally. As a matter of fact, I didn't even realize that I was in love with her until very recently. I didn't mean to hurt anyone, least of all your daughter, whom I still hold in the highest esteem."

"Mr. MacKenzie, I doubt that my daughter would want to have anything to do with you now, even if you were still under the impression that you were in love with her and wanted to ask for her hand. The brawl last night was bad enough, but now I understand that you have refused to accept Emery Haskwell's challenge."

News traveled fast in Boston. And Frederick Reynard's eyes were cold as he waited for an explanation. Not that Frederick approved of dueling. Nevertheless, no man, nor any woman, could have any respect for a coward, no matter how much of a donkey Emery Haskwell was to have issued the challenge.

"Certainly I refused. I have no wish to murder a man in cold blood."

Frederick's eyebrows rose.

"Mr. Reynard, I'm a dead shot. And I'm fast. Emery Haskwell wouldn't have a chance against me. If I were to delay long enough so that he could get off a shot, he might just be lucky and hit me. And if I did not, he would be gravely wounded at the very least. I'd try not to hit a vital spot, but accidents happen, and there isn't much room for taking careful aim when you're faced with a man intent on killing you if you don't kill him first. It would be nothing short of murder."

Frederick's eyebrows resumed their normal position on his face. So Donal had a valid reason after all, and it was one that he was forced to respect.

"I accept your explanation." He didn't doubt for a moment that Donal was telling the exact truth. "About the duel, that is. About the other matter, I'm afraid there's nothing I can do to help you. You'll have to get yourself out of that one the best you can."

Donal, who had half expected to be met with a horsewhip, felt less relief than he might have. "Then you don't forbid me to call at your home?"

Nadine would probably never forgive him, and it was doubtful if Lucy would speak to him for a month, but Frederick wasn't going to forbid it. The matter had to be resolved, and the sooner it was resolved the better so that Nadine could begin to get over it. As for Cordelia, Frederick held her in no way responsible for Donal's change of affections. He knew without a shadow of a doubt that the girl had done nothing to encourage the young Englishman. On the contrary, she'd gone out of her way to avoid him.

In spite of the gravity of the situation, Frederick had to fight against the smile that twitched at the corners of his mouth. By all that was sacred, he was glad that he wasn't standing in Donal's shoes.

"I do not forbid you. But I can make no guarantee about your reception if you do call."

"Should I talk to Mrs. Reynard first?" Donal wondered aloud.

"I can't help you there, either." Clearly, this interview was at an end. Donal felt more of a fool than ever for having asked.

Once outside Frederick's office, his feet did their best to turn back toward the Liberty Arms rather than toward the Reynard house. Facing Cordelia, facing Lucy and Nadine Reynard, was without doubt the most difficult thing he had ever been called upon to do. Resolutely, he forced his feet to follow the direction his brain gave them. Putting it off wouldn't make it any easier. Besides, he had an ulterior motive for wanting to get it over with. If he went now, there was a chance that they would not yet have heard of his supposed cowardice in refusing to meet Emery with pistols at dawn.

The parlor that he had found so charming on his previous visits seemed cold and forbidding this morning while he cooled his heels waiting for the ladies of the house to appear after Gertie had admitted him. The day was bright and sunny, in contrast to his mood. He only hoped that Emery was suffering one-tenth as much as that nincompoop's actions of last night were causing him to suffer now.

Heaven's Horizon

"Mr. MacKenzie?" Lucy's voice wasn't quite as cold as the younger ladies' eyes, but neither was it filled with the warm welcome that had always been his on previous occasions.

"I've come to offer my apologies for last evening. What happened was inexcusable, and although I didn't start the altercation, I should have taken steps to prevent such a thing from occurring."

"Indeed you should have, Mr. MacKenzie. If you had wished to speak to Miss Leyland alone, you should have chosen a different time and place."

"But that's just it. There never seemed to be another time or place! Mrs. Reynard, may I speak to Miss Leyland now? It is of the utmost importance."

Cordelia's face flamed, and Nadine's paled. Without a word, Nadine turned and left the parlor, and her mother followed her. Both of their backs were stiff.

"Mr. MacKenzie, you heap indignity upon indignity!" Cordelia said. "Asking Nadine and Mrs. Reynard to leave the room, in their own home! Is this a way a gentleman behaves in England?"

"I have no idea. In England, I was never faced with this dilemma. Miss Leyland, you must have understood me last night when I told you that I love you and I want you to marry me. I didn't mean to hurt Miss Reynard! I'd give anything if I could undo that hurt. But it's you I love, Miss Leyland. I love you and nothing can change that. You must have some feeling for me. When I kissed you last night, I felt your response and there's no way it could have been either anger or indifference."

"You took me by surprise! I was caught off guard. If you think that I'd do anything to hurt Nadine, if you think that I could ever marry you knowing that it would hurt her, then you must be the most obtuse man ever to walk on two legs! I will not marry you! I wouldn't marry you even if I loved you!"

"Even if?" Donal couldn't help it, his hands went out with no direction from his brain and grasped her shoulders and pulled her against him. She had no choice but to meet his eyes even as she struggled. "Are you being truthful, Miss Leyland? Are you trying to convince me, or yourself?"

"Let me go! How dare you, and in Nadine's house!" Cordelia stormed.

"It has to be somewhere, and I can hardly waylay you on the street! But I will, I promise you that I will, if you don't give me an honest answer! Would you have considered marrying me, if Nadine had never been in the picture at all, if all of this had been between the two of us from the beginning?"

"No, I wouldn't have, I would not have! I don't even like you!" The falsity of her statement was so blatant that Donal had to fight down a desire to laugh. She didn't even believe it herself!

"You don't have to like me. That will come later, after I've had a chance to earn your liking. What I'm asking is if you love me."

Cordelia's mouth opened, but no sound came out. Then she wrenched herself free. "Mr. MacKenzie, please leave. I do not wish to see you again, and I'm sure that Nadine never wants to see you again. You will do all of us the greatest favor if you get out of our lives."

"I'm not going to get out of your life. You've given me your answer. And you might as well say you're going to marry me, because I'm going to be your shadow, dogging your footsteps, until you do. I'm not going back to England without you, and you might as well get that through that stubborn head of yours."

"Then you will never go back to England at all." Shaking in every limb, Cordelia wanted to run from the room, but her dignity made her walk, and at a ladylike pace at that. "Good morning to you, Mr. MacKenzie. Gertie will show you out."

Nadine was waiting for her in her room. Her face as she turned it toward Cordelia made Cordelia's heart twist.

"I heard him," Nadine said. "His voice has a carrying quality, and he didn't bother to lower it. He loves you, he wants to marry you! Not me, it wasn't me at all, it was you, ever since he came to Boston! I'll never forgive you, Cordelia. I'll never forgive you for as long as I live!"

"Nadine, I had no idea, I swear that I had no idea in the world! How could I have had, he never gave the least indication!"

"Maybe it wasn't your fault, but I'll still never forgive you."

Heaven's Horizon

Sobbing, Nadine threw herself down on the bed, her shoulders shaking.

Her heart heavy with tears that she couldn't shed, Cordelia said, "I'll go back to the academy. I'm afraid I won't be allowed to return to Georgia until the school year is over, but I won't inflict myself on you any longer, I promise you. I'll keep out of your way as much as is humanly possible."

Nadine went through one of the lightning changes that only she was capable of. She sat up, glaring at Cordelia, her face blazing with anger.

"You'll do no such thing! You'll stay right here today and tonight, and tomorrow, and next weekend and the one after that, just as if nothing had happened! Do you think I could bear to have fuel added to the fire, to have everyone in Boston know that we've fallen out because you took Donal away from me? You can at least help me to hold my head up, and not to have to endure that additional humiliation!"

"Nadine, don't treat me like this! I'm not going to marry Mr. MacKenzie. If you could hear us, you know that I told him that I won't. You're the only friend I have in the world, the only real friend, I can't bear it for you to hate me!"

"You'll have to bear it, because I do hate you! But you'll bear it right here in this house! And you'll bear Mr. MacKenzie's coming to call as well, because I am not going to be pointed at and laughed at as the heartbroken, jilted sweetheart! We will let it be known that I decided against Donal myself, until he goes back to England."

It was impossible, Cordelia thought. How could she go on spending the remaining weeks in this house, enduring Nadine's hatred, having to see Donal when he came to court her right under Nadine's nose? But she could understand Nadine's demands. Nothing was as pitiful as a girl who had been scorned, and Nadine couldn't bear pity, and Cordelia couldn't find it in her heart to blame her.

"All right, if that's what you want. And I promise that I won't see Donal when and if he comes to call."

Nadine took a deep, shuddering breath. "You really aren't going to marry him? You don't really love or want him?"

"I'm not going to accept him." Would Nadine notice that she hadn't said that she didn't love him?

Apparently, Nadine didn't. "All the same, I still hate you. You took him away from me even if you didn't mean to. In public, we'll still be the best of friends, but all the rest of the time just stay away from me, don't even talk to me!"

She's being childish, Cordelia thought. She'll soften, she has to, because I can't bear it if she doesn't. But her heart was filled with doubt. Nadine's life had been too easy—she didn't know how to stand up under heartbreak.

The days that followed were an agony. At school, she and Nadine walked with their arms around each other, laughing and chattering as if nothing between them had changed. Nadine prattled on and on to the other girls who attended the academy, making fun of Donal, mocking his accent, telling them how neither she nor Cordelia could abide him now that they'd come to know him better, and how he'd made a fool of himself trying first to win her, and then Cordelia, after she'd turned him down.

"A boor! But Mr. MacKenzie showed his true colors soon after he arrived in Boston. Public brawling, trying to court two young ladies at once! When he saw that I wasn't about to fall victim to his charms, he turned them on Cordie. Oh, he was determined that he'd return to England with an heiress! He must have thought that American young ladies are fools. Papa and Mama tolerate him for the sake of their friendship for his parents, but only barely. Thank goodness his visit is nearly at an end, we'll be happy to see his back when he boards ship!"

Cordelia felt physically ill.

"And then he turned out to be a coward to boot! Imagine his refusing to accept Mr. Haskwell's challenge! I can't help but hope that word of his craven behavior gets back to England. Perhaps no girl will ever accept him now. But, then, perhaps they already knew his true colors back there, and that's why he came to America to seek a wife!"

The other girls were convinced against their wills. It would have been vastly more exciting if Nadine had been jilted, if there had been a flaming romance between Cordelia and Mr. MacKenzie. It was a pity that they had to accept the lesser excitement, but even so it was better than nothing.

Miss Virginia Baker, with years of experience behind her and a mind so discerning that few of her young ladies had ever managed to deceive her, held a different opinion.

Cordelia had always been one of Virginia Baker's favorite pupils. Privately, of course, because Miss Baker did not play favorites. The bewildered, heartbroken girl who had been sent to her four years ago, her eyes so wounded that Virginia's heart had twisted, had reached out to every stifled motherly instinct.

Austere in manner, her hair gray now instead of the soft brown it had been when she had been a girl, her face lined, Miss Baker was still a romantic at heart, and her private domain, the little room on the first floor, which no one else ever entered, was filled with both great literature and novels of love and courtship and romantic adventure. And she knew, she felt in her heart, that Cordelia was playing a part, that Cordelia was facing a tragedy that might well ruin her life.

Cordelia was, in fact, shaken to her core. She managed to get through the week, although she felt as though she were screaming inside and that any moment the screams would break out and she would go on screaming until someone came to take her away to one of those places where mad people were confined.

The school hours, which were long, weren't so bad. But the nights were a study in misery, as she had to parry the avid curiosity of the three other girls who shared her room. Somehow she managed to give them the impression that every word that Nadine said was true, without saying more than a word or two herself.

And now it was the weekend and she had to stay with the Reynards again, just as though everything were normal. There was no way she could get out of it. Both Lucy and Frederick had agreed with Nadine that it was the best way to handle the situation with the least embarrassment, and she owed the Reynards too much to refuse to do as they wished.

She was in Nadine's room, sitting very straight in a rocking chair that was pulled close to the table where a lamp shed its light on the book she was holding in her hands. Nadine was in her parents' room, and she wouldn't return to her own and to Cordelia's unwanted company until it was time to go to bed. And downstairs, Donal had come to call, but neither girl would go down, and again for appearance's sake, Donal must spend at least two hours in stilted, painful conversation with his host and hostess before he could take his leave.

Cordelia's face was as stiff as her back, and her eyes stared at the page in front of her without seeing a word. She fought against straining her ears, but all the same, even though the house was well built and the bedroom door was closed, she could catch an occasional murmur of voices. Donal had a nice voice, deep and firm, nearly always holding a warmth that drew people to him. Cordelia had never realized until now how she had used to listen for his voice, that hearing it had pleased her even when she had been telling herself that he was insufferable. What was he saying, what could he find to say to the parents of the girl he had cozened, leaving the entire family open to the sniggerings or the pity, according to people's personalities, of all of Boston?

Frederick Reynard would have been within his rights to refuse Donal entry to his house. But although Donal had been wrong to take Cordelia to the garden, Emery had without any doubt struck the first blow, and Donal was in Boston under the aegis of the Reynards, who held his family in high esteem, and there was the need to avert as much scandal as possible by behaving as though he had done nothing wrong. It was a mercy that he had had the good sense to refuse Emery's challenge.

Frederick had told Lucy Donal's reason for refusing to meet Emery, and Lucy, who had a sense of fairness even in the present circumstances, had told Nadine and Cordelia. But to the rest of Boston, Donal was regarded not only as a bounder but a coward. It would be a relief to everyone when Donal returned to England and when Cordelia returned to Georgia. Maybe then life would return to normal for the Reynards, if only that ass Emery would leave off bragging that Donal had been afraid to meet him.

Heaven's Horizon

As for Emery himself, again it was a mercy that his father had forbidden him to call at the Reynards' or to seek Donal out in any way, the elder Mr. Haskwell having a mind to keep his son and heir alive and in good health so that he could one day take over the family enterprises. A man didn't go to all the trouble of rearing a son to have him maimed or killed in a duel over a girl who obviously did not reciprocate his affections.

Cordelia's wrists began to ache from holding the book. Surely two hours must have passed! It was hard to judge time anymore, every minute dragged like an hour, every hour like three. Drat convention, anyway! It would have been better if Nadine had yanked every hair out of her head and the Reynards had refused Cordelia further entry to their house. This pretense was maddening. And even after Donal left, she would still have the night to face, lying in the same bed with Nadine hostile and unforgiving beside her, and after that she must live through going to church tomorrow, and sitting in the same pew with both Nadine and Donal while everyone at the services speculated about them instead of attending to the service.

There! There were footsteps and voices in the entrance hall, and the sound of the front door opening and closing. Against her will, Cordelia found herself on her feet and at the window. Nadine's bedroom was at the side of the house, but she'd be able to see Donal when he passed the corner of the house on his way back to the Liberty Arms.

There he was, walking fast, and even from this perspective she could see that he was dejected. As he had every reason to be! And, then, to her horror, he turned and looked directly up at her window, where she must be clearly visible to him, watching him, with the light behind her in the room.

"So!" Nadine's voice cut through her like a knife. "You are in love with him, you're mooning over him right now, spying at him through the window! You've been out to take him from me all along, why don't you admit it?"

"That isn't true. I was only making sure that he had left."

"Don't bother to talk to me! Just be quiet!" Nadine stormed.

There wasn't any use in crying. Tears had never healed a thing since the beginning of time. Cordelia lay awake for hours, aching, her throat painful when she tried to swallow. As bad as it would be at Leyland's Landing, she wished that she were leaving tomorrow!

She in Leyland's Landing, Donal in London, halfway around the world. She'd never see him again, never as long as she lived. But she'd remember him. No day would pass when she wouldn't wonder how he was, what he was doing, if he had found someone else and was happy. And Nadine would still hate her, even though neither of them would ever see him again.

Let the tears fall, let them soak her pillow. What did it matter? She could cry without making a sound, or if she couldn't, then she had better learn. Only, she wouldn't cry.

In the morning, after a night that had seemed endless, her face was pale and there were shadows under her eyes, and in spite of her effort to control them her hands trembled as she dressed her hair.

"You look dreadful," Nadine told her. "Pinch your cheeks to bring some color into them, and put a smile on your face! Don't you know that everyone will be looking at us? Don't you dare disgrace me, or I'll . . ."

"You'll what?" Cordelia asked, her voice bleak. There was nothing left that Nadine could do to her, she had already done it all.

Breakfast with the family was an ordeal. The boys were unnaturally quiet, even Mark, who had always been irrepressible, darting furtive glances first at his sister and then at Cordelia.

"I wish that dumb old Donal MacKenzie had never come here!" Mark finally burst out. "I wish he'd stayed to home where he belongs! Everything's spoiled, 'cause of him! Cordie isn't any fun to play with anymore, and all Nadine does is sulk and pout!"

"Mark, that is enough. Finish your breakfast and get ready for church," Lucy told him.

Mark finished his breakfast, although his eyes were still angry under lowering brows. Cordelia couldn't finish hers, and no one urged her.

They walked to church, smiling and nodding and greeting others who were bound in the same direction. Nadine walked beside Cordelia, her smile sunny. Cordelia hoped that her bonnet hid enough of her face so that no one could see how pale she was, how smudged her tired eyes.

She had to nod to Donal when he entered their pew. Nadine did the same, and then she poked Cordelia sharply in the ribs with her elbow and whispered, "Smile!" Cordelia smiled.

She survived the service, she survived the walk back to the Reynard house. She survived the afternoon, which she spent alone in Nadine's room. She even survived Sunday night supper, to which Donal had been invited as usual. They sat at opposite sides of the table, and Cordelia refused to look at him although his eyes seldom left her face. Nadine's eyes were fixed with hostility on Donal, and she was as silent as Cordelia. If Donal didn't wish that he were a thousand miles away, something must be the matter with his brain.

Cordelia excused herself immediately the meal was over, and went back to Nadine's room. Nadine went to her parents' room. Fifteen minutes later, Lucy came up to ask Cordelia if she would talk to Donal.

"No," Cordelia said.

"I quite agree. He should have known better than to ask. All this will be over soon, Cordelia. I'm only sorry that either of you girls has to go through it."

Cordelia picked up the same book that she had held last evening, and once again she sat without turning a page until Donal had left.

Chapter Five

Virginia Baker closed the side door of the academy behind Donal, her eyes troubled. She had broken a cardinal rule in allowing him inside the academy at all, but her sense of fairness had compelled her to listen to Donal's side of the story and determine if there was any way she could help. Her fondness for Cordelia had demanded it.

Bounder the young man was not, Virginia had decided before the first five minutes of the interview had passed. He had been indiscreet, and he had been foolish, but he had also been the victim of circumstances. How could he have prevented himself from falling in love with Cordelia, who, in Miss Baker's estimation, was worth a dozen Nadine Reynards, for all that most people would consider that Nadine was more beautiful than Cordelia?

Virginia had sympathy for Nadine, but her heart broke for Cordelia. If something wasn't done, two lives were going to be blighted, perhaps beyond repair. Nadine would recover as soon as some other personable young man came into the picture and laid siege to her heart. But Cordelia was different, her emotions ran deep, and if she loved Donal MacKenzie she would go on loving him for the rest of her life. And she believed that the same held true for Donal MacKenzie.

There being no one else who was willing or able to do something about it, Virginia set herself, as trembling as she was inside at the idea of actually interfering in a real-life romance, to be the one to try. She sent Lizzie, her girl-of-all-work, to fetch Cordelia to her room.

"You wanted to see me, Miss Baker?"

"I did. Sit down, Miss Leyland. I have just received a visit from Mr. MacKenzie, who was most anxious to see you. Of course I could not give him permission without consulting you, and even then it would be strictly contrary to the rules of this establishment."

"I don't want to see him, Miss Baker. Thank you for refusing."

"Cordelia..." Virginia broke another rule by addressing a pupil by her first name, "...are you very sure that you do not want to see him? If you love him, you will be making a grave mistake."

"How could I love him, after the havoc he has caused?" Cordelia cried, her voice ragged. "And even if I did, I could never accept him, after what he did to Nadine! He broke her heart, how could I ever be happy, knowing that I'd taken him away from her?"

"And you're quite sure that you don't love him?"

"How can I know, how can I tell?" All of Cordelia's torment was in her voice. "I've never been in love before!"

"I believe that you do not wish to return to Leyland's Landing, that the prospect of returning there for the rest of your life is distressing to you." At Cordelia's startled expression, Virginia held up her hand. "I am an observant person, Cordelia. I am aware that you and your father are not close. And I am certainly aware of the state of your emotions when you first came to me, and of your distress every summer when you had to return to your home."

Cordelia didn't answer. There was nothing to say.

"Suppose, Cordelia, that by some farfetched strength of the imagination, that Mr. MacKenzie's life were in danger. Suppose that only by returning to your father, for all the rest of your life, you could save Mr. MacKenzie's life. Suppose that there would be no escape. Would you do it?"

"Of course I would!"

"Just so," Virginia said. "You love him, Cordelia. And he loves you."

"But there's still Nadine. There's no way I can ever marry him!"

"Now suppose that there are three people, one of whom must be sacrificed unless all three should perish. Of what avail would it be for all three to perish, when two could live out happy lives together? For all three to perish would certainly not help the one. It would be a waste for no purpose. And please use the intelligence that I know very well that you possess. Nadine will not perish. Nadine will not even suffer unreasonably. Only her pride will suffer, and that will soon be healed. She is a very young and very beautiful and very fortunate young woman, possessed of a loving family, of loyal friends, sought after, admired. Within a few months she will be in love with someone else, and what good will your sacrifice do you then? Your friendship with her has already been destroyed. I dislike to say it, but Nadine is not a person who takes being disappointed with good grace. I expect that she's being spiteful to you right now, that she's making your life miserable. Is that not true?"

Cordelia looked down at her hands, which were folded tightly in her lap. "It may be true. But it doesn't change anything. I would always know that I'd been disloyal to her, and I owe her so much, Miss Baker! She made my life bearable when I was so unhappy that I wanted nothing more than to die. The Reynards have been kind to me, unfailingly kind, how could I repay them with such a betrayal?"

"At least think about it. And think with your head, not your heart," Virginia said. "And remember that not only your life will be affected by your decision, but Mr. MacKenzie's as well. Do you have the right to ruin his life because of your loyalty to a family that befriended you? You have repaid them many times over, just by being yourself, by loving them and adding richness to their lives, by being Nadine's constant friend and companion. The Reynards have no further claim on you. You have done nothing wrong. And your life is your own, and it is your duty both to yourself and to God to make the most of it."

After Cordelia had left her, Virginia sat for a long time in thought. She had done her best, but she wasn't at all sure that Cordelia would take her advice. The girl's loyalty to her friend and to the Reynards was too deep-rooted for her to bring herself to do anything that might cause them embarrassment or grief.

Cordelia no longer went home with Nadine after school during the week, as she had often done before this rift between them. And that evening, Virginia did something that only last week she would never have dreamed of doing even in her wildest romantic imaginings. She sent a message, by Lizzie, who was threatened with such unknown punishments if she ever opened her mouth that she was reduced to shaking terror, to the Liberty Arms, asking Mr. Donal MacKenzie to call on her immediately he had received her message.

Unfortunately, it was Betty Cristy to whom Lizzie turned over the note she had been entrusted with, to be taken up to Donal's room. And Betty being the person she was, pried up the seal and read the note before she delivered it, carefully sticking it down again with a drop of candle wax after she had read it. The contents of the note filled her with excitement. Miss Virginia Baker, that paragon among women, asking for a secret meeting with Mr. MacKenzie!

It had to do with Miss Nadine Reynard and Miss Cordelia Leyland, and Betty searched for some means to turn her knowledge to their disadvantage. The Nadine Reynards and the Cordelia Leylands of the world were the objects of Betty's deepest envy and hatred, simply because they had been born beautiful and wealthy and with a place in society that had been denied her. If she could do those two young ladies a hurt, Betty would take the greatest pleasure in the doing.

Cordelia's heart was heavy as she once again approached Miss Baker's closed door, having been summoned by Lizzie. She didn't think that she could bear another such session as she had gone through this afternoon. Miss Baker was kind, and Cordelia appreciated that the headmistress was trying to help her, but words wouldn't change anything. Even if she loved Donal until she thought she'd die of it, she couldn't marry him.

She rapped, and Miss Baker's voice bade her enter. She opened the door, and Miss Baker nodded at her and stepped through it immediately Cordelia had entered, and closed the door behind her.

Cordelia had no time to recover from that surprise before she received another that nearly jolted her off her feet.

She wasn't alone in the room. Donal was there, looming over her, his face alight with the intensity of his feelings as he swept her into his arms without so much as a by-your-leave.

"Cordelia! Bless Miss Baker, if she hadn't let me see you I think I would have cut my throat! Cordelia, I love you! You belong to me, you know it and I know it and God knows it, so why go on trying to deny it?"

"No!" Cordelia said. "Mr. MacKenzie, please let me go this instant!"

"Cordelia, if you call me Mr. MacKenzie one more time, I swear I'll wash out your mouth with soap! My name is Donal. Say it, Cordelia. Donal!"

"You're mad! I can't conceive of what possessed Miss Baker!"

"Common sense possessed her. She knows that we belong together even if you don't."

"I don't, and I won't!"

"You will!" Donal's mouth came down over hers, and this time it was even worse, better? than it had been when he had virtually kidnapped her into the Schynders' rose garden. It was the same, exactly the same, only even more so and that wasn't possible, but all the same it was. Cordelia's bones were melting, they wouldn't even hold her up, she had to cling to Donal to keep her knees from buckling, and she cursed them even as she responded to his kiss, no more able to help herself than if she had been struck dumb and helpless by an act of God.

"Donal!" Donal prompted her, releasing her mouth just long enough to say his own name before he kissed her again. "Say Donal."

"No!"

"Then I'll go right on kissing you until you do."

"You wouldn't dare! This is a young ladies' academy!"

"What are you going to do about it? You can hardly scream for help, in a young ladies' academy. Think of the scandal! You'd be ruined for life!"

"I'm already ruined for life. Donal, don't!"

Lydia Lancaster

"You said it!" Donal exulted. He held her closer than ever, she couldn't breathe. "You're going to marry me, we're already engaged. Blast it, I don't have an engagement ring for you! Never mind, I'll get one tomorrow. And I'll write your father tomorrow, and ask his permission to visit Leyland's Landing to court you officially. It's a good thing that tomorrow will be a school day, because I'm going to be busy and I wouldn't be able to see you until evening anyway. I must write to my family as well, and see to booking passage on a fast packet that will take me to Georgia as soon after your own departure as I can manage. I suppose it wouldn't be proper, even here in America, for me to travel on the same packet with you, but I won't be far behind you."

"We can't be engaged! Think what it would do to Nadine!"

"You can wear the ring around your neck. She need never know, nor need anyone else in Boston. It will be our secret, and Miss Baker's. I don't want to hurt Nadine, or the Reynards, any more than you do. We'll be married in Georgia, and there's no way that word could get back to Boston. Your arguments aren't valid, Cordelia."

Wasn't that what Miss Baker had said? Cordelia wasn't sure, her head was swimming, she couldn't think straight. She didn't want to think straight, she didn't want to think at all, she only wanted Donal to go on kissing her and never stop. Her conscience told her that she wasn't playing fair, but then what Mark had said that first night Donal had visited the Reynards popped into her mind. They'd been playing hide-and-seek, and Mark had said, "If you always play fair, then you hardly ever get to win!"

She'd told Mark that he was wrong, but in this case she'd make an exception. Fair or not, this time she was going to win! She was going to marry Donal and go to England, fair or not, and Nadine would get over it just as Miss Baker had said.

Not to England. To heaven! She'd marry Donal and go to heaven. Two people would survive, and Nadine could sink or swim as it pleased her, and now at last Cordelia admitted that Nadine was a very good swimmer indeed and in no danger of drowning.

She still felt guilty. But she wasn't going to let it bother her. She'd been born tonight. Tonight was the first day of her life.

If Cordelia and Donal thought that they could keep their involvement with each other a secret, they were brought up short the next day. Betty Cristy had put a flea in the ear of the town's most inveterate gossip, a well-meaning man who talked too much when he was in his cups. She knew that by the time twenty-four hours had passed, everyone in Boston would know that Mr. MacKenzie had visited Miss Virginia Baker's Academy for Young Ladies in the evening, and everyone in Boston would come to the conclusion, as Betty had, that his visit had been concerned with Miss Cordelia Leyland.

But there was no proof that Donal had seen Cordelia at the academy. Her roommates attested that Cordelia had been summoned to Miss Baker's private quarters that evening, but there was no way they could swear that she had seen Donal.

Questioned by a delegation of fathers of the students, Miss Baker told them firmly that she had been conducting a private investigation and that she was satisfied with the results of her investigation. It was no more than the truth. She did not feel obligated to tell them what the results of her investigation had been or how thoroughly satisfied she was. The gentlemen concluded, in view of Miss Baker's flawless record, that she had only been doing her duty in protecting her school from any scandal concerning one of her young ladies. Lizzie could tell them nothing except that she had delivered a message, and she wouldn't have dared to open her mouth if she had known more.

Virginia drew a heartfelt sigh of relief when the gentlemen left. She might have been ruined, but the risk had been worth it. As it was, her institution would not suffer unduly. A few overly suspicious families might withdraw their daughters next semester, but she would stay afloat. Virginia's heart felt warm. At last, after all of her sterile life, she had lived a little.

But Nadine believed the worst, and if she had made Cordelia's life a torment before, it had only been a preview of the fury of which she was capable. Even Lucy and Frederick were ashamed of their daughter.

Suffering Nadine's tongue-lashings, Cordelia would have thrown the truth in her face if it hadn't been necessary to protect Virginia Baker. As it was, she gritted her teeth and bore it.

What was even harder to bear was that she and Donal were unable to see each other at all before she returned to Georgia. Because of Nadine, Donal was no longer invited to the Reynard home, and Frederick had to tell him that he wouldn't be welcome in the Reynards' pew on Sundays. For Donal to risk another visit to the academy was out of the question. Another visit would certainly bring about Miss Baker's ruin. And there was no way for Cordelia to contact Donal or for him to contact her, as Nadine insisted that Cordelia should accompany her home every afternoon and spend the night, as well as spend every minute of the weekends there.

By the time the school year was over, two more weeks that dragged like eternity, Cordelia was reduced to a quivering mass of nerves. Had Donal written to her father? Would he follow her to Georgia as soon as he could? Or would he have second thoughts, and return to England without ever contacting her again?

The entire Reynard family saw her off on the packet. Nadine threw her arms around her and kissed her and wept. If Cordelia hadn't felt the stiffness of Nadine's body and seen the icy fury in her eyes, she might almost have been convinced that Nadine was sorry for all the misery she'd caused her. As it was, she knew that Nadine was putting on a show for the other onlookers in order to keep her pride intact.

Donal was nowhere to be seen. In spite of the fact that she knew that for Donal to have come would have set tongues to wagging again, Cordelia felt such sharp disappointment that it cut through her like a knife. How could she go on waiting in this suspense without going mad?

But if Donal was not present, Emery Haskwell was, very much so, bearing a box of bonbons and a slim volume of verse to help Cordelia while away the time until she arrived at home.

Emery took Cordelia's hand and held it until her face burned. "Miss Leyland, I beg you to forgive me for any embarrassment I have caused you. You must be aware that it was only because of my

Heaven's Horizon

deep and abiding affection for you. As soon as circumstances allow, I shall journey to Georgia so that I can present myself to your father for his approval."

Don't you dare kiss me, Cordelia thought. Don't you dare! For a moment she was convinced that he was going to, right in front of everybody. But propriety won out. Emery contented himself by pressing her hand even more tightly, while his eyes looked for all the world as if they belonged to a sick calf. And then he released her, giving every appearance of a young man who was going to die of love. Cordelia didn't know whether to laugh or to cry, so she did neither.

"I'll write to you every week, Cordie! And you must write to me every week, without fail!" Nadine choked. What an actress she was! Thank heaven, it was time to board the packet. Miss Emmaline Frampton, the senior of Miss Baker's two assistants at the academy, was escorting her as chaperon, all atwitter at still another adventure, even though this time would be the last. She had accompanied Cordelia in the same capacity every year, and those trips were the only bright spots in her life.

"We'll practice our French while we are traveling," Miss Frampton said. "You were one of my best pupils, Miss Leyland, it will be a pleasure to continue our French conversation for this little while before we have to part, never to see each other again."

Cordelia thrust the bonbons and the book of poetry into her hands. "Dear Miss Frampton, I want you to have these as a token of my affection."

Almost overcome, Miss Frampton had to turn away to wipe the tears from her eyes. Perhaps there had been rumors that Miss Leyland had not always comported herself as a virtuous young lady, but Miss Frampton, for one, was not going to believe it.

Andrew met the packet at Savannah. Escorting his daughter to Leyland's Landing was something that could not be left to servants. Miss Frampton did not accompany them, her duty was ended when Andrew took charge of his daughter.

Andrew had brought the trap, a utilitarian conveyance. He hadn't used the phaeton since his wife had died. He had no use for the trappings of luxury, no interest in impressing his neighbors. Even his plantation house was modest, a plain, four-square clapboard edifice built by his own slave labor, lacking the grace of columns and balconies such as a few of the wealthier plantation owners were beginning to flaunt as a testimony to their prosperity.

Andrew, like a good many others, had started out in a two-room log cabin with a dogtrot connecting them. The house had been built to welcome the birth of his first child, the son he had been convinced would be his. He'd intended to add to it as other sons were born, to make it a showplace, a worthy setting for his heirs.

As no son had been granted him, the house still stood as it had been at Cordelia's birth. Andrew did nothing for its appearance other than to see that it had a fresh coat of paint as soon as the old started to weather.

Even knowing what to expect, Cordelia's heart contracted with grief when she stepped inside the door. While her mother had lived, the inside of the house, at least, had been cheerful and comfortable. Lorelei had kept the rooms filled with flowers, there had been decorative touches of statuettes and pictures. But now the statues and other pretty bric-a-brac had been stored away in the attic, the staff of house slaves had been cut to the bone to release the servants to more productive work. Dear God, I can't live here, I'd go mad! Cordelia thought. Why hadn't her father mentioned Donal, hadn't Donal written him after all? She herself hadn't quite dared to break her father's indifferent silence by asking him. If Donal hadn't written, there would be no point to it, and if he had, her father would tell her when he got around to it.

And then there was a rustle of starched calico, and the clean smell of soap and water. Two thin arms enfolded her and she was held against Aunt Zoe's shrunken breast as the black woman crooned words of thanksgiving for her safe arrival.

"I've been waitin' and waitin'! I never took my eyes off that drive, only I just slipped out to the kitchen for a cup of leftover coffee to keep up my strength for the waitin'! And that's when you came, as soon as I took my eyes off the drive. Cordie, baby, my own baby, home at last!"

Heaven's Horizon

Cordelia kissed her, touching her wrinkled cheeks, her fingers tracing the lines, filled with love. "We'll have to do something about the house. It's awful!" she said.

"Won't take no time at all. I know where everything is stored. We'll have it all back the way it's supposed to be before you kin blink an eye. Your mama's flower gardens are all ruined, but now that you're home you can ask your papa to let you have a man to weed 'em out and get them goin' again. A few of the roses are still pretty, I weeded them myself so's Miss Lorelei's prize bushes wouldn't die."

Cordelia's room was a revelation. The windows sparkled behind white organdy curtains, the crocheted bedspread had been freshly laundered and painstakingly mended, the sheets had been stored in lavender. There was a vase of roses on the mantel. Aunt Zoe had made sure that her darling's room, at least, would be in order.

Dear, dear Aunt Zoe! Would she be willing to travel to England, to sail across the ocean, and make her home in London when Cordelia and Donal were married? Was she too old to stand the voyage, would she be willing to leave her only living relative, her son Runt, to live with Cordelia for as many years as she had left on earth?

Andrew was sure to allow her to go. The slave was too old to be of any value to him. The only reason he hadn't sold her off was that to have gotten rid of his dead wife's beloved personal servant would have put him beyond the pale of decency among men he had to do business with.

Cordelia took Zoe's hand in hers and drew her with her to sit on the edge of the bed. "Aunt Zoe, I have so much to tell you! I met a young man in Boston..." Now at last she could let it all out, she could talk about it to the one person in the world who would understand, who would love her even if she were wrong.

"...and that's the way it stands," Cordelia finished, at last. "Oh, Aunt Zoe, I don't even know if he'll come!"

"Of course he'll come! How could any young man not come, when it's you waitin' for him? And course I'll go to England with you! Do you think I'd let you go alone, to a heathen place like that?"

Cordelia had to laugh, in spite of her worry about Donal. "England isn't a heathen place, it's more civilized than America!"

"All the same, they're foreigners. But we'll put 'em in their place. Now we gotta git busy and unpack your things and git this house fittin' for your sweetheart."

"Later. I prefer to eat without discussing matters of importance," Andrew told his daughter at the supper table.

Cordelia waited, only picking at her food, shoving it around on her plate. It was only tolerably palatable in any case. What had happened to Opal, who had been such a talented cook? Sold off, for a high price, no doubt. Andrew's tastes were simple, and as he never entertained and Cordelia had been away, he had had no need of a cook who was an artist in her own right. Donal would just have to make the best of it when he arrived. At least she knew now that he'd written to her father, that he intended to come.

At last Andrew finished his coffee and pushed his plate aside. He fixed Cordelia with his emotionless gaze, and said, "I received a communication from a Donal MacKenzie, as you asked me. The young man's credentials seem to be in order. If he is a friend of the Reynards, he must be acceptable. I take it that you are in favor of accepting him and making your home in England?"

"Yes, Father. That is what I wish."

"He informed me that he would follow on your heels, so we may expect him any day. He expressed a wish that a conventional courtship might be dispensed with, so that you may be married at the earliest convenience and leave for England."

Cordelia's heart was pounding almost right through her bodice. If her father would allow it, it would be too good to be true! Not to have to wait all that long time, to be able to marry Donal right away and leave Georgia and Leyland's Landing behind her forever! "Yes, Father, that is what we would like."

"I can see no obstacle to your wishes. As we have no friends or neighbors who take an interest in our affairs, there is no reason you should not be married immediately on Mr. MacKenzie's arrival. Provided, of course, that he meets with my approval after I have interviewed him in person."

"Thank you, Father." Cordelia felt like laughing at how totally inadequate those three words were when she wanted to jump up and run around the table and throw her arms around her father and kiss him, when she wanted to weep and sing and dance with pure, unadulterated joy.

But looking at her father, she kept her place at the table. He only wanted to be shut of her, a constant reminder that he had no son but only a daughter. There was no place for her in his life. The sooner he could marry her off and get rid of her the better it would suit him.

"May I be excused, Father?"

At his nod, Cordelia's feet took her flying up the stairs, where she burst into her room, where Aunt Zoe was waiting, and grabbed her around her waist and waltzed her around and around the floor until the old woman begged for mercy.

"I'm going to be married! Aunt Zoe, I'm going to be married! And I'm going to live in England, and you're coming with me. I'm sorry we can't take Runt with us, but Father would never let him go. But you can write to him. I'll write the letters for you, and he'll find somebody to read them to him."

"That Runt, he kin take care of hisself. Besides, he prob'ly ain't goin' be here at Leyland's Landin' much longer."

"Not be here? But Father would never think of selling him! Why, Runt's the best worker he ever had, everyone knows that!"

Aunt Zoe's face lost its smile and now it was serious and sad, with a trace of apprehension that faded as quickly as it had been born as she studied Cordelia's face.

"I kin tell you, 'cause you won't go tellin' your father. Runt's a-gonna run off."

"Run off! Aunt Zoe, he can't! He'd be caught, and you know what would happen to him then, he'd be beaten until he was nearly dead, no slave has ever gotten away with running off from Leyland's Landing! Even if he managed it, he'd be sure to be tracked down by the slave catchers, and they'd bring him back."

"Not where he's gonna run," Aunt Zoe said. "He's got it all figgered out, Cordie, he's been studyin' on it for a long time. He's gonna git him down to Florida, to the Seminoles, and ain't nobody ever gonna ketch him there an' bring him back."

"The Seminoles?" Cordelia's brows knit. "But aren't they Indians?"

"Of course they is. There's many an' many a slave managed to git to them, an' they take them in, an' they treat them good, an' they're happy there an' free. The Seminoles make them their slaves but it ain't like bein' a slave on a plantation, belongin' to a white man, ain't nothin' like that. The Seminoles love their slaves, they treat them just as good as they treat themselves; the slaves have their own garden patches an' their own houses to live in an' they kin git married and know their children will never be sold off. Sometimes they marry Seminoles an' then they're Seminoles themselves, real members of the tribe, with all the rights that go with it. Yes, Miss Cordie, that's where Runt is a-goin', an' I won't tell him not to 'cause if he kin make it, then he'll be the same as free, and he'll live happy all the rest of his life."

"I hope he makes it, then! I hope he does! And you'll be in England with me and everyone will be happy!"

"That's what I'm hopin', baby. That's what Zoe is hopin'," Aunt Zoe said. "An' prayin', too, and now you'd better add your prayin' to mine, to make sure it all comes out the way we want."

Cordelia would never doubt the efficacy of prayer again. Hadn't her prayers added to Aunt Zoe's brought Donal to Georgia in a matter of days after her own arrival, hadn't they caused her father to approve of Donal, wasn't she, in this month of June of 1829, this thirtieth day of June, already Mrs. Donal MacKenzie, a married woman for all of five days?

And nights, Cordelia thought, and her face turned bright red right there at the supper table, with her father's eyes on her as he asked a question for the second time because she hadn't been paying attention the first time, her mind too filled with those nights, to the exclusion of everything else.

It was no wonder that she hadn't been paying attention to what her

Heaven's Horizon

father was saying. She'd been too busy reliving the moment Donal had stepped off the coastal schooner, the first evening he'd spent in this house while her father had closeted himself with him in his study, to emerge half an hour later and tell Cordelia, who had been waiting in a frenzy of suspense, that he saw no reason the marriage could not take place.

They had been married three days later, the ceremony performed by the Reverend Samuel Rockford, whose Presbyterian church Cordelia had never set foot in until that moment. Donal had been insistent that the marriage be performed by a clergyman, in a church, his upbringing had precluded anything less as not being quite legal.

Cordelia had no attendants. Andrew had given her away, and the sexton and the clergyman's son had acted as witnesses. Cordelia had worn white, and carried a bouquet of roses that Aunt Zoe had picked from Lorelei's garden. She'd wanted to be married in her mother's wedding dress, but Aunt Zoe had told her, sorrowfully, that Lorelei had had no wedding dress, that Lorelei's marriage had been as simple as Cordelia's was to be.

A simple ceremony or not, Cordelia was still married, legally married in church before the eyes of God, but she hoped that God's eyes hadn't been on her on her wedding night. What under the sun made teachers like Miss Baker and Miss Frampton think they had educated their young ladies when not one word had ever been said about the glory of being a wife?

If it hadn't happened to her, Cordelia wouldn't believe it even now. If her awakening to the facts of being a wife had been a shock, accompanied by a moment's pain, what had come after had wiped it all away in a delight that had astounded her. She didn't have to wait to go to England to be in heaven. Heaven's gateway was right here in this house that she had always hated, and she had already stepped through it.

"Are you quite sure that your wardrobe is adequate? I will have you driven to Savannah to purchase anything you think you might need."

"Father, I have enough clothes to last me for years! Mrs. Reynard saw to that. Donal will have no cause to be ashamed of me, nor his parents either."

Donal's eyes on her face were so adoring that she felt her flush deepen. "As, if I could ever be ashamed of you! You'd be beautiful even if you were dressed in rags. Sir, it was good of you to consent to let Aunt Zoe accompany Cordelia to England. Her heart would have been broken if she had had to leave her behind."

Andrew waved his hand as if Aunt Zoe were of no consequence. "If my daughter wants her, there is no reason she shouldn't have her. What are your plans, Donal? How soon will you be sailing?"

"Not for a while, sir. But we'll be leaving Leyland's Landing by the day after tomorrow at the latest. I promised my mother, before I came to America, that I would visit friends and relatives of hers in Virginia, and bring her back firsthand news of them."

"In Virginia?" Andrew's face was suddenly still, his eyes had gone hard in a face that revealed nothing. "I understood that your mother, like your father, was native to England."

"She is English now, very much so!" Donal laughed. "But she originally came from Virginia, sir. She and my father made their home in England immediately after they were married."

"Then your father isn't an Englishman, either?" Andrew's brows went up.

"It's all something of a tangle, I'm afraid. I haven't thought about it for so many years that it never occurred to me to explain. You see, my father, Duncan MacKenzie, isn't my actual father, he's my stepfather. My mother married him when I was only three years old, and he gave me his name when she provided only daughters for him. My actual father, Lester Ross, died when I was two. My mother's maiden name was Flemming, Marguerite Flemming, from Virginia, and I am to visit the remaining Flemmings."

In the doorway that led to the kitchen, Aunt Zoe, who had insisted on supervising the meal herself, dropped the tray of cakes and plates that she had just been carrying in for her family's dessert. Her face turned an ashen gray, the color of pewter, every muscle in her body went rigid, as she stood there in the ruins of broken crockery and broken cake.

Heaven's Horizon

"God in heaven have mercy!" she whispered, although no sound came from her throat. "God have mercy on us all!"

"Aunt Zoe! My goodness, what a mess! Never mind, it can be cleaned up. That tray was too heavy for you, you shouldn't have tried to carry it," Cordelia exclaimed. "Donal, you'll have to be patient until we see if there are more cakes in the kitchen."

"If there aren't, it won't matter in the least. Don't look so stricken, Aunt Zoe. I promise you, in London you won't have to carry trays at all, much less heavy ones! Cordelia and I have decided that your only duty will be to be with Cordelia and keep her happy."

Andrew's fingers tightened around the stem of his wineglass until it seemed that the fragile stem must snap. Neither Cordelia, down on her knees helping Zoe pick up the broken plates, nor Donal, noticed.

Marguerite Flemming! His fiancée, his Marguerite, the girl he had loved more than life itself, was Donal MacKenzie's mother! And Lester Ross, the cursed thief who had stolen her from him and left him crippled, was Donal MacKenzie's father!

My daughter is married to Donal MacKenzie. My grandchildren will carry Lester Ross's blood in their veins, Andrew thought. And on the heels of that thought came a denial, so fierce that it thundered through his brain, blotting out everything else with its force.

No! It would never happen. He'd see Donal MacKenzie dead first!

Chapter Six

Cordelia and Donal had gone out into the ruined gardens directly after supper, seeking whatever breeze might cool off the sultry evening. Although Donal didn't complain, he was glad that they would be gone from Georgia before the real heat of summer set in, and he was even more glad that Cordelia would never have to live on this plantation again. Andrew Leyland might be a wealthy man, but although he had been pleasant enough to Donal, Donal could see that his cold formality would blight the life of anyone who had to live with him day in and day out, much less a girl like Cordelia.

The state of the abandoned flower gardens appalled him. What sort of a man would let his dead wife's gardens fall into such desolation? He put his arm around Cordelia, drawing her close. She'd delight in his mother's gardens, so lovingly tended that they overflowed with scent and color. He could picture her in a wide-brimmed hat, strolling among the flower beds with a basket over her arm, helping Marguerite select blossoms for the house. Cordie and his mother were bound to hit it off. Marguerite was naturally friendly and warm, naturally gay. She'd take Cordelia to her heart and the two of them would be the best of friends.

Cordelia had told him a little about her childhood, although he could see that it still hurt her to talk about it. There had to be something fundamentally wrong with any man who could treat his wife and daughter the way Andrew Leyland had treated Lorelei and Cordie, banning friends and neighbors or any human contact at all. It was no wonder that Cordie's eyes darkened with grief when she talked about her mother. Leyland's Landing was a bleak place, and the sooner he could get her away from it the better.

In his study, Andrew paced the floor, a glass of brandy in his hand. Not ordinarily a drinking man, this evening he had sent for a bottle. His face, always still, was as cold and hard as granite, and his eyes were deep, black pools of hatred.

For over twenty-two years, Andrew had not known where Marguerite and Lester had gone. He'd spent months after the duel that had left him crippled trying to find them, swearing that nothing would keep him from exacting full vengeance, but his efforts had come to nothing. By the time his shattered body had healed enough so that he could undertake the search in earnest, there was no trace of them, and neither their families nor their friends would tell him a thing, intent on protecting the couple.

Andrew had suspected, he had been certain, that his own family knew where Marguerite and Lester had gone. Determined to keep Andrew from carrying out the vengeance he swore, they had refused to tell him anything, advising him to accept his loss and set about rebuilding his life instead of brooding about something that was over and could not be repaired. In his rage, he had turned against them, convinced that their disloyalty to him proved that they weren't worth his caring for them, that blood ties no longer meant anything.

Marguerite! Even now, more than twenty years later, Andrew's heart twisted at the thought of her. Always, even when he had been enjoying the favors of some other girl or woman, he had known that there was only one woman for him, Marguerite Flemming, and once they were married he would never look at another woman for as long as he lived.

Heaven's Horizon

Andrew had been attracted to Marguerite ever since he had turned twelve and she was only eleven. With his first stirrings of curiosity about the opposite sex, he'd realized that no other girl in the world was half as beautiful, half as desirable, as the girl who had been fated to be his.

It had never crossed his mind to doubt that he was one of the favored of the gods. The Leylands were an old Virginia family, aristocrats, proud, wealthy. Their plantation was a showplace. All of the Leylands were handsome, but Andrew, the eldest son, was head and shoulders above the others. He took his good fortune for granted, as no more than his right.

The Flemmings were also an old Virginia family, as wealthy as the Leylands, as aristocratic, as favored by fate. The Flemmings' plantation bordered the Leylands'; the children grew up together. His and Marguerite's marriage would be ideal, something that dreams were made of. Andrew so darkly handsome, Marguerite so glowingly golden-fair with her violet eyes and her hair like spun silver and a body so deliciously perfect that it set him on fire just to look at her. Every movement she made was filled with grace. Her laugh was light and filled with joy, her smile melted him, and he had cursed the years that would have to pass until he could claim her as his own.

When Marguerite was fifteen, she was so exquisite that it stopped the breath just to look at her. When she was sixteen, she was even lovelier as her womanhood blossomed into the promise of full flower. And when she was seventeen and their betrothal was at last an accomplished fact, Andrew's world was as perfect as it could be until he reached his ultimate goal, their marriage.

Marguerite's eyes were like stars as she discussed their wedding. It would be the most magnificent wedding that had ever been celebrated in Virginia.

"Lorelei will be my chief bridesmaid, of course," Marguerite said. "She's to wear pink, we've been planning her dress for a year. Our mothers sent to Paris for the design, both for my wedding gown and the bridesmaids' dresses, but you mustn't ask what they will look like, it would be bad luck."

Andrew couldn't have cared less what color the bridesmaids

would wear. Only Marguerite mattered, and she would have been beautiful if she'd come to the altar in calico.

Put to the question, Andrew supposed that he liked Lorelei well enough. There was nothing about the girl to dislike except that she seemed always to be there, getting in the way when he wanted Marguerite all to himself. He could probably have come up with the fact that Lorelei's hair was a sort of a golden brown, that her eyes were blue, that she had a sweet disposition and a sweet smile. He supposed that she was pretty, although all other girls faded by comparison with Marguerite.

Three or four of Andrew's friends were interested in her, she never lacked for an escort, but so far she had not settled on any one of them. She seemed content to be Marguerite's shadow, never resenting the fact that Marguerite was so much more beautiful. A goddess and her handmaiden, Andrew sometimes thought, amused, only a handmaiden ought to be sent away when her presence became irksome.

Not that Lorelei lacked tact. She faded into the background or disappeared completely when it became obvious that her presence wasn't wanted. All the same, she and Marguerite were inseparable, and Andrew thanked all the fates that bridesmaids were not included on honeymoons.

The engagement was celebrated in late June, the summer before Andrew would be finished with his formal education. Once the summer was over, the rest of their engagement would have to be spent apart, but as soon as Andrew returned home after his final year at Harvard, they would be married.

It seemed to Andrew that he was the happiest man ever born of woman, on that night of the engagement ball. The Flemmings' plantation house was ablaze with candlelight, the long drive leading to it was illuminated by torches placed at short intervals on either side, the gardens were hung with decorative lanterns, the strains of soft music filled the air. Marguerite looked as though she had stepped from the pages of a book of fairy tales, her silver-gilt hair accented with gardenias whose heady fragrance went to Andrew's head so that he trembled when he led her out onto the ballroom

Heaven's Horizon

floor, where their reflections were duplicated dozens of times in the mirrors that lined the walls.

Everybody who was anybody in the county was there, and there was one guest who wasn't from Virginia at all, Lester Ross, a classmate with whom Bertram Flemming had formed a friendship so close that Lester had been invited to visit the Flemmings for the summer.

Andrew liked Lester, although he wasn't as close to him as Bert was. Lester was a pleasant-mannered young man, the second son of a Boston shipping family, eminently acceptable even in the rarified atmosphere of Virginia aristocracy. He wasn't nearly as handsome as either Andrew or Bert, his hair was brown, his eyes a warm, friendly hazel that drew people to him. Andrew scarcely gave him a second thought. It certainly didn't enter his mind that Lester's staying at the Flemmings' plantation house could be any threat to him. In Andrew's perfect world, a perfection that would reach its zenith when he and Marguerite were married, it was inconceivable that anything could go wrong.

There was a spate of entertainments in the engaged couple's honor after the ball. Lester, as the Flemmings' guest, was invited to all of them. And still it never crossed Andrew's mind that his world was on the verge of toppling. His own happiness was so great that he hardly noticed that Marguerite seemed preoccupied, that there were shadows in her violet eyes, as July melted into August. If he thought about it at all, he put it down to the fact that she wasn't getting enough sleep as the parties went on until the small hours of the mornings.

"Marguerite, darling, don't look so sad!" Andrew cajoled her one evening when, by some miracle, he had her to himself. They were in the Flemmings' rose arbor, the starlight was so bright that he could see her almost as clearly as though it had been daylight. "You haven't smiled for the past half-hour! Are you upset because I have to return to Harvard so soon? The year will pass quickly even though it seems like an eternity to us now."

"It isn't that," Marguerite said. Her eyes, when they met his, were so stricken that Andrew was jolted. "Andrew, I have something I must tell you, but I don't know how."

Andrew tried to laugh. Nothing could infringe on his happiness, his life. "Has your father refused to allow you to have a new dress for the Emmersons' garden party, then? As if anyone would notice what you were wearing! You're so beautiful that they look only at you, not at your gowns. Or have you had a tiff with Lorelei? Where is Lorelei, by the way? I've been expecting her to pop out of the shadows all evening."

"Andrew, stop it! I can't bear it!" Marguerite cried. "I have to tell you, and I'd rather cut off my arm. I'm not going to marry you, Andrew."

For a moment he just stared at her. She couldn't have said that she wasn't going to marry him, there was no way she could have said such a ridiculous thing.

She repeated it. "I can't marry you, Andrew. I'm not in love with you. I love you, but I'm not in love with you, if you can make any sense out of that. I'm in love with someone else."

"You're ill! You have a fever, you're in delirium!" Andrew burst out. "Marguerite, you aren't making sense! Of course you love me, we've loved each other for years, we've loved each other all our lives! I can't conceive of what's come over you!"

"Neither can I." Marguerite's face and voice were so miserable that Andrew was forced to accept that she was telling him the truth. "I never dreamed it would happen, and then it did happen. It seems as if I've loved you forever, that there could never be anyone else. It was always you. I was sure that it could never be anyone else but you. Only it is. I've fallen in love with someone else, and I have to ask you to release me from my promise."

"No! It isn't true!" The words were torn from Andrew's throat, a cry of furious anguish as every atom in his body refused to accept such a possibility. "There isn't anyone else, how could there be? You don't even know anybody else, anyone you haven't known and hadn't decided against years ago!"

"I'm sorry, Andrew. I'm so sorry that I could die of it."

Andrew grasped her shoulders, and began to shake her until her head snapped back and forth. She screamed in terror. "Who is it? Tell me! I'll kill him!"

"Andrew, stop it!" Marguerite cried. But it took Bert and Lester Ross, who had come sprinting into the garden on hearing Marguerite's screams, to wrench him away from her and pry his hands from her shoulders.

"Your sister's gone mad!" Andrew flung at Bert. "Stark-raving mad! She's trying to tell me that she doesn't love me, that she isn't going to marry me!"

"Andy, take it easy! Calm down, get ahold of yourself!" Bert commanded. "Margie isn't crazy, she's simply found someone else. It happens. It's too bad, but it does happen, and you'll have to accept it. I think you'd better go home and stay there until you have control of yourself. You're in no state for anyone to talk sensibly to you."

"Who is he?" Andrew shouted. "Bert, tell me! You know, I can see that you know. Damn it, you're going to tell me if I have to beat it out of you!"

"That won't be necessary," Lester Ross said. His face was pale, but he had complete control of himself. "Andrew, I'm sorry, but I'm the man. Marguerite and I love each other."

He'd barely got the words out of his mouth before Andrew was on him. He had to kill this man who had dared to come between him and the girl he loved. With Marguerite's screams splitting the air, screams that Andrew, in his rage, didn't even hear, his hands fastened around Lester's throat and he was exerting every ounce of his strength in the attempt to choke him to death.

Now Marguerite's older brother, Carl, was there, shouting for his father. It took all three men to subdue Andrew, and by the time they had pried his hands away from Lester's throat Lester's breath came in agonized gasps.

But Andrew wasn't completely subdued. Although a small measure of sanity had returned to him, his hatred blazed as fiercely as ever. Wrenching himself free from the hands that restrained him, he struck the still-gasping Lester across his face.

"The choice of weapons is yours," he said, each clipped word

Lydia Lancaster

falling like ice. "I'll meet you at dawn, by the creek in the Flemmings' south meadow, Bert will show you the place. Bert, I assume that you'll act as Mr. Ross's second?"

"Andrew, I am not going to fight you," Lester said. "This is ridiculous. I'm sorry that you've been hurt. But facts are facts, and for one of us to kill the other would solve nothing."

"Coward! Unprincipled, northern coward!" Andrew raged. "Marguerite couldn't love you, no girl could love a man who's afraid to face his rival in a fair duel!"

"Andrew, stop it! Lester is perfectly right. A duel would be ridiculous. Even if you killed him, I would never marry you. And if he killed you, I would still marry him. Do as Bert said, go home until you're able to think straight." Marguerite's face was as white as the starlight, her eyes burning as she put her hand in Lester's.

All three of the Flemming men accompanied Andrew back to his own plantation, afraid to let him go alone for fear he would come back and that his return would result in the direst consequences.

Marguerite collapsed into Lester's arms, sobbing, while her mother and her younger sister came hurrying to take her in charge as she wept until she was too exhausted to weep any longer. Hurting Andrew had been the hardest thing she'd ever had to do in her life. They'd grown up together, they'd always loved each other, and she loved him still, just as she had told him, only it wasn't the kind of love that would make for a lifetime as a happily married couple.

At home, closeted in his father's study while his father attempted to talk some sense into him, Andrew was silent, but his rage burned the deeper for all of that.

"You can't hold Miss Flemming to her promise if she loves someone else," Granger Leyland told his son. "I'm sorry that it happened. I always wanted for you and Marguerite to marry. But you should be thankful that Marguerite found the man she really loves before it was too late, before you were married."

Andrew's lifelong habit of courtesy to his father compelled him to listen to the older man, but Granger Leyland's words made no impression on him. In his hurt and rage, he was incapable of listening to reason. Marguerite had been his before Lester had entered the picture, she had always been his, and if Lester were removed she would be his again. Marguerite didn't love Lester, she couldn't, she was simply intrigued with him because he was someone new, and being from the North he was different from any of the young men she'd been familiar with all her life.

Up until this had happened, Andrew's drinking, what he had done of it, had been purely social. He'd engaged in his share of carousals at Harvard, but he had seldom overdone it as many of his classmates had done. His father was moderate in his habits and he'd instilled that quality in his son. A man should always have control of his faculties in order that he should have control of his life.

Now Granger Leyland did not raise an eyebrow when Andrew helped himself to a liberal portion of the brandy that Granger kept in his study to offer gentlemen guests when they were discussing business. The cut-glass decanter gave off arcs of color as Andrew tilted it over the snifter. Granger winced inwardly when Andrew downed its contents without regard for savoring the aroma and body as a gentleman should.

"It's an old adage but true for all that," Granger told his son. "Time heals. In a year, two years, you'll realize that this was for the best. You'll find someone else, and you'll be happier with her than you would have been with Marguerite. If Marguerite had truly loved you, she wouldn't have succumbed to Lester Ross so soon after meeting him. There's Lorelei Evans, for instance. She is a lovely girl, and I've always thought that if it hadn't been for Marguerite, you and she would have made a match of it."

"I won't be considering any other girl for some time, Father," Andrew said. "If you will excuse me, I'll go to bed." Without as much as looking at his father for permission, Andrew picked up the decanter and took it with him to his bedroom. Granger Leyland sighed. Drinking himself into oblivion wasn't the solution he himself would have chosen, but Andrew was young, and beyond waking up in the morning with a throbbing head and nausea roiling in his stomach, he'd be all right.

When Andrew awoke late the next day, his hangover was monumental. Pompeii, the slave who had been his personal servant since

Lydia Lancaster

he'd been old enough to walk, regarded him with sympathy that he didn't dare show. Only a year older than Andrew, Pompeii'd been chosen as his young master's playmate and companion as well as his servant, and Andrew had always been kind to him.

This morning, Pompeii could almost feel the misery that Andrew was suffering. And knowing the remedy, he was quick to offer it.

"Hair of the dog, Master Andrew," he said. "I know it'll be hard to get down, but once it's there it'll settle your stomach if you can hold it down."

The smell of the brandy made Andrew gag, but he steeled himself to swallow it. For a moment he thought it was going to come up again, but he struggled against retching, and when the first acute impulse of his stomach to reject it had passed, he took another.

"That's the way, Master Andrew. Take it cautious, though. You don't want to overdo it lest you get sick again. You stay right there in bed. I'll fetch you some breakfast. Lots of strong coffee is what you need now, and some ham and eggs to get your strength back."

His eyes closed, his face pasty, Andrew lay back against his pillows. Oh, God, Marguerite! His hand reached for the decanter that Pompeii had left on his bedside stand. The fiery liquid on his empty stomach hit him full force. The nausea was gone, the throbbing of his head had eased, but he needed more before he could face the day and all the days that would follow.

Outwardly, Andrew presented a calm face to the world, and his family and friends breathed a collective sigh of relief. Marguerite's jilting of him was a scandal that rocked the county, and as the county gentry were clannish, Lester Ross was looked on as an interloper and everyone was solidly on Andrew's side. But the Flemmings' standing in the community forced them to tolerate the northerner, and still include him on social occasions.

Andrew's pride forced him to accept the invitations that came his way, and it was inevitable that sooner or later he and Lester would meet. This happened less than a week after the disastrous evening when Marguerite had told him that she loved Lester and that he must release her from her engagement. Jeffery Cummings, whose family owned one of the finest plantations in the neighborhood, had arranged an evening of cards for a number of young gentlemen. Whist was still a highly favored game, and Andrew was one of the dozen friends who gathered at the Cummingses' plantation for an evening without the distracting company of ladies.

Bert Flemming was there, and he had brought Lester. There were a few uneasy glances before it appeared that Andrew had control of his emotions and was going to behave as a gentleman.

Brandy flowed freely, although none of the young gentlemen drank to excess, preferring to keep clear heads so that they could win if the cards fell their way, or lose as little as possible if luck ran against them.

But if the other young gentlemen's heads were clear, Andrew's was not. He held his liquor well, but he had been drinking steadily ever since the night he had drunk himself into a stupor and Pompeii had urged him to drink a little more the next morning in order to avoid the worst of his hangover. He hadn't done his drinking overtly. Even his father was unaware of the amount he had consumed. He'd been drinking before he'd arrived at the Cummingses' plantation, and he continued drinking during the game. Only Bert, who knew him so well, was uneasy.

"Andy, aren't you overdoing it a little? You won't be able to see the cards if you keep on, and you still have a long ride ahead of you tonight."

Andrew's eyes were level, his hands steady. He showed no outward appearance of having had too much to drink. But inwardly he was seething. To have to spend a social evening with the man who had betrayed him, to have to play a gentlemen's game of cards with him, pushed his endurance to the breaking point.

He flashed a smile at Bert, but it didn't reach his eyes. "I'm fine," he said, as he lifted his glass again, "except that the cards are hexed. I haven't had a decent hand for the last half-hour."

The cards were running against him, but not as much as they would have if his head had been clear. Twice he'd failed to follow the lead and had to concede the game because of his misplay. Even a young man of his magnificent constitution could not drink steadily for days without feeling the effects. And as frequently as he lost a trick because he lacked trump or his trump was low, Lester Ross won one.

The stakes were high. Virginia gentlemen did not play for shillings, but it wasn't the money that Andrew was out of pocket that bothered him, it was the fact that it was Lester Ross who was winning.

Another round was dealt and played, with Lester having the deal. Once again, Andrew lost trick after trick. It had to be more than coincidence. His brandy-fumed mind leaped to the most logical explanation. If a man would cheat another man out of the girl he loved, he would cheat at cards. Lester was a northerner, and like most of his class, Andrew was of the opinion that nearly every northerner was unprincipled. With an oath, he flung the remaining cards in his hand on the table and fixed his eyes on Lester.

"You, sir, are cheating," he said.

There was an electrified silence. To accuse a man of cheating was virtually unheard of, especially in what was a casual game among friends.

"Andy!" Bert protested, while Lester's face went white and two white lines appeared between his nostrils and the corners of his mouth.

"He's cheating. He stacked the cards and dealt himself the winning hand. It isn't the first time tonight, either." Now that he'd said it, Andrew believed it.

Lester retained control of himself. "You are mistaken, Mr. Leyland. I will put it down to the fact that you've had too much to drink."

"Are you calling me a liar?" Andrew rose, his own face deathly white. "I'll have the satisfaction of meeting you tomorrow at dawn."

Now every face in the room was white. This was a challenge that could not be sidestepped. To be accused of cheating at a card game was a mortal insult, and Lester would have to defend his honor or be disgraced for--as long as he lived. If he refused, even Marguerite would turn her back on him. Raised as she'd been in the southern tradition, there was no way she could marry a man who'd been branded a coward as well as a cheat.

Lester's eyes had turned from hazel to a fiery black. He also stood up, and bowed. "At your service, sir. I take it that the choice of weapons is mine? Pistols, then. I'm afraid that I'll have to impose on Mr. Flemming for a set of dueling pistols. Not being a southerner, I have none in my possession."

If there had been any way Bert could have put a stop to this insanity he would have done it. But his sister's honor was at stake as well as Lester's, and he had no choice but to agree.

The card game was over. Andrew flung himself on his horse and galloped home, filled with exultation. He hadn't been able to kill Lester Ross for stealing Marguerite's affections from him, but a gentleman had every right to shoot a man who cheated at cards.

He experienced several moments of light-headedness as the clear air filled his lungs after hours spent in a smoke-filled room. His magnificent horsemanship saved him from going off, and his mount, one of the best in Virginia, kept up a pace so steady that he was able to keep his seat. A measure of sanity returned as his brain adjusted to the change in the air. Marguerite would never forgive him. His standing in the county would be jeopardized, a challenge such as he had issued, without palpable proof, was something that would not be looked upon with favor. His reputation would be ruined, his family would be disgraced.

But the challenge had been given, and there was no way that he could withdraw it beyond making an abject apology and retracting his accusation. His pride would not permit that. His honor was on the line.

So be it. On his arrival at home, Andrew helped himself to two or three more liberal drinks of his father's best brandy, and then let Pompeii put him to bed after giving him orders to wake him two hours before dawn.

There were a dozen witnesses the next morning when the two young men met at a spot halfway between the Cummingses' plantation and Virginia's Pride. Bertram's face was the color of putty as he had to stand by and watch the man who had been his friend from earliest childhood, and the man who was going to be his brother-in-law, attempt to kill each other. It was doubtful that both of them would leave the field alive, and whichever one was the victor, Bert would suffer a lifetime of regret for the loss of the other.

Andrew himself had no doubts as to who would emerge the victor. He was a dead shot, and he was fast. He'd been familiar with firearms from the time he had learned to walk. His emotions were unclear about how he would feel about being a murderer, but he'd have the satisfaction of knowing that he had erased a scoundrel from the face of the earth. His hands were steady, his eyes were clear, in spite of the brandy.

But if his hands and his eyes were steady, his reactions had suffered. At the command of "Fire!" he spun to face Lester, his timing a split-second off as he pulled the trigger. Both reports sounded like one and for an instant he thought that Lester hadn't got a shot off at all. And then he felt a shock that knocked him off his feet. There was no pain, only an astonished numbness before the sky that had only just brightened into day turned dark again and he wondered if a storm had closed in to obscure the sun without his noticing.

His shot had only grazed Lester's shoulder. Lester, much less expert as a marksman, had miscalculated so that his shot was low, smashing into Andrew's hip as Andrew had stood with his side turned toward him so as to present the smallest possible target, as was the custom. It was fortunate for Andrew that the shot had been low. If it had been higher, striking his torso, it would have been certain to kill him.

The consequences were serious enough as it was. Ross's bullet had shattered his hip. For weeks, Andrew lay drifting in and out of consciousness, while both the physicians who had been summoned and his family and his friends feared for his life. Even if he lived, he would be crippled, only half a man. Realizing that, in his rare moments of full awareness, Andrew had no desire to live, and everyone who loved him was in despair.

Only Lorelei refused to give up. She was there constantly. Immediately on learning what had happened and how desperate the situation was, she had packed a box and, defying her father and mother, had moved into Virginia's Pride until Andrew should either

Heaven's Horizon

recover or die. She loved Andrew, she had loved him as long as he had loved Marguerite. Born with all the pride of a southern gentlewoman, she had hidden the love so thoroughly that even Marguerite had not suspected. When her bridesmaid's gown was being planned, she had smiled for Marguerite's joy. But now Marguerite didn't matter. Gentle by nature, she was capable of fighting like a lioness when Andrew's life was at stake.

Constance Leyland, Andrew's mother, welcomed Lorelei with gratitude. The constant nursing that was demanded taxed her strength to its limits, and Andrew's one sister was only thirteen, too young to be of much help. Pompeii was a godsend, seeming to be able to function without sleep as he tended his master's more intimate needs, but it was Lorelei who sat beside Andrew's bed, holding his hand, talking to him, commanding him to fight, to live, not to give up. She bathed his forehead during the sweltering August days when the suffering man was in torment from the pain and the heat. She spoon-fed him, coaxing, cajoling, demanding, until he would open his mouth and swallow the broths and gruels that his insulted body needed if it was to survive at all. She moistened his cracked lips, she fanned him to cool his sweat-soaked body, she waged a personal vendetta on every fly or mosquito that dared to invade his room.

Even during the first semiconscious days after the duel, Andrew was aware that she was there. Her cool hand on his burning forehead soothed him. Her gentle voice, filled with love and confidence, gave him the courage to go on fighting his pain, to start fighting to live. And as the weeks passed, as summer receded into autumn, Andrew found another reason to live.

Vengeance. He'd live, if only for the reason that he must track Lester Ross down and kill him for having ruined his life.

Once he had begun to heal, the convalescence was long. His hip didn't knit properly, the damage to the bones had been too severe for the medical science of that day to repair. It was gravely doubted that he would ever walk again, or that if he did walk, it wouldn't be merely to drag himself around on crutches. His body wasted away until he was little more than a skeleton, and there was little doubt that it was Lorelei, who could manage to coax food down his throat when everyone else failed, who was the deciding factor in whether he would live or die.

It was late October before Andrew could attempt to get on his feet. Only he and Pompeii knew the agony of those first attempted steps, undertaken in the dead of night so that no one else would know, with Pompeii holding him up while his body was a dead weight that seemed to press down on his legs as though he weighed a ton instead of being skin and bones held together by fragile skin.

But Andrew had a driving purpose to keep him trying. His hatred for Lester Ross, his thirst for revenge, drove him on. One faltering step, followed by one more, became one more and yet another under his own power before he staggered and would have fallen but for Pompeii.

And still Lorelei stayed on, helping Constance with the nursing, freeing her to attend to the myriad other duties demanded of a plantation mistress. By now the county had accepted the situation. With the entire family there, there was no breath of scandal. Still, if Andrew didn't ask her to marry him as soon as he was well enough, he would be looked upon as a cad.

Lorelei never thought of that. Her only concern was that Andrew should get well. Sleeping with one eye and both ears open because of her concern for him, she became aware of the stealthy movements in Andrew's room and went to investigate. Horrified, she gathered all her courage and set herself to aid and abet the determined invalid, adding her support to Pompeii's, telling him that he could do it, that he could take two more steps tonight than he had the night before, and then that he could take three or four.

"You can do it, Andrew. Just see how much you've improved, your strength is returning by leaps and bounds! Try again, just two more steps, come to me, I'm only a little way away."

"I lurch as if one of my legs was a foot shorter than the other!" Andrew raged.

"Not that bad. You're exaggerating. Of course you'll have a limp, but what matter is that? Just walking is the important thing! Try again, just one more step before you rest!"

By the time Andrew astonished his family and the physicians by

Heaven's Horizon

walking downstairs with only Pompeii assisting him, Marguerite and Lester Ross had disappeared without a trace. All of Andrew's efforts failed to unearth them. It had been inevitable that word of Andrew's ravings that he would exact revenge should reach them, and they knew that Andrew would carry out his threats if they didn't cover their tracks so that he could never find them.

The Flemmings knew where they were, but even Bert refused to divulge their whereabouts, and no one else would tell him. It was as if they had stepped off the surface of the earth.

"It's for your own protection as much as for theirs," Bert told him. "I don't understand you anymore, Andy. Don't think that I don't realize how hard it is for you. You've been through hell. But the duel was your own fault, and if you'd been your normal self, you would have killed Les. Let it go, pick up your life and go on from here. That's the only advice I can give you. I will not, and I never will, tell you where my sister and Les have gone, and I pray to God that you never find them!"

Frustrated, twisted inside as badly as his body was twisted, Andrew at last gave up his search. But he could not bear to go on living in Virginia, where memories taunted him at every turn. He refused to consider finishing his education at Harvard, where he would be an object of pity and speculation after he had been the campus idol, envied and admired. What he needed was a new life in a new country where no one would know him or the reason he had chosen to exile himself from family and friends.

He settled on Georgia, and his father, filled with grief, agreed to finance him until he had made a start and could go on on his own. Granger Leyland had to arrange for an additional mortgage on Virginia's Pride in order to raise the money, but he did it without a second thought.

"There's just one thing, Andrew. You need a wife, a woman who will work shoulder to shoulder with you, and give you children. You'll never have any kind of a life without that, no matter how much of a success you make. I'm convinced that Lorelei would accept you. Her devotion to you all through your illness proves that you couldn't make a better choice."

Lydia Lancaster

"I will not ask her to risk such a venture with me, Father. Georgia is still largely wilderness, there will be danger, and certainly there will be hardship. No gently bred lady should be asked to follow her husband into such an uncertain future."

"The future is only as uncertain as you will allow it to be," Granger told his son. "And as for Lorelei, she has the courage to face whatever might have to be faced. You owe it to her, for one thing. The whole county expects you to marry her. If you leave her behind her life will be ruined. She loves you. She's loved you ever since you were children, and she's a woman who will never change. She'd follow you into hell, if that were the only way she could have you, but you can see that she follows you into a heaven of your own making if you so choose."

Eventually, because he knew that his father was right, Andrew agreed. He didn't love Lorelei. He knew that he would never love another woman for as long as he lived. But Lorelei was gentle and agreeable, she was lovely enough to be a credit to him among his peers, and her unquestionable loyalty to him was the deciding factor. She would never desert him, she would never turn her back on him. And she would give him the sons that were the only thing he had to live for now.

In view of the circumstances, they were married quietly at Lorelei's parents' home, with only their two families as witnesses. There were no parties, no celebrations.

As early the next spring as was feasible, they set out for Georgia to carve out a new life for themselves. Lorelei set out with shining faith in the future, leaving all else behind her, taking only Zoe, who had been her nurse from the day she had been born. Andrew refused to take even Pompeii. He wanted no reminders, he wanted no one, not even a loyal slave, to know of his humiliation, and so he took only his determination to succeed and to build a dynasty that would compensate him for all he had lost. The few slaves he took with him to help with the move would be sold off as soon as they arrived in Georgia, all except Zoe and Zoe's young son, who was too young to realize what had happened, hardly more than a toddler.

Chapter Seven

Now, more than twenty-two years after Andrew Leyland had come to Georgia, he paced his study at Leyland's Landing, all of the rage and frustration of those years roiling inside of him.

He had succeeded in carving out a huge plantation in this wilderness. His success had been all that he had dreamed of. But without sons to carry on after him, it meant nothing, and Lorelei had failed to give him sons. There was only Cordelia.

He might have married again, but he dreaded being perceived as an object of pity, at best—at worst, contempt. The almost constant pain he had to endure had etched deep lines on his face, his lurching gait was something that was bound to repel any woman of breeding. Lorelei had known him when he was whole and attractive, when he could have chosen from any number of suitable young ladies. And Lorelei had loved him, her love had been so strong that it had endured even through all the years of loneliness that he had inflicted on her.

He acknowledged his debt to her. Without her love, without her loyalty, it was doubtful that he would have survived at all. But

Lydia Lancaster

gratitude falls far short of love, and although he had been unfailingly courteous to her, unfailingly gentle, he could not forget that she had failed him in the most important aspect of his life. A man without sons was as nothing, all that he had achieved would die with him.

He had never lost sight of the fact that Cordelia would marry and provide him with grandchildren. Grandsons were better than no heirs at all. His sending her to Boston to be educated had been calculated. He hadn't wanted her at Leyland's Landing, where her sex and her complete difference from the daughter Marguerite might have given him were constant reminders of all he had lost. He had hoped that she would find a man to marry among the Reynards' friends, and that she would make her home in Boston, well out of his way.

He had no interest in having his future grandchildren near him, in seeing them grow and develop into adulthood. All that was necessary was for Cordelia to provide him with a grandson who would be named Andrew Leyland as his given names, who would have Leyland blood flowing in his veins and who would take over Leyland's Landing when the time came, so that his line would go on.

When he had received Donal MacKenzie's letter, he had been satisfied. An Englishman would be eminently suitable, even more suitable than an American because he would take Cordelia to live in England with him and he would not be inflicted with any of them until his namesake was sent to Georgia in order that Andrew could acquaint him with his heritage and train him to manage the plantation. As that would be another eighteen or twenty years in the future, Andrew was content.

And now, this evening, Donal had dropped his bombshell. Marguerite's son, Lester Ross's son! As impossible as the odds were, and Andrew was aware of the astronomical odds, fate had decreed that he should suffer this final blow, the certainty that his daughter's children, his grandchildren, would carry Lester Ross's blood in their veins.

It was intolerable. He could not, he would not, accept it. As he had thought in the first instant after Donal had told him of his true lineage, he'd see him dead first. Cordelia would marry again, she

Heaven's Horizon

was young and even if it took her two or three years to recover from her grief she would marry again and provide him with an heir. Although he had cut himself off entirely from his family and the friends he had known in Virginia, he would get in touch with them if necessary and arrange to send Cordelia to Virginia, where she would be thrown into the company of any number of suitable men, where the social life she would lead would be certain to result in her remarriage.

But first Donal MacKenzie must be disposed of, and it would have to be done immediately.

Andrew lurched to his leather chair and lowered himself into it, placing his unfinished glass of brandy on the table beside it. The pain in his hip had intensified from his pacing. He could not walk for any distance without tiring and having the pain grow. He was able to sit the saddle, using his legs, pressed against the horse's sides, to ease the pressure on his hip, so that he could ride nearly as well as he had when he'd been a young man, but staying on his feet, active, for any length of time was agony for him. Damn Lester Ross for having crippled him, damn the doctors who hadn't known enough to be able to set his shattered hip and repair the damaged muscles so that he would have healed into a whole man again. And damn Donal MacKenzie, who had wooed and won his daughter, who thought to give him grandchildren of Lester Ross's blood!

In the garden, Cordelia and Donal were happy, filled with plans for the future. First the stopover in Virginia, which Cordelia looked forward to with shining eyes and a heart that was bubbling over. How social Virginia was, how glamorous the society there! And as Donal's wife, as a kinswoman to Donal's mother's family, she would be swept into the thick of things, welcomed, feted. It was like a fairy tale come true. And, then, early in the autumn, while the weather would still be fair, they would sail across the Atlantic Ocean, the voyage their real honeymoon, to enchanted England where she and Donal would live happily ever after.

She'd never return to America, she'd never return to Leyland's Landing. There was nothing to hold her here now. Her mother was dead, her father a stranger to her, Nadine and the Reynards estranged from her. She would visit her mother's grave tomorrow, she'd strip what was left of Lorelei's garden to cover her grave with flowers, and then she would turn her back on Leyland's Landing forever. The only thing she wanted to take from this place had already been granted her, the assurance that Aunt Zoe would go with her.

"Donal, sometimes I think I'm dreaming, that I'll wake up in the morning and realize that none of this is true."

"Shall I pinch you?" Donal asked. But he had a better idea. He kissed her instead, and no dream could convey the intensity of that kiss, the flood of feeling that rushed through her body as she responded to him without reservation.

"It's too early to go to bed," Donal murmured close to her ear, nibbling at its lobe.

"But I'm tired," Cordelia lied. What a delightful lie it was, and one that was sure to be forgiven. "It isn't too early for me."

Their arms around each other, they entered the house. As they passed Andrew's study, the sound of their footsteps made his mouth compress into a grim line. Let them enjoy tonight. It would be the last night they would ever have together.

Donal looked about him with interest as he and Andrew reined their mounts to a stop. It had been his father-in-law's suggestion that Donal see something of the country around Leyland's Landing before he and Cordelia left on the first leg of their journey.

"Georgia isn't all cultivated plantation land by any means. You'll want to see the forests, the prime hunting lands. Cordelia and Aunt Zoe will be busy all day, packing, she'll want to take everything she owns with her and it will be wise of us to remove ourselves while she changes her mind a dozen times about what to take and what to leave behind. I'll have to send a wagon after you, all the way to Virginia. We men are fortunate in that respect, we can travel light with a minimum of luggage."

"I'd enjoy that, sir." And Donal was enjoying it. It had been too long since he had been in the saddle, mounted on a fine piece of horseflesh, and Andrew Leyland's mounts were fine indeed, nettle-

Heaven's Horizon

some, perfectly trained, eager to go. Beautiful animals, horses that even a hunt-enthusiast Englishman would be proud to add to his stables.

This was not a hunting expedition, but each man had a pistol and Andrew carried a rifle in a saddle sheath. The Georgia wilderness in 1829 was no place to go unarmed. Donal had first been amused, and then impressed, when Andrew had insisted on arming him.

"This isn't England, Donal. We're nowhere near as settled and civilized as your country, although I understand that road agents are a danger even there. For myself, I'm glad that there are wide stretches of wilderness, because without them Leyland's Landing would not exist today. This is a big country, and the larger share of it is unsettled. We still have all of the West, clear to the Pacific Ocean, to conquer. However, I'm satisfied with Georgia and what we have right here."

Andrew had hesitated about providing Donal with a pistol, but in the end he had thought it necessary. Cordelia might remember afterward, if he hadn't armed her husband, and wonder why. The pistol at Donal's side provided no danger to Andrew, because Andrew had no intention of letting him use it.

"What's that just ahead of us, sir? Some kind of a bog, it looks to be."

"It is. Don't ride Commander any closer to it, the ground won't bear his weight, but it's safe for you to dismount and take a closer look." Andrew too got down from his horse, and the men tethered them to a nearby sapling. "Go on ahead, don't slow your pace for me, I'm not a champion walker anymore. I'll catch up with you before you've examined the spot to your satisfaction."

Donal strode ahead, realizing that to slow his pace would be an insult to the older man.

The ground under his boots became more marshy as he neared the stretch of the bog itself. Its surface seemed to quiver, and there were no animal tracks around it, the wild things avoiding it as the death trap their instincts told them it was. There were places like this in England, Donal had seen more than one during stays with friends who had country estates, and they were similarly avoided.

Lydia Lancaster

The quiet was almost a living presence as he stopped when he thought he had gone as far as was prudent. He didn't want to ruin his boots, much less get caught in the mire. All around him, the forest seemed to be as primeval as it must have been at the beginning of time. All sorts of game abounded here. Indians, notably Creeks, had used it as their hunting grounds, their moccasined feet leaving no trail discernible to a white man. Andrew Leyland had had trouble with the Creeks in the past, before Andrew Jackson had defeated them and cleared most of them out, sending them to reservations somewhere far to the west.

Donal felt a coldness in the small of his back, the short hairs at the nape of his neck stiffened, almost as though there were danger of being ambushed by a party of warlike Creeks at this very moment. He shook the feeling off, laughing at himself. The smile had no more than twitched at the corners of his mouth before the bullet struck him just beneath his left shoulder, and as it spun him around, his mouth falling open with surprise, another one caught him at the side of his forehead.

He fell, his eyes, already glazing, hardly recognizing his father-in-law, who stood with his rifle lying at his feet and his still-smoking pistol in his hand. His father-in-law had shot him, but why? It was incomprehensible. In the name of heaven, why?

And then there was nothing. Andrew Leyland stood where he was for a moment, making sure that his shots had been effective in wiping the life from this man who had come so near to wrecking what was left of his own.

There was no doubt of it. Donal MacKenzie was dead. Slowly, walking with his painful lurch, Andrew covered the ground between them. He dragged Donal's body to the edge of the bog, sinking in to his knees himself but sure of his footing because he was thoroughly familiar with this place. And then he pushed the inert body from him, as far as he could, and Donal began to sink. In a few moments his body would be covered. No one knew how deep the bog was, but it was certain that anything as heavy as a man's body would disappear from sight forever, never to be found.

Andrew made his way back to solid ground. The going was hard,

Heaven's Horizon

it would have been hard for a whole man, much less one who walked with Andrew's difficulty. But his muddied boots and clothing were all to the good, they would confirm his story when he returned to Leyland's Landing and told Cordelia that Donal had wandered into the bog, despite his warnings, and been trapped before Andrew could get to him to help him. No one would ever be able to prove that it had happened in any other way, even if anyone would have any reason to suspect that Andrew might have wanted Donal dead.

He leaned his back against the trunk of a tree while he waited, breathing heavily from his exertions. Donal's body was already half submerged, it would only be a few moments now. The horses had shied at the sound of the shots, but they had been tethered firmly, and they were quiet now, their ears pricked forward. In a moment, he would mount his own and lead Commander home with an empty saddle. In the meantime, he'd clean both of his firearms and reload them. He'd taken pains to bring rags and oil in his saddlebag, as well as the food that they had brought along for their dawn-to-dark expedition.

His breath coming evenly now, he moved to the horses and was just reaching into the saddlebag when he thought he heard something. It wasn't a sound an animal would have made, it had a human quality to it that put him on the alert. Another glance toward the bog showed him that Donal's body had all but disappeared, only his face was still showing above the surface. Cleaning the guns would have to wait. It was probably nothing but his nerves, but it would be expedient to mount and get away from here just in case some traveler or hunter was approaching.

Behind the shelter of a thick growth of bushes, a pair of eyes watched until Andrew was out of sight. Then a pair of hands, sun-browned, rough from heavy work, but small and shapely, parted the bushes and the rest of the face came into view. It was a girl's face. She was young, no more than nineteen or twenty. She was dressed in a shapeless calico dress that had faded until the original pattern was all but indiscernible. Her hair, a rich, bright auburn, was plaited in one thick braid that hung down her back, fastened with a leather thong. Her feet were bare, and not too clean.

She pursed her mouth and whistled, the whistle indistinguishable from that of the blue jay that answered her from its perch on a limb a few yards away. The whistle was answered by a second. Nate had better stir his stumps and get here, or it'ud be too late. Maybe it was too late already, but Rebecca McCabe wasn't going to concede that fact until she'd given it her best try.

Her feet made no sound as she raced to the edge of the bog and threw herself full length onto the marshy ground that surrounded it. Her arm reached out, and she strained to the limit her muscles would endure, and her hand grasped Donal's hair and clung. She used every ounce of strength in her body to hold his head above the surface of the treacherous slime that was determined to engulf him.

"Nate, you git here, hear me?" she called. It was safe enough to use her voice now, the man on the horse, the man who had murdered this man, was long gone, out of earshot. "You hurry, I cain't hold on to him much longer!"

An adolescent boy, perhaps fourteen, loped into the clearing from the spot he had wriggled to, unseen and unheard, immediately after Andrew had thrown Donal's body into the bog. He'd been the one who had made the noise that had sent Andrew away, and he'd done it deliberately, for just that purpose. There hadn't been much danger in it. Wasn't no way that man was going to find him iffen he didn't want to be found. And once that body sank, there'd be no gittin' it back, an' there might be something of value on it, a ring, a watch, a watch chain. Even money. And there was the pistol in its holster. It was a good pistol, an expensive pistol, a piece such as neither Nathan McCabe nor his father or his older brother who wasn't right in the head ever since he'd fallen out of a tree and all but bashed his brains out when he'd been five, could hope to own.

"Grab aholt of my ankles!" Rebecca commanded, the cords of her neck standing out above the neckline of her dress. "Pull, durn it! You kin pull harder'n that! Pull, or we'll lose him fer sure!"

Nathan pulled. He was small for his age, but he was strong and wiry. He pulled harder, and inch by inch, as he pulled, Rebecca worked her flattened body backward, bringing Donal's head farther out of the bog, then his neck, then his shoulders.

Heaven's Horizon

The struggle to extricate the body from the bog took a full twenty minutes, and by the time Donal's torso lay on marshy ground that would support its weight, both Rebecca and Nate were covered with sweat and their muscles jumped and quivered from the strain that had been placed on them.

"Got 'im! He's safe enough now, he ain't about to sink. Leave us rest a minute," Rebecca panted. "Glory, he's a heavy un! But he's a rich un, too, or else he was afore that other un did him in. Did you ken who it was, Nate? Wasn't it Andrew Leyland, from Leyland's Landing? He sure-lord limped when he walked, an' I don't know of any other man in these parts that limps like that. I've heered tell of him. Mean cuss, from all accounts, don't hev nothin' to do with nobody."

" 'Twere old Andy Leyland fer sure," Nate gasped. "I seen him oncet, in town, Pa pointed him out to me. Looked like he wouldn't spit on the likes of us iffen it'ud choked him holdin' it in."

"Now why'd he go murderin' somebody?" Rebecca wondered. Not that it mattered to her. The gentry's affairs held no interest for her. People like Andrew Leyland and the other plantation owners were worlds apart from the cabin she and her mother and father and her two brothers lived in, scratching a bare existence from their patch of ground, eking it out by hunting and berrying and nutting. Crackers, folks like Andrew Leyland called them, or red-necks. Whatever they were called, it was derogatory.

They'd rested long enough. "All right, let's haul him the rest of the way out, an' see what we kin find," Rebecca said.

"The pistol's mine," Nathan told her, glaring at her from underneath sun-bleached eyebrows. His eyes, a pale blue, blazed with determination. "You gotta tell Pa it's mine, Becky. I'm the one did the work of gittin' him outa the bog, so it rightly belongs to me. Pa kin have the money, and Rufe kin have that ring that's on his finger. Ain't no stone in it but it's sorta purty. Iffen he has a watch, it won't be no good now, arter bein' in all that mud an' slime, but the pistol kin be cleaned as good as new."

They tugged and hauled, and the going was easier now. Donal's legs came out of the bog, and they dragged him away from the marshy ground to where they could work his clothing over more easily. It was hard enough as it was, all sodden and filthy, and it stank. The bog didn't smell exactly like Ma's lilac bush in the spring, the one that didn't do good because it'ud come all the way from Pennsylvania an' the roots had been all but dead by the time Etta had got it planted. And it was too warm in Georgia for it anyway, but some springs it made some blossoms that were the sweetest things Rebecca had ever smelled. It was the only pretty thing around their cabin, flowers were too much trouble and there were enough wild ones in the woods so it would be downright foolish to try to grow them in the packed earth of their overgrown yard.

Rebecca grasped Donal's hand and tugged at the ring. It was a tight fit over the knuckle, and it took her a little while. Nathan snatched the pistol from its holster; it was the best of luck that it was still there and not at the bottom of the bog. He extricated the pocket watch and chain from the fob and watch pockets. Ma'ud likely like the chain, iffen Becky didn't latch onto it for a pretty.

"We'd best git to strippin' him," Nathan said. "Look at them boots! They's too big fer me, but mebbe Pa kin git his feet in 'em. And them clothes is expensive, they's real quality. You reckon Ma'll be able to git the mud an' stink offen 'em so's they kin be used?"

"Certain sure. We ain't goin' to let good material like that go to waste! C'mon, haul them britches off! We'll take the underwear too, ain't no use leavin' anythin'."

The buttons of the shirt were hard to manage, sodden as the buttonholes were. Nathan knelt with one knee on either side of Donal's chest as he worked at them, his eyes puckered up from the effort.

"Handsome cuss, weren't he?" Rebecca said, as she removed the studs from Donal's cuffs. "Will you look at that! This here's gold, Nate. Wonder if I could find some way to make 'em into a pair of earbobs?"

"Your ears ain't pierced," Nate said, always practical. "You gotta hev pierced ears to wear earbobs. 'Sides, we couldn't do it anyhow, and even iffen we could you wouldn't dast wear 'em. We

Heaven's Horizon

don't want nobody askin' questions 'bout how we come by anythin'." He yanked at the last button, impatient to get this task over with.

His yelp of pure terror made his sister drop the cuff links she had wiped free of mud and was admiring.

"Nate! You skeered the daylights outa me! Look there, you went an' made me drop them cuff links! Iffen I cain't find 'em, I'll skin yer hide right offen yer back!"

"He ain't dead! He's a-breathin'!" Nate yelped.

"Yer outa yer head. Course he's dead. Shot, ain't he? Deader'n a doornail an' it's a pity too 'cause he sure is handsome! A real handsome gentleman, I'd of liked to see him alive an' all cleaned up, he'd of been somethin' to see."

"He's alive, I tell you! He's a-breathin'!"

Rebecca left off searching for the cuff links, and crawled over to Donal's half-naked body. She put her ear to his mouth, and sure enough he was breathing. Not hardly breathing, but enough so that she knew that there was still a spark of life somewhere in his body.

"Crimminy! We'd better hurry an' finish strippin' him an' dump him back in the bog!" Nate said. "We-uns don't want to get us mixed up in anythin' like this. He's supposed to be dead an' we'd best put him back where he's supposed to be!"

Rebecca was hardly listening to him. She used a corner of her skirt to wipe the mud and slime from Donal's face. The crease along his forehead was deep and oozing blood, and there was blood coming from the hole in his shoulder. Rebecca had never spent a day in school in her life but there were things that she knew, and knowing that a dead man doesn't bleed was one of them.

"He's alive all right. Glory, but he's purty! I never seed such a purty man before," Rebecca said.

"Hurry up an' help me git this danged shirt offen him! We wanta make tracks away from here fast as we kin!" Nathan demanded. "We'll git all he has to git, an' dump him back in the bog. He won't never know the difference, he's most dead anyhow, he'ud been dead already iffen we hadn't fished him out."

"If we hadn't been checkin' your trapline, we'd never of seen it happen," Rebecca said. "It's fate, like."

"Sure is. Lookit all the stuff we woulda missed."

Lydia Lancaster

"I don't mean that. It's fate we got him out whilst he's still alive. We ain't gonna throw him back in, Nate. We-un's gonna carry him home and see iffen Ma kin patch him up."

"You're daft!" Nate stared at her as though he was afraid that she'd start raving and frothing at the mouth. "You're sartin outa your mind! He's a-gonna die, an' the sooner we git outa here an' back home, the better it'll be fer us. We won't throw him back in iffen you don't want to. That'ud be hard, seein' as he's still a-breathin'. I wouldn't like to dream how we'd kilt him ourselves, it would almost seem like we done the murder. But we don't want to be anywhere near around this here place. Them plantation folks ain't nobody to go a-tanglin' with."

"We're totin' him home," Rebecca said. Her voice gave no room for argument. "I likes him. An' mebbe he'll give us somethin' fer our trouble, iffen Ma kin save him. Iffen she cain't, then we kin cart him back and throw him back where we found him."

Nathan sighed. He knew there would be no use in arguing with his sister. Rebecca was not only older, but she always got her way. It didn't pay to cross Becky. She was a wildcat, she was a holy terror, if she was crossed. It didn't happen often, mostly she was nice and agreeable, but if she set her mind to something, there was no way to make her change it.

"He's heavy, an' it's gonna be a mighty far piece to tote him."

"Then we'd better git started. Gather up them duds, sling'em around your neck. I don't wanna go joltin' 'im around tryin' to git him dressed agin, it might set the bleedin' off more'n it already is. Put the boots on, half-wit! It'll save carryin' 'em. No, don't put 'em on! They'd leave tracks an' our bare feet won't. Tie 'em in the britches so's they won't fall out."

Slowly, because Donal was as dead a weight as he would have been if he had been as dead as Andrew Leyland thought he was, the two young people picked up their burden, Rebecca carrying the shoulders and Nathan the feet, and turned their footsteps toward their cabin, clear on the other side of this patch of woods, so isolated that strangers seldom passed by. That was the way Eben McCabe liked it, away from interference from the outside world, a law unto himself. And if this man who was supposed to be dead and wasn't, didn't die, that isolation that Eben liked because he wanted to be far enough out of the way so that no sheriff was going to come along and evict him, like he'd been evicted from his farm back in the north when he'd fallen behind on his mortgage payments, that isolation would be a mercy because there wasn't any chance in the world that Andrew Leyland or any of the other high and mighty plantation owners would come wandering along and recognize him.

"Don't know," Etta McCabe said. Stripped naked, washed, Donal lay unconscious on the corn-shuck pallet on the rough bed in a corner of the cabin, her bed and Eben's. Rebecca and Nathan and Rufe slept in the loft, reached by a straight up-and-down ladder, cold in the winter and stifling in the summer, and there were no bedsteads for their pallets. Now, because her daughter had stubbornly brought this near-deadman to their cabin, she and Eben would have to sleep on the floor for as long as the stranger lived, because there was no way Becky would let them put the stranger out of their bed as long as there was breath in his body. Besides, it wouldn't be hospitable.

Etta McCabe reproved herself for her unchristian thoughts. It was just that life was hard, and she was worn out from it, and a real bedstead for her bed was the only real comfort she had.

"You kin try, Ma. You's good at doctorin'!"

"I ain't never removed no deep-set bullet like this here. Your pa got hisself shot oncet, but it went clean through. This here one's still inside an' we gotta git it out an' that's as like to kill him as leavin' it inside."

"Then let's git to it."

"Pa, I'll need your knife. Hone it up, it's got to be good an' sharp. I'm a-gonna hev to cut him some, ain't nothin' in the cabin'll latch onto a bullet an' draw it out. Becky, you find some clean rags and be ready to try to stop the bleedin' oncet I git the bullet, iffen I kin git it. Nate, you go find Rufe an' bring him here to set on his legs in case he comes awake an' needs to be held down oncet I start cuttin' an' probin'. Pa an' Nate'll hold his shoulders, likely it'll take the both of 'em to hold him quiet."

"Knife's sharp enough. You know I allers keep it sharp." Eben McCabe was thin and stoop-shouldered, his face was bearded because wearing a beard was a heap less trouble than shaving, and there was a perpetual tic under his left eye. Life had not been kind to Eben. His oldest son, the one big enough now to do him some good, was half-witted and that was a pity, because Rufe had been as bright as any other boy when he'd been a tad, before he'd fallen out of that tree. Nate was only fourteen and small for his age and allers runnin' off into the woods, snarin' an' huntin', when there was shot to spare. Couldn't keep him to home in the corn patch nohow.

Becky weren't so bad, she'd take her turn with the hoe to keep the weeds from chokin' out the corn, and'ud turn her hand to helpin' Ma too, but she was a woman growed now and even as isolated as they were, she'd be takin' up with some man one of these days and go off and leave them. Rufe, he couldn't be trusted nohow, he'd chomp down the corn as fast as he'd chomp down weeds, iffen you didn't keep a sharp eye on him. Heavy totin' was about all Rufe was good for. Strong as an ox, he'd of been a real help to his pa iffen he hadn't gone and fallen outa that tree.

It was Rufe who'd toted this stranger the last half-mile, when Becky and Nate had tuckered out and Nate had come scootin' to the cabin yellin' fer help. Toted him like he didn't weigh no more'n a baby, and laid him on the bedstead, and then he'd gone scootin' off agin to watch a squirrel scamperin' up and down the oak tree at the far corner of their dooryard, tryin' to figure out how it could jump from one far branch to another most like it was flyin'. Rufe liked little critters an' he wouldn't let Nate shoot this one fer the stewpot, he said it was hissen an' he called it Scamper. Durned if the critter wouldn't take food, a chunk of corn bread or the like, right from Rufe's fingers.

Now Eben figured that Etta was right, the stranger was like to die no matter what they did for him, and if he were found here, in their cabin, there'd be a peck of trouble, mebbe they'd even end up hangin' by the neck because men like Andrew Leyland weren't a-goin' to take the blame, and who'd believe a McCabe against Andrew Leyland?

Heaven's Horizon

His face screwed up with concentration, because he didn't like to do something wrong and have his mother sigh, Rufe moved to the foot of the bed and sat on Donal's legs, gingerly because he was afraid he was too heavy and he'd hurt him and he didn't like to hear his mother sigh when he didn't do something right. His face was childlike for all his sixteen years, because his mind had stayed the same age he'd been when he'd fallen out of the tree. It was a mercy that he was a good boy and minded what he was told, else they'd have had a deal of trouble with him, as strong as he was. Seemed like the Lord had given him size and strength to try to make up a little for his brain being weak.

"Becky, stand outa my light. If we're gonna do it, we might as well git it over with. He ain't goin' to git any stronger, layin' there with that bullet in him. Keep them rags handy, I don't know how much he's a-gonna bleed."

Etta's face was pale, but her hands were steady. What had to be done had to be done, she'd learned that a long time ago. She'd birthed Nate right here in this cabin with no other woman to help her, and she'd set Eben's leg when a tree he was felling had fallen on him before he could get out of the way, and treated Rufe's foot with water leached through wood ashes when he'd stepped on a rake. Soaked it for days on end, and it hadn't festered and killed him like it might have. Etta could help skin out a hog after Eben had butchered it, and make her own lye soap, and when doctorin' had to be done she did that too, and so far she'd been lucky and maybe her luck would hold and maybe it wouldn't.

Her mouth compressed, Etta made the incision, trying not to cut it any wider than she had to. Donal's eyes flew open and his body arched and a sound like a painter screamin' in the night burst from his throat, and then he went limp and she didn't know whether she'd killed him or not. She hesitated, but Becky's voice was sharp as she said, "He's still breathin', Ma. Go on, git it over with."

Grimly, Etta went on. The bullet was lodged deep in his shoulder, and the cut had to be deep, and Becky was kept busy mopping up the blood so that her ma could see what she was doing. The surgery was crude, Etta hadn't had any experience in anything like this. The important thing was to find the bullet and get it out, flesh and blood would heal itself if the patient didn't die first.

The tip of the knife grated against the bullet and Etta's mouth thinned still more. She wished she had a pinch of snuff under her upper lip, it would be a comfort about now. Snuff rotted your teeth but a body had to have something to ease the strain of living. Eben always brought her some when he took the corn squeezin's in to town to sell it to the trader, after he'd saved enough corn for their meal for the winter, but it didn't last long enough and she was out now.

She pried at the bullet with the tip of the knife. It slipped away and she had to probe again. Donal's breathing was shallow, you could hardly tell he was breathing at all, and Becky held her own breath, willing him to go on breathing. He mustn't die, he was the purtiest man she'd ever laid eyes on, and she wanted him to live.

"Come on, Ma, come on! You've almost got it!" she urged, her voice tense. Rufe looked at her with his eyes wide with wonder, but he kept on sitting on Donal's legs even if Donal didn't move. "He cain't feel what you're a-doin' to him, go ahead an' git it!"

In the end, Etta had to stick her middle and index fingers into the incision and latch on to the bullet herself. It was a slippery devil, but she hung on to it, and then she had it. Bitty thing like that to cause so much trouble, how could anything that small kill a man?

"Don't lose it. It kin be melted down to eke out what we got," Eben cautioned her. The McCabes wasted nothing, because they had nothing to waste.

"Gotta sew him up," Etta said. "Nate, fetch me my needle an' a hank of thread. Thread the needle fer me, my hands is all over blood."

"I'll do it," Becky said. "You done enough an' my eyes is better'n yourn."

The edges of the sewn wound were ragged, if it healed it wasn't going to be pretty to look at, but his shirt would cover the scar and it wouldn't matter. Becky did the best job she could, even though her hands, unlike her mother's, trembled a little. Sewing human skin was a sight different from sewing cloth. But it was finished at last, and it didn't look too bad.

"He's still breathin'," Etta said. She laid her head on Donal's chest. "But his heart ain't too strong. I cain't hardly hear it. Don't go gittin' yer hopes up, Becky. We done all we could, but I'm thinkin' he's gonna die anyhow."

"We'll hev to bury him, then," Eben said. "In the corn patch, that'll be the safest place. Bury him good an' deep. Rufe'll hev to dig the grave, he's got the heft fer it."

"I kin dig good!" Rufe said proudly. "I kin dig real good. You want I should do it now?"

"No! He ain't dead yet, you idiot!" Becky lashed out at him.

"Ain't no call to go snappin' yer brother's head off," Etta reproved her. "He don't know no better. Don't dig the hole yet, Rufe boy. We'll tell you when to do it."

"The pistol's mine," Nate said. He glared at his family, defying them to deny him his rights.

"Course it is, Nate. You just mind you keep it outa sight once you got it cleaned," Eben told him. "But we'll hev to bury the stranger's clothes and all his other things. Cain't take no chances."

"Not the ring or the watch chain, or the cuff links! They's purty," Becky protested. " 'Sides, he ain't dead yet. Ma, how long do you think it'll be afore we know?"

"Cain't tell. But he's a-gonna die, I'm thinkin'. You'd best make up yer mind to do like yer pa says. Cain't take no chances. Baubles won't do us no good iffen they're found here where they got no business to be. I'm gonna wash up. Becky, go stir the mush, it's about to burn. It's a pity you didn't hev time to check all yer snares, a rabbit would of gone good with the mush."

On the bed, Donal lay as though he were already dead. Looking at him, Etta shook her head. He was a fine-lookin' man, all right, and she had sympathy for Becky's wanting him to live, but the girl had better get ready to bear disappointment because there wasn't a hope that he'd make it. From the looks of him, he'd be gone by sunset.

Chapter Eight

Zoe sat beside Cordelia's bed, listening to the rain that lashed against the windows. The room was stifling, closed up as it was to keep the rain out. Outside it might have been a little cooler, but the summer heat that had been trapped inside the house was still there, made all the more unbearable by the humidity that accompanied the rain.

Behind the mosquito bar, Cordelia's face was flushed as though she were running a fever, and her eyes were swollen shut from all the crying she'd done once the first shock of the news of Donal's death had worn off. Zoe had thought that she would never leave off crying, but that was a good thing, because all of that grief inside her had to go somewhere and if its pressure wasn't relieved by tears, she'd have died of it.

It had been two weeks since Andrew Leyland had returned to Leyland's Landing leading Donal's horse, its saddle empty. His face had been grim as he'd told them what had happened.

"Donal rode on ahead of me. We'd been in the saddle for hours and my hip was bothering me. I'd warned him about the bog and it never occurred to me that he might dismount and try to get a closer look at it.

"I heard him shout for help, but I was too far away to get there in time. He was already nearly submerged when I caught sight of him. The ground wouldn't support a horse's weight, and I had to dismount and walk. By the time I'd broken off a tree limb to hold out to him, he was gone."

For the first several hours after her father had told her of Donal's death, Cordelia had moved about the house like a ghost, her face white, her eyes dark and enormous in their blankness. She hadn't screamed, or cried, or carried on. She'd even sat at the table, picking at her food, her face as dead and expressionless as a marble statue's.

She'd gone to bed early. Zoe had helped her, had tucked her in and arranged the mosquito bar around the bed so that no flying insect could penetrate it to keep Cordelia awake. She had made up a pallet for herself in Cordelia's room, unwilling to leave her baby alone in those first hours of her grief.

It happened in the middle of the night, that long, agonized scream like a soul being tormented in hell. The scream had gone on and on, chilling Zoe to the bone, making the hair at the nape of her neck stand up. By the time she'd struggled from her pallet, Cordelia had been threshing and fighting invisible demons as her nightmare of Donal's horrifying death held her in its grip, and the mosquito bar was pulled down around her, enveloping her, trapping her, while those awful sounds had gone on, the sounds of a grief too great for any human being to bear.

Zoe had left a candle burning, in case Cordelia had awakened during the night and needed her. "Hush, baby, hush," she'd crooned. Her old hands had been shaking so badly that it had taken her minutes to get Cordelia untangled from the mosquito bar and the sheets. She'd gathered the girl into her arms, holding her, rocking her, comforting her. "Hush, hush, it was a dream, it will pass. Not tonight and not tomorrow, and not for a lot of nights and a lot of tomorrows, but it will pass." The soul-deep grief of her race told her that, a race that had been steeped in grief ever since white men had

Heaven's Horizon

discovered that black men could be enslaved. "You can't bear it now, Cordelia child, but the day will come when you can."

Andrew had come into the room, carrying a decanter of brandy. He poured a little into a glass and held it to Cordelia's lips. Gradually some color had come back into her face and sanity returned to her eyes.

But Zoe had been right about the unbearableness of the grief not passing in a night, or in many nights to come. Every night since Donal had died, Cordelia had waked in the depths of the same nightmare, every night she woke after only an hour or two of sleep, screaming and struggling, nearly mad with the grief that the nightmare brought back to her in its fullest force.

"She's taking it hard," Zoe told her master. "She's taking it mighty hard, Master Andrew. She loved that man."

"I know she did. But other women have lost their husbands and survived. She'll find someone else in time, she'll marry again."

Zoe shook her head. She didn't believe it and she didn't believe that Andrew believed it. She was glad when he left the house to ride his fields, glad when he was out of sight. There was a sickness growing inside of her, because there was something that she didn't want to believe, and that was that Donal's death had not been an accident.

She'd seen Andrew's face the night Donal had told him that his true name was Donald Ross. She'd seen the murder in his eyes. And now Donal was dead, and Zoe believed that Andrew had killed him.

It was a belief that she would have to keep to herself, forever locked up inside of her. Cordelia's grief was hard enough to bear now. If she suspected that her father had murdered Donal, she'd never have another moment of peace for as long as she lived.

It wasn't like anything could be done about it. Accusing Andrew would serve no purpose. It certainly wouldn't bring Donal back to life, and there was no way to prove that Andrew had killed him, and to bring him to justice. Cordelia had enough to bear in the years that lay ahead of her without this additional, unbearable burden.

So Zoe sat beside Cordelia's bed every night, almost as torn with grief as Cordelia herself, and watched and listened as Cordelia struggled with her recurring nightmares even though by day she moved and spoke and acted as normally as any woman in her circumstances could.

"I'm sorry, Aunt Zoe. I woke you up again. I don't mean to carry on like this. It just seems as if I can't help it."

"Cry," Zoe told her. "You go right ahead and cry. It's the only way, you can't start healin' until your cryin's done."

The men who had made the journey to the spot where Donal had met his death had returned with word that there was no trace of him, that there was no way that his body could be recovered for burial. Their faces had been grave and embarrassed, as men will be when they have to convey bad news. It would have been better for Cordelia if there had been a body. If she could have seen Donal lowered into his final resting place, she would have had to begin to accept the fact of his death.

"Aunt Zoe, I only had him for such a little while! Just such a little while! And now it has to be enough to last me for a lifetime, and it isn't, it isn't! I want him, Aunt Zoe. I want him so much!"

"I know." And Zoe did know. But there was no way she could help her baby. Cordelia would have to bear her grief alone because no one else could help her bear it. So how could she bear it at all if Zoe told her what she suspected, if she told her the truth about Donal's ancestry, that he was the son of the man who had stolen Andrew's sweetheart and had left him crippled, only half a man, for life? And that there wasn't any doubt in Zoe's mind that Andrew had exacted his revenge, over twenty-two years later, on the man Cordelia had loved and married?

"I wish that I could die too," Cordelia said. "It's unreasonable to have to go on living when there's nothing to live for."

"That's wicked. You gotta go on living. God has a plan for you, even if we can't see what it is. If He'd wanted you to die too, you would have been with Donal when it happened, and gone down into the bog with him."

"I know that that's what I'm supposed to believe, but right now I can't." Cordelia's hands were clenched tightly in her lap, her eyes were dark pools in a face that was so pale that it twisted Zoe's heart.

"Oh, Aunt Zoe! I have to write to Donal's parents, to his mother and father, and tell them what happened, and how can I do it? He came to America to marry Nadine, and instead I took him away from her and now he's dead! If it wasn't for me, he'd be alive, he and Nadine would have married each other and been happy."

"Don't you talk like that! Don't you even think it!" Zoe said fiercely. "It was you he loved, not Nadine. It wasn't your fault."

"What can I say to them?" Distracted, Cordelia got up and paced the room. "How can I find the words to tell them? They loved him, I know from the way Donal talked about them that they loved him very much. And now I have to tell them that he's dead, that they'll never see him again."

"Folks have lost sons ever since the world began. There's sickness and accidents and war. They'll survive, Cordelia child. People survive."

Cordelia knew that they did, she just didn't know how. There didn't seem to be any sense to it. Still, the letter must be written, and she turned to her escritoire. The quill dug into the paper and made scratches and blots as she struggled to control her mind, and she spoiled four pieces of paper before she managed to make an acceptable copy. The letter was pitifully short. All Cordelia could think to say, beyond the bare facts of Donal's death, was "I loved him too, I loved him too!"

"They'll hate me," she said. "They won't be able to keep from hating me. It's beyond human nature not to hate the one who caused you so much grief."

Zoe's mouth clamped shut. It wasn't Cordelia they'd hate, but when they learned the name of the girl Donal had married they would know, as Zoe knew, that Andrew Leyland had reentered their lives with this disastrous result. And they would be bound to suspect that Donal's death hadn't been an accident. Zoe only hoped, and prayed, that they would not let Cordelia know of their suspicions. If there had been any way she could have prevented the letter from being sent, she would have done it. At least it would be months before there could be an answer, and there was a wild, nearly impossible chance that Marguerite MacKenzie would have the intuition and the human kindness not to let Cordelia know of her suspicions.

Andrew was also aware that Marguerite would know who he was when she received Cordelia's letter. But unlike Zoe, he was glad that Marguerite would know. He'd loved her once, loved her more than life itself, but she had betrayed him and it was because of her betrayal that his life had been shattered. She'd robbed him of the sons he might have had. She'd given Lester Ross a son, she would have given him more sons if Lester hadn't died, while he, Andrew, had only a daughter.

A widowed daughter, now. The widowed wife of Donal MacKenzie. Yes, Marguerite would know, and Andrew hoped that she would suffer, and that her suffering would be multiplied tenfold because she would know that there was nothing she could do about it, that Andrew had had his revenge at last and that there was no way she could make him pay for it. The sins of the fathers, the sins of the mothers!

One day dragged into another. The heat of summer settled down over Georgia. August was always the worst month, and this year there was more rain than usual, bringing with it the humidity that made breathing almost impossible and that bore down on flesh and blood until bodies felt weak and heads throbbed and it seemed that summer would never end.

For Cordelia, the days were longer and more unendurable than they were for anyone else. If she had had something to do, things that had to be done, it would have been easier. But there was little for her to do, beyond helping Zoe doctor a few minor injuries among the field hands, a summer fever or two among the oldest and youngest of the slaves. The house that had run without her for four years went on running without her hand directing things. Andrew would give her no real authority, he was satisfied with things as they were. If dust collected on the furniture he never noticed it, there was only Cordelia to notice, and Andrew himself unlocked the storerooms and doled out the supplies of foodstuffs, as he had ever since Lorelei had died. The house seemed to settle in around the stricken widow, its walls moving in on her, its weight suffocating her.

Someday, she would have to leave this house. There was no way she could go on living here where she had known so much grief. First her mother, and now Donal. But she wasn't strong enough to go yet, she couldn't face it yet. If she could have gone back to Boston, to the Reynards, it would have been different but that escape was closed to her now. Nadine hated her for taking Donal away from her and she would hate her all the more now that Donal was dead as a result of that theft.

She didn't cry as much now. She had better control over her grief, even during her sleeping hours. But still the nightmares recurred. If Cordelia got one night's sleep without the dreams, they came back the next night with the horror intensified as though they were making up for the lost time.

There had been a nightmare last night. Zoe had listened to her crying, her heart breaking. It had been almost dawn before Cordelia had calmed and was able to drift off to sleep again. Now with the first light of day, a cloudy morning with the rain pouring down as though it would never stop, Zoe's face was sad as she studied the swollen eyelids and the flushed face behind the mosquito bar.

Cordelia would be waking soon. She always woke early, no matter how exhausted she was from her nightmares. The first light brought her awake, even when Zoe drew the draperies to keep the room in gloom.

Zoe sighed and got up, her bones and muscles stiff from the damp. The water in the ewer would be lukewarm. She'd fetch some fresh so that Cordelia could cool herself a little when she washed, and soothe her swollen eyes. And she'd tell Ruby that the poached egg for Cordelia's breakfast must be just right, not all runny and not too hard, and the biscuits had better be as light as a feather and the coffee fit to drink. Cordelia had lost weight, she was so thin that Zoe was afraid for her; she couldn't get her spirits back unless she kept up her strength and she had to eat to do that.

Cordelia woke slowly, reluctant to come fully awake even before she remembered why she wanted to go on sleeping and never have to wake up and remember what she couldn't bear to remember. While she was still half asleep, her hand reached out, seeking the sleeping form beside her, her fingers eager to touch him, to reassure herself that he was still there, that she hadn't just dreamed that she and Donal were married and that he would always be there beside her when her eyes opened in the morning.

There was nothing for her hand to touch.

Her eyes flew open and full awareness washed over her, all the tide of grief that was lying in wait for her washing over her until she wanted to scream and go on screaming and never stop.

Donal wasn't in bed beside her. He would never be in bed beside her again. Donal was dead.

Aunt Zoe came into the room, backing in because she was using her hindquarters to push the door open while her hands were busy holding a tray with a poached egg and biscuits and preserves and a silver pot of coffee. Cordelia sat up, pushing her pillow higher against the headboard so that she could lean against it and accept the tray. She'd eat her breakfast this morning if it choked her, because Aunt Zoe's eyes were stricken every time she left most of it.

"I thought you'd be awake, so I just brought your breakfast along," Zoe said, settling the tray on Cordelia's lap. "I watched Ruby fix that egg, it's just the way you like it. She went and burnt the biscuits a little but I cut off the burnt parts and they're all right. Let me pour your coffee. I sure do wish it would stop rainin'! It feels like the whole house is filled with steam."

There was a film of perspiration on Cordelia's forehead. The smell of the coffee that Zoe was pouring reached her nostrils, and a wave of nausea rose up in her throat and she clapped her hand over her mouth and fought against retching.

"Aunt Zoe, take it away, I'm sick!"

Zoe set the tray on the floor and ran for the slop bucket. She supported Cordelia's head as it hung over the edge of the bed, while Cordelia retched until her stomach was sore. When it was over she lay back against the pillow, weak and spent.

"I'm sorry, Aunt Zoe. It must be the heat. I'll try a little of the coffee now. Maybe I can keep that down."

She kept it down, and about half of the egg and a nibble of one biscuit. But she still felt weak and shaky. Aunt Zoe was right. If

Heaven's Horizon

only the rain would stop! It had been raining for two days, and Cordelia's nerves were on edge. It seemed as if the sound of the rain pounded against her head until it felt as though it might burst.

"You ain't feverish," Zoe said, testing Cordelia's forehead with the palm of her hand. "Not real feverish, like you was comin' down with something. It's probably just the heat, like we figured."

"Yes, that's what it is. I'll get up and wash in a few minutes, and then I'll feel better."

She did feel better. She washed and dressed and let Zoe help her with her hair. She occupied herself with some needlework, the constant mending that had to be done in any household, but because of the rain the light was poor and the eyestrain made her head ache again.

She put the mending aside and sent Zoe to fetch Ruby from the kitchen. "The whole house needs dusting," she said. "It's a disgrace. Mama would never have let it get like this, we must do something about it."

The two women fell to work under her direction, eager to do anything to please her and take her mind off her grief. It wasn't easy to keep the house clean since Miss Lorelei had died and Master Andrew had sent the house girls to the fields, where their labors would bring him profit. This wasn't a proper kind of a house nohow.

Cordelia was sick again the next morning, even though the rain had stopped and a watery sun promised to strengthen and dry some of the dampness out of the air. But the sickness passed, and Cordelia, frantic with idleness, decided that the drapes in the living room and dining room must come down and be beaten clean of dust, that the carpets must be taken up and carried outside to be beaten, that furniture must be polished and moved around.

Andrew, not pleased by this feminine activity, still let her have two field women to help her with the beating and cleaning and polishing. But Zoe looked at her darling with her eyes filled with a question.

Zoe had seen the like of this before. All of this cleaning, of scrubbing, of rearranging things. The readying of the nest, Zoe thought, the instinct of any female creature to get things ready to receive a new being. And with the nausea every morning, things fell into place.

She said nothing. It was too soon to speak, to raise hopes in Cordelia that might be dashed if Zoe was mistaken. Cordelia had enough to bear, she'd never be able to bear the additional grief of a disappointment of this magnitude. There wasn't any hurry about saying what she thought, there was all the time in the world.

But the morning sickness went on, and the flurry of domesticity. All of the silver must be polished, cupboards cleaned out and scrubbed, dishes that were seldom used washed and put away again. Cordelia was implacable. "Do it!" she said. "Mama would be horrified if she could see how this house has run down. No, not like that, get into the corners, get it really clean!"

Praise the Lord, Zoe thought. Praise Him from whom all blessings flow! Cordelia didn't know it yet, but she had a reason to live, and when she held Donal's child in her arms she would be happy again. Not as happy as she would have been if Donal hadn't died. That was impossible, and Zoe wasn't asking for miracles. But part of Donal would live on in his child, and bring Cordelia comfort, and there would be the years of raising the child, and loving it, and watching it grow. Full years, now, not empty and sterile, without joy or hope. This was miracle enough to make Zoe sing as she worked, humming under her breath so that the others wouldn't hear.

"Aunt Zoe, what in tunket is the matter with me?" Cordelia demanded a few days later. "I'm sick so often, and then it goes away, but I'm so restless that I can't stay still and I'm driving you and Ruby ragged doing things that don't need to be done at all." Her eyes, as she looked at Zoe for reassurance, were filled with fear. "Aunt Zoe, do you think I'm losing my mind? Am I going crazy?"

"If you hadn't been sheltered like you were, you'd know you wasn't losin' your mind. You're gainin' something, child, not losin'. I didn't say anything before because I wanted to be sure for certain, but I'm sure enough now. You're going to have a baby."

Cordelia cried. She couldn't believe it, she didn't dare to let herself believe it. "What if you're mistaken, what if it isn't true?"

"It's true. There ain't any doubt about it. That mornin' sickness every mornin', and when I help you dress and undress I can see that your nipples have darkened. Ain't your breasts a little tender feelin'?"

"Yes, they are, but I never thought, I never dreamed..."

She must have been simpleminded not to have known, not to have guessed! But her mind had been so filled with grief that she'd had thoughts for nothing except Donal's death. They'd been married for such a little while! But it had been long enough to make her pregnant, she was going to bear Donal's child. She cried for an hour, tears of pure happiness, and, like Zoe, she thanked God for this gift that had already made her life worth living.

She told her father that night at the supper table. "Father, I'm going to have a baby. I'm going to have Donal's child."

Andrew Leyland went on eating, but the food tasted suddenly bitter. It wasn't possible! Fate, that had been so unfair to him, wouldn't dare to perpetrate this last, unforgivable unfairness! It couldn't be true, Cordelia must be mistaken, it must be her own wishful thinking. The shock and grief she'd been through was making her suffer from delusions.

"I wouldn't get my hopes up too high," he warned his daughter. "You may be mistaken. You're run-down, not yourself."

"I'm not mistaken, Father. There isn't any doubt about it at all. Aunt Zoe says so, and she'd know. I've been sick every morning, and all that housecleaning is a symptom, Aunt Zoe says. And I missed my—" she broke off, flushing. Monthly periods were not mentioned to anyone, much less one's father! "We're sure. You're going to have a grandchild."

"We'll wait and see before we start making plans," Andrew said. Cordelia bit at her lower lip. As cold and remote as her father had always been, still you'd think that the news that he was about to become a grandfather would have pleased him.

"If it's a boy, it will be exactly like Donal, I know it will," she said. "And I don't have to wait and see, because I know. I'm going to write to the MacKenzies right away, and tell them the wonderful news. It's certain to make them happy. They'll want me to come to England, they'll want their grandchild, Donal's child, to be born there. It's their right to have him. I must start planning to go to England as soon as I hear from them."

The thought made her glow. Donal's child, Donal's son, to be raised in Donal's home, to have the love and protection of grandparents who doted on him, of two young aunts who would adore him! And she herself would escape from Leyland's Landing after all. It was as though Donal had reached out from the grave with his love to rescue her.

Surely the MacKenzies would want her to come! Even if they disliked her because Donal's having married her had been the indirect cause of his death, they would want their grandchild. And when they understood how much she had loved Donal, how much she still loved him, they would forgive her even if they blamed her at first.

She wrote to them that evening, and this time the letter was easy to write because she had this wonderful news to give them. It chafed her to think how long it would take for the letters to reach them. They probably didn't know, even now, that Donal was dead! This second letter, coming so close on the heels of the first, would be earthshaking.

Her chin came up, her mouth firmed. She wouldn't wait to receive their reply to her letter. She'd have faith that they would want her and welcome her, for the sake of the baby if not for herself. She would go to England as soon as passage could be arranged, her child would be born there, in his father's country where he belonged, just as he would have been if Donal hadn't died.

Her mind was made up. Now that she had a reason to live and plans for the future, her tears were all behind her. Donal's son deserved a mother who smiled, who was happy, who wouldn't burden him with a grief that he couldn't understand. She would not allow herself to think for one moment that she would not be welcomed in England with open arms.

There was so much to do! She must pack, Father must make arrangements for her passage. She held a stick of sealing wax to the candle flame and sealed the letter, writing the address in a firm and legible hand. Now she would go upstairs and tell Zoe that they would be leaving as soon as it could be arranged.

Andrew seemed to be agreeable to her plans, as Cordelia had been sure he would be. She couldn't picture her father as a grandfather, much less a loving one. He'd been pleased at the thought of getting rid of her when she had married Donal, and he seemed equally pleased at the prospect of not having a young mother and a toddling child under his roof, disrupting the austere life he had made for himself.

Cordelia busied herself planning what to take with her. There was little of Donal's, only the personal effects he had brought with him to Leyland's Landing. She felt the tide of grief rise again as she handled his clothing, his extra studs and cuff links. It was a pity that he'd taken his pocket watch with him on the day he had died. His child would have liked to have it as a memento. But there was his toilet set, the silver-backed brushes, as well as his clothing. She would leave nothing of his behind.

She and Zoe went through the house and the attics searching out what things of Lorelei's that they could take. The crystal vase that her mother had used to fill with roses for the drawing room table, the sampler she had made when she was a little girl in Virginia, each cross-stitch perfect, the border of leaves and flowers still unfaded. The bedspread that Lorelei had crocheted for Cordelia's bed, the cameo brooch that she had worn at her throat, a few other pieces of jewelery that she had seldom worn but that Cordelia would treasure. So little to show for a lifetime! One daughter and no sons, a handful of articles of little intrinsic value, and a husband who had never loved her as she had deserved to be loved. But Cordelia had loved her, and Zoe, and these few things Cordelia gathered together they would take with them as remembrances.

The year was wearing on. For all of July and part of August Cordelia had battled with her grief, not caring from one day to the next whether she should live or die. Now it was nearly September, and it was time that she should be leaving.

"Wait a little longer," her father advised her. "Going to England, planning to make your home with people you have never seen and whom you are not sure will welcome you is a grave step, one you should think over carefully. At least wait until you've heard from the MacKenzies."

"I have thought it over, Father. I can't afford to wait for weeks until I could hear from them. I need to go while the weather is good, I wouldn't want to risk a rough passage. Nothing must happen to Donal's child."

Her father shook his head, but then he nodded and told her that he would see to her passage at his earliest convenience. But still he stayed at the plantation, telling her that there were a few things he had to see to before he could travel to Savannah. A week went by, and then another.

"Father, I must sail soon!" Cordelia told him. "There's no point to delaying any longer."

Her father left for Savannah the next morning, and Cordelia breathed a sigh of relief. Now that everything was packed, she couldn't wait to leave Leyland's Landing and all of its unhappy memories behind her. But when Andrew returned he told her that he had been unable to book passage.

"There were no accommodations," he told her. "You will have to be patient. A few more weeks will make no difference."

"But Aunt Zoe is old, and I wanted to make the crossing while the weather holds, for her sake as well as for my child's."

Her disappointment was so acute that she felt physically ill. "Did you find out when there will be another ship? How long will it be?"

"Ships seldom come in on schedule, Cordelia. It depends on a number of factors, whether they pick up good winds or run into storms. I'll keep a close check, and book the first available passage. You will have to be content with that."

Another week passed, and still another. Cordelia kept at her father, but each time she asked he told her that there was still no ship available. At this rate, it would be winter before she set foot on a ship! The house closed in around her again, and the days dragged interminably.

If Cordelia was depressed, Zoe was troubled, so deeply troubled that she didn't know what to do. Knowing little of life outside of the

Heaven's Horizon

plantation, she was still a keen observer of human nature, and she knew Andrew Leyland well and how his mind worked.

He ain't going to let her go, Zoe thought. He's goin' to keep her right here until the child is born. And knowing Andrew, knowing that he didn't want this grandchild for himself, that he would be glad to see Cordelia's back if it weren't for the child, Zoe was convinced that he meant harm to the baby.

Donal was dead, and Zoe knew in her heart that he had died by Andrew's hand. And the child would carry Donal's blood. Zoe smelled danger, and her heart trembled with terror.

She had to tell Cordelia.

Chapter Nine

The effect of Zoe's story on Cordelia was even worse than Zoe had feared. Cordelia's face was so white that it was as if every drop of blood had been drained from her body. The fact that Donal had been the son of Andrew Leyland's enemy, the man he hated so much that it had ruined his life and Lorelei's along with it, was such a shock to her that for a few moments Zoe was afraid that she might miscarry.

And, then, before Zoe could raise a hand to stop her, to beg her to be cautious, Cordelia was out of her room and running down the stairs and out of the house. It was early morning, and her father was somewhere in the fields, supervising the work that he had always refused to entrust to an overseer. He needed to be kept busy at all times, to push back his black memories by filling his mind with other things, and tiring his body so that he could sleep at night.

Cordelia slowed her steps as she approached the stable. She mustn't trip or fall, she was carrying a precious burden under her heart. But she was going to confront her father now, demand that he take her to Savannah. She was not going to spend another night under his roof.

"Zeke, saddle Misty for me. And where is my father?"

Zeke, a man over sixty whom her father would have sold off while he was still capable of doing a full day's work except that he was the best hand with horses he'd ever had on the plantation, looked at his young mistress with consternation. He took his orders from his master, it had always been that way. Even when the other mistress had been living, he had never saddled a horse for her, or hitched up a carriage to drive her anywhere, unless Andrew himself had told him to do it.

"The master's to the north field, Miss Cordelia. But I cain't saddle a horse fer you to go lookin' fer him. Ladies don't go traipsin' off to the fields, and the master wouldn't like it."

"Saddle her!" Cordelia demanded.

Zeke still shook his head, backing away. He'd never been faced with such a dilemma before and he had no idea how to handle it. But he knew that Miss Cordelia was going to have a baby, the plantation grapevine had spread the news among all of the slaves almost as soon as Cordelia herself had known it, and he knew that white ladies were delicate and shouldn't ride when they were in that condition, and he knew that Andrew would be angry if he obeyed Cordelia's command.

"I'm sorry, Miss Cordelia. I cain't do it."

"Then get out of my way! I'll do it myself!" Cordelia brushed past him, and Zeke's face turned gray. He dasn't lay a hand on Miss Cordelia to stop her. For a black man to touch a white lady was an infraction the results of which were something that was only whispered, with rolling eyes and dread in the heart.

Cordelia's first impulse was to straddle Misty bareback, in order to face her father the sooner, but even in her agitation she knew that that would be taking a foolish chance. She didn't even know how to ride bareback, she'd never done it, and she might fall.

As she moved to lift the sidesaddle from its peg, Zeke made up his mind. Wasn't any way he could stop her, the state she was in, so he'd best do it himself.

Heaven's Horizon

"Don't you go liftin' that heavy saddle!" He trembled violently as he saddled and bridled the mare, but if the young mistress was to hurt herself lifting the saddle, or fall because the girth wasn't tight enough, he'd be in even worse trouble, his life wouldn't be worth a whistle.

There was no mounting block at the stable. When ladies rode out, the horses were led to the door of the plantation house where they could mount without dirtying their boots. And Cordelia wasn't even wearing boots, but only flimsy slippers, and a day gown instead of a riding habit, and Zeke didn't even dare wonder what had put her in such a state. He cupped his hands so that Cordelia could step into them and lifted her into the saddle.

"You be keerful!" he dared to warn her. "Keep her to a walk, Mistress, don't you go trottin' or gallopin'! If you'll wait a little minute, I'll mount up and follow you so's to be sure you don't come to no harm."

But Cordelia wasn't waiting for anything. She wheeled Misty around and her heel set the mare into a gentle trot. Zeke's heart was heavy with foreboding as he watched her leave the stable yard, bound for the north field.

Andrew, himself mounted the better to oversee the work in progress as the field slaves worked to clear this already stripped field, turned to see who was coming when he heard the approaching hoofbeats. Visitors to Leyland's Landing were so rare that he couldn't imagine who had found occasion to invade his acres.

He scowled when he saw that the rider was Cordelia, and his eyes went hard as he saw her white face and the furious anger in her eyes. Something had happened, and he wheeled General and trotted to meet her.

"Cordelia, go back to the house immediately! What is the meaning of this, riding out to the fields alone, and not even properly dressed? Turn your mare, I'll escort you back."

Instead of obeying, Cordelia reined Misty to a stop and sat the saddle staring at her father, her eyes burning with a fury of which Andrew would have thought her incapable.

"You killed Donal," Cordelia said. "You killed him, Father! You killed my husband, simply because he happened to be the son of the man you hated! Don't try to deny it, I know that you did it, just as I know that there's no way I can ever prove it and you'll go to your grave unpunished for it. But I'm leaving Leyland's Landing, you are to take me to Savannah immediately, and arrange passage for me. If I have to wait for passage I'll wait there, but I am never going to spend one more night at Leyland's Landing!"

"You're ill," Andrew told her. "You're raving. Will you be kind enough to tell me what brought this on?"

He already knew. There was only one person who could have told her about Marguerite and Lester Ross.

"You killed him," Cordelia repeated, and the hatred in her eyes struck Andrew with such force that he was jolted. "You killed Donal and now you're planning for something to happen to my baby. But you aren't going to get away with it, Father. I can't punish you for killing Donal, but I can see that you never have a chance to lay a hand on Donal's child!"

How had she come so close to the truth? Zoe again, of course. The old woman was virtually a witch, she could read people's minds. The only detail in which Zoe had guessed wrong was her suspicion that he would kill Cordelia's baby.

That had been his original purpose. Kill the child, wipe the last drop of Lester Ross's blood from the face of the earth! But then he had thought better of it. Even he quailed at the thought of murdering an infant, his own grandchild. So he would not kill the child, he would find another means of disposing of it.

Zoe was old, it would surprise no one if she were to be discovered dead on her pallet some morning, having to all appearances died in her sleep. It was essential that Zoe be removed before he could carry out his plan.

Cordelia, knowing nothing of the past, would be easy enough to convince that her baby had died in its cradle the first night after it was born. Still weak from childbirth, she would not be able to get up to see her child buried, so an empty box could be laid in the ground beside Lorelei's grave.

He'd take the infant to New Orleans, it wouldn't be hard to find some settler who would be willing to raise it, given the sight of a gold piece or two. The infant, boy or girl, would be raised in poverty, never knowing its true heritage. That would be revenge indeed, greater and more satisfying than killing it, and he would be rid of it forever without having to stain his hands with infanticide.

But now all his plans seemed to be crumbling around his feet. Cordelia knew, and Cordelia had enough of his own blood in her to fight back. There was only one way to handle the situation, and that was to maintain that she was temporarily unhinged by her grief and to confine her, so that she could not escape with the child she was carrying and cheat him of this last phase of his revenge.

Once Andrew had made up his mind what must be done, he acted. Without warning, he swept Cordelia from her mare and placed her in front of him on his own horse, holding her pinned so that her frantic screams and struggles were of no avail. Misty would follow them back to the stable. He set spur to his mount, and carried Cordelia back to the house, where the terrified Zeke watched them coming. But Andrew wasn't thinking of Zeke or Zeke's infraction about having saddled the mare for Cordelia.

"Take care of the horses. Your mistress is ill," Andrew said, half-carrying, half-shoving her into the house. Andrew thrust her into her bedroom and locked her in.

"You will stay there, for your own protection, until you have come to your senses," he told her from the other side of the door. "I advise you to try to calm yourself so that no harm will come to the child."

Zoe had followed them up the stairs, her heart filled with dread for what was to come. If only Cordelia had stopped to listen to her, they might have been able to devise some plan to circumvent the devil who now had her darling in his complete power.

"Let me go to her, Master Andrew," Zoe begged. "She needs me, she mustn't be locked in there all alone."

"No." The word was curt. "As long as my daughter persists in acting like a madwoman, she must be treated as one." Depriving Cordelia of the comfort of having Zoe with her would bring her to her knees all the sooner. Nothing was going to interfere with his

Lydia Lancaster

plans, no mere slip of a girl and an ancient black woman were going to stand in his way. On this plantation, he was the absolute master.

He was breathing hard, and beads of perspiration stood out on his forehead. Controlling his wildly struggling daughter, carrying her up the stairs, had taken a lot out of him. His hip pained him, sending needles of fire through his body, but there was no expression on his face as he descended the staircase again and went into his study, where he poured himself a glass of brandy and sat down until his trembling passed. The immediate danger was over, he had found the strength to act in the only way possible if he was not to be thwarted.

After her first frenzy of outraged fury, Cordelia stopped beating against the door. She must be calm, if she continued to carry on like this she might lose her baby. Her father couldn't keep her locked up forever. She'd get away, she'd get to England and Donal's parents somehow, but hysteria wouldn't help her to plan. Damn him, damn him! She should have taken a gun from the locked case in her father's study and taken it to the field with her and shot him. An eye for an eye, a tooth for a tooth!

Even in her despair, she knew that to have done any such thing would have ended in disaster. If she wasn't hanged for it, she'd certainly be confined in some prison for the rest of her life, or locked away in an insane asylum, and what would have happened to her baby then? Murder was murder and there was no way she could have gotten away with it. It was likely that the MacKenzies would have come for or sent for their son's child, but even the satisfaction of having killed Donal's murderer could in no way make up for that same child being branded as the child of a murderess.

Forcing herself to breathe calmly and evenly, she lay down on her bed to wait. Her father had the upper hand now, because of her own stupidity in not having fled the plantation while he was in the fields, but somehow, sometime, she would have a chance to escape and that next time she would make no mistakes. Now she must use her head instead of her emotions, because the fight for the survival of her child was the most important thing in her life.

There were noises in the corridor outside her door. She sat up, her heart pounding. Was it her father, come to let her out? Or was it

Heaven's Horizon

Zoe, come to bring her her lunch? But the door didn't open, and the scratching, drilling and pounding noises against the door's heavy surface were like nothing she had ever heard before.

She got up and crossed the room. "Who's there? What are you doing?" she demanded.

There was no answer. The sounds went on. And, then, incredulous, she saw that an opening less than a foot wide was being cut into the upper portion of the door, and she had to struggle against the despair that flooded over her, making her want to scream and beat on the door again in futile frustration.

The purpose of the opening was obvious. It was being cut so that food could be passed in to her and the soiled dishes and her chamber pot passed out. Her father had no intention of releasing her anytime soon, perhaps not until after her baby was born!

She ran first to one window of her room and then to the other. She'd knot her sheets together and let herself down that way as soon as darkness had fallen, why hadn't she thought of that before? It would be dangerous, but she was strong, she'd manage not to lose her grip and fall no matter how much strength she had to conjure up. She'd get into the stable, she'd take Commander, he was the fastest horse on the plantation and she knew that she could handle him because her desperation would give her the strength and skill to handle him.

Even as her mind raced, her disbelieving eyes saw that a ladder had been placed under each of the windows, and that stalwart black slaves were scaling the ladders. Now the heavy shutters were being closed and nailed shut. The room was plunged into gloom, only a little light coming in through the close-set slats. She was a prisoner indeed. There was no way she could escape until her father chose to let her out.

Her eyes were swollen shut from crying when Zoe's soft voice summoned her to the door hours later, when the streaks of light that filtered through the shutters were tinged with red from the setting sun.

"Miss Cordelia? Are you awake, child? Here's your supper. I

Lydia Lancaster

want you should eat it, every scrap, mind? You gotta keep up your strength."

"Aunt Zoe, can't you get me out? Can't you find the key and unlock the door?"

"Cain't, child. Your father's got the key, it's in his pocket. You eat your supper, then try to sleep. We'll think of something."

The dishes were handed in to her one by one, the opening in the door wasn't large enough to admit a tray. There was a plate of fried chicken and baked yams, another of biscuits and preserves, there was a pot of coffee. Cordelia wanted to hurl the food against the wall, but her baby must be nourished even if the food choked her. When she placed the last dish on the bureau, Zoe's hand came through the opening and she went back to take it, clinging to it just as Zoe clung to hers.

"I gotta go. Your father said I couldn't stay an' talk to you. I'll be back for the dishes later. Keep your courage up, child, and pray. If there was ever a time for praying, it's now."

But prayers couldn't open a locked door, prayers couldn't pull the nails that fastened the shutters shut, prayers couldn't cause her father to drop dead so that Aunt Zoe could get the key and let her out. Cordelia ate. She hadn't been brought anything at midday, and after the first few bites she found that she was ravenous. She ate it all, down to the last crumb of biscuit, and drained the pot of coffee. The food was good, Zoe had seen to that. Cordelia would have been able to eat more if there had been more.

It seemed hours before Zoe returned to collect the dirty dishes. She made a sound of satisfaction when she saw that the dishes were empty. "That's right, child. You gotta eat. An' remember that I'm here, and I'm prayin', and I'm thinkin' an' figurin', too. Now you git to bed, and rest. We'll have a few minutes again in the morning."

A minute or two of futile conversation in the morning, again in the evening. Zoe was helpless to save her, there was no way that it could be done. Cordelia was alone, and for the first time in her life she fully understood the meaning of being alone. It was the most desolate feeling in the world. And she wondered, with terror springing into her heart, if this was part of her father's plan, to drive her mad so that he could keep her confined for all the rest of her life, and so be able to do what he willed with her child.

Well after midnight a week later, Zoe sat hunched in the darkest corner outside of the hut that housed her son Runt along with three other womanless and childless field hands. Runt had had a woman once, but Zeelee had died, she'd caught a misery from being soaked through in a cold winter rain, and she'd been gone in a matter of days.

They'd had two young'uns, Runt and Zeelee had, but both of them had been girls and Andrew Leyland had sold them off when they were hardly more than knee-high. They hadn't brought much, but they were two fewer mouths to feed and two fewer bodies to dress, and Andrew had no use for girl children who wouldn't be able to turn him any profit for years to come. He had determined, a long time ago, that it was cheaper to buy full-grown, healthy slaves than to raise them from babies.

Runt had been given another woman, but there hadn't been any more children. Andrew didn't know it and the woman didn't tell him, but there hadn't been any more children because Runt hadn't had intercourse with the woman. He wasn't of a mind to beget more young'uns to be raised up to be slaves, sold away when they were babies if they were girls, worked to the limit of their strength when they were still tads if they were boys. He didn't love the new woman and she didn't love him. Zeelee had loved him even if he was short, shorter by a head than the next shortest slave on the plantation, measuring only a fraction over five feet if he stood as tall as he could.

That's why he was called Runt. He'd been small when he'd been a boy and he'd gone on being small. But his shortness hadn't affected his strength. Or rather, the strength that might have gone into making him grow taller had somehow seemed to go toward making him strong. His shoulders weren't heavy and massive the way some small men's shoulders were, and his arms didn't bulge with muscles. To look at him no one would think that those arms had the strength of the arms of any two ordinary men. The sinews were corded and when Runt swung a hoe or lifted a bale, they counted. He could do the work of two ordinary field hands without tiring, he was the best worker at Leyland's Landing, and Andrew had kept him even after he'd taken the second woman away from him and given her to somebody else. Runt was still a valuable hand even if he hadn't passed on his phenomenal strength to male offspring, but had fathered only two girls.

Beside Zoe, Runt also crouched on his hunkers, making himself as small as possible. The plantation was silent, all of the other slaves in the quarter had been asleep for hours, the sleep of exhaustion as they gathered their strength for the next day's work.

They kept their voices so low that they could hardly hear each other even though they were side by side.

"Ain't no way I kin do it," Runt said. "I been a slave all my life, and once I git away from this plantation I ain't fixin' to be hampered by any white lady holdin' me back."

Runt was past thirty now. He hadn't kept count of the years but he knew he was past thirty, and that was a long time to be a slave, never knowing the taste of freedom. Zoe hadn't taken a man for a long time; back there in Virginia, she'd been too busy taking care of Miss Lorelei's mother and then Miss Lorelei. He'd only been a tad when Andrew Leyland had brought his mother along to Georgia to go on taking care of Miss Lorelei, and Miss Lorelei had raised such a fuss about Zoe having to have her boy with her that Andrew had given in. Andrew had thought that he was a whole lot younger than he was because he'd been so small, too young to know anything of what had gone on, so young that he'd forget even if he had known anything. And with Zoe knowing that if either she or the boy dared to talk, they'd both be sold south, Andrew hadn't thought there was much danger. Mother and son had been separated at Leyland's Landing, with Zoe in the house daytimes to care for Lorelei, and Runt put in the fields to do what he could when he was hardly big enough to swing a hoe.

Runt had been planning his escape for too long to jeopardize it now for the sake of a white lady, even if she was Miss Cordelia and the blood of his mother's heart. There just wasn't any way that he was going to do it.

"You gotta. There ain't no other way. You gotta take her, else Master Andrew's goin' kill that baby when it's born, he's goin' to kill it sure as I'm sittin' here."

"An' we'll be cotched. Ain't no way we wouldn't be cotched, iffen I took her with me. And ain't no way we kin git her outa the house even if I was willin' to take her. I'm sorry, Mama, but it cain't be done."

"You're smart. You're way and above smarter than any other man I ever knew. You got your plans all laid, you know exactly how you're goin' to git away and git free, clear to Florida and the Seminoles. Miss Cordie's strong and she's smart, too, Runt, you got to take her. I'm askin' it. You want to see that baby dead, and for all we know Miss Cordelia too? Ain't no tellin' what that devil might do, now he knows that Miss Cordelia knows."

"If I was to take her, and I ain't, Master Andrew'd know you had a hand in it and he'd kill you," Runt said. "You'd have to come too an' you're old, you couldn't make it, not one of us would git away if you was to come too."

"I won't be goin'. Like you said, I'm old. If Master Andrew wants to kill me, then he kin. It won't make no nevermind to me as long as you an' my child is safe." Even in her near whisper, her voice carried absolute conviction, and Runt knew that she meant it. If her beloved Lorelei's child was safe, and if that child's child was safe, Aunt Zoe would lay down her life for her part in it without regret. Then she would know that God had had a plan for her all along when he'd made her to be a slave, and she'd know that she had fulfilled that plan and she could die easy in her mind even if her body screamed with torture under Andrew Leyland's hand. And his hand would be heavy, because he'd be determined to force Runt's plans from her before he let her die.

But he wouldn't be able to force her to tell, because she wasn't going to know what route Runt was going to take, she wouldn't let Runt tell her. No matter what Andrew Leyland did to her, she couldn't tell him something she didn't know. Runt hadn't ever told her for just that reason, because she wouldn't let him tell her, and now it was more important than ever that she shouldn't know.

They had been silent for a full fifteen minutes now, mulling over their own thoughts. It was Runt who broke the silence.

"I could git her outa the house," he said. "I know a way. It wouldn't be easy, but I could do it."

"Then do it."

"We have to wait. Now ain't the time. It's gotta be just right. We need a storm, one granddaddy of a storm."

Zoe didn't ask him why. She knew that Andrew would get bloodhounds, that he'd stretch every resource at his command to the limit to track Runt and Cordelia down. A storm, with gullies of rain to wash away their scent so that the hounds couldn't pick it up, was essential.

Even if God sent them such a storm as they needed, even if Runt could get Cordelia out of the house, and away from here, Zoe closed her mind to what would happen if they were taken. For a runaway slave to be taken carried dire enough consequences. For a runaway slave to be caught with a white girl was something that demanded that the mind be blanked out against. That Runt's life would be forfeit would be the least of it. Hanging would be an easy death compared to what Andrew Leyland would probably do to him for daring to try to help his daughter to escape whatever fate he had in store for her and her child.

"Git back to your bed," Runt told his mother. "Ain't no profit in chewin' it over any more tonight."

Zoe went back to the house, slipping noiselessly through the shadows. She was the only slave on the plantation who did not sleep in the quarters. Lorelei had insisted that she must have a room, and the privacy it afforded, to herself when the Leylands had first come to Georgia, and Andrew had had a lean-to built against the kitchen quarters, a small place but one Zoe could call her own, and that upheld her prestige as Lorelei's personal attendant. She had a real bed rather than a cornhusk pallet on a cot, a rocking chair and a chest of drawers, a rag rug on the floor. For a slave, it amounted to luxury.

But tonight Zoe took no comfort from her pleasant quarters. What was left of the night she spent in prayer. Lord, let it rain, she begged. Let it rain like it had never rained before!

In the days that crawled past, Cordelia thought she would go mad with suspense. Zoe dared talk with her for only a moment at a time, when she tended to her needs through the opening in the door.

"Runt's gonna git you outa here. I don't know how but he'll do it. You be ready, and don't get scared and scream when he comes for you," was all Zoe could tell her.

Another time, Zoe added, "You cain't take nothin' with you, only the clothes on your back. Make sure to have 'em ready. Strong, sturdy shoes, the sturdiest you got. You kin wear two dresses, maybe, one over the other, but you dasn't wear too much or it'll slow you up. Wear your ridin' clothes, they'd be best, an' a dress under your habit."

Cordelia touched the things of her mother's that she had already gathered in her room for packing, and wept over Donal's things that must be left behind. But there was no use in weeping. She couldn't take them, except for the cuff links and a set of studs that she sewed into the skirt of her riding habit, along with her mother's cameo brooch. Her mother's three rings she put on her own fingers. None of them were valuable, Andrew hadn't believed in investing money in jewels, but in land and slaves, but they would bring a little if she could find a safe place to sell them, perhaps enough to get her to Boston, where she would beg Frederick Reynard to lend her passage money to England.

Despairing again, she realized that her father would expect her to try to get to the Reynards, that he would be sure to apprehend her somewhere along the way. He would convince everyone that she was mad, and bring her back here where she would never have another chance to escape. If she and Runt, by a miracle, made it all the way to Florida and to the Seminole Indians who had taken in so many runaway slaves, she might have to stay with the Seminoles for a very long time before it would be safe for her to try to get to England.

The prospect filled her with dread. She knew almost nothing about the Seminoles. She'd heard rumors that they were a savage people, that they were cannibals. Zoe had told her that Runt had told her that they were civilized and kind, or else so many slaves wouldn't have taken the risk of escaping from their masters to go to them. But even if they would take in slaves, black people, what assurance did she have that they would take her in?

It didn't matter. Whatever had to be faced must be faced, and she wouldn't think about it now. First she had to get out of here, and how Runt was going to manage that was something that her wildest imaginings couldn't fathom. Zoe had said that he would do it, and she clung to that. So she waited, and, like Zoe, she prayed for rain, because Zoe had told her that if there were a real storm, at night, that would be the time.

The thunder woke her shortly before midnight, and even through the narrow slits between the slats of the shutters she could see flashes of lightning. The thunder was loud, and a moment later the rain began, falling in torrents. Outside, although she couldn't see it, the wind lashed the branches of the trees in a fury. Zoe had prayed for a storm, and God had sent a real one in answer to her prayers.

Without lighting her candle, Cordelia found her clothing, the things she had laid out against this moment. She was careful not to make a sound even though she knew that even the sharpest ears wouldn't be able to hear her moving around over the noise of the storm.

She waited, her hands trembling as she clasped them together, hardly daring to breathe. The pounding of her heart all but suffocated her. When would Runt come, and how?

Outside of her west window, where an oak tree stood too far from the house for the window to be reached from its longest branches, Runt was already scaling the tree, his bare toes clinging to the bark to give him purchase. If he'd wanted a storm, he had it, and tonight was the night or he might have to wait for weeks or even months for another storm of this magnitude, and there was no time to wait if he was to take Cordelia with him.

There was a rope coiled several times around his waist, a long length of rope. He'd taken it from the tack room, having for weeks now made it a habit to lend Zeke a hand after the day's work in the

Heaven's Horizon

fields had been finished and the evening mush consumed. Zeke was getting old, and Runt's strength never failed him, he was still able to give Zeke a hand without feeling the effort. Zeke welcomed his help, and Runt told him, after the first few nights, that he could do what had to be done alone.

"Rest yourself, Zeke. I kin do this."

"You mind you git it done afore Master Andrew comes to lock the stable," Zeke told him. The stable was locked every night. No plantation owner risked leaving his stable unlocked so that some foolhardy slave might make off with a horse in a bid for freedom.

"I'll git it done, don't fret yourself. Go and git your sleep."

The tree limbs were lashing back and forth and Runt's perch on one of the highest of them was precarious, but he did what he had to do with steady hands. He tied one end of the rope to the limb, making sure that the knot was secure, and he knotted the other end to make a sure purchase for his hands. Then he propelled himself from the branch and began to swing in ever-widening arcs. Almost close enough this time, a few more inches would do it. He swung again, and his fingers groped for and found a purchase on the shutter that covered Cordelia's window.

It took every ounce of his tremendous strength to cling there with one hand, his feet braced against the wall of the house to steady him. With the rope tied around his waist now so it wouldn't fall away from him, he grasped the shutter and pulled, straining until he was afraid that his muscles would rupture and his heart would explode.

With a screech of nails pulling away from wood that would have roused the entire house if it hadn't been for the storm, the shutter began to pull loose. Runt exerted still more effort, summoning up a strength that even he hadn't known he possessed, and the shutter gave way so that he could swing it back.

Inside the room, Cordelia was already at the window, pushing up the sash as far as it would go and propping it with the stick that was used to hold it open in hot weather. The full fury of the wind and rain lashed in at her, driving her back until she braced herself to face it.

"Git your arms around my neck an' hold tight," Runt told her. "Make sure you got a good grip, 'cause I won't be able to ketch you if you slips."

"Runt, you can't do it!" Cordelia gasped. The height of the window from the ground appalled her. Runt was so small, how could he bear her weight?

"Do it!" Runt said. He was in the room now, and he turned his back to her. Not daring to think, not daring to look down again, Cordelia closed her eyes and did as she was directed. Her hands, clasped around his neck, clung to each other so tightly that they felt numb.

Runt wasted no time or breath giving her further directions. She had a good tight hold, and now was the time.

With Cordelia clinging to his back like a leech, he wriggled through the window and launched himself into space, swinging once, twice, three times before his hands grasped at a branch of the oak. He scrambled for a firm purchase, and then he had it, and then his feet felt for another branch and his toes curled around it. There was no way to tell Cordelia to keep holding on tight, the wind would whip the words from his mouth and drown them before they reached her ears.

Cordelia didn't need to be told. Rigid with fright, she clung as if her life depended on it as Runt began his descent of the tree. Her life did depend on it, hers and the baby's that she carried inside of her.

Now they were down, she couldn't believe it but they were down, Runt's feet were on the ground and an instant later hers were too. Runt grasped her arm and pulled. In the light from another flash of lightning she saw his mouth form a word, but the clap of thunder that followed it drowned it out. She didn't need to hear what he had said. The word was *Move!*

Bending almost double into the teeth of the wind, they began to run.

Chapter Ten

Cordelia kneeled on the covered platform of one of the small structures that had been built around the cookhouse. She was grinding corn into coarse meal with a pestle. The work wasn't hard. Neither she nor any of the other slaves who labored in the small Seminole village was overworked, and they were all treated kindly and with consideration. She hadn't been required to work at all until she had recovered from the ordeal of her nightmare flight with Runt.

Even now, she shrank from thinking about that flight. Although she was able to push the memory of it into the back of her mind during the daylight hours, it still returned to haunt her when her mind was defenseless in sleep.

Nothing in her life had prepared her to accept that a pregnant woman, who should be safe at home with a loving family, who should be pampered and coddled and cared for every moment, should be required to run like a hunted animal, run until she dropped from exhaustion, until she was convinced that she would never be able to get up again and go on running, while the driving rain soaked her and weighed her down until she could scarcely stagger in her sodden clothing, while the wind buffeted her so that she could not have kept on her feet at all if it hadn't been for Runt's supporting arm around her as he half carried and half dragged her. If she had been further along in her pregnancy, she couldn't have survived.

She'd never realized before how cold rain was, how it could chill the body to the marrow of the bones. Even in Boston's frigid winters, she had never felt this cold. She had been dry, then, and if her clothing had become damp she had known that in a matter of minutes she would be under shelter, with a leaping fire to warm her, clean dry garments to comfort her, a cup of fragrant, steaming tea to give her a sense of well-being.

But during that first night's flight, there had been nothing ahead of her but cold and wind and rain and the exhaustion that filled her with terror that she might lose her baby right there in the cold and the wind and the rain, lying in writhing agony on the sodden ground with only Runt to help her.

"Keep goin'!" Runt had commanded her. "You gotta keep goin'!" And somehow, although her mind had told her that it was impossible, she had.

They had run for hours, pausing for brief moments to rest when Cordelia collapsed. Several times, Runt had swept her up into his arms and gone on running until her labored breath had stopped tearing at her lungs, until she'd been able to stand on her own feet and run again. It was as if the undersized black was tireless, as if her weight meant nothing to him. But even Runt's strength had to be conserved. He couldn't carry her all the time, and he couldn't run as fast when he was carrying her, and they had to cover ground, a lot of ground, before the daylight came to bring Andrew Leyland, with a pack of hounds, on their trail.

Cordelia had no idea of the direction they were taking, but Runt knew exactly where he was going. Not toward Florida, this early in their flight, because that was the direction Andrew would think they had taken, and that was the direction in which he would begin his search.

He never hesitated, he'd planned his route for months, and the lack of moon or stars to guide him hadn't confused him. He kept going, dragging Cordelia with him. He knew, far better than she, whose life had been sheltered even though she had lost her mother and her father had no love for her, the consequences of being taken. If they were caught, he would have nothing left to pray for except a swift and merciful death, and Andrew Leyland would not grant him that.

If it hadn't been for the storm they would have had no chance at all. That was why Runt had waited, biding his time. Now, with the rain coming down in floods to wash away their scent, they had a chance, although even he dared not calculate how much of a chance, lest he lose heart.

They had run through the night, far from any road or town. They had come at last to a branch of a river, and Runt had panted, "Take off them boots, an' that ridin' habit."

Cordelia had gaped at him, not understanding, too exhausted to try to understand.

"Take 'em off! They're too heavy, they'd weigh you down." He'd half pushed her to a sitting position, and himself yanked at her boots, and with fingers numb with cold and slippery with wet, Cordelia had struggled with the sodden serge of the riding habit. Runt had wrapped the boots in the habit, bundled the skirt into the jacket and knotted the sleeves of the jacket around Cordelia's neck. And, then, before she could protest or even think what he was about, he had pulled her into the water, deeper and deeper until he had been forced to swim, one arm holding Cordelia up. Her head went under water two or three times until, strangling, sure that this was where she was going to die, she had learned to keep her mouth closed and to hold her breath until she could adjust herself to this outrageous mode of travel and keep her head up and make some effort to help the man who bore her along instead of hindering him.

By any reasonable manner of thinking, it was impossible for any man with such a burden to swim as long as Runt had that night. And eons later, an eternity of time so long that Cordelia felt as though she had already died and was floating in some nightmare limbo, they had found a log and her arms had clung to it, with Runt's body pressed against hers and his arms stretching around her in order to make sure that if she lost her grip she wouldn't sink into the water.

Only Cordelia's determination to survive in order that Donal's child might live gave her the strength to continue.

They emerged from the river an hour before dawn. It was still raining, but not as hard as it had before, and the wind had died down. They were in wooded country now, and Runt had forced and prodded her to keep going, deeper and deeper into the dense growth. Only when the first watery light of morning had begun to penetrate the shadows had he found a shelter of sorts underneath a fallen and rotted-out tree. Her teeth chattering and her body shaking and icy from the hours of being wet and chilled by the wind, Cordelia had huddled there and Runt had huddled with her, as close together as possible for what warmth they could derive from each other.

Incredible as it was, Cordelia had slept. Her spent, racked body had demanded surcease from its pain. It was full daylight before she had opened her eyes, still cold and shaking, for a moment not realizing where she was and then feeling blind terror as she realized that she was alone.

She'd huddled there, not daring to move, not even caring. It was all over. She had failed, Runt had deserted her, and even in her despair she hadn't been able to blame him. He'd never make it to freedom, burdened with her, and in the end, every human being, man or woman, grasped at their own survival. I'm sorry, Donal, she thought. I tried, but I failed.

And then Runt was there, coming so silently that she had no awareness of his approach until he was hunkered down beside her. Even as she gaped at him, too filled with relief to say a word, he took her hand and opened it, palm up, and placed a heap of berries in it. "Eat 'em," he said.

There was so little! Cordelia's stomach twisted with protest as the small amount of food awakened her hunger and there was nothing more to assuage it.

But there was. There was a fish. A raw fish that Runt had caught in the river, using only his hands. Cordelia turned her head away and gagged. Runt didn't press her. She wasn't hungry enough yet. He ate it himself.

"We gotta git goin'," he said. "Git up."

She couldn't. There was no way that she could do it. Every step sent agony shooting through every centimeter of her body. She was still wet, her stockinged feet were torn and bleeding, but Runt wouldn't let her put her boots back on, they would make indentations in the soggy ground that a half-witted child could follow, much less a determined man. He swept her up into his arms and carried her to a stream, shallow enough so that it came only to her calves, and there he put her down into the water, with her skirt bunched up in her hands to keep it from dragging and becoming sodden. They followed the stream, wading, for miles. Cordelia's feet were torn on sharp stones, but the coldness of the water kept her from feeling too much pain.

He carried her again when they left the stream, not daring to let her leave blood on their trail. He found another hiding place, deep in brush that tore at her clothing and hair and skin, and he left her there while he set a rabbit snare. She couldn't keep going on a few handfuls of berries, she had to have real food, something that would give her strength. Then he came back to her and they slept again. Before dawn he rose and found a rabbit in his snare.

While Cordelia still slept, he spent over an hour coaxing sparks from two stones that he struck together until the little heap of damp tinder he'd gathered finally began to smolder. When he had a bed of coals, he dug out a hole and pushed the coals into it and put the skinned and gutted rabbit on top of them on a thin layer of earth and damp leaves, and covered it all. He buried the entrails.

The rabbit was tough and stringy and poorly cooked, but Cordelia ate her half and wished that there were more. The bones were buried. The skin, scraped as clean as he could manage, he carried with him, to fashion into moccasins for Cordelia as soon as it had dried enough. In the meantime, he either carried her or they kept to the water, which served to soothe her cut and bruised feet as well as to hide their scent.

That was the story of their flight. Run until they were exhausted, wade, swim, always taking to the water when it was possible. They ate what the land provided, fish when Runt could catch one, a rabbit when he could snare one, berries and roots when he couldn't.

Cordelia lost track of time, and she had no idea when Runt began angling toward their final destination. They had lost days going in the opposite direction to throw Andrew off the track.

The rabbit-skin moccasins were a godsend, as crude and ill-fitting as they were. Cordelia watched as Runt buried her boots, but then she closed her eyes and slept. She had no regret for their loss. She was no longer a civilized human being. She was a hunted animal and the only thing that mattered was survival.

The country they traveled through grew ever wilder. There were times when they had to fight their way through tangled brush so thick that Cordelia's sturdy riding habit was reduced to tatters. Runt missed no shred of cloth or single thread as he plucked them from branches and spines. Tearing at her portion of still-smoking rabbit, Cordelia looked at her hands as if she had never seen them before. The nails were broken to the quick, the hands themselves roughened and as thin as claws. But they weren't really dirty because they still took to water at every opportunity, and she scrubbed them as clean as she could, as well as her face and arms.

There was little danger from Indians. The tribes were at peace; the Creeks, who had been the terror of the settlers and plantations for so many years before they had been subdued, had largely been removed to reservations in the west. But there were other dangers, wildcats and possibly bears, larger cats called painters, although they never saw one and Cordelia hoped that there were none in this wilderness although Runt kept a constant eye out for them. How had she managed to live for so many years without realizing the dangers of the wilderness, how weak and puny human beings were in the face of such creatures?

They had little protection. Runt carried only an ordinary kitchen knife, honed to razor sharpness, all that Zoe had been able to provide him with, to stand between them and the terrors of the wilderness. That, and his strength, were all they had to rely on to get them through.

Heaven's Horizon

They saw no one, neither Indian nor white man, as they kept to the depths of the wildest land. They might have been the only two human beings left on the face of the earth.

Exhaustion, rain, hunger. They were almost the only words that had meaning for Cordelia. But there was one more word that had even more meaning. Survival, for herself and her child.

There was little time for talk, even if she and Runt had had any common ground for conversation. But sometimes, at night, their mutual loneliness drew them together and they conversed in low tones, their never-ceasing vigilance making them speak quietly even though they were sure that there was no one near them to hear.

"Runt, why were you so eager to escape and run away to the Seminoles?" Cordelia wanted to know. "You were safe at Leyland's Landing, and you knew that as long as you did your work you'd be fed and clothed and not mistreated." Andrew Leyland did not mistreat his slaves, for the same simple reason that he would not mistreat any other object that gave service to him. Wagons and machinery and tools were kept in repair, and a mistreated slave could not give as good a day's work as a well-treated one.

Runt had thought about it for a long time before he'd answered. "Safe ain't everything, Miss Cordelia. Bein' fed ain't everything. A man has to be free."

"But even if we get to the Seminoles, you won't be free. You'll never be able to leave them, and the Seminoles will own you."

"I'll be more free. Won't no white man own me. When I was owned by Master Andrew, I wasn't a man. With the Seminoles, I'll be a man."

"But what will I be?" Cordelia was almost afraid to ask the question. "Will I be a slave too?"

"Don't know. I reckon as you'll be a slave. I been thinking about it, and I reckon you'd best tell them that you're already a slave, a quadroon. Don't know if they'd take you in if they was to know that you're white and free, we'll have to study on that after we git to know them, wait and see if they'll accept you for what you are."

That was the trouble, that they didn't really know. Runt had only heard rumors, whispers that spread from the slaves of one plantation to another. For all they actually knew, they might be burned at the stake, or eaten. The slaves whispered one thing, the masters told them another. Runt had preferred to believe the slaves, and Cordelia had had no choice.

Neither of them mentioned Zoe. They were afraid to open their minds to what might have happened to her when Andrew had found that they were gone. What if he had had her beaten? Zoe was old, she wasn't strong, the thought was unbearable. But she had told them to go, and because of the baby, Cordelia had had to obey her. Dear Zoe! If Father hurt her, if he's had her beaten, he'll burn in hell, Cordelia told herself fiercely. And if I ever have the chance, I'll go back to Leyland's Landing someday and I'll exact my revenge on him, if he hasn't died first!

They didn't know when they passed from Georgia into Florida. The country had no clearly definable difference. They'd been traveling through pine forest for days, tired, hungry, worn down to skin and bones. Runt was never in doubt as to which way was south. And he was never in doubt that the farther they went the more danger they were in, because the Florida Indians had been removed from the richly fertile and valuable lands of northern Florida, and forced to make their home farther south on less fertile, less desirable land that the tide of land-hungry settlers didn't want yet. And white people would take them captive, would hold Cordelia for her father to claim, and turn Runt over to the slave hunters for the reward that was by now on his head. Runt redoubled his caution, making sure to give any settlement, any farm or cabin a wide berth.

They spent the larger part of one day high in a pine tree, after Runt's ears had picked up the bayings and yappings of dogs. They'd barely gained their place of concealment, with Runt boosting Cordelia ahead of him, when the dogs came into view, two of them, their noses to the ground, and Cordelia's blood had congealed with terror.

But the dogs weren't bloodhounds, they were coonhounds, and the two unkempt, bearded men in homespun who followed them weren't members of a search party looking for them. Dogs and men had passed by their hiding place, on the trail of whatever animal they were hunting. All the same, they'd stayed in the tree until nightfall. The memory of the rifles the men had cradled in their arms still made Cordelia tremble. Runt took more than his usual care that night in finding them a hiding place.

As well hidden as they had been in the center of a dense thicket and as careful as they had been to leave no trace of their passage, they woke in the morning to find three Indians looking down at them. Cordelia would have screamed if her throat hadn't been too constricted with fear to let a sound escape.

They looked nothing like Cordelia had thought they would. She'd pictured scalp locks and breechclouts, glistening naked torsos covered with painted designs. These Indians stood tall and proud, their hair was worn loose around their shoulders under turbanlike head coverings with feather plumes in them. Their bodies were covered with a sort of long loose blouse that came to their knees, belted in with bright sashes, and their leggings were high, disappearing beneath the hems of their blouses. They cradled rifles in their arms, and their coal black eyes surveyed them without expression.

"We found 'em," Runt said, but Cordelia knew that he was as frightened as she was in spite of the bravado of his words.

She stood up. She tried to stand as tall as she could and look confident. Her success was indifferent, but it didn't matter. The Seminoles were looking at Runt, not at her.

"Escaped slave?" The English words startled Cordelia. She hadn't expected that any Seminole would speak English.

Runt nodded. "Runt," he said, pointing to himself. "This here Florida?"

The one who had spoken nodded. They looked at Cordelia now, and waited.

"She's runnin' too," Runt said. "She's a quadroon, a slave like me."

One of the Seminoles was carrying the carcass of a deer over his shoulders. Swiftly, with no wasted movements, they built a small, smokeless fire and cut chunks of venison from the slain animal, which they impaled on long sticks over the fire. The smell of the roasting meat made Cordelia's mouth water even in her fright. Would they let her and Runt have a little? Well, she thought wryly, even if they make us go hungry they aren't roasting us! The thought gave her a little comfort.

They gave her her fair portion, and Runt his. The venison was delicious, it was a feast, Cordelia's stomach purred with contentment. And then they walked, behind the Seminoles who were either their rescuers or their captors. Cordelia tried not to think about that. She was still alive, they hadn't laid a hand on her, they had fed her. But if she couldn't keep up, what then? She had no way of knowing, so she gritted her teeth and kept walking even when she became so tired from keeping up the pace that she was staggering.

The Seminoles looked at her and called a halt so that she could rest, and her spirits rose. She and Runt were fed again, fed generously, and after Cordelia had eaten she was allowed to sleep for an hour before they started walking again. She estimated that it was about two o'clock in the afternoon when they came to a river, and there was a boat, an Indian dugout, pulled up on the bank, and two more deer and several wild turkeys had been suspended from the branches of a tree, out of reach of any predator.

The spoils of the hunt were stowed in the dugout and then Cordelia was helped in, once it was in the water, to sit behind one Seminole and in front of another while all three men began to paddle. Cordelia closed her eyes and sighed. To ride instead of walk! Every muscle in her body responded with gratitude, and her feet most of all. It was luxury unimaginable. She basked in it, held it close, reveled in it.

The dugout followed the twistings and turnings of the river all the rest of the afternoon. The Indians seemed tireless, the rhythm of their strokes was perfect and so lulling that Cordelia slept again until the craft was beached and they had to walk again. Runt carried his share of the game but Cordelia wasn't burdened. Her spirits soared. One of the rumors that Runt had heard was certainly true. The Seminoles were kind, they saw that she was exhausted and asked no more of her than to walk at a pace she could maintain.

The dogs were the first to greet them as they came to the village. There were over a dozen of them, vicious, snarling, snapping. Cordelia screamed. The Seminoles ignored them and kept on walking, paying them no heed, and somehow fangs never connected with human flesh.

It was a small village in a large clearing, and Cordelia learned later that it was called an istihapo. People were moving about, and no one paid any attention to them as they made their way to the center of the settlement. There was a large structure there, erected on a raised platform. The roof was thatched with palmetto fronds and the sides were open to the air. Mats and furs were spread on the floor, and one of the Seminoles pointed to it and indicated that this was where she and Runt were to stay.

"The cookhouse is there," he said, nodding toward another structure. "Take what you want from the kettle."

The kettle, suspended over a fire, was filled with a kind of stew of ground corn and venison. Cordelia learned later that it was called sofkee, and it was the Seminole staple. Right at the moment she called it ambrosia, and gave no thought to the fact that it was partaken of by everyone in the istihapo right from the kettle, with wooden spoons. Her spoon traveled from the kettle to her mouth until she could eat no more. Runt waited until she had satisfied herself before he lifted his own spoon. The conditioning of a lifetime could not be stamped out in such a short time.

Cordelia's body seemed to fold up of its own accord as she collapsed on one of the mats in the structure where she had been told to stay. She was asleep again before she was fully stretched out on the mat.

She slept all of that night without stirring, and no one disturbed her. It was full light when she woke, and she was alone, Runt was up and gone and it took her a moment to orient herself. But her body, so long half-starved, remembered the cookhouse and once again she ate until her stomach was full to the bursting point. Around her, the people of the village went about their business, paying no attention to her, but when Cordelia left the cookhouse a young woman approached her.

She was little more than a girl, probably of Cordelia's age or close to it. She wore a shapeless garment that reached to the ground and her feet were bare. Her hair was long, hanging loose down her back.

She looked at Cordelia, and then she reached out her hand and placed it on Cordelia's stomach, and then she smiled and placed her hand on her own stomach. No words were needed. Cordelia was pregnant, and the Seminole girl was pregnant, and it was a bond between them.

The girl was graceful and lithe, her face was pretty and her eyes were intelligent and kind. She examined the filthy rags that were all that remained of Cordelia's clothing, and studied the gaunt face and emaciated body. She took Cordelia's hand and led her back to the guest lodge and indicated that she should rest more, and a few moments later she returned carrying a garment like her own, shapeless but clean and whole, and placed it in Cordelia's hands.

Cordelia's eyes filled with tears of gratitude. Her relief was so overwhelming that she wanted to weep. All the rumors that Runt had heard about the Seminoles were true. They were civilized and kind, their slaves were treated with as much consideration as if they had been free Indians, she was in no danger here, she had reached true haven.

"Donal, I made it." She said the words aloud. The Seminole girl looked at her with curiosity, but there was no way that Cordelia could explain. She could only cry, and after she had changed into the clean, whole garment she slept again. It was as if she couldn't get enough sleep, as if she would have to sleep for days until her exhausted body had finally rested enough.

Now, with her time drawing near, she squatted on the covered platform near the cookhouse and pounded corn. It was the only task assigned her, something that would not task her strength. She was still wearing a Seminole dress, and her hair hung loose around her shoulders and down her back.

The village that surrounded her was simple in its efficiency. The structure that she had slept in when she had first arrived was at the center, a place used for general assembly and council meetings and used as a guesthouse. The individual dwellings were built on platforms, the sides open to the air, the roofs thatched with palmetto fronds. There was storage for grain and potatoes, and a private, open room on the second level for the man of the family, where he could sit in comfortable solitude no matter how hot the weather.

A second building was separated by a twenty-foot yard from the first of the single dwelling units that held the storage places, or garitas, as they were called. This second structure was where the family lived, and it was of one story and also served as the family's sleeping room.

The istihapo was clean. The ground was kept swept and free of litter. The inhabitants were clean as well, taking frequent baths in the nearby streams. They were a highly civilized people, with strict laws to govern their conduct. Stealing and lying were forbidden and brought swift punishment. If a man took another man's woman he was put to death, and if the woman gave herself to him willingly she followed him in death. This had not happened while Cordelia had been at the village, and she was sure that it never would.

In all the time Cordelia had been here, she had never seen a Seminole man raise his hand to his wife, or even raise his voice to her. The women were treated with consideration and respect. She couldn't help thinking that the large majority of white men she had known, cultured and wealthy as they were, could profit by the Seminoles' example.

There were individual gardens, as well as a large communal field that the slaves tended. The slaves had their own dwelling places, or chikees, as all the single dwelling units were called, and their own gardens, and the Seminoles treated them as dignified human beings in their own right, never mistreating them. The fondness, the genuine love, between the slaves and their Seminole masters was a revelation. This was not only a haven for runaway slaves, it was freedom and contentment such as could never have been found elsewhere in the world.

Cordelia had her own chikee. Runt had helped to build it, as well as his own. The work she was expected to do was far from arduous, even before she had come so near her time. Pounding corn into meal, stitching garments, tending the cook-fires. At first she had worked a little in the fields, hoeing or pulling weeds, but never until she had become tired, and now that her pregnancy was so far advanced she was not allowed to work in the fields at all, or to carry anything heavy, or to lift or to stretch.

She had picked up a smattering of the Seminole language, and Weleka, the girl who had been the first to welcome her, had learned a little English from her as well as from runaway slaves, so that between them they were able to communicate even if sometimes they had to resort to sign language that left them both laughing until their sides ached. It was assumed, without ever being stated, that Cordelia was the property of Weleka and Wacassa, the young brave who was Weleka's husband. Because they were so near in age and in the advancement of their pregnancies, it was considered fitting.

But Cordelia did not feel like a slave. She was Weleka's friend, and Weleka was hers. If their chatter was restricted because of the language barrier, their smiles and gestures were not, and when Cordelia was sad, as she often was when she was overtaken by her grief over Donal's death and the uncertainty of her future and that of her unborn child, Weleka would lay her hand on her arm and her eyes would be soft with sympathy.

Cordelia had made Weleka understand that she, too, had had a husband, and that he was dead. She made no attempt to tell Weleka that she wasn't a quadroon, that she had never been a slave, that she was the daughter of a white plantation owner, that she had spent years in Boston among wonderful friends, living in a luxury that Weleka would have had no way of comprehending.

Cordelia had had only one bad fright since her arrival. Weleka had come to her where she was pounding corn, and urged her out of the village, through the pack of snarling dogs, and deep into the forest. Runt had joined them, his face grave, and helped them find a place of concealment in heavy brush.

"White men comin'," Runt told Cordelia. "Slave hunters, likely Master Andrew sent 'em to hunt us out in one of the Seminole villages. Don't move and don't make a sound."

Weleka had come for them at midmorning of the following day. The white men had left, satisfied that the village had neither sheltered nor heard of the two fugitives, the slave and a white girl of eighteen.

Heaven's Horizon

Runt had picked up more of the language than Cordelia, and he told her that the slave hunters had tried to take one of the male slaves, claiming that he was a runaway, but that they hadn't dared, even backed by the guns they carried. "The Seminoles don't look kind at slave hunters tryin' to steal their slaves," he said. "All the same, iffen they'd seen us they'd tell Master Andrew we was here and he'd find a way to git us even if he had to send in the army with an order to turn us over. And I ain't going to go wandering off by myself, and don't you do it either."

Cordelia had no intention of wandering off by herself. Where could she go, she thought sadly. She tried to push the thought that she might have to spend the rest of her life in this village into the back of her mind, the thought that her child might be raised as a slave of the Seminoles, no matter how kindly treated, that its only chance for a better life would be to marry a Seminole and become a full member of the tribe, with all tribal rights, as slaves did when such marriages took place.

If only there were something better to look forward to! She loved Weleka, and she had come to love Stillipika, Weleka's mother, and Hilolo, another Seminole girl of her own age. She liked and respected Wacassa, Weleka's handsome young husband, who treated her with teasing good humor, almost as though she were his sister. They were her family now, but no matter how much she loved them, loved them for themselves as well as for their kindness to her, they weren't her own people. And her child, Donal's child, had a right to his heritage, a right to be raised in England and take his place there with Donal's family. The present impossibility of bringing this about was depressing and she often had to fight back tears.

She thought about the Reynards, about Lucy and Frederick and the boys, and about Nadine and Miss Virginia Baker and the Academy for Young Ladies. Miss Baker would be horrified if she knew where Cordelia was now, Lucy and Frederick would be no less horrified, filled with consternation because there would be no way for them to rescue her from her predicament.

But Nadine? Cordelia wasn't sure about Nadine. Maybe Nadine

still hated her, maybe Nadine would laugh, and be glad that she had been punished so severely for having taken Donal away from her.

No, Cordelia told herself. Nadine wasn't like that. She had been hurt and heartbroken when Cordelia had come between her and Donal, but she wouldn't have wanted such harm to come to either of them.

There was no profit in thinking about it. And there was no profit in wishing that she could get away from here, or trying to plan ahead. The only thing of importance now was for her baby to be born, and to be strong and healthy.

But someday, she would get away from here. Someday, it had to be possible that she would live again among her own people, that her child would take his rightful place in the world. There had to be a way to make her way to England and to the love and protection of Donal's parents, and then she would be able to look back on this experience with grateful memories, something she would never forget but something she would never have to worry about again.

She clung to this hope as the days moved toward the birth of her child. It was possible that it could be done. She still had her mother's rings and cameo, they would bring something. If they would bring enough for passage to Boston, Frederick Reynard would advance the money for her passage to England. But that lay a long time in the future. Her father would have had to give up hope of finding her and be convinced that she was dead, her child would have to be old enough to travel.

Two years, three? Would it be as long as that? But someday, no matter how long it took, she would do it.

She imagined her child in England, surrounded by the love of his grandparents and aunts. In the meantime, she waited, and merged into the Seminole community. She laughed and made jokes with Weleka and Hilolo, she pounded corn, and she was learning to make beaded ornaments—her fingers were naturally dextrous and it was challenging to fashion the intricate patterns. The hard thing was to follow the Seminole rule that no manufactured product must be perfect, that there must always be an imperfection because only istohollo, or, as the Seminoles pronounced it, ist-o-hollo, God, could make anything perfect. But she abided by the rules, deliberately leaving out two or three beads or forming a line that was not quite true. Her child would be perfect, and that was enough for her.

She wondered whether her child or Weleka's would be born first. The two girls had counted on their fingers and determined that their pregnancies were the same number of months along. It would be nice if the two babies were born just far enough apart so that she and Weleka could help each other, but that, as all else, was in the hands of istohollo.

She was so deep in her thoughts that she didn't notice the man who had approached her and who stood now looking at her intently while her pestle moved up and down. He was a tall man, his shoulders were broad and he was in his early thirties. He was dressed in the traditional Seminole dress but his black hair was cut short in the fashion of a white gentleman, and although his skin was dark, it was a good deal lighter than the Seminoles', and his eyes under thick, dark brows were a startling blue.

His hand fell on her shoulder, and she gasped with surprise and looked up, seeing only the blue eyes, and her heart leaped with terror as he said, in perfect English, "If you're a quadroon, I'm a Hottentot!"

Chapter Eleven

Donal woke slowly, and lay for a few moments as he always did in the morning, not remembering for a moment where he was or why he was here. The ceiling of the cabin where he lay on a roughly made bed was unfamiliar to him, alien. A ragged patchwork quilt covered him, and there was no pillow under his head, no sheets between his naked body and the quilt.

Memory returned painfully, and he winced. Memory that was all too short, all too incomplete. He knew that he was in a settler's cabin somewhere in Georgia, in a clearing that had been hacked out of the surrounding forest. He knew that he had been here for months. He knew that he had been shot, that he had hovered for weeks between life and death, and he knew that he owed his life to the auburn-haired girl who had fought for his life with every ounce of strength that was in her.

Becky. Her name was Becky, and this cabin belonged to the McCabes, to Eben and Etta McCabe and their three children, Rufe and Rebecca and Nate. Rufe's name was actually Ruben but somewhere along the way they had begun to call him Rufe. Etta had told him that, her eyes filled with resignation at her middle child's retardation.

Rufe was standing beside his bed now, looking down at him with that happy, childlike expression that never seemed to change, a great, hulking boy of sixteen whose mind was that of a five-year-old child.

"He's awake, Becky!" The words came out of Rufe's smiling mouth like a crow, as though this were something remarkable of his own doing. "He'd done wokened up!" He lumbered to the door of the cabin and called out again, petulantly now, "Becky, you done a-tolt me to call you when he wokened up! An' I did, so what does you want me to do now?"

"You kin stop that stupid yellin', fer starters!" Becky's voice came back. She entered the cabin, pushing her brother aside. "Go set down an' keep quiet."

Obediently, Rufe shuffled over to the stick-and-clay fireplace and squatted down, his arms locked around his knees, watching Becky as she crossed the cabin to Donal's bed.

"Mornin', John. You ready fer some breakfast? Git up, then, an' I'll dish you out some mush."

Donal pulled the quilt higher around his neck, and Becky laughed. "Ain't you modest!" she mocked, but there were imps of merriment in her eyes. Her hair was braided into a long pigtail that hung over one of her shoulders, and a few tendrils had escaped around her forehead and the nape of her neck. Her calico dress was faded, but it was reasonably clean and so was she. Donal had no way of knowing that Becky took a sight more pains to keep herself clean and neat since he'd first come out of the unconsciousness he'd been in for days after she and Nate had toted him home when they'd pulled him out of the bog.

Donal didn't know about the bog, either, or who had shot him, until Becky had told him. He had vague memories of tossing and raving as his wounds had festered and sent infection through his weakened body, his fever so high that Etta McCabe had warned her daughter that there was no way he could live through it, that she might as well give up and accept the fact that they were going to lose the fight for his life.

"Shall I start diggin' the grave?" Those words came back, he was sure he'd heard them more than once, eager words from Rufe's smiling mouth as the dim-witted boy wanted to do something that would earn him a pat on the head for being useful. "Shall I start diggin' now?"

"No! He ain't dead yet an' he ain't gonna die!" Those words had been fierce, and it was Becky who had said them. "Go sit down, Rufe, an' keep outa my way! No, go fetch some cold water, I gotta wet down his forehead, he's burnin' up."

"You'll give him a chill an' kill him quicker," Etta had warned her. "Keep him kivered, keep him warm, but it ain't gonna do no good."

"He's hot!" And then there had been a cool, wet cloth on his forehead, and it had eased him. And there had been broth spooned between his lips, and Becky's voice commanding him to swallow. "Swallow it, dang you! You gotta eat else you'll starve to death iffen the fever don't git you first!"

John. His name was John Martin, Becky had told him that. And he'd been shot by a lawman while he'd been running after he'd shot and killed another man in a fight, and been thrown into a bog because the lawman hadn't been inclined to either go to the work of digging a grave, or of toting his body back to town. Only he hadn't been dead, by some miracle Becky and Nate had found him and pulled him out of the bog and carried him here to this cabin and these people had saved his life. He couldn't remember it, but he knew he'd been shot because of the scars and so it must be so.

But his life before he had waked up in this cabin was a complete blank to him. He wouldn't even know his own name if Becky hadn't told him that he'd told her in his delirium, and told her that he had no family, that he'd muttered and raved about his father being killed by a marauding Indian when he'd been a small lad, about his mother and his sister and his two brothers being taken by sickness and dying when he'd been in his teens. He'd got in a fight with the man he'd worked for, because the man had cheated him, and he'd killed the man and he'd been hunted down and shot.

He had his life, and that was all he had. He didn't even own a stitch of clothing of his own, but had to make do with what Rufe could spare him, Eben's and Nate's being too small. He owned no weapon, that had gone down in the bog, he had no money, he was completely dependent on these people who had found him and taken him in and saved his life. And for all he could remember of his former life, he was to all purposes a newborn babe, and, he reflected not without bitterness, as weak as a newborn babe as well.

The derisive merriment in Becky's eyes deepened as Donal pulled the quilt higher around him, waiting for her to leave the cabin so that he could get out of bed and get dressed. He'd been getting up for a little while every morning ever since he had gotten a little of his strength back, to move around with Rufe supporting him to try to regain some of his strength. In the late afternoon he'd tried again, and would sit outside the cabin door on a stump, soaking up the late autumn and early winter sun as it warmed the cabin wall on its westerly orbit toward setting.

"You ain't got nothin' to hide that I ain't seen afore!" Becky said, teasing him. "You was naked as a jaybird fer weeks, an' me tendin' you, so you might as well git up and crawl into them britches whilst I dish up yer breakfast."

"I'd prefer not to," Donal said. His voice was stiff and formal, and Becky laughed again. She was a pretty girl, astonishingly pretty to be the daughter of a backwoods family. Her hair seemed to glow with a life of its own, her eyes were a deep violet blue rather than the pale watery blue of her brothers and her father. She must have inherited them from her mother, although Etta's eyes were so surrounded with crow's-feet that it was hard to be sure of their color. Maybe Etta had been pretty once, when she'd been a girl, but life had left its mark on her, aging her prematurely so that she looked closer to sixty than forty. Her teeth, what was left of them, were stained from the snuff that she kept tucked under her upper lip, and her hair had faded to an indeterminate color that held more gray than brown or red.

It hurt to think that in twenty years Becky would be a replica of her mother. The girl was so lovely, so fresh and filled with life, her body so lithe and shapely. She deserved better than that, better than a life of bending over a washtub, and hoeing corn, and raising babies on some backwoods place no better than this while the years robbed her of her beauty and her zest for life, until she would become as withered and worn out and as without hope as her mother.

The thought was unpleasant, and he had enough troubles of his own. He was hungry, and while cornmeal mush had no appeal for him, it would be welcome. In the past several weeks, while his strength had begun to return so slowly that it was difficult to tell from one day to the next whether he had made any progress, his appetite had returned as well, as his body demanded more and more food to continue its recovery.

"All right, I'll turn my back," Becky humored him, her teasing smile still flickering at the corners of her mouth. She went to the fireplace and stirred the kettle of mush, and gave Rufe a gentle slap alongside his head at the same time. "You let it scorch," she told her brother. "I tolt you to keep yer eye on it."

"You tolt me to keep my eye on John," Rufe protested, wounded.

Becky sighed. So she had, and it was beyond the realm of possibility for Rufe to keep his eye on more than one thing at a time. But she'd wanted to primp in front of the shard of broken mirror that was all that was left of the glass her mother had brought with her to this cabin. It had been broken while it was being moved, and only the largest piece had been worth keeping. It wasn't large enough by half to suit Becky, who would have liked to see more than most of her face and part of her hair, but it was a sight better than nothing.

The mirror was propped on a narrow ledge that she herself had pegged to the outer wall of the cabin just outside the door where a pail of water stood for such ablutions as her family indulged in. She'd secured the mirror with more pegs, so that it wouldn't blow or be jarred off and lost forever in even smaller fragments. She'd rather have kept it in the loft, but there wasn't enough light there, or anywhere inside the cabin with its one door and two windows that were covered with deerskins scraped so thin that they were almost translucent so that they could let in a little light as well as keep out the cold and the flying insects.

Donal reached for the britches, which were hanging on the bedpost, and skinned out of bed and into them. A homespun shirt, its butternut brown faded to gray, followed. There was no underclothing, and both pants and shirt were too large for him. Once he was dressed, he stepped outside the cabin to splash cold water on his face, and run his fingers through his hair.

The face that was reflected in the piece of mirror was unfamiliar to him. His hair had grown long and unkempt around his shoulders, and the lower half of his face was covered by a beard, lighter in color than his hair. There was a deep furrow on his forehead where the lawman's bullet had creased him, coming within a fraction of an inch of taking his life. It ran from his hairline to his left eyebrow, inflicted as he'd turned when the first shot had struck him in the shoulder from the back.

You're no beauty, whoever you are, Donal told himself wryly. Becky and Nate should have thrown him back into the bog after they'd rescued him, after they'd taken a closer look at what they'd rescued. Maybe he hadn't looked so bad, clean-shaven.

His fingers lingered at his beard. Some vague conviction that he should be clean-shaven nagged at the inner recesses of his mind, but there was nothing he could do about it. Eben owned no razor, when his beard grew long enough to itch him he scraped it off with the edge of the knife he kept so sharp for his unending whittling, and Donal had no desire to cut his own throat by trying to shave with a knife. The beard would have to stay.

He wished that he had his own clothing, whatever he'd been wearing when he'd been shot, but Becky had told him that it had been ruined, that there hadn't been any way to get it clean and get the stink out, so they'd burned it.

"Why do you keep lyin' to him like that, Becky?" Etta had demanded, although Donal knew nothing of this. "You keep fillin' him chock-full of lies, an' it ain't right."

"It ain't wrong, neither," Becky had countered, her chin stub-

Heaven's Horizon

born. "Were we to tell him the truth, he might take it in his head to go lookin' fer Andrew Leyland, an' this time he'd be kilt fer sure. Iffen he as much as steps foot off this place, Andrew Leyland might git wind of it an' come lookin' fer him to finish the job. He's gotta think he's a hunted man, that iffen anybody fins out he's alive he'll be taken an' hanged."

"What if he remembers, all by hisself?" Etta wanted to know.

"He ain't remembered yet, and mebbeso he'll never remember. That there crease in his forehead prob'ly did somethin' to his brains so's he'll never recollect who he is or what happened."

"Becky's sweet on him," Nate jibed at his sister. "Becky's got her eye on 'im."

"You shut up! 'Tain't none of yer business!" Becky flared. "An' don't you dast go openin' yer mouth to him, neither, or I'll skin you raw, and don't believe I won't!"

Etta could see which way the wind was blowing, and although she knew that what Becky was doing was wrong, she let it go. The rigors of life had worn her down, and there wasn't enough spirit left in her to go against her strong-willed daughter. Eben wasn't any help. Always an ineffectual man, he had grown even more so over the years, one defeat after another bowing his shoulders and taking the will out of him as it had taken it out of Etta.

One of the younger sons of a reasonably prosperous farmer, Etta had thought she'd done well enough for herself by marrying him. She was the middle daughter of the owner of a general store, but her family, like Eben's, was large, and hers had run to girls where Eben's had run to boys, and the town of Martinsville, Pennsylvania, hadn't been large enough to make her father's store prosperous. There were too many girls in Etta's family to be of any use, and too many boys in Eben's for the land to go around. Two bad crops in a row had sent Eben to Martinsville to seek employment, and he'd found it at the miller's, lifting and carrying heavy sacks of meal and flour. Eben and Etta had met at a church social, and been drawn to each other because they were so much alike, neither of them needed or wanted at home.

Eben had saved enough out of his wages to make a down payment on a few acres of his own. He and Etta had married, filled with hope for the future. But the little farm had not prospered in spite of the fact that both of them had worked hard, giving it all they had. They'd been disappointed at the birth of their first child, who had been a girl, and elated when Rufe had been born. But Rufe had fallen out of a tree when he was only five, and addled his brains; and then Eben's two cows had sickened and died; a cold, wet winter had killed off most of their chickens; a late, wet spring had delayed planting until it was too late to raise a good crop of anything and an early frost had been the final blow.

Unable to meet the payments on his farm, Eben had sold his interest in it for what he could get and they had struck out for Georgia, where they'd heard that they could hack out a piece of land without cash to pay for it, and get a fresh start where the climate was kinder to farmers.

But with only Eben and Etta, with Etta having to tend two children and then another when Nathan was born, the going had been hard. The few chickens they had brought with them had been taken by varmints. They had no cow, and they would have had no way to get it serviced if they'd had one. Always undernourished, the work backbreaking, they'd submitted themselves to fate, living from day to day without either joy or hope. If they thought about it at all they supposed they were lucky that they had survived. Rufe was handy at heavy work if he was watched without taking your eye off him, and Nate was of an age now where he could have been of real help except that he was forever off tending his traplines, or hunting when there was shot to spare, anything to escape the tedium of the corn patch.

It was the worst for Becky. She was pretty and smart, and she deserved better. It saddened Etta to think that her comely girl had nothing really pretty to wear, that she had only the education that Etta had been able to give her, her ABCs and a little counting. Etta had learned to read and write after a fashion, because her mother had been better educated and she had attended two years of school, but with no books in the cabin except the Bible, and no pen or paper or slate, it had seemed pointless to try to teach Becky and Nate.

Heaven's Horizon

The worst of it was that living like they did, in the middle of nowhere, there weren't any men as prospects for Becky, either. Small holdings like the McCabes' were widely scattered, and what young men were on them were backwoods crackers, and Becky would have to settle for one of them and for a life no better than her mother's, or never marry at all.

Anybody, even someone as beaten as Etta, could see why Becky was so taken with the stranger she'd hauled from the bog. He was a fine-looking man, and it was obvious that he was a cut above the McCabes or any other family that Becky might have personal contact with. No town man would take Becky no matter how comely she was. The crackers were looked down on, held to be lower in the scale of things than a good black slave. The plantation people and the prosperous farmers didn't acknowledge their existence.

But here was this pretty man, young, and anybody could see that he was smart even if that bullet crease on his forehead had taken away his memory. Given enough of a story, just credible enough, he might stay around, he might even marry Becky if he was convinced that it would be worth his life to leave. It was taking him a long spell to recover to any condition where he could leave, in any case, and Becky had had all this time to work on him and she'd have more.

Lying was a sin, and Etta knew that. But Donal, whom she called John, the name Becky had made up for him, was going to be strong and able-bodied once he'd got his full strength back. With his help, more land could be cleared, more crops grown, and if God granted them decent weather, they might even end up with a cow or two, and a good stout fence to keep chickens from straying and a henhouse to protect them from varmints that hunted by night.

Etta would dearly love to see Becky in a new dress, and a pretty sunbonnet, and with shoes on her feet instead of going barefoot all summer and wearing moccasins in the winter. And Etta would dearly love to see Becky married and raising a passel of young'uns of her own so long as their place produced enough to feed them and it would if Becky could persuade John to stay and to hitch up with her. Rufe wouldn't ever be anything but what he was now, and Nate might take it in his head to go off and leave them once he had a little more growth. They needed John, and that was a fact.

Donal finished his inspection of himself in the mirror. His growling stomach pleased him even if there would be nothing to satisfy it this morning except cornmeal mush. He was gaining strength rapidly now. Every day, he stayed up longer and moved around more. Nothing made a man feel more useless than to be helpless, sick and good for nothing.

Beyond regaining his strength, Donal had no plans. It would take thinking about, that was certain. He knew without it being pointed out to him that he was different from the McCabes, but the degree of difference was something that he didn't know. His speech was entirely unlike theirs, for one thing. Nate laughed at him and said that he talked funny, and although Donal was too polite to retaliate in kind, the McCabes' accent was strange to his ears and their grammar made him wince.

And there was another thing. There were no signs on his hands of having done hard physical labor. Even as long as he'd been sick, lying in bed doing nothing, there would have been traces of calluses, his hands would have been roughened if he had done hard manual labor. And one of his fingers, the ring finger on his right hand, was a little smaller at the base as though a ring had been there for a long time. There was no ring there now and the McCabes disclaimed that he'd been wearing one when they'd found him, but he was convinced that he had worn a ring at one time, and extremely poor manual laborers were not likely to wear a ring.

"That bounty hunter what 'most kilt you must've took it," Becky told him. "A man that'ud shoot another man in the back wouldn't go leavin' no ring on your hand. Mebbe he took it so's he could prove he'd kilt you, an' collect a reward."

Now that he was getting stronger, not being able to remember was driving Donal crazy. It seemed to him that if he tried hard enough, something would be bound to come back. But it didn't, his mind remained as blank as it had been on the first day when he'd realized that he was lying in Eben and Etta McCabes' bed in the McCabe cabin.

Heaven's Horizon

"I'm goin' with Nate this mornin' to check his snares," Becky told him while he ate his mush. "You want to walk with us fer a spell? Reckon you could find yer way back alone, if you was to tucker out?"

It wasn't in her mind that Donal should have to find his way back alone. It was in her mind to come back with him, without Nate's company, and be alone with him for the first time since she and Nate had rescued him from his buried-alive grave in the bog. And high time, too, because she was itching to be alone with him; there was a need for her to be alone with him that had to be satisfied soon or she'd go plumb out of her mind.

Donal's face brightened. It would be good to get out of the cabin, to stretch legs that had been idle for too long. His lungs hungered for the fresh pine-scented air of early winter, an escape from the cabin that was perpetually clouded with smoke from the poor-drawing chimney, a cabin that was hardly big enough to turn around in as it was. For the past week or two his confinement had been irritating him, setting his nerves on edge. Besides, he needed to get out, to study the lay of the land. It wasn't good not to know exactly where he was, and the way out if he should need it.

"Me too!" Rufe said, his eyes bright with eagerness. "I'm goin' too!"

"No, you ain't. Not this time," Becky's voice was final, and Rufe hunkered closer in onto himself, his face a picture of disappointment. But Becky didn't weaken, although she felt a little guilty. "John's goin' to need your coat and moccasins. I'll just go tell Ma that we're leavin', so's she kin keep an eye on you."

Etta gave her daughter a sharp look when Becky found her with Eben in the woodlot where Eben was making a halfhearted effort to get out enough fuel to last them the winter and Etta was helping him load the crude sledge with Stubborn, the mule that was their only domestic animal, hitched to it. But she changed her mind about objecting when she saw the shining expectation on Becky's face.

"All right. I'll fetch Rufe back here with your pa an' me, he kin help me load an' unload. Mind you don't let John git too tired."

Letting John get too tired was the last thing in Becky's mind. She wanted him to get just tired enough to want to go back, but not too tired for the other things she had in mind for him.

The weather was crisp but not cold. Becky wrapped herself in a shawl, the knitted wool still thick although it was rough to the touch from being washed with lye soap, and raveled in places. She pulled her homemade moccasins on her feet, moccasins that she wore only out-of-doors even in the winter. Rufe's moccasins, the hide as poorly cured and as roughly fashioned as Becky's, were so big that Donal's feet felt lost in them, and again he experienced that sense of the alien, of something entirely outside of his experience, as he looked at them.

There was a light dusting of snow in the more sheltered spots, where the sun hadn't got to it yet. It was winter, Donal knew that, but he had no clear idea of the exact date. Becky had told him that she calculated that it was getting on toward the middle of December. It had still been summer when she and Nate had found him, and that made it five months or more ago, and that was a big chunk of a man's life to be lost without a trace of memory. He knew, because both Becky and Nate had told him, that the McCabes had given him up for dead half a dozen times during those months while the infection-fed fever had consumed him, and only Becky had refused to give up trying to save him. Each time that Etta had said that he was beyond hope, that he would be gone before morning, Becky had yelled at Rufe to put the shovel away, that it wasn't time to dig a grave yet.

He owed Becky for that. He was alive, he was on his feet, he was strong enough to walk in the forest, drawing the clean air into his lungs, savoring it, savoring the sense of well-being that flowed through him just to be among the living and able to walk again.

One thing was certain to Donal as they walked. There was no discernible trail, but Becky and Nate both seemed to be following one that he couldn't make out. He wasn't a woodsman, he could be sure of that. He didn't know the first thing about making his way through wild land with which he was unfamiliar.

"You'll git the feel of it," Becky assured him. "Won't take no time at all. Come spring, you'll be as good at it as Nate and me."

Heaven's Horizon

Come spring! The thought that he would still be here in the spring was like a blow to his solar plexus. But where else would he go, where could he go, a hunted man, a man who would be taken and hanged if he were to go back to any kind of civilization? He had no money, no means of support, and if he had had any skills or talents that would enable him to earn a living, he didn't know what they had been. Who was he? Why couldn't he remember?

There was a rabbit in the third snare. The fourth had held a rabbit, but something else had got there before they had. Nate cussed, using language that made Donal flinch. Becky, seeing his reaction, chided her brother. "Watch yer mouth, Nate. That ain't no way to talk, dammit!"

Nate watched his mouth, because Becky could be vicious if she was crossed. She wasn't mean very often, but she had the capability for it, and Nate wasn't eager to find out firsthand just how mean she could be.

The fifth snare also yielded a rabbit, and Donal was tiring. Becky concealed her satisfaction as she saw that his steps were slowing.

"We'll head on back now. Nate don't need us nohow. We'll jest take the rabbits we already got along. Ma'll be wantin' to skin 'em and drop 'em in the pot."

She carried the rabbits on a thong, careless of their limp bodies swinging at her side. Donal wondered whether he'd been squeamish in his former life, because he felt pity for the furry creatures although his newly awakened hunger made his mouth water at the thought of the meat he'd have for supper. There was a sudden flash of conviction that he had hunted, but that his quarry had been birds, quail or grouse, and then it was gone, leaving him feeling empty and frustrated. Where had he hunted, when?

Becky was deep in her own thoughts. She had to make a move because it was obvious that Donal wasn't going to. She knew nothing of flirting, none of the wiles she would have known if she had lived in a town where there were young men to flirt with. But girls know some things by instinct, it's born in them, assimilated with their mother's milk.

Turning her ankle would do, but that was too obvious. Without an instant's hesitation, she brought her moccasined foot down on a sharp spine that a baby could have avoided. Her yelp of pain, not in the least feigned, brought Donal to a halt.

"Got a spine in my foot. Gotta git it out," she said. "Let me lean on you, John, so's I won't go fallin'."

She removed the moccasin. The spine, or part of it, was still embedded in the sole, but the rest of it was in her foot, broken off. Becky wasn't too happy about that. She'd been hoping that enough of it would still stick out so that she could get ahold of it and yank it out. The pain she was experiencing meant nothing to her. It smarted, but she'd had worse hurts.

"Cain't git it. You'd better try," she said. She sat down on the ground and Donal knelt in front of her, taking her foot in his lap. It was a shapely foot, narrow and well-arched, in spite of having been broadened from running barefoot all her life, and in spite of the calloused soles, almost as tough as the moccasin leather itself.

"I'm afraid it's in deep," Donal said. He tried to get ahold of it with his finger and thumbnail, but not enough of it showed.

"This is a hell'uv a note, ain't it?" Becky asked cheerfully. "We'll jest hev to wait till we git back, an' Ma'll take it out with her needle. I'll hev to lean on you, an' hop."

Leaning on him, being in close physical proximity to him, had been her object all along. She leaned on him, a good deal more heavily than was necessary. Donal was acutely aware of the warmth and aliveness of the body pressed against his. He ought to carry her, but he wasn't sure that his strength was up to it. They'd just have to do the best they could.

"Does it hurt badly?" he asked, his voice anxious.

Becky hopped along. "Not too bad. I kin manage." They grasped at each other to keep their balance, three-legged as they were. Becky was pressed up against his chest, laughing up into his face, her mouth only inches from his. A tantalizing mouth, soft and pink and curved in a smile, and her eyes were soft and filled with a shining he hadn't seen there before, and her cheeks were pink and she was in every way desirable and Donal knew, without being able to remember, that he had held a woman's body in his arms before, that he had kissed her and that he had liked it, that it had been intensely satisfying to him.

He wasn't ill anymore, he just didn't have his full strength back. And whatever girl he had kissed, whenever it was he had kissed her, had left his body with the memory and he wanted more, it was a male hunger that would not be denied after so long of doing without.

Becky's eyes flew wide when his mouth came down over hers, and then she closed them. Her lips opened under his of their own accord, as if she'd been kissed before, although she hadn't, as if she knew how, which she didn't, but she was learning fast and darned if it wasn't the most surprising thing she'd ever learned. Her arms crept around his neck as the rabbits fell unheeded at their feet, and they went on kissing each other and something was happening to Donal, kisses weren't enough and she wasn't helping him to control himself, clinging to him as she was, pressing her soft, rounded breasts against his chest, pressing herself, the whole delicious length of her, against him.

Becky wasn't sure what would have happened next but she knew that she was sorry that it didn't happen, and it was all she could do to keep from letting out a string of cusswords that would have put anything Nate had ever said to shame, when Rufe's lumbering body bore down on them. Rufe's feet were bare and he was wearing only his trousers and his homespun shirt, but his face was shining with joy as if he felt no trace of the sharpness in the air.

"I found you! I done found you! I knowed I could!" he crowed.

"Rufe, you shouldn't of come out alone, you knows you ain't supposed to!" Becky snapped at him. Drat, consarn and drat, why had Rufe had to pick today to slip away from Etta's watchful eyes and come trailing them?

But if Becky was furious, Donal was relieved. What he'd been about to do was beyond the limits of decency. What kind of a man would repay the people who had saved his life, who had taken him in and nursed him and fed him and clothed him for all these months, by seducing their daughter in the woods the first time he got her alone? Even McCabe would have had every right to shoot him, and he wouldn't have blamed him.

"It's all right, Rufe. Come along."

"You wuz kissin' each other," Rufe prattled. "I seed you, you wuz kissin' each other. Are you gonna hev a baby now, Becky? Will there be a little bitty young'un fer me to play with?"

Becky's face flamed, and she had to hold herself back from slapping Rufe's face so hard that it would send him squalling home and never dare to venture out again where he wasn't wanted.

"Don't be any crazier'n you already are! Of course I ain't gonna hev a baby!" she said.

Rufe's face fell, but it brightened again immediately. "But mebbe you'll kiss each other again, an' then you will," he said. "Hey, you done dropped the rabbits!" He scooped them up himself and set off toward home, hopping and skipping like any five-year-old turned loose in the woods.

"Don't pay him no mind. He'll forgit it afore we git home," Becky told Donal.

"I'm sorry. I didn't mean to take advantage of you," Donal said, fumbling for words. "It was unforgivable of me."

"Ain't nothin' to be sorry fer. Nothin' happened." And Becky added, "Damn it!" but she said that silently.

All the same, she'd made progress. Donal was looking at her with different eyes, not as a man looks at a woman who nurses him when he's sick but like a man who looks at a woman, knowing that she's a woman. And he liked what he saw, and he'd liked kissing her, and if Rufe hadn't come barging in who knew what might have resulted from it and it would have been all over but the shouting because Becky knew that once Donal had had her, she'd be able to hold him. If she wasn't able to hold him, then she didn't deserve to be called a woman.

Rufe had outdistanced them, eager to show his mother the rabbits. Becky turned to Donal, and before he had the least idea of what she was about she stood on tiptoe and kissed him again. Her arms were around his neck, and as before, her tongue flicked out and he felt as though he were going to explode from his need for her.

"That's just to hold us until next time," Becky told him. And there would be a next time, and the next time she'd make sure that they weren't interrupted. "We'd better git on back now, or Pa'll likely come huntin' us if Rufe's too far ahead totin' them rabbits so's he'll know Rufe was with us. You mighta tuckered out, or fallen an' hurt yerself.''

Donal's whole body felt as if he had fallen and hurt himself. But beyond the aching need for Becky, there was another, eerily-fast impression of some other girl, only he couldn't put a name or a face to her.

He tried not to let it bother him. It was certain that he was no adolescent, he was bound to have had experience with some girl or woman before he'd got in the trouble that had sent him running and ended by nearly costing him his life. And Becky's words pushed that fleeting moment of almost remembering something still farther into his subconscious. Like Becky, he knew that there would be a next time, and he wasn't sure how he'd be able to endure waiting until it came.

Chapter Twelve

Still squatting on the platform, the pestle motionless in her hand, Cordelia looked up at the man who had addressed her with such an astonishing statement and felt the terror grow in her heart. It was compounded when the man went on.

"You're that runaway girl a man named Andrew Leyland's hunting for, or I'll eat my moccasins! You're Cordelia Leyland, and there's no use denying it because if a sawed-off slave called Runt is here as well, I'll know for sure."

It was too much for Cordelia. After all these weeks of believing that she was safe, that there was no way her father could ever get his hands on her again, to be discovered now and dragged away and returned to him was more than she could bear. Her eyes filled with tears, and the sound that escaped from her throat was one of pure anguish.

"What the devil! Stop that, Miss Leyland. I'm not going to eat you. What I'm wondering is what the devil I'm to do with you now that I've found you."

Cordelia gaped at him. She must look like an idiot, but she

couldn't help it. What did he mean, what was he going to do with her? He'd take her back to her father, of course, or send word to Andrew that she was here. Any white man would. Runaway daughters of plantation owners had to be returned, even more than runaway slaves.

"And look at you!" the man said. "You're seven months gone at the least. And your father turning all of Georgia and Florida upside down looking for you, and will you start talking and tell me what the devil you mean by being here, by running away from a luxurious and coddled life to take refuge with the Seminoles?"

"And what the devil do you mean by saying what the devil over and over again as if you didn't know how to say anything else?" Cordelia's spirit had returned, if not in full force at least enough to make her retaliate. "Who are you, anyway? If I'm no quadroon, you're no Seminole!"

The blue eyes were laughing at her now, warm and humorous. The stranger's teeth flashed very white against the tan of his face. He was clean-shaven, and he wasn't handsome, but there was something about him that was attractive. His nose was just slightly crooked where it had been broken at one time and hadn't been set quite properly, and his eyebrows quirked up at the ends, giving him a slightly devilish appearance that was compounded by a crooked smile. It was sort of a lopsided face, but an appealing one.

"You're only half right about that, Miss Leyland. I'm only half Seminole. The other half is Spanish."

"But you don't belong in this village! What are you doing here, if you didn't come to hunt me?"

"I came to see my grandmother. I come to see her when the fancy strikes me, and my visits aren't too far apart or she'd crack me on the side of my head hard enough to make me see stars."

"Your grandmother?"

"Little Acorn," the man said, and there was unmistakable fondness in his voice as he uttered the name. Cordelia knew Little Acorn, she knew everyone in the village. Little Acorn was old, her face was marked by many wrinkles, and she lived alone, doing what share of the work of the village she could still manage and taking her sustenance from the common stores. No one in a Seminole village went hungry or unclothed, the sick and the old were entitled to their share of the stores that were set aside for that purpose.

Little Acorn had rapped her fingers when she'd first tried doing beadwork, because she'd completed a design with no flaw, and indicated that she must take a few beads out. But her eyes had held no malice; she was only teaching a woman who knew no better the correct way of doing things. And she observed the size of Cordelia's stomach, comparing it to Weleka's, and she smiled when she did it, and sometimes she came and spelled Cordelia when Cordelia sat pounding corn, sitting in companionable silence after she'd taken the pestle from Cordelia's hand and motioned for her to rest. She never let Cordelia forget that she was the senior and entitled to respect, but she never did or said anything to remind Cordelia that Cordelia was a slave. Cordelia liked her, as she liked everyone in the village. She realized, almost with surprise, that there was no one here who was worthy of dislike. If it wasn't for the boredom, for the lack of books, for the lack of people who could talk to her of things she knew, it would have been next door to Eden.

"I don't think I understand. If you're a Seminole, why don't you live here? The men belong to their mother's family, I know that, so this should be your home, shouldn't it? Or was Little Acorn your father's mother, and he married a girl from another village?"

"As I have never married, I still belong to this village. My mother was Little Acorn's daughter. But I live on a plantation a good distance from here, to the north."

"So that was what all the yapping and snarling of the dogs was about this morning. You had arrived to visit your grandmother. Does your master allow you to visit Little Acorn often enough to keep her from boxing your ears?"

"He does. I happen to own the plantation. Carlos DeHerrera, at your service, ma'am."

Cordelia felt like a fool, but she was so relieved to learn that she wasn't to be dragged back to Leyland's Landing that she didn't care. "I didn't know that there were plantations in Florida. Farms, and small settlements, but not real plantations."

Lydia Lancaster

"We learn something every day," Carlos DeHerrera said. "Or we do if we keep our eyes and our ears open. There are large plantations in northern Florida, Miss Leyland."

Cordelia's face flamed. In her condition, for him to call her Miss Leyland! It wasn't to be borne, not even from a half-Seminole.

"I am not Miss Leyland. I am Mrs. Donal MacKenzie," she said, her voice sharp. "I am a widow, Mr. DeHerrera."

"Señor DeHerrera," Carlos corrected her. "Lesson number one. There are plantations in Florida, and Spanish gentlemen are called Señor, not Mister. And I accept your apology. I also accept your lesson, that you are Mrs. Donal MacKenzie, a widow. That still doesn't tell me what I am to do with you now that I have discovered you."

"You don't have to do anything with me. I'm perfectly all right. Everyone in the istihapo is kind to me. They will care for me when my baby is born, and they will allow us to go on living here for as long as we wish. It doesn't have anything to do with you." Then her curiosity got the better of her. "Señor DeHerrera, is your plantation a large and prosperous one? Is it like the large plantations in Georgia?"

"Very like, Señora MacKenzie. I have done quite well for myself since my grandfather Filipe DeHerrera died and left me enough to get a start."

"Then, will you lend me enough money to get to England, after my baby is born? My husband's parents will pay you back, I promise that they will! They'll want me and the baby, you see, because the baby will be their only grandchild and he'll belong in England, with them, and I have no way to get there and they don't know where I am and so they can't help me—"

Carlos held up his hand, laughing although his eyes were serious. "Hold it! You're going a little too fast. Would you mind telling me why your father didn't send you to England after you were widowed, and why you ran away from him?"

"He killed Donal," Cordelia burst out. "He shot him and killed him and threw his body into a bog so that it could never be proved against him, because of an old grudge against Donal's father! I have no way to prove it, there were no witnesses, but he did it! And he wouldn't let me go to England, he wanted my baby, Donal's baby, to be born at Leyland's Landing so that he could harm it, so that he could kill it just as he killed Donal!''

It all came flooding back, and Cordelia began to cry. Her shoulders shook and she scrubbed at her eyes with the backs of her hands but still the tears came, she couldn't stop them, it was as if she'd never be able to stop them now that they had started.

"Zoe said so, and Zoe knew, because she knew about my father and Donal's father although we didn't know that Donal was the son of my father's enemy when I married him, his name was different because his mother had married again, you see..."

Strong hands raised her to her feet, and she was pulled against a strong shoulder. Oh, God, but it felt good to lean against a strong shoulder, to feel strong arms around her, she'd been so alone, even if the Seminoles were kind to her, even if Weleka and Hilolo were her special friends, even if Runt was here. She had been so alone that she hadn't dared to think about the future and how she could make her way to England if she couldn't manage to get as far as Boston and beg the Reynards to help her. But if this man, this half-Spaniard who was Little Acorn's grandson would help her, she needn't ever be alone again. She'd have her child, and Donal's parents, and his sisters, and it was too good to be true and so she went on crying, getting Carlos's blouse wet and soaking the shoulder underneath it.

"Stop it. Stop it now! You'll do something to yourself, I don't want you to drop that baby on my feet right where we're standing! I'll help you, you don't have to go on crying like a baby with a stubbed toe. But it'll take some thought and even more time. If your father is as powerful as you've indicated, so powerful that he could kill your husband and hold you prisoner, he'll no doubt still have men hunting for you, and every port watched. I'll have to do a lot of checking before we dare to make a move. Not that it matters. You wouldn't be able to leave for several months in any case. First you have to control yourself so that you won't have your baby right here this minute, and then you have to let it, he or she—whatever it happens to be—get big enough to travel, and we have to make very sure that we can smuggle you through whatever network of agents your father has employed to apprehend you. All right? Which is your chikee? You need to lie down and rest, you've had a shock. And I want to hunt up Runt. I've heard about him from the men who've been scouring Florida looking for you and I want to see if a man who's as small as they say he is can actually be as strong as they say he is."

"He'll be in the fields with the other slaves," Cordelia gulped. "And he is small, and he is strong, he couldn't have gotten me away if he hadn't been so strong, and I'll never be able to repay him. And I don't know what my father has done to Zoe and I can't bear it . . ."

"I'll find out." The voice was gentle now. "I too know how to employ spies. Come along, you must rest."

Cordelia went with him willingly. No one in the village paid any attention to them as he escorted her to her chikee. The Seminoles were never so impolite that they pried into the affairs of others until they had been expressly invited. It was another of the traits that Cordelia admired so much. She knew many white people who were supposed to be civilized and cultured who could take lessons from them and profit by it.

She lay down as soon as Carlos left her, but she couldn't sleep. She was too excited, her heart was still beating too fast, and she felt her baby move, a sharp kick as though it were out of sorts with her for her upset. She put her hand on her stomach. "Be patient, little one. And for mercy sake stop that kicking, didn't you hear Señor DeHerrera tell me that I must rest?"

What a remarkable man he was! Cordelia had never known anyone like him and she doubted that there was anyone else like him among all the people she would ever know. Half Seminole, but well educated, certainly, wealthy and cultured and kind. To think that he was Little Acorn's grandson! And she thought, not without amusement, that now she could find out how the old woman had come by such an odd name. Her few Seminole words gave her no way to ask Weleka, and, besides, such a question might be considered impolite.

Lying there, feeling her breath become steady and her heart quiet,

Heaven's Horizon

she admitted to herself for the first time how afraid she'd been in her loneliness. And she hadn't even been saying her prayers! But still God had sent Señor DeHerrera to her. Zoe must have been praying for her, and that meant that Zoe must still be alive. She would know soon, because Señor DeHerrera had promised to find out.

By nightfall, before Cordelia woke up after having slept even though she'd been sure that she wouldn't be able to, the entire village knew that she was not a quadroon and not a slave, that she was a white girl who had run away from her wealthy and powerful father. Some of them had suspected it, but they had never said so, or asked her. And even now, no one looked at her with curiosity. They hadn't been invited to, yet, and they would not until she indicated that she didn't mind.

Weleka came to her while she was eating. She looked into Cordelia's eyes, and then she placed her hands on Cordelia's arms and smiled. There was sympathy and understanding on her face, and love. It was a good feeling. When Cordelia left the istihapo, when Señor DeHerrera thought it would be safe for her to go to England, she would miss Weleka, and she would remember her all the rest of her life, and all of the other Seminoles and the slaves who had been so kind to her.

Señor DeHerrera was waiting at Weleka and Wacassa's chikee. Little Acorn was there as well. They sat in a circle on the platform, the women's blankets pulled snugly around their shoulders against the chill of the evening. Cordelia pulled hers tighter, the blanket that Weleka had given her when she had first arrived in the village. She'd take her Seminole clothing and the blanket with her when she left, she'd keep them always, for remembrance. She'd show them to her parents-in-law and later to her child, and make them understand the gentle majesty of these people who had befriended her.

There was amusement in Carlos DeHerrera's eyes when he looked at her. "You could almost pass for one of us," he said. "In that getup, and with your skin so brown from all your exposure to the sun, you're nearly as dark as we are. You could certainly pass for a mulatto, or at least the quadroon you claimed to be. You'll be safe enough here for the time being. I'll start inquiries when I return home, but I wouldn't count on your father having given up the search for you yet, Mrs. MacKenzie."

"Mrs. MacKenzie," Weleka said, her tongue having difficulty in forming the words. And then she laughed and pointed to herself, "Mrs. Wacassa." The name pleased her and she repeated it, giggling at her husband, who laughed back at her.

They talked for an hour. Weleka's curiosity was as great as that of any woman, no matter her color. Through Carlos's interpretation, she tried to visualize the plantation on which Cordelia had grown up, the house, the clothing Cordelia had worn. It was even more difficult to give her a picture of Boston and Miss Virginia Baker's Academy for Young Ladies. For young females to go to school was incomprehensible to her. Her face was filled with wonder, and Wacassa shook his head, as puzzled as his wife.

Looking at Little Acorn, who was following the conversation with as lively an interest as Weleka and Wacassa, Cordelia remembered to ask Carlos how she had come by her name.

"She earned it as a toddling child." Carlos laughed. "She liked to play with acorns, but she always chose the smallest, for a reason no one else could understand. Perhaps it was because she was small and had an affinity for small things."

How cultured his speech was! Although he looked very much a Seminole in his Indian dress, no one who heard him speak in English would mistake him for a red man, no matter how civilized. But when he spoke Seminole, the transfiguration was startling. Only his shorter hair struck a discordant note, and the blue eyes that seemed to have no place in his dark face.

There was activity at the central structure where council meetings were held. A fire had been built there, and the men of the village were gathering, young and old. Carlos stood up, his movements fluid. "I'll talk to you again before I leave," he told her. Wacassa too stood up, and the two men went to join the others at the council house.

Cordelia wondered what was going on. There had been no such meeting since she had come to the village. Carlos's face had been grave, and Wacassa's as well, when they had gone to join them.

Heaven's Horizon

And Weleka's eyes were shadowed, and although Little Acorn rarely showed any emotion, she looked sad.

Cordelia shivered in spite of the blanket wrapped around her shoulders. Whatever it was, it must be important. The village was unnaturally quiet. The women kept to their chikees and kept the children close to them. Cordelia could see that the male slaves were also gathered around the council fire, Runt among them, and that the slaves were also allowed to stand and talk.

"Is there trouble?" she asked Weleka.

Weleka didn't understand the word and there was no combination of words and signs by which Cordelia could make her understand. Maybe Señor DeHerrera would tell her about it when he talked to her before he left. For tonight, there was nothing to do but return to her chikee, walking the long way around to avoid the men, and try to sleep.

Sleep was a long time in coming. Now that her deliverance was within her grasp, her heart ached for Donal more than it had for weeks. She had never stopped grieving for him, and she never would, but the necessity of surviving and of adapting herself to her new way of life had taken up part of her thoughts. Now she pressed her face into her sleeping mat and wept. The thought that she would never feel Donal's arms around her again, holding her safe and close, filled her with such desolation that she almost wanted to die.

But it wasn't permitted her to die, to matter the depth of her grief. She must go on living so that her child might live. It was the last and the only thing she could do for Donal, to see that the child of his flesh and blood grew up to a happy and fulfilled adulthood.

It was late before the council meeting broke up, and the men's faces, both red and black, were grave as they walked to their separate chikees. Carlos slept in the council house rather than in the lodge where the young unmarried men slept apart from their families. He wanted no more questions put to him tonight because he had no more answers. When he learned more, when he had something definite to tell them, he would come back.

"There's no trouble," he told Cordelia in the morning before he left to return to his plantation along the Apalachicola River to the northwest. "Not at the moment, at any rate, and I think it will be a long time in coming. But there will be trouble, although no one can predict how soon."

"But the Seminoles are at peace with the whites!" Cordelia protested. "They've been at peace for years, and they haven't broken their treaty!"

"A peace not of their own making, but one they were forced to accept," Carlos told her, his eyes as serious as if he had been talking to a man. "They were defeated, and they had to accept what they were given. And the terms were harsh, Mrs. MacKenzie. They were exiled from their rich, fertile northern lands where they had been prosperous and contented, where they had extensive trade with their cattle and grain, their furs and hides, where their dugouts dotted the rivers as they transported their goods to ports for sale and export.

"The Seminoles have kept to the treaty, remaining in the lands given to them here. But white men have not. More and more white settlers are moving in, and like those who drove the Seminoles from their homes in northern Florida, these white men now demand that the Seminoles be driven from these lands so that they can have it for themselves."

"But that's not right! This land belongs to the Seminoles! How can the government allow white men to drive them out?"

"The country is land hungry," Carlos told her. "The tide of settlers waiting to move in is beyond comprehension. And in spite of the treaty, there is talk now of the United States government passing a removal act, to force the Seminoles to quit Florida entirely and agree to be resettled in Arkansas, to be reunited with the Creeks from whom they broke off generations ago when they left Georgia and migrated to Florida to become their own nation. The word *Seminole* has derived from a word that means 'those who broke off,' or 'those who went away.' They came here because they wished to live in peace, to raise their cattle and grow their crops and engage in trade and watch their women and their children wax fat and content. But the white men will not have it so.

"If the act is passed, there will be trouble. The old men want peace at any price, but the young men will fight. They will not be

Heaven's Horizon

moved again, driven from their lands, without resistance that may well flare into a full-scale war.

"Those fools who run our government have no idea of the fury that will be unleashed if they pass their act and attempt to enforce it. With the hordes of land-hungry settlers, land speculators—standing to make fortunes by opening up this Seminole territory, buying now for a pittance and planning to sell for unimaginable profit when the Seminoles have been removed—are demanding that the act be passed, and that the army be sent in to force the Seminoles to go if they will not go peaceably. Trouble is certain to come."

Cordelia's face had gone pale under the tan she had acquired since she had come to the village, and now Carlos put his hand on her arm.

"There is nothing for you to worry about for the present. As I said, if there is trouble, it will be a long time in coming. We can let ourselves believe that before it happens you will be safe in England with your husband's family."

"But what about Weleka and Wacassa? What about Hilolo and Stillipika? What about your own grandmother, Little Acorn, and all of the others? They can't go running off to England!"

"And they wouldn't if they could." Carlos smiled at her. "It's out of your hands, Mrs. MacKenzie, and out of mine. We can only wait and hope that this time the white men will honor their treaty. For you, the only sensible course is to put it out of your mind and concentrate on having your caccosoci, your child, and project your thoughts to the day you will join your family in England." His smile deepened. "It is a fitting thing for you to do, after all. Under Seminole law, a man belongs to his mother's family, and as your Donal's mother is now your mother-in-law, that is where you would have been if Donal had not been killed."

"Señor DeHerrera, will you write to my parents-in-law, will you tell them that I'm alive and safe and that they are going to be grandparents and that I'll come to them as soon as I can?"

"Certainly. It will be a pleasure. Will you give me their address so I can see to it immediately?"

Cordelia's brow furrowed. Their address! What was the matter with her mind, why couldn't she remember it? She'd written to them twice, once directly after Donal had died and again when she had discovered that she was pregnant. She knew that they lived somewhere in Mayfair, but the street and the number eluded her. She'd had no need to commit it to memory, it had been written down for her to refer to whenever she needed it.

"It's somewhere in Mayfair, Mr. Duncan MacKenzie. I can't remember the rest, how could I be so stupid?"

"Never mind. I will find a way to get the letter to them. There can't be that many Duncan MacKenzies in Mayfair."

Cordelia felt a moment of panic as she watched Carlos ride away from the village. He sat tall and straight on his horse, a magnificent black, as fine as any she had ever seen in Georgia, finer than any her father's stable boasted. He used no saddle, but rode Indian-style, on a blanket. She wondered what he would look like dressed in white men's clothing, or did he always dress as a Seminole, even when he was on his plantation? She knew so little about him!

But that was unimportant. He was leaving, and her tenuous link with civilization, with England and the MacKenzies, was leaving with him. How long would it be before he returned to the village, how long would it take him to find out if it was safe for her to leave the protection of the Seminoles?

Weleka came and stood beside her and put her arm around her. She indicated that Cordelia should busy herself at something, and Cordelia knew that her friend was right. She would need to keep very busy in the days that followed, or she wouldn't be able to get through the time until Señor DeHerrera came back.

Cordelia counted on her fingers. June, July, August, September, October, November, December, January, February, March. She wasn't sure what month it was, she had lost track, but she knew that the winter was past, that it was early spring, and that her baby should be born very soon.

Carlos DeHerrera had not returned to the istihapo after that first visit, and she was filled with apprehension that something had happened to prevent him, or that he had changed his mind and decided not to help her after all.

Now, with her baby's birth so close at hand, she fell into a fit of depression. Was her child, Donal's child, to spend his life as a Seminole after all? Or would she have to somehow make her way to Boston to throw herself on the merciful generosity of the Reynards? Alone, unprotected, with only her mother's few jewels as assets to buy her passage, afraid at every turn and every footstep behind her that one of her father's agents had found her as she searched her way through Saint Augustine seeking someone to buy the rings and the brooch so that she could board a coastal schooner?

Runt had told her that that would be the best way. Having picked up much more of the Seminole language than Cordelia had, he had found out that the Seminoles would attempt to take her safely to Saint Augustine, as soon as her child was old enough to withstand the journey, but once she had reached that city she would be on her own.

Her baby had stopped moving. After weeks of enduring its kicking and squirming, its stillness was ominous to her. It was dead, it must be dead or it would move! That terror was worse than the terror of the pain she would be forced to endure, worse than the terror that she would never be able to leave this place. If her baby was dead, how would she be able to go on living?

Stillipika and Little Acorn laughed at her, seeing her distress and knowing its cause. With a few English words, a few Seminole words, and many signs and gestures, they made her understand that her baby had stopped moving because it had dropped, positioning itself for its birth. It would be soon now, very soon. Weleka too was counting the days, her face serene, her own baby still.

Little Acorn had moved her few possessions into Cordelia's chikee late in February, and with kind but firm insistence, she forced Cordelia to move, to walk, every day. The old woman, Señor DeHerrera's grandmother, watched and waited and Cordelia lost some of her fear. And Little Acorn was there on the night that Cordelia's water broke, and she held Cordelia's hands and talked to her and soothed her all through the long hours of labor, through pain such as Cordelia had never dreamed existed. Cordelia cried, but she didn't cry out. Little Acorn patted her cheek and nodded, well pleased. The birth of a first child was hard, and Cordelia wasn't a Seminole, she wasn't trained as the Seminoles were to endure pain without flinching but she was doing very well.

Cordelia's baby was born at dawn, as Cordelia at last screamed Donal's name in that last wave of agony. Little Acorn received the child, she smiled and held it up for Cordelia's pain-dimmed eyes to see. The baby was already wailing, its lungs powerful and its cries filled with fury at being thrust so unceremoniously into the world.

It was a boy. Exhausted but triumphant, Cordelia marveled at what she had wrought. And before the morning sun had reached its zenith, Hilolo came to her chikee to tell her that Weleka had also given birth and that her child was also a boy.

Chapter Thirteen

Donal woke in a cold sweat, fighting to retain the dream that was already slipping away from him, beyond recall. He was convinced that if he could remember even a part of the dream he would be able to reconstruct the rest of it, that all of the pieces would fall into place and he would be able to remember his past.

But the dream was gone. All he could remember was a fleeting impression of a garden, a rose garden, the beds beautifully kept with flagstone paths between them. There were no roses on the McCabe place, no flowers of any kind except those that grew wild. Becky sometimes brought a handful of violets and placed them in a cracked cup on the table. She loved pretty things and it was a shame that she couldn't have more of them.

Although there was no indication of it, Donal knew that dawn was near. There was that silence that seemed to come just before the dawn, when the dark is at its deepest. In a little while the first birds would start twittering and moving about on their branches, and their twittering would grow in volume until the clearing was alive with it. What kind of clock was concealed beneath their feathers, that they should always know when dawn was at hand even though it was still dark?

Donal no longer slept in what he thought of as the main cabin. For the past two months, he and Eben and Nate and Rufe had labored at felling trees, clearing more land, and throwing up this second cabin that was attached to the main cabin by a dogtrot. It was a rough structure and it still needed a good deal of work. The floor was pounded earth, and Becky was still filling in the chinks in the walls with clay.

The new cabin, as rough as it was, was a great satisfaction to Donal. He couldn't go on putting Eben and Etta out of their own bed, and it was impossible for him to sleep in the loft where Becky slept with her two brothers. The cot Eben had fashioned for him was even more pitifully inadequate than this new cabin, laced and pegged together from branches and with a network of leather thongs to hold a thin corn-shuck mattress. Donal was afraid that one of these nights the whole thing would collapse and send him to the floor, but so far it had held, and soon he'd get around to reinforcing it. In the meantime, it was his own, and the privacy it afforded meant everything to him.

He would have liked to go back to sleep, but he knew that there wouldn't be any use trying. He put his hands under his head and thought about Becky. He was going to have to do something about her, and before much more time had passed, There wasn't any way he was going to be able to keep his hands off her much longer, and once he'd taken what she offered so freely, he'd be committed. The question was, did he want to be committed or not?

If only he could remember! It drove him half-mad, not being able to remember the least detail of his life before he had come out of his unconsciousness here in the McCabes' cabin. Damn that crease on his forehead that had stolen his memory, and damn the man who had given it to him!

It was an uneasy feeling, to think that he had killed a man. It didn't rest well in his mind, especially as he could recall nothing of the man he had killed or his reason for having killed him. He must have had a reason, but had it been a good reason, or a bad one? Had

Heaven's Horizon

he killed him for revenge, or for profit? If it had been for profit, he thought with wry humor, it had availed him nothing, because God knew he had nothing now. But the thought that he might have killed a man for a reason that wasn't good enough weighed heavily on him, disturbing both his waking hours and his sleep.

"You'd be knowed iffen you left," Becky told him, her violet eyes dark with fright. "Even with that beard you'd be knowed. You ain't easy to forgit, an' from what you said when you was ravin', there was a mighty big passel of folks lookin' fer you afore that one that thought he'd kilt you picked up your trail. But you're safe here. So long as you don't show your face off this place, everybody'll think you're dead."

There wasn't much comfort in being dead, even if he knew that he was alive. It gave him even less of an identity, and it was an empty feeling and one that he didn't like. But either he had to pull up stakes and get out of here and take his chances, or he had to do something about Becky, and it was a hard decision to have to make.

The birds were at it now, scolding and making more racket than you'd think such small creatures could make. From the doorway of the other cabin, he heard Rufe's excited crowing. Rufe was always the first one up, the first one to scramble down the ladder from the loft to greet the new day. Etta and Eben were slower in rising, having none of their simpleminded son's enthusiasm for facing what another day would bring. One day was a replica of another, holding only monotony and work and the ever-present fear that some disaster would befall them and wipe them out. Donal didn't relish the thought of living like that, even if his strength and work would make a big difference in the McCabes' prosperity.

And he did work. He took his place behind Stubborn and fought the crude plow to turn the earth to receive the new planting of corn. His hands blistered and bled while he used every ounce of his strength to manhandle tree roots out of the ground, and stumps. There were a good many half-rotted stumps, left where they were when Eben had felled the first trees to make his clearing, and dug the earth and planted around them. Rufe lent his own strength, proud to help Donal, but still this place was a long way from being a well-run and prosperous farm.

He'd never known that work like this existed, and that thought startled him. Why hadn't he known, how had it happened that he didn't know? But he felt, somewhere deep inside of him, that such backbreaking manual labor was alien to him, that he had never done it before. He couldn't have, or he wouldn't have been so utterly inept the first time he had tried, so that even Rufe had laughed at him and Eben had been filled with disgust.

"You worked in a town, in a store," Becky told him, drawing on her never-failing imagination to make things plausible to him. She had to give him an identity, a former life, in order to hold him here. "Don't let it fret you, John. You'll learn, it ain't all that hard."

Donal tried to conjure up images of a dry goods store, a general store, of standing behind a wooden counter measuring out bolts of calico and totting up figures, but his mind remained blank. Why was it that he seemed to remember things in his dreams, only to have them disappear without a trace the moment he opened his eyes?

But if his mind didn't function properly, he had to admit that the same thing didn't hold true for his body. He was whipcord lean, hickory-wood hard, and the stirring of his blood every time Becky got too close to him proved that he was as whole a man as he would ever be.

Becky, and the rest of the McCabes, took it as a thing that was settled that he would stay on here.

"Come next winter, we'll fix your room up, we'll hev plenty of time then. I've got it in mind to build a good fireplace, stone 'stead of stick an' clay. It'll bear thinkin' on. Rufe'ud come in handy helpin' to tote the stone. I never got the hang of fittin' such together but betwixt us we could figger it out. A stone fireplace'ud be nice, with a mantel to set dishes on and such."

There was a new light in Eben's eyes these days, a new spring in his step. It was because he had hope, where hope had been lacking. Hope for a son-in-law, for a strong back and a smart set of brains to help him make something of this holding after all. It bothered Donal to see him, not being sure if he was going to stay or not.

Heaven's Horizon

It bothered him even more to see the smile on Etta's face. Those first weeks he'd known he was still among the living, he'd seldom see her smile. But now she looked from Becky to him, and the smile was there, not much of a smile but hovering at the corners of her mouth and eyes as though it wanted to get out but didn't quite dare, just yet. Donal could almost read her thoughts. It would be nice to have Becky stay at home, to see their holding take shape after all these years and to see a little cash money come in. It would be nice to have her grandchildren grow up under her feet. If Becky married someone else, a man who wasn't hunted, she'd go off with him to his place and Etta would be more trapped in her loneliness than ever.

But most of all, Becky bothered him. How did he know what sort of a husband he might turn out to be? What if his memory returned and he found reason that he had to leave?

Good Lord, he thought, startled. I don't even know how old I am! With his beard, he could have been anywhere from twenty to his mid-thirties. But one thing was certain. He was old enough so that living without a woman was unnatural.

It was a fine day, and it was too bad that he couldn't enjoy it. Beating his brains out because he couldn't remember his past wouldn't solve anything. It was almost certain by now that he would never remember, and he couldn't simply stop living because of it. However old he was, all the rest of his life was ahead of him. The question was whether or not he wanted to spend all those years alone just because he couldn't remember.

Etta smiled at him as she ladled up his mush. "Nate's out checkin' his traps," she said. "There'll be meat for supper, an' the greens is comin' up. A good mess of greens will go good with rabbit. They ain't very tasty come summer, they git tough an' bitter, but in the spring like this they're good. A body gits a cravin' fer them, after goin' all winter with nothin' but meat an' cornmeal."

Donal had never heard her utter so many words at one time before, and he knew that he was the reason and he swallowed. With the return of hope, however tenuous, it was as if her need to communicate had returned, her need to feel close to people and to share her thoughts with them.

"Furniture won't be no problem," Eben said, wolfing down his portion. "All we gotta do is hew it out an' peg it together. I reckon my hand'll be better at it now, arter all the practice I got when I made the fixin's fer Etta an' me years gone, when we first got to this here place. I ain't fergot how. Nate an' Rufe kin help with the smoothin', Nate's turnin' right handy when I kin keep him to home 'stead of runnin' the woods."

They expected him to stay. And he owed them. He owed them his life, and he owed them for keeping him all this time, and he owed them for not turning him in in case there might be a reward on his head.

If he left here, if by some lucky chance he was not recognized and he got free away, it was almost certain that he would never find another girl as pretty as Becky, or one who could promise the excitement that possessing her was sure to bring. Just looking at her was enough to bring his blood to the boiling point. There was a sensuality about the backwoods girl that would stir any man, young or old. It had been born in her, and it reached out and drew a man to her like a magnet. Donal had an idea that it would have been that way even if she hadn't been so disconcertingly pretty.

Maybe it was only his body that wanted her, and not his mind. A man's body was a troublesome thing, when it came in contact with a desirable female. The most surprising thing about his attraction to Becky was that he hadn't done anything about it yet. It wasn't as if he hadn't had the opportunity. Becky had become a master at creating opportunities, only somehow he had always backed off up until now. But the way she had of brushing up against him, the way she had of leaning over so that the tops of her breasts showed above the neckline of her dresses, the way she had of standing against the light that came in through the open door now that spring had come, so that he couldn't miss the delectable curves of her body in profile, was driving him out of his mind. If he hadn't known how simply she'd been brought up, knowing nothing of the ways of the world, he would almost have thought that she did it on purpose!

"Yes, sir, we'll git at that furniture soon's the corn's high enough to fend fer itself, an' fix up that there cabin fitten fer a king!" Eben said. "Ain't no reason to wait till winter, come to think on it. With you here to help, the work don't pile up on me the way it usedter an' there's no reason we cain't git at it right soon. We'll build that there good stone fireplace, an' a table an' a couple of chairs an' a cupboard an' a better bed. This here place is goin' to shine, what with a bigger crop come fall, an' the extry room to the cabin. Well, we'd best git to hoein'. Them weeds ain't goin' to sit still just 'cause we are!"

Donal winced. He had a very good idea that it had been years since Eben had been so energetic about keeping the weeds down and looking forward to extra work as well, like building fireplaces and furniture. And it would have been obvious to a blind man that all of this activity was designed with himself and Becky in mind.

The sun was halfway down toward setting when Donal straightened, easing his back, at the end of a row of corn. It was unseasonably warm for April, and Eben had gone back to the cabin an hour ago and Nate had never showed up at all but had taken off into the woods. Rufe had tried to help but they'd had to send him back to the cabin when his enthusiasm had made him mistake the tender young shoots of corn for weeds.

Donal's shirt, or rather Rufe's shirt, clung to his back. He could use a bath, he must smell like a bear when it comes out of hibernation. But a full bath, the kind he thought of longingly, was difficult in the overcrowded cabin. Even now that he had his own room, he never knew when someone would come barging in, and as likely as not it would be Becky.

His mind went to the creek half a mile from the cabin. It would be running full and deep from the spring rains, and the water would be clear and cool. He could almost feel it even when he still stood there in the corn patch. There would be plenty of time to take advantage of it before supper, and it would feel almighty good to be clean all over again. He'd dunk the clothes he was wearing while he was at it, let them dry on some bushes while he wallowed.

He stopped at the cabin only long enough to poke his head in and tell Etta that he was going swimming in the creek. Becky was nowhere in sight, and neither was Rufe. Likely Becky had taken

Rufe with her when she'd gone to hunt for the greens Etta wanted to boil up for their supper.

The woods felt wonderfully cool after the hot sun in the corn patch, and the creek was as cold as he had hoped it would be. He stripped off his clothes and sloshed the stink out of them and hung them to dry, and then he wallowed and dunked himself under and came up to shake the water out of his eyes and off his hair and simply floated, letting the coolness relax him, while he stared up at the patches of blue between the overhanging branches and mulled over his problems.

He was so deep in his thoughts that he caught only a glimpse of a pale figure streaking toward the creek. Becky's silvery laughter reached his mind before his eyes fully picked up her image. And then she jumped into the water with a splash that all but swamped him.

"Wonderful! You had the right idea, John. I never thought anything could feel so good!"

"Becky, get out of here! I'm not dressed!"

"Well, neither am I, except I've still got my shift on, I left my dress on a branch. But your idea is better, I'm gonna shuck the shift right now, it doesn't feel good all wet and tangled up."

She stood up, and with one graceful motion she peeled the clinging shift over her head and sent it sailing to the bank, where it landed in a sodden mass.

For a moment, he was so mesmerized that he couldn't say a word. She stood there, smiling at him, not quite up to her waist in the water. Her arms were still over her head as she stretched them, luxuriating in the stretching. Her waist was small, accenting the graceful curves of her hips. Her breasts were upthrust, firm and slightly pointed, the nipples puckered from the shock of the cold water and as pink as tightly furled rosebuds just getting ready to spread their petals. She looked like a marble statue, except that her torso and upper arms were several shades whiter than her face and lower arms that were exposed year-round to the weather. Her auburn hair was darkened from its wetness, wisps of it clinging to her face, the rest hanging loose across her shoulders and back, and even as he

Heaven's Horizon

watched, small rivulets of water dripped from her hair down across her breasts and Donal felt such a flood of heat infusing his body that it was a wonder that the creek didn't start to boil.

"Becky, you know better than to pull a trick like this! What are you trying to do, drive me mad?" His voice returned at last, filled with angry protest.

She waded over to look down at him, her eyes filled with laughter. "Of course I'm tryin' to drive you mad! Nothin' else has worked, an' I'm sick an' tired of waitin'! Consarn it, John, I'm a woman, an' you're a man, an' it's about time you realized it an' did somethin' about it! Time don't stand still and I ain't fixin' to be an old maid."

Again without warning, she ducked completely under and then he felt her hands on his ankles, pulling his legs out from under him. They were all tangled up together, their legs entwined, Becky's arms around his neck, her mouth seeking his in a watery kiss that threatened to make his brain explode.

He struggled, breaking the surface gasping for air. "Damn it, Becky, you stop that!"

"Ain't goin' to stop. It feels too good," Becky told him. She too was standing, pressing herself against him, her breasts hard against his chest, hard and soft and warm and cold all at the same time, but her mouth was all warm, warm and hot and ripe as it offered itself to his and then pressed against his while her body started to tremble.

"God A'mighty, John, ain't it time you put me out of my misery?" The words were whispered against his mouth, hers slightly open, her tongue darting and making flame dart all through his body. Now she wasn't the only one who was trembling. His whole body was shaking, as he pressed her closer and still closer to him, as his hands sought for and found all the secret, maddening places of her body that haunted his waking hours as well as his dreams for weeks past.

"It's gonna happen sometime, there ain't no way on God's green earth that it ain't, an' it might as well be now as later," Becky told him, her voice husky with passion, her eyes deep with longing. "You're my man an' there ain't ever goin' to be any other, an' I'm ready, I been ready this long time an' I ain't goin' to wait any longer."

Groaning, knowing that his battle was lost, Donal gathered her up in his arms and carried her to the creek bank. He laid her on the soft new grass, in the sun-dappled shade, and as he kissed her again his floodtide of passion burst.

There wasn't any use fighting it. Donal was only human, and he'd been a long time without a woman, and Becky was a woman to set any man's blood on fire.

Becky's scream when he took her was one of triumph, of longing fulfilled, more than of pain. She'd never had a man before; that much came through to Donal even in his urgency. She was untouched, and she was his, and if he wasn't the luckiest man who'd ever lived because she'd been the one to find him and save him from death, then he didn't deserve any luck at all. He was free, and he was young, and he had this girl who offered him all the delights that any man could dream of.

They returned to the cabin as full dusk settled in, their clothing still damp and clinging to their bodies, their hands clinging to each other's as they stepped through the door. Abashed, Donal thought that even if Eben and Etta were blind they'd know what had happened out there by the creek. And then something inside him began to laugh, because if they thought that he'd seduced their daughter they had another think coming. He'd been just about the most seduced man who'd ever lived.

Etta looked up from where she was stirring the kettle, and her eyes brightened in their network of wrinkles.

"Ma, we got somethin' to tell you," Becky said. Her face was flushed, her eyes shining.

"I reckon you hev. It's writ all over you," Etta said.

"We-uns is gonna git married. Only how's we to go about it, Ma? There ain't no parson hereabouts, an' we dasn't go into any settlement lest John gits knowed an' taken. All the same, we're bound to do it."

Etta gave the matter thought, her mouth pursed and her forehead creasing. Then she laid aside the ladle and crossed to the bed in the corner of the cabin. She knelt down and rummaged under it, finally drawing out a dog-eared Bible.

"Here 'tis," she said. "My ma and pa gave me this, when I married up with your pa. Every fambly ought to hev one, even if we ain't used it as much as we should hev. See here, there's a place in the front to write things in. Births, an' deaths, an' marriages. We'll write yer names in it, an' hit'll do. There's many an' many, in unsettled places, hev had to do the same, till there come a time they could git it finished up by a parson. Writin' yer names in the Bible, under marriages, is most as bindin' as if it were done in a church, 'cause it's a promise to God, like."

Donal wasn't so sure about that, but under the circumstances, it made sense. People couldn't go on being single just for the lack of a man of the cloth to say the words over them.

"We'll do it tonight, then," Becky said, her eyes taking on an even deeper glow. "With you an' Pa an' Nate to witness. Rufe kin watch. Ain't it lucky I'm already clean from the creek! All I need is to put on my other dress."

"I'll hunt out a ribbon fer your hair," Etta told her. "I know I got some somewheres that I fetched along when we come to Georgia, your grandma give it to you one Christmas right afore we started, an' I laid it aside to keep fer somethin' special oncet we got here."

"Couldn't be nothin' more special than gittin' married," Eben said. There was a light on his face that made Donal feel guilty because he knew that Eben expected that he would stay on here forever, and the same light was in Etta's eyes. Nate looked gratified. With Donal here permanently, he'd have more time to tend his trapline, to roam the woods that he loved. Rufe only looked bewildered, but a wide grin split his face because his family was happy.

The simple ceremony was performed that evening, just as Becky wished. She glowed with happiness, and even without the blue ribbon that tied back her hair she would have been the prettiest girl in Georgia. The faded blue of her calico dress, the better of the only two she owned, only served to bring out the brilliance of her hair and the deep violet of her eyes.

Lydia Lancaster

Eben started out officiating, but he stumbled and stopped. "You do her, Ma," he said. "You got more words'en I hev."

Etta did her best. "Lord, standin' before You and these witnesses, this man an' this woman wants to be joined in wedlock. Without no parson to hitch 'em, we're askin' You to give 'em Your blessing. Amen."

Donal felt a stinging in his eyes. He couldn't have felt more married if Becky had been wearing a satin wedding gown and a lace veil, with a bishop presiding in a church packed full of friends and well-wishers.

They wrote their names in the proper place in the Bible. A quill from a wild turkey was their pen, the ink was berry juice mixed with a few grains of gunpowder. Donal wrote his name first, John Martin, and then he guided Becky's hand as she wrote hers. Eben's signature as witness was all but illegible, but Etta's hand was steady, the letters carefully formed. Nate, who had resisted all efforts at being taught, made his mark beside the name Donal wrote in for him, and at the very last, Rufe had to be allowed to make his mark as well, because his face twisted up and his eyes puddled at being left out.

It was done. "Now we'll eat," Etta said. "Iffen I'd had more notice, I'd hev tried to come up with somethin' more fitten fer a weddin' supper."

"It's fine, Ma. It's real good," Becky assured her.

Their own cabin across the dogtrot was waiting for her and Donal, and that was all that mattered. They were married, and they had their own place, and Becky was happy enough to burst.

Looking at her, Donal told himself that if he wasn't as happy as she was he ought to go out and shoot himself. But that feeling lasted only until they were in bed together. Then there was only Becky, her arms around him, her mouth setting him on fire, blotting everything else out.

Chapter Fourteen

Donal leaned on his hoe, stretching his shoulder muscles to relieve the tension brought on by hours of chopping at the weeds that seemed determined to grow faster than any man-made crop. The soil, which was so fertile that even corn as indifferently sowed as Eben's thrived, seemed to spur the weeds to even greater efforts as they contended for the cleared space under the hot July sun.

The clearing was unnaturally quiet. Nate had been supposed to help him, but after the lad had worked for two hours he'd gone back to the cabin to get a drink of water and he hadn't come back. The young scamp had taken off for the coolness of the woods, there wasn't any doubt about it, just as there wasn't any doubt that he'd come back before dark.

There were only the three of them, Donal and Nate and Rufe, on the place today. Becky and Etta and Eben had set off at first light to walk to the Grubbs' place, the nearest clearing to their own, if you could think of a five-hour walk as being near. Norma Grubb was getting near her time and Etta wanted to check up on her, there being only her husband Job to help her because the two young'uns they already had were too young, a shy-eyed, towheaded girl of seven and an even shyer-eyed, towheaded boy of five. There'd been one other boy, but he'd been snake-bit two years back when he'd wandered off from his ma and met up with a cottonmouth by the creek. It was a hard life for women, here in the wilderness, and those within traveling distance of each other had to lend a hand in time of need or none of them would be likely to survive at all.

There hadn't been any need for Becky to go, but contact with another woman besides her mother was an event in her life. Who knew but what the Grubbs might have picked up some gossip, news that hadn't infiltrated to the McCabe clearing, where no one except Job Grubb had set foot when he'd come to let Etta know that Norma's time was getting close. And Eben hadn't had any need to go except that womenfolk shouldn't go gallivanting off through the woods without a man along to protect them.

"Mebbeso I kin give Job a hand with somethin' too heavy fer one man," Eben had said. Donal had a very good idea that the only hand Eben would raise would be to lift a jug so that Job wouldn't have the work of emptying it all by himself. Donal only hoped that he'd remember that he had to walk all the way back, before he got in a condition where Becky would have to support him.

Lord, but it was hot! Hot weather was good for the corn but there wasn't any need for it to be this hot. It was humid, too. Donal felt as though the air was crushing him. It had started out as a clear day, but the humidity had built up and now the sky was overcast, with that particular glow that foreboded a storm. Looking up, squinting his eyes against the glare, Donal saw that ominous-looking clouds were already gathering toward the west. It was going to rain as sure as he was standing here, he could feel it in his bones, and it looked to be a real storm.

He'd done enough for one morning. It was too hot to go on working and his stomach was growling and his thirst couldn't be denied any longer. He glanced around for Rufe, but the simpleminded boy had disappeared. He'd been underfoot most of the morning, so that Donal had had to tell him to move before his hoe chopped off one of his bare toes, but now he was nowhere in sight.

Heaven's Horizon

Donal didn't worry about it. There was nowhere Rufe could have gone except back to the cabin. Probably he'd been thirsty too, and bored with not being trusted with a hoe. Likely as not he was curled up in a corner fast asleep.

Donal could have gone with the others, leaving Nate to watch after Rufe, but by tacit understanding it was agreed that the less Donal saw of any neighbor, with time for questions to be asked, the better. Eben had given out that Donal was the son of people he'd known back in Pennsylvania, who had come to Georgia looking for a piece of land of his own, and who had been so taken with Becky that he'd married her and thrown in his lot with the McCabes.

The clouds were gathering fast, pushed by a wind that had sprung up out of nowhere. If it came on to storm hard, Becky and Etta and Eben would have to spend the night with the Grubbs. He wondered how it would feel not to have Becky snuggled close to him in their bed that night. Not having to sleep alone was one of the best things about being married. It was a satisfaction to a man to be able to reach out and gather a pretty woman into his arms anytime he took the notion, and the excitement of possessing Becky's delectable body hadn't had time to wear off yet. She was all woman, and Donal still couldn't quite believe in his good fortune.

If it hadn't been for those maddening fragments of dreams that almost but never quite told him things that he wanted to know, Donal would have been content. Eben and Etta were easy to get along with, so happy to have him married to Becky that they deferred to him in everything, and he liked the boys. And when he was working, or making love to Becky, everything was all right. But after the day's work was done, and after he lay sated with lovemaking, the puzzle drove him crazy. A piece here and a fragment of a piece there, but nothing that he could put together to make a whole picture.

There was the rose garden, for instance. And an echo of a woman's voice, a voice that he knew that he had loved but that he couldn't place. Once he had dreamed of a woman with dark hair and dark eyes and a soft laugh that had thrilled him, but when he had tossed in his sleep Becky had reached out to hold him and the dream was gone before he could lock it into place, fading as his dreams always faded, into nothingness.

The first drops of rain sent Donal's legs striding toward the cabin. He stopped outside the door and splashed his face and arms with water from the bucket, washing off some of the dust and sweat before he stepped inside, narrowing his eyes against the sudden gloom to look for Rufe.

There he was, over in the far corner by the fireplace, his own special place where no one would stumble over him. He was playing with something, but for a moment Donal couldn't make out what it was until his eyes had adjusted to the change of light. The fire needed poking up and replenishing, he thought. They were careful never to let it go entirely out, even in this hot weather, because it was so much work to start it again.

"What's that you have there?" Donal asked. There weren't any toys in the cabin, except for the wooden top that Eben had whittled out for Rufe, and a corn-shuck doll that Etta had fashioned for Becky when she'd been little, almost disintegrated now but still cherished because it was the only doll that Becky had ever owned.

Rufe looked up, guilt written all over his face, and he thrust what he held in his hands behind his back. "Nothin'," he said. "It ain't nothin'."

Rufe being Rufe, Donal knew that he had to see what it was, to make sure he hadn't got hold of something he shouldn't. "Let me see," he repeated.

Rufe began to cry. "Don't tell Nate. Don't go a-tellin' Nate, he'll be mad, I'll put it back, I ain't hurt it none!"

His curiosity thoroughly aroused, Donal reached out to draw Rufe's hand around in front of him again, and then his eyes widened.

It was a pistol, and a fine one. It had been kept clean and greased. It had a mother-of-pearl handle and silver mountings, and Donal knew that it had cost what to the McCabes would be a fortune beyond their wildest dreams.

Rufe gave it up reluctantly, still crying. "I didn't hurt it none!" he repeated. "Lemme put it back 'fore Nate finds out I looked at it!"

Heaven's Horizon

Donal turned it over and over in his hands. Something inside of him flared into excitement. There was a familiar feel to it, as if he had held it before. Was it his, something from his former life? But Becky had told him that he'd had nothing on him when she and Nate had pulled him from the bog, that if he'd been armed the gun had been lost, never to be recovered.

His voice was sharper than he'd intended as he demanded, "Where did Nate get this?"

Rufe jumped up and ran to scramble up the ladder to the loft. Donal followed him. The loft was hardly more than a crawl space, so he had to double over to make his way around the pallets where the boys still slept. Rufe was already crouched in a corner scrabbling at a place where one of the logs had been hollowed out, with a slab of bark to cover it so that if anyone hadn't known it was there it would never have been discovered.

"Put it back," Rufe sniffled. "Put it back 'fore Nate comes home and kotches me!"

There was something else in the hiding place. Donal held it in his hand in the dim light, and his fingers closed over it, and with a feeling of nausea greater than any he'd ever experienced after one of his dreams, the object turned the key to his locked memory and the door inched open.

It was a ring, a gold ring, a man's signet ring. And even as his fingers opened again and he looked at it, he could see the slender, graceful hand that had put it into his own.

"Happy birthday, Donal. Now that you're eighteen, your father and I thought that you should have your own signet ring, so that you can seal all of the love letters to all of those beautiful young ladies with your own seal."

They had been at the breakfast table, spread with a snowy linen cloth and gleaming with silver and fine china. Glass doors stood open to the August morning, letting in the scent of the formal garden that was just outside, the aroma of roses predominant. Across the table, a heavyset man with gray hair and a kind face and twinkling eyes had chided his wife.

"Don't tease him, Marguerite. A young man's sweethearts are a

Lydia Lancaster

private subject. Donal, many happy returns of the day. Eighteen! And a man grown, for all you won't be legally of age for another three years. A satisfactory young man in every respect, a son I've never had occasion to be anything but proud of, even when you got into scraps in places you had no business to be, in your younger days. At least you gave good account of yourself, nefarious as your activities were, and never came home sniveling that you'd taken a beating."

"How did you know?" Donal's surprise had been genuine. "I thought I'd covered my tracks better than that!"

"Ah, but I was young once myself, so I knew what to look for." Duncan MacKenzie had laughed. And his mother, Marguerite, had looked at them both with amused resignation.

He was Donal MacKenzie, and the house was in London. He worshiped the beautiful woman, twelve years younger than his stepfather, and he loved his stepfather and his two younger stepsisters and his life was full and content.

For a moment the loft seemed to darken, and he struggled against dizziness, until he realized that the loft actually had darkened, that the full force of the storm was upon them, with thunder crashing overhead and the rain beating against the shingles so close to his head.

"Is there anything else?" he demanded.

Rufe cowered. He was afraid of thunder, afraid of storms. Donal berated himself for being so abrupt with the simpleminded boy, but he had to know. He asked again, his voice stern.

"Becky done burned yer clothes. An' she wanted to bury the purty gun an' the purty ring, but Nate tookened 'em an' said as he wouldn' ever let you see 'em. John, the thunder's gonna git me!"

But Donal wasn't listening. Other memories were crowding back. Cordelia! Oh, my God, Cordelia! And Boston, and the Reynards, Nadine and Lucy and Frederick, and his journey across the ocean to court Nadine, only he'd found Cordelia instead, and they had been married, and Andrew Leyland had invited him to explore a part of Georgia before he and Cordelia had started the first leg of their journey back to England.

Heaven's Horizon

Andrew Leyland had shot him, had shot him in the back when he'd dismounted and gone to investigate the bog that Andrew had said was bottomless. He could feel the impact of the bullet again as it tore into his shoulder, spinning him around as another shot burned against his temple.

Beside him, Rufe whimpered again, and Donal put his arm around him and comforted him. "Come back downstairs. I'll poke up the fire. The thunder isn't going to get you, Rufe. I'll take care of you."

He brought the pistol and the ring down with him, and put them on the table, telling Rufe not to touch them. He replenished the fire, blowing on the new wood until it caught. He pulled the kettle over the flames. Rufe would be hungry and he had to be fed, and the kettle was half filled with rabbit stew.

He dished Rufe a bowl when it was hot enough, and one for himself. But he did all of these things automatically, without thinking about them. He was Donal MacKenzie and he was married to Cordelia Leyland, and he had to go back to Leyland's Landing and face the man who had tried to kill him, and find out why he had done it. And most important of all, he had to go back to Cordelia.

Becky had turned into a wildcat, fighting for her life. Her hair was disheveled, her eyes frantic, she pummeled Donal with her fists. "You ain't a-goin'! You hear me, John? You ain't a-goin'! That Mr. Leyland tried to kill you oncet, so what's to keep him from finishin' the job if you go back? You'll be walkin' into a trap just like some poor dumb woods critter that don't know no better! You're my husband, we're married, we writ our names in the Book, you belong to me 'an' I ain't goin' to let you go!"

Donal captured her hands. He had to use all his strength to control her. "Becky, we aren't married. I know it's hard on you, and I'm sorry. But I'm married to someone else, I'm married to Andrew Leyland's daughter, and I must go back. Now that I know who I am, there's no way I can stay here and you know that as well as I do. It'll be easier for both of us if you accept it. I'll do what I can for you, once I get things straightened out. I have a little money, I'll see that you get something, enough to help you and your folks. But I have to go, and I'm going now, because there's no point in delaying it."

"Damn you! Damn you to hell, John Martin! I hate you, you promised me you was mine, you married me!"

"My name isn't John Martin. It's Donal MacKenzie. Becky, why go over it again and again? It won't change anything. Good-bye. I appreciate everything you and your family did for me and I'll appreciate it as long as I live, but it still doesn't change anything. It would be nice if you could let me go without causing both of us so much grief."

He must go. Ever since he had remembered his past life, ever since Cordelia had come back to him in a flash so painful that he still trembled from it, he had been straining to get to Leyland's Landing, his whole purpose and being centered on that one objective. There was nothing that the McCabes and Becky could do about it. If they had saved his life and nursed him and supported him, he'd made up for it by all the work he'd put in on the place.

It was a pity that Becky had to be so torn by his leaving her, he hated having to hurt her. She would suffer, but she was young and she would get over it. She was far too lovely to remain single for long, once he was out of the picture. Donal wished her every happiness, but now he had to go.

He had already said good-bye to Etta and Eben, to Nate and to Rufe. He'd kissed Etta's withered cheek and thanked her for all she had done. Now he made the mistake of trying to kiss Becky's cheek, to show her that he meant it when he said he was sorry.

Becky hissed at him, her eyes blazing rage. With a sudden twist of such strength that Donal marveled that so slender a girl could be possessed of such strength, her hands yanked away from his grasp and she struck him across the face, following that action by raking his cheek with her fingernails until the blood ran.

"Go, then, an' damn you to hell an' damn that high-falutin' girl you married! She ain't half the woman I am an' she never will be! An' if you ever dast to set foot on this place agin, I'll shoot you an' don't you forget it, John Martin!"

Heaven's Horizon

"Becky, it ain't fittin', the way you're carryin' on," Etta said, her face working. " 'Tain't John's fault he remembered an' has to go."

"You shut up!" Becky screamed at her. Donal was already out of the door, his pistol stuck in the waistband of Rufe's too-large trousers, the signet ring on his finger, and a small pack of victuals slung over his shoulder in a scrap of cloth—boiled squirrel and corn bread—enough to stay him until he could find something else. Becky darted after him, and now she was on his back, clinging like a monkey, her voice shrieking at him. "You ain't goin', you ain't!"

He managed to shake her off, but it wasn't easy. "Becky, do I have to tie you up so that I can get out of here? I will, if you keep this up."

She sank to the ground, her face in her hands, weeping wildly. That hurt Donal as much as her invectives, as her recriminations. Feeling like the worst scoundrel who had ever walked the face of the earth, he strode away from her, out of the clearing, to plunge into the woods. It was a relief when he had walked far enough so that he could no longer hear her crying.

He stiffened his back and kept on walking, because only Cordelia mattered now, Cordelia, and the man who had tried to kill him.

Behind him, Becky kept on weeping. She'd wanted him more than she'd known it was possible to want anything, she'd wanted him so much that she'd been willing to risk eternal hellfire to get him. Yes, and she'd take him back now, if only he would return to her, and live with him in sin. Right or wrong had no meaning when you loved someone as she loved Donal. A lifetime with him would be worth a dozen eternities of burning.

Ma was right. Ma said that God sees everything, and that no sin goes unpunished. She had sinned, and this was her punishment. She wouldn't have to go to hell when she died, because her hell had been meted out to her now, the sentence of living out her life without the man she had got by lying. But if she could have her druthers, she'd rather die right now and go to hell than to have to accept this other punishment.

Rufe, his face crumpled and tears running down his cheeks, tried to go to her. Becky hurt, and he loved Becky. But Etta put her hand on his arm and held him back.

"Leave her be. Ain't nothing we kin do to help her. Jest pray, Rufe boy. Pray that her hurt will stop in time."

Maybe God would listen to a good, dim-witted boy. For herself, in spite of her faith, Etta had lost her faith in prayer for anything that might happen on this earth. The ways of the Almighty were beyond understanding, and it was the lot of mortals to accept them without protest, and go on doing the best they could.

Donal made no attempt to approach the plantation house at Leyland's Landing until the evening was well advanced. He had to be sure that no slaves were still about and that Cordelia would be asleep. He had to confront Andrew Leyland and wring the truth of his attempted murder from him without a woman, even Cordelia, going into hysterics at the sight of him.

He took care not to be seen as he kept to the shadows of the trees that dotted the lawn, although he thought grimly that even anyone who had known him well would have trouble recognizing him now. With his full beard, and wearing Rufe's shabby and too-large clothing, his feet shod in ragged moccasins, he bore little resemblance to the clean-shaven young man clad in tailor-made apparel, his boots shining like mirrors from the polishing Aunt Zoe had given them, who had set out a year ago to explore this part of Georgia with his father-in-law.

All the long and arduous walk back to Leyland's Landing, his mind had been in a ferment. He had no more idea now than he'd had when he'd regained his memory at the sight of the pistol that was now jammed in his waistband, of what possible motive Andrew Leyland could have had for shooting him.

He had no watch, and he wasn't adept at telling the time by the position of the moon or stars, but he judged that it must be somewhere near eleven before he approached the house on soundless feet. Only one light was showing, and that was in Andrew's study. Not as much as a chink of light showed through the curtains of the other downstairs rooms or the bedrooms upstairs.

Heaven's Horizon

The doors were locked and, Donal realized from the nights he had stayed at Leyland's Landing, barred as well. No plantation owner, no matter how secure he felt in the loyalty of his slaves, slept without the doors being barred. But the window that opened into Andrew's study was not yet shuttered for the night, open to allow the cool night air to penetrate the room where the master of the plantation was still going over his accounts. Donal saw him at his desk, which was placed so that the daytime light would fall over his left shoulder. When he went in, it would have to be quickly, or the element of surprise would be lost. The chances were that Andrew kept a pistol in his desk drawer. He knew that his father-in-law never left the house without it.

The window was high from the ground, but not too high for Donal to grasp the sill and with one fluid motion that he wasn't sure he would have been capable of before his months of work on the McCabe place had hardened him, he heaved himself up and slid headfirst through the opening, doubling up to land on the balls of his feet. Andrew saw him, but his reaction came too late. With a motion as fast as that of a striking snake, Donal was behind him, his arm crooked around the other man's neck, cutting off his breath and pinning him to his chair before Andrew had time to reach for his pistol.

"Who the devil are you?" Even in mortal danger, Andrew lost none of his cold arrogance. "If it's money you're after, I'll see you in hell first! I don't keep enough in the house to make it worth hanging for in any case, so if you know what's good for you you'll leave the same way you came and put enough distance between us so that I won't be able to catch up with you!"

"You aren't very observant, are you, Mr. Leyland? I'd have thought you'd recognize your son-in-law, even in such a quick glance."

He felt Andrew stiffen, felt the disbelief that flooded through him. "My son-in-law is dead. He met with an accident months ago."

"He met with an accident, all right. The accident of not suspecting that you intended murder! Why, Mr. Leyland? I'm filled with

Lydia Lancaster

curiosity and I mean to have it satisfied. Why did you see fit to try to kill me, when I'd never done you any harm?"

He loosened his grasp just enough so that Andrew could turn his head to look him full in the face. Even then, Andrew's face showed a moment of doubt. It was Donal's voice, that unmistakable voice with the trace of an English accent, that convinced him before he could picture the man who held him prisoner without the beard and the outlandish clothing.

"I had good and sufficient reasons, I assure you. Your father was my bitterest enemy. If I'd been able to track him down, I'd have killed him before you were conceived, and then I wouldn't have been faced with the necessity of killing you!"

"You never saw Duncan MacKenzie in your life! He's never set foot outside of England!"

"I was not referring to your adoptive father. I was referring to your actual father, Lester Ross. I assure you that I knew him very well indeed, although not nearly as well as I knew your mother, who was my fiancée before your father took her from me and left me in this crippled state when I challenged him, as I had every right to do. The coward took Marguerite and fled while I was hovering between life and death. Of course I tried to kill you when I learned your true identity! Do you think that I'd allow any grandchild of mine to carry Ross blood in his veins? With your death, the debt would be wiped out, Lester Ross's blood eliminated from the face of the earth!"

Donal had no idea of what he had expected, but Andrew's words took him by such complete surprise that he could scarcely comprehend it. Not in his wildest speculations had he expected anything like this! And there was no mistake. The man knew his father's name, and his mother's, and he spoke with such conviction that there was no room for doubt. His mother had come from Virginia, even though she had never mentioned Andrew's name or told him any more about her background before she and his father had made their home in England.

A blood grudge, all these years old! And even now, he could feel Andrew's hatred as if it emanated from him in some physical form that could be seen and touched.

Heaven's Horizon

"I ought to kill you," Donal said. "By every moral right, I have the right to kill you. I doubt that any jury in the civilized world would find me guilty. But for Cordelia's sake, I'm going to let you live. As much of a scoundrel as you are, it wouldn't be pleasant for her to be married to the man who had killed her father! But I warn you, Mr. Leyland, that if you make any attempt to follow us or harm us in any way, once we've left this plantation, that I will be watching for you, that I'll never let down my guard, and that I'll kill you without a second's compunction!"

"You won't be taking Cordelia away." There was a vicious satisfaction in Andrew's voice. "I have no idea how you managed to survive, but you're far too late to claim my daughter, Donal Ross! She isn't here, she's dead, she's been dead for months."

Donal felt as though every drop of oxygen had been taken from his body. He was suffocating, he had trouble keeping on his feet, keeping his grip on his father-in-law.

"You're lying!" He tightened his arm around Andrew's throat. "Cordie isn't dead, how could she be dead? She's young, in perfect health! She isn't the type to have died of grief over me, no matter how deep her grief was and I know that it was deep. She's a survivor, and she always will be."

Filled with a rage that all but blinded him, he used his free hand to tear Andrew's own belt from his body and bind his hands behind his back. Andrew made no move to resist. The cord from the window draperies served to bind the man's feet, and Andrew's handkerchief was stuffed into his mouth and secured by the stock that had been around his neck only moments before. And still, even as Donal left him to race up the stairs to find Cordelia, he had an uncanny feeling of dread at the way Andrew's eyes spat malice and triumph at him.

"Cordelia! Cordie!" Donal burst into Cordelia's room, the room that he had shared with her so blissfully and so briefly, but he'd no more than stepped across the threshold when that sense of an empty room, long abandoned, struck him like a blow.

Cordelia wasn't here. The bed was still rumpled just as she had left it the night Runt had taken her out of the window on their flight for freedom. Her toilet articles were on the dressing table, her dresses still hung in the wardrobe, but the room was musty, long unaired, and a thin, gritty film of dust covered every surface. Wherever Cordelia was, she hadn't been in this room for months, and no house slave had been sent to clean it and keep it in order.

With rising panic, Donal inspected all the other bedrooms. Still fighting against the belief that what Andrew had told him was true, he ran back downstairs, and unbolted the door that led to the covered passageway that led to the kitchen quarters. Aunt Zoe would be there, she had a lean-to room off the kitchen, the only slave on the plantation who wasn't sent to sleep in the slave quarters at night.

Seething with frustration, Donal found that the door to the kitchen was locked. Everything on a plantation of this size was kept under lock and key, to prevent petty pilfering by the slaves. He had to return to the study and rummage through Andrew's desk to find the keys that Andrew kept there, with Andrew's eyes still spitting hate at him.

There was another maddening delay as Donal had to try four keys before one of them unlocked the kitchen door. The room was in darkness except for a faint glow from the banked fire on the hearth, and he stopped just inside the door, not wanting to crash into a table or chair in this unfamiliar place.

"Zoe! Aunt Zoe? Are you here?" Desperate, he raised his voice. "Answer me! For the love of God, answer me!"

There was a scrabbling noise behind the door that led into Zoe's cubbyhole room. "Who's there? Who's that callin' me in the middle of the night?"

Thank God! Donal followed the sound of her voice, and his hands encountered her door and, to his astonishment, a heavy bar across it. Good Lord, she was locked in!

"It's Donal. Donal MacKenzie. I'll let you out."

"You ain't Donal MacKenzie. What kind of a trick you pullin'? Mr. Donal MacKenzie, he's dead."

"I am Donal MacKenzie, and I'm not dead." He lifted the bar and yanked the door open. But Zoe cowered away from him in the darkness, before she scuttled around him and groped for the stub of

Heaven's Horizon

a candle on one of the kitchen shelves. Kneeling by the hearth, she lighted it and held it up so that its glow reached Donal's face.

"Lord have mercy! Oh, Good Lord have mercy! Is that you, under all them whiskers? How kin it be you, when you're dead?"

"Where's Cordelia? What has Mr. Leyland done with Cordelia?" Donal demanded. He felt like grasping Zoe's shoulders and shaking her, but shame flooded over him at the thought of laying hands on such a frail body even if he hadn't come to be so fond of her during the short time he'd known her.

"It is you! I knows you, and you ain't no ghost! Master Donal, she's gone, Cordelia's gone, she's been gone these months, ever sicce I told her about your father an' her father. I had to tell her, because I figgered that Master Andrew had kilt you and I was afraid that he'd harm the baby."

Donal felt nausea rise up in his throat, and dread greater than any he had ever known made him light-headed for a moment.

"Zoe, make sense! Are you trying to tell me that Cordelia is pregnant? And don't you dare go gibbering at me, tell me where she is!"

Zoe's face seemed to waver in the flickering light of the candle, and tears welled up in her eyes and spilled over to run in rivulets down the creases and wrinkles of her face. Her voice was filled with grief as she answered, "I don't know, Master Donal. She an' Runt, my Runt, they hit out for Florida to try to get through to the Seminole Indians, where they'd be safe. But I don't know iffen they ever got there. Master Andrew says not. He knew where they'd head, and he spent months searchin' for them, he had agents all over that place tryin' to track them down but he never got no whisper of them at all. Runt was so sure he could make it, he had it all planned out for a long time before you and Miss Cordie were married, but with Miss Cordie with him, slowin' him down, I just don't know. My poor baby, an' my Runt, gone, both of 'em gone, an' no way to tell whatever happened to them! But I got me a feelin' that they made it, I got me a real strong feelin', even if Master Andrew says they're both dead."

She turned to place the candle on the deal table, and the loose night shift she was wearing slipped down over her shoulder. Donal's face registered horror as he saw the scars that crisscrossed her back and shoulders. He reached out to touch them. They were old welts, poorly healed, and he was sure that Zoe hadn't been scarred before, that she'd never been whipped or mistreated in any way, or Cordelia would have told him.

Zoe pulled the nightgown back up over her shoulder, and there was a look almost of shame in her eyes as she turned to meet his.

"He done it, when he found Miss Cordelia had got away from him. He had her locked in her room, he said she was crazy. But Runt got her out, he climbed that big old tree outside her window and swung over on a rope an' took her out, an' they ran, an' when Master Andrew found she was gone he whipped me to make me tell where they was goin'. I thought as how he was goin' to kill me, but I didn't tell. An' when he saw I wasn't goin' to tell him, he had me locked up, an' he set out a-searchin', 'cause he knowed where they'd be headin'. Only one place a slave kin go without friends or money to help him, an' that's to the Seminoles. He sent men to watch all the ports, and to Boston to see if Miss Cordelia could of got there to the Reynards, and he had all the passenger lists checked to make sure she hadn't got on any ship to take her to England, but there wasn't any trace of her, her nor Runt neither, an' all I been doin' ever since is prayin' that they made it to them Indians and they're safe. But ain't no way of knowin' for sure. Master Andrew, he still has men searchin', he only locks me up nights anymore, an' I've heard him talk to some man he put in charge of the search now that he ain't off searchin' for Miss Cordie himself no more."

Donal groped for a straight-backed chair and sat down, his face in his hands. "Zoe, you said she was pregnant. Did I hear you right?"

"Yes, Master Donal. You heard me right. Miss Cordelia never came out of her grief till we found out about the baby, an' then she pulled herself together 'cause she had somethin' to live for. She was goin' to go to England, to your folks, an' live with them there so's the child could grow up where you grew up. It was all she talked about. But Master Andrew wouldn't book passage for her, he lied an' lied an' said there wasn't no passage just then an' he'd keep tryin'. That's when I knew he never meant to let her go, 'cause of the child, an' I told her about your father an' her father, an' Master Andrew locked her up so's Runt had to git her out of her bedroom window an' run with her."

Donal's voice was thick with fury. "He'll pay for everything he's done, I swear that he will! But not now. I have to find Cordelia, Andrew Leyland can wait. Zoe, can you pack what you'll need and leave here right now? I'll take you to the people who befriended me when they found me after he'd left me for dead. They'll care for you and you'll be safe there."

Having to see Becky again would be agony, but he couldn't leave Zoe here to be mistreated. Cordelia would never forgive him if she were still alive and he managed to find her. He could pay the McCabes for caring for Zoe, and he knew he could trust them to keep her whereabouts a secret. People like the McCabes had nothing to do with the plantation owners, and no good word to say for them, they were naturally suspicious of strangers and of anyone who was wealthy and fortunate.

But Zoe shook her head. "I 'preciate it, Master Donal, but I can't do it. Master Andrew, he'd turn this here state of Georgia upside down lookin' for me an I can't go gittin' no good folks in that kind of trouble. I'm all right where I am. 'Sides, iffen there's any way, Runt will git word to me that he an' Miss Cordelia are all right. You go find her, Master Donal, that's all that matters."

Donal wanted to argue, but he knew that Zoe was right. He rose and took her into his arms and kissed her withered cheek.

"God keep you, then," he said. "When I find Cordelia, we'll come back and take you away with us, and that's a promise."

"I know it is, Master Donal, and God bless you. I'll be prayin' for you, I won't never leave off prayin'."

Heavyhearted, Donal left the old woman and returned to Cordelia's room. His clothing was still there, undisturbed since the day Andrew had thought he had killed him. The opening in the door, cut to pass food through, filled him with even greater fury. But there was no time for that now.

Money would be no problem. There was money enough in his

traveling bag to carry him for a long time, and he had a letter of credit from a bank in London that would be honored anyplace.

His mind was working rapidly as he stripped out of Rufe's clothing and got into his own. By all rights, he should turn Andrew Leyland over to the law, bring charges of attempted murder against him, but that would take time, he'd be required to remain for the trial, and he wasn't willing to give up even one day before he started his search for Cordelia.

He'd have to take one of Andrew's horses, the best one the stable had to offer. And he had to make sure that he had a long head start before Andrew, filled with rage because Donal was still alive, started his own search for him, this time fully intending that his plans wouldn't miscarry.

He returned to the kitchen to raid it for food that he could carry in a saddlebag—ham and corn pone—enough so that he wouldn't have to lose time searching for sustenance for two or three days. Then he went back to the study and helped himself to one of Andrew's rifles by shattering the glass of the rifle case while Andrew glared at him with hate-reddened eyes. He checked Andrew's bonds and gag. It would be late tomorrow before any slave dared to enter by the open window to discover him. He'd already warned Zoe not to make an outcry when Ruby tried to enter the kitchen.

The stable was locked, but it took him only seconds to find the right key to open it. Zeke, who slept on a pile of hay in a corner, came staggering to his feet, still foggy-brained from being awakened so suddenly.

"Man, what you doin'? Who you? You cain't come in here an' help yourself to one of Master Andrew's horses! Master Andrew didn't tell me to let you take no horse!"

"Go back and lie down, and keep your mouth shut!" Donal commanded him. The pistol in his hand gave authority to his words, although he knew that he'd never be able to bring himself to use it against a defenseless slave. "Go back to sleep. On second thought, I'm going to have to tie you up. If I don't, your master will punish you. I'll have to gag you as well, but I won't tie or gag you tightly, you'll be quite comfortable."

Heaven's Horizon

Even in the darkness of the stable, Donal could see the whites of Zeke's eyes as they rolled. "Master Donal, is that you? Is you a ghost?"

"I'm not a ghost. You have nothing to be afraid of. Someone will let you out sometime tomorrow. I'll throw the keys back into your master's study before I leave."

Working swiftly, Donal secured the old man, being as gentle as he could, and Zeke made no resistance. He saddled Andrew's own horse and, changing his mind about leaving Andrew to be discovered early in the morning, the horse he had ridden on that fateful day last July. A better plan had come to him while he had been tying Zeke up.

He led both of the saddled horses to the front of the house. Entering again through the window, he unbolted the front door and carried Andrew outside, forcing him to mount before he retied his feet underneath the horse. He left the door to the kitchen unbolted so that Zoe could get out and release Zeke in the morning, but the slaves would have no idea what to do when they found their master gone, and so they would do nothing. Zoe would see to that.

A sharp kick set his horse trotting down the avenue, his free hand leading Andrew's. He kept to a good pace, but not one fast enough to overtire the horses. He remembered, clearly, the route Andrew had taken him last summer, and he followed it roughly, deep into the wilderness of uncleared forestland.

They rode all night, and after the sun had been up for a full two hours Donal stopped to rest the horses and to catch two or three hours of sleep himself. He propped Andrew in a sitting position against the trunk of a tree and tied him there. He knew that the man must be suffering, but he felt no sympathy for his pain, but only a sense of deep shame that he should have been reduced to making another human being suffer.

Shame or not, he fell asleep immediately, not even feeling the hardness of the ground underneath him. His body was exhausted. It had been a long walk from the McCabe place to Leyland's Landing, and a long ride last night.

When he awoke, he untied Andrew's hands long enough to share the corn pone and ham with him. In spite of his deathly weariness and pain, in spite of the dryness of his mouth after having been gagged, Andrew found his voice, filled with venomous scorn.

"So now you're a thief, a common horse thief! Like father, like son. Your father stole a woman, but you have sunk to stealing horses!"

"Better a thief than a murderer, Mr. Leyland," Donal said, and the mildness of his tone surprised even him. "I'm going to leave you now, but you can comfort yourself with the assurance that I'll be back to deal with you as soon as I've found my wife."

"You'd leave me, afoot, in the depth of the wilderness? A crippled man?"

"You'll have a better chance than you gave me when you shot me and threw me into the bog." Donal kept his voice as emotionless as his face. "I'll loosen your bonds so that you will be able to work yourself free, after a while."

Leaving a crippled man stranded in this forest, miles from civilization, was monstrous, but it had to be done. He had to have as long a head start as possible because Andrew would launch a search party for him with the intent of killing him as soon as he made his way back to Leyland's Landing. If Andrew had had reason to want him dead before, now his death was imperative.

His face grim, Donal reflected that what lay ahead promised to be interesting, to say the least. He searching for Cordelia in an unknown and uncharted wilderness, himself hunted by Andrew and his minions. Leading Andrew's horse, he covered a good ten miles before he released the animal and gave it a sharp slap on its rump.

"Go!" he shouted. "Get out of here, go on home!"

Tired, confused by Donal's shout, the horse headed for its own safe stable. By the time it got home Zeke would be released from his bonds and ready to take care of it.

There was no way that Andrew could catch up with Donal now, and Donal set his own mount back in motion, his only concern to make his way to the territory of Florida in the shortest possible time.

Chapter Fifteen

Outwardly, there was nothing to indicate that this day was different from any other day. The people of the istihapo were going about their normal business, and there wasn't as much as a knowing smile from one woman to another, or a wink between men, to indicate that this was Hilolo's wedding day.

Nevertheless, the ceremony was going on as Cordelia sat pounding corn. The October air was balmy, the sky so blue that it hurt the eyes to look directly at it. Only a few fluffy white clouds drifted near the horizon, and there wasn't a hint of rain. It was a beautiful day for a wedding. Cordelia was only sorry that the Seminoles didn't make more of a ceremony of it. Where were the maids of honor, the friends of the groom? Where, for that matter, was the man who would join them in wedlock?

But things were done differently among the Seminoles, and Cordelia accepted that. And no matter how little ceremony there was to the proceedings, she was still excited and happy for Hilolo. The pretty girl, who was Cordelia's own age, was her best friend after Weleka herself. The three of them were like sisters, and Cordelia

Lydia Lancaster

had more sense of belonging to a family here than she had ever had at Leyland's Landing, where she had spent her growing years.

Watching out of the corners of her eyes, careful not to betray unseemly interest, she saw Hilolo approach her bridegroom. Sam Brent was a slave who had run away from his master five years ago when he had hardly been out of his boyhood, a lad of fifteen. Tall and straight and strong, Sam's face reflected pride of race and of his manhood, and when he had visited this village from his own several miles to the south, he and Hilolo had looked at each other and fallen in love.

It was fortunate that Sam came from another village, because under Seminole law no man could marry a woman from his own village. The rule prevented inbreeding, and Cordelia could see that it was a good rule with a lot of sense behind it. Even in her own limited experience, she had seen the results of first cousin marrying first cousin. The children of such marriages might not be quite bright, or be actually mentally deficient or have other defects. The Reynards had not approved of such marriages, and Lucy, who was more outspoken than many other ladies of her station, had explained her reasons to Nadine and Cordelia without mincing words.

Now that the ceremony was actually under way, the istihapo still went about its regular routine, with no one paying the least attention. It would have been considered impolite to gather around and gape. Cordelia was glad that she had a front-row seat, so to speak, so that she could watch without being obvious about it.

Hilolo walked between her parents. The day before, Sam Brent had left a gift at their chikee, a fine young deer, and it had been accepted by being taken inside after he had left. Now Hilolo's mother bore a gift for Sam, a deerskin shirt that Hilolo had made. It was a fine shirt, lavishly decorated with beadwork, and Hilolo had been working on it for weeks, her love for Sam going into every stitch. The mother of the bride left her husband and daughter and advanced to where Sam was waiting and handed him the shirt. He accepted it, and she walked back to take her place again at the other side of her daughter.

Now Hilolo stepped forward and went to stand beside Sam. This,

Heaven's Horizon

Weleka had told Cordelia, symbolized that her parents were relinquishing her to her husband. Hilolo was radiant, her soft eyes glowed, she held her head high and proudly as she took her place at the side of the man who was now, by her taking these few steps, her husband.

It was done. Hilolo and Sam were man and wife. And now the istihapo came to life. The men, laughing and gesticulating, making Sam the butt of their jokes, hurried to help build a chikee for the newly married couple, while the women gathered to set out a feast, not only sofkee, but corn cakes and boiled corn on the cob, pumpkin, beans, smoked and fresh fish, roasted venison and wild turkey, and conte, a jelly made of chopped roots of the China briar, boiled and then strained and the sediment allowed to dry in the open air to a powder that was then mixed with water and honey and could be eaten either alone or used to sweeten other foods. A hot beverage called cazina, made of a weed and nonintoxicating, was prepared in quantity.

The harvest had been good this year, and there was no stinting. At the Green Corn Dance, Weleka had told Cordelia that thanks had been given for the bountiful harvest of corn. Cordelia had been disappointed that she couldn't attend this most important of all Seminole ceremonies. Only Seminoles were allowed to participate, and it was held well away from any village, with large numbers of Seminoles from different settlements gathered together. The Seminole women went along to tend the fires and do the cooking, as no slaves were allowed to attend.

In the Green Corn Dance the warriors partook of the Black Drink, an emetic that purified them by making them give up the contents of their stomachs, after which councils were held to settle disputes and wrongdoers were sentenced to their punishment, confinement in the sweathouse being a standard punishment. The ceremony lasted for several days and Cordelia had been lonesome while the village was virtually deserted and its inhabitants feasted and danced at the Green Corn Dance far away from non-Seminole eyes. But Weleka's and Hilolo's accounts of it, after their return, made her feel almost as if she had been there.

Lydia Lancaster

The new chikee went up in record time with so many hands to help. Shy and proud, Hilolo regarded her new home as though she were already dreaming of the happiness she would know there.

Cordelia's eyes were distracted as she saw Carlos DeHerrera walk, laughing at some joke, between two strange young Seminoles who had also come to celebrate the wedding. Osceola, the tall one's name was, and Cordelia sounded it silently on her lips so that she would not forget it. The syllables sounded like music. How strong the warrior was, how proud his face and bearing! It was obvious that Carlos respected him, and that he had an especial fondness for the shorter Seminole who walked on his other side.

Coacoochee. These syllables were harder to say, harder for Cordelia to remember. Coacoochee. Wildcat. Slender and wiry, the young man bore claw marks on his body from an encounter with one of the beasts when he had been a boy. The name suited him. There was something wild and unconquerable about him, as though he were indeed related to the fierce wildcats of the forests. But as fierce and proud as both young warriors were, today they were laughing, their faces filled with good humor.

Whooping, a young warrior from the istihapo instituted a ball game. The ball was fashioned of deer hide stuffed with hair, and the object of the game was to strike the trunk of a tree that had been stripped of all but its topmost branches. One of the opposing teams was made up of young men, the other of young women. The girls were allowed to throw the ball with their hands, but the men had to use a racket made of looped palmetto laced with thongs.

Cordelia's eyes sparkled with excitement and she jumped up and down and clapped her hands. Of all the players, Osceola and Wildcat and Carlos were the best, darting here and there, seldom missing the target. Weleka and Hilolo were the fastest and most accurate among the girls, their laughter ringing out in triumph every time they made a hit and scored.

Cordelia couldn't stand it any longer. Although she had determined not to join in the game because she was afraid that her inexperience would be a handicap to the girls, she plunged in and made a wild grab for the ball and captured it, and an instant later the ball struck the tree. She'd done it, she had scored! Weleka and Hilolo beamed at her, crying out with pleasure, and Cordelia's face flushed with triumph. This reminded her of the games and romps she'd had with the Reynard boys, while Nadine had looked on with disapproval. How much more sensible and natural the Seminoles were, with young women allowed to romp and play as a matter of course, and even compete with the men!

Thoroughly involved in the game now, Cordelia ran and dodged and grabbed, pitting all of her speed and natural skill to help the girls win. She scored twice again before she saw Stillipika, Weleka's mother, come from her chikee with a baby on each arm. Cordelia ran to take Donal Frederick from her and toss him into the air. It was incredible how big he was at seven months, he was already crawling, going like greased lightning after anything that caught his eye, and attempting to pull himself to his feet and stand.

How proud Donal would have been of him! The thought brought a lump to her throat and tears to her eyes, but she blinked the tears away. Today was no day for tears, today she must be happy for Hilolo, even though the thought of how happy Hilolo and Sam would be, for all the rest of their lives, made her eyes sting harder so that she had to fight to hold back the tears.

Donal Frederick bounced up and down in her arms, crowing with excitement, his face glowing with it, his eyes snapping. He clapped his hands together and struggled, wanting to be put down. Whether he could walk or not, it was obvious that he had every intention of getting into the ball game if he could only get loose from his mother.

"I'm afraid not, Donnie boy," Cordelia told him. "Not until next year, when you'll be a man!"

Donal Frederick gave her a dirty look. Cordelia could have sworn that he'd understood. Donal Frederick MacKenzie already had a mind of his own and he wasn't shy about letting it be known. When he wanted something, he bent every effort to get it, and if he didn't get it, he made his displeasure known to the entire istihapo. There were times when Cordelia felt like smacking him good and proper to teach him who was the mother and who was the baby, but punishment of that sort was virtually unknown among the Seminoles.

Children were treated with tolerance and kindness and respect, and only the most severe infraction would bring about reprisal.

The ball game was over at last, with both sides claiming victory. The good-natured banter flew back and forth as the men pretended to concede defeat while the girls knew perfectly well that they had lost. There was no ill will among any of the players, none of the anger or sulking that Cordelia had come to expect among her own people if there happened to be a poor loser among them.

She let Donal Frederick crawl while she ate. Instantly, the child made a beeline for Coacoochee, crawling as fast as he could go until he reached the young warrior, where he immediately attempted to crawl up onto his lap.

Wildcat grinned and patted his head, and then he lifted the child and tossed him into the air and caught him again. Donal Frederick crowed with excitement. Wildcat tossed him again, and again, before he set him back down. Cordelia went to retrieve him, embarrassed, but the instant she turned him loose he was scrambling back to Wildcat.

Wildcat laughed, obviously delighted to be singled out. He said something in such rapid Seminole that Cordelia couldn't understand. Osceola looked at her, his face grave, his voice courteous. He could speak English. His widowed mother, of the Creek Red Stick tribe, had married a Scotsman named Powell when he had been a boy.

"Coacoochee says that this will be a fine warrior," Osceola told her.

Cordelia smiled and nodded, but her heart turned cold with dread. Donnie, her Donnie, Donal's son, to grow up among the Seminoles and become a Seminole warrior? He would be accepted as a Seminole if they stayed. He would be as much Seminole as if he carried Seminole blood in his veins. And there was no doubt at all in Cordelia's mind that he would be happy, that the life would suit him. But he wasn't Seminole, he was white, and he didn't belong here no matter how kind the Seminoles were to him or how fully they accepted him as one of their own. He belonged in England, with Donal's family, and no day passed that she didn't feel despair at her inability to take him there to claim his birthright.

Heaven's Horizon

Carlos was amused. "Your son made a real impression on Osceola and Wildcat. How does it feel to be the mother of a brave Seminole warrior?"

"Don't joke about it!" Cordelia snapped at him. She was sorry immediately. Carlos was nothing but kind, he had only been teasing her. "We won't be here that long, I'll get him away somehow, I swear I will!"

"It isn't a bad life," Carlos told her. "Or it wasn't, in the old days. Now, I'm afraid that things will be different. The Removal Act has been ratified, and when these people are ordered to pick up and move to Arkansas there will be trouble such as Florida has never seen."

"But they can't force them to go! You told me yourself that the Seminoles were promised these lands!"

"Promises mean less than nothing when white men become greedy for the lands the Indians own." There was no laughter in Carlos's eyes now, no amusement on his face. This was a subject that touched him deeply. "And white men are land hungry, there are thousands of would-be settlers demanding that the Seminoles be removed so they can take their land. And there are the southern plantation owners as well, clamoring for their runaway slaves to be returned to them. The United States government is being besieged on all sides, and they will find it expedient to remove a few thousand Seminoles from the lands of their fathers in order to please the white men who put them in office."

"Do you think it will actually come to that, that it will actually happen? The government will try to force the Seminoles to go, and the Seminoles will fight?"

"Look at Osceola. Look at Coacoochee. Do you think that they will leave meekly, without fighting? The old men will want to agree, they are tired and they want peace, but the young men will fight to the last drop of blood in their veins. You can count on it, Cordelia Leyland MacKenzie. And you are right. This will be no place for you and your son when the tinder that will start the war catches fire."

"What does Micanopy think?" Cordelia demanded. She had

never seen Micanopy, and it was doubtful that she ever would, but she had heard about him, a great deal about him. Micanopy's official title was Pond Governor, and he was the chief of all the Seminoles.

If it hadn't been for political disagreement among the other chiefs, Micanopy would never have been elected Pond Governor, never would have been the leader of the Seminole nation. Carlos had told her that the man, fat, lazy, and far from brave, was a laughingstock, that he had been chosen only because the chiefs could not agree and he had been their compromise. Sam Jones should, by rights, have been chief, as he was the oldest chief among them, venerable and brave and wise.

"Micanopy will not want to fight. He will care for nothing except being allowed to keep his riches and his slaves, and these will be promised him. Not that the promise is likely to be kept. But Micanopy will believe the promises because believing them will be the easiest thing to do, and as long as he is chief, removal will have to be considered."

Cordelia felt suddenly cold in spite of the mildness of the evening, and she edged closer to the fire. Donal Frederick had eluded her again, and was sitting on Coacoochee's knee, while Coacoochee popped bits of conte into his mouth. Donal Frederick patted Coacoochee's face with his plump hands, traced the claw marks, and crowed. He was entranced with Wildcat, who was the son of King Philip and a minor chief in his own right. Osceola, sitting next to him, kept his face impassive. There was a majesty about him, a dignity, that was overpowering even though he was not a chief of any kind, even a minor one. What, the thought passed through her mind, would be the outcome of the trouble that Carlos was sure was coming, if Osceola, rather than the weak Micanopy, had happened to be the chief?

"How soon?" she asked, and there was dread in her heart.

"Not tomorrow," Carlos spoke easily. "Even wars take time to get started, Mrs. MacKenzie. A delegation of chiefs will have to be sent to inspect the lands in Arkansas that the government wants to allot them, and a treaty drawn up and signed. You can sleep tonight without fear of being awakened by a tomahawk in your pretty hair."

Heaven's Horizon

"If only the MacKenzies had written to me! Do you think the letter you sent them for me ever reached them, Señor DeHerrera? Donal had such respect for Duncan MacKenzie, perhaps he would be able to come up with some plan that would make it safe for us to go to them in spite of my father."

"I'm sure the letter arrived in England. Whether or not it ever reached the MacKenzies, with its incomplete address, is another matter. The chances are that it did. There's no use speculating about it, Cordelia. Anything might have happened. Mr. MacKenzie might even be dead. Or there might be a letter from him soon. In the meantime, we have to think what to do about you. You are quite right in thinking that you can't stay in this istihapo forever. You must certainly be well established away from the Seminoles before the trouble starts."

"I'll hate to leave my friends. I'll die of loneliness without Weleka and Hilolo. Everyone's been so good to me, so kind!"

"If that isn't just like a female! Itching to show this place your heels one minute, and weeping because you have to leave it the next! But you won't have anything to say about it. I have no intention of leaving you here much longer, I have other plans for you and you have no choice but to go along with them."

"If that isn't just like a man!" Cordelia exploded. "No choice, indeed! Just because you're male you think you can dictate to me!"

Carlos spread his hands, rolling his eyes heavenward. "So help me, nothing's more unreasonable than a woman! Do you want to stay here, then, and find yourself running and hiding, dragging young Donal along with you, with every white man in Florida and a large part of the army of the United States on your heels intent on killing you?"

Cordelia could feel the blood leave her face, leaving it white and drawn. Dear Lord in heaven, not that! Not her Donnie, hunted, harried, in danger of losing his life with every breath he took! Surely they wouldn't kill children, surely they wouldn't!

As if he could read her thoughts, Carlos said, "Oh, yes, they would," and his voice was entirely grave. "Dressed as you are, your skin darkened by the sun, they'd kill you, and Donal Frederick, before they realized that you were begging for your life in English! Make no mistake about that. And as your father is still searching for you, and as I am convinced that he already has an agent posted in England to keep the MacKenzies' home under surveillance, in case you should happen to go there, going to your husband's people is out of the question, or to your friends in Boston. It follows that you have no choice but to do as I say, and be kind enough not to give me any arguments about it, or I might just wash my hands of such a stubborn, unreasonable female and leave you here to take your chances!"

His eyes, usually laughing, were like steel, and the expression on his face left Cordelia with no doubt that he was deadly serious.

"Consider," he told her. "Even if—when you were hunted down as the Seminoles are going to be hunted if they choose to fight rather than to be removed from the land they love—you were able to make yourself known to the soldiers who captured you, you'd be returned to your father. What else could they do with you? Do you think for one moment that they would put any credence in your story that your own father murdered your husband and wanted to harm his own grandchild? A respected planter, wealthy, influential! They'd think you were demented. At the very least, they would hold you until your father could be contacted, and then he would come to get you, and what chance would you have then?"

Trembling, all the joy gone out of the day, Cordelia sat with her arms wrapped around her knees. Everything that Señor DeHerrera said was true. Carlos had already told her that her father's agents had given her description to the commandants of each army post in Florida. If she were taken she would be recognized, and there would be no escape.

Carlos nodded, satisfied by what he read in her face. "I'm taking you to my plantation," he told her. "I have already made it known that my niece, the young lady who married my nephew, is now widowed and that I have offered her a home as it is my duty to do. You will have to learn a little Spanish, as you are supposed to have been married to a Spanish gentleman. There's no way I could pass you off as Spanish, you could never learn enough of the language,

Heaven's Horizon

with a pure enough accent, in time, because I cannot spend all of my time here in the village to tutor you. Now say *"Yo comprendo, Señor, y gracias."*

The expression of dismay on his face when Cordelia's tongue struggled with the unfamiliar words made her laugh, even in her present mood of depression.

"¡Por Dios! You'll have to do better than that! Say it again, and try to make it intelligible!"

"Yo comprendo, Señor, y gracias," Cordelia attempted.

"Better, but not much. *Mañana,* we will leave for Solopi Heni. You will leave Donal here. Weleka will care for him until I bring you back; he's too young to make the journey but I want you to see what you will be letting yourself in for. There are no white people on my plantation and my slaves are trustworthy, no word will get out of your visit. While we travel and during the time you spend at Solopi Heni on this initial visit, you will speak Spanish. Every morsel of food and every drop of liquid that passes your lips will be asked for in Spanish, or you will go hungry and thirsty. It will be a start."

"Why are you doing this for me, why are you so kind?" The words were torn from Cordelia's heart.

Carlos twirled the ends of an imaginary mustache, and the leer on his face made her dissolve into laughter.

"Because I intend to ravish you, my dear. What other reason could I have? Be sensible, for the love of *Dios!* I simply don't want to see you and Donal killed or captured and sent back to Leyland's Landing. Now stop asking foolish questions and go and retrieve your son. He's crawling all over Coacoochee again. Not that Wildcat seems to mind, but if Donal swallows any more conte it'll start coming out of his ears. And you'd better go to bed early and get all the sleep you can, because we'll leave at daybreak. *Buenas tardes, Señora."*

Why was he helping her, indeed! Behind his amused expression, Carlos was deeply troubled. Ever since he had discovered Cordelia here at the istihapo, she had preyed on his mind. He'd sworn that he would never allow himself to fall in love, that he would never marry.

251

A Seminole woman would not be accepted in the life he had made for himself, a life as a white man. Outside of the istihapo, and the Seminole people at large, no one knew that he was half Indian. If it had been known, he would not have had the opportunity to build his plantation, to amass the fortune that gave him all of the finer things in life, things that his Spanish blood wanted and needed as his right.

And there was no way he could marry a white woman, without telling her the truth, and if he told her the truth, what white woman of breeding would accept him, would want to bear children of mixed blood? The other kind of woman, the coarser kind, held no appeal for him.

But now here was Cordelia, and he felt so drawn to her that it caused him sleepless nights and troubled days. He was every kind of a fool to take her to live at Solopi Heni, where her presence would be a constant torment to him. Even if she would not have rejected him because of what he was, she still loved her dead husband, her heart still belonged to Donal MacKenzie and it would be years before her grief subsided enough to allow her to love another man.

All the same, there was no way he could leave her here, no way he could put her entirely out of his life and eventually out of his mind. And so only one course remained open to him. He must school himself to think of her as the niece he had already told his friends and neighbors would soon be making her home with him. A man does not fall in love with his niece, much less hope to marry her! And until he learned, he must take every care that Cordelia never suspected his true feelings for her, because if she suspected, she would not accept his help and protection.

He tore his gaze away from her face, afraid that something of his feelings might show on his own, and immediately such a look of anger was there that Cordelia was startled. Following his gaze, she saw that a jug was being passed from hand to hand, and that even some of the women were drinking from it.

"Rum!" he said, his voice as angry as his face. "Where the devil did they get it? Go to bed, Cordelia. In a little while, things will be going on that you won't want to see."

Osceola had risen to his feet, his ordinarily immobile face black

Heaven's Horizon

with anger even greater than that which Carlos showed. His voice rang out, and although Cordelia could follow little of what he said, the fury in it was enough to start her trembling again. Wildcat too got to his feet, placing Donal Frederick carefully on the ground.

The young men who were drinking rum only grinned at Osceola, and went on imbibing. Clearly, they had no intention of stopping. Osceola was not a chief, he had no special standing, his anger could not hurt them or make them desist from their pleasure.

Osceola stared at them, his face showing all of his anger and pride and scorn. Together, he and Wildcat stalked to the compound where the horses were kept and led their own to the outskirts of the village before they mounted and rode away into the silent darkness.

"Osceola has reason to hate all white men," Carlos told Cordelia softly. "He hated his stepfather, Powell, for taking his mother's love from him and making him an outcast from his own people. And he doubly hates them for supplying the Indians with spirits that take their wits from them and allows the white men to cheat them. Go to bed, Mrs. MacKenzie. But first try to persuade Weleka and Hilolo, at least, not to drink the rum. Maybe you can convince them that it can't do them anything but harm."

Cordelia moved to obey him, and placed her hand on Weleka's arm. "Sister, don't drink that poisonous stuff," she begged. "It will only make you sick."

She saw that her warning had not been necessary. Both Weleka's and Hilolo's eyes were filled with a sadness that made her feel like crying. But they made no attempt to stop their husbands. They already knew that it wouldn't be any use.

Damn those white men, damn those traders who gave or sold or traded rum to the Indians! Cordelia gathered Donal Frederick into her arms and went to her chikee. It took her a long time to comfort her son, who was undergoing his first frustrated desolation at the departure of Wildcat. To quiet him, she gave him her breast, but even after his howls of fury had stilled, her spirits were at their lowest ebb.

What did the future hold for her friends, lied to as they were by the white men who wanted their lands, ordered to emigrate from their home to a new and unknown country, supplied with the drink that kept their minds befuddled so that they could not defend themselves from the white man's forked tongue? And what did the future hold for herself and Donnie? They too would be uprooted, facing an unknown future.

It won't happen tomorrow, Carlos had said. But his words and his voice and the bleakness in his eyes had told her that it would happen, that it was inevitable.

In spite of Carlos's suggestion that she get a good night's sleep, she lay awake for hours, listening to the ever-increasing revels as the celebration went on. Women as well as men were drunk, their shrill laughter and their excited cries disturbing the night that should have been peaceful and quiet. They were dancing now, their feet pounding the earth, and now and again a new cry rent the air, so ominous that it made Cordelia shiver and her blood run cold. *"Yo-ho-hee!"* It was a cry that she had heard before only during the little boys' games as they played at war. It was the Seminole war cry, and it portended nothing but evil.

She felt tears flood her cheeks in a sudden spate and there was no way that she could hold them back. If it hadn't been for her own people, these Seminoles would have lived in peace and happiness for generations to come, unspoiled by the vices that the white men had brought to them. She turned her face into her sleeping mat and cried until she could cry no more.

In the morning, still tired from having slept so little, she left the istihapo with Carlos, leaving Donal Frederick in Weleka's care. She was glad to leave the village behind her, both men and women were struggling to their feet from where they had fallen the night before, or staggering with glazed eyes and trembling limbs from their chikees to retch and retch again.

"Don't dwell on it. There's nothing you can do about it," Carlos told her. "You have your own future to think of, and that's enough for you to have to contend with without taking on the miseries of a whole nation, Mrs. MacKenzie."

Cordelia's knees tightened against the sides of the horse she was riding, saddleless as was the Indian custom. "If you call me Mrs.

MacKenzie one more time, I'm going to scream! Sometimes you call me Cordelia, and if I'm going to be your niece you'd better always call me Cordelia!"

Carlos threw back his head and laughed, his mirth bringing tears to his eyes. "Then you'd better start calling me Uncle Carlos! But don't start now. For the purposes of this first visit, you're only a young Seminole woman. The time for our great charade has not yet come. And remember, no speaking English once we arrive at the plantation, even in front of the slaves. Use what Seminole you have, if you can't think of the correct word in Spanish. They'll never know the difference. Now save your breath for the journey. It's a long one, and you'll need all you have."

A mile to the east, traveling by another route, Donal approached the istihapo scarcely half an hour after Cordelia and Carlos DeHerrera had left it. He heard the dogs even before the village came into sight, and the Seminole guide he had picked up at one of the trading posts indicated that they should dismount and enter the village on foot.

Donal was used to this by now. To ride a horse into the village would be discourteous. They made their way, leading their horses, Donal's bearded face gaunt with fatigue and the disappointment of having investigated countless villages without finding any trace of Cordelia. The buckskins he'd bought to replace his civilized clothing were filthy, stiff with dirt and grease from the even more countless meals of campfire-broiled game.

Even if the istihapo had been beginning an ordinary day, rather than suffering from the quantities of rum that had been drunk the night before, no notice would have been taken of him and his guide as they made their way to the guest lodge and the cookhouse. They would be welcome to eat their fill from the sofkee kettle and to sleep in the guest lodge, and the Seminoles would wait with no evidence of curiosity for them to tell them why they were here.

A stripling came to lead their horses away. Donal was ravenous. He no longer felt the slightest compunction about eating from the common pot, using a wooden spoon that others had used before him. The sofkee was delicious and filling, it satisfied his hunger, but even as he ate he strained his eyes to note and examine every woman who moved about the istihapo. None of them were white, although several of them were young and slender.

It was obvious that something unusual was going on in this particular village. The few men he saw looked the worse for wear, even ill. His guide, whom he called Oscar because that was as close as he could come to his actual name, exchanged a few words with the stripling who had taken care of their horses, and then told Donal, in halting English, that there had been a wedding and much rum had been drunk. Oscar's eyes gleamed with wistful envy, and Donal winced. The Seminoles he had seen idling their time away at the trading posts had been possessed of a magnificent dignity except when their trading had allowed them to purchase rum if they were so inclined. The change in these people when they were drunk struck him to the core, and like Cordelia and Carlos, like Osceola and Wildcat, he cursed the white men who had brought this evil to a simple and dignified people.

Both Runt and Sam were working in the common fields when Donal arrived. Neither of them was the worse for drink. As soon as the white man had approached the outskirts of the village, Runt had gone to ground, while Sam returned to the village to see what the white man wanted.

Because he spoke English and could interpret much better than Donal's guide, Sam was questioned about a young white woman who would now have a baby, who might have taken refuge with the Seminoles.

"Her name is Cordelia. She would have come with a runaway slave called Runt, a small man but very strong. I am Donal MacKenzie, Cordelia's husband."

All of the faces, including Sam's, were blank. They knew of no such young woman, Donal was told. They all knew that Cordelia's husband was dead, that he had been slain by her wicked father. In the Seminole nation, Andrew Leyland would have been put to death for his crime. This white man was one of Cordelia's father's agents, come to spy.

Donal was allowed to search. The Seminoles stood impassive

while he looked into each chikee, while he studied every young woman. Weleka kept her eyes modestly averted as she held a baby to her breast, its face concealed from him. Nearby, Hilolo held another baby. Not being possessed of supernatural mental powers, Donal had no way of knowing that the infant Weleka was nursing was named Donal Frederick MacKenzie, that it was his own son, and that the baby Hilolo held was Weleka's baby.

Cordelia wasn't here. This phase of his search had turned out to be as fruitless as all the others. Donal and Oscar rested for two hours, and then resumed their journey. Donal's heart was heavy. He had searched so many istihapos, he had talked to so many Seminoles, and there wasn't even a trace of the girl for whom he was searching.

Sam went back to the field, and Runt joined him.

"What did he want?" Runt asked.

"He was looking for Cordelia and Donal Frederick," Sam told him. "This one was smarter than the others who have come searchin'. He said he was Donal MacKenzie! A bearded man with a scar on his forehead, lean and strong."

Runt's white teeth were in startling contrast to his black skin as he grinned. "He sure is smarter'n them others! Only, Master Donal didn't have no beard, and he didn't have no scar. Besides, Master Donal's dead." He picked up his hoe and went back to his work, cursing Andrew Leyland's persistence. Damn the man to hell! But he wouldn't find Miss Cordelia, not if he searched for a hundred years and sent a thousand men to fetch her home. And he wouldn't find Runt either. Runt hoped that the bearded, scarred man who had dared to say that he was Donal MacKenzie would fall into a river and be eaten by a crocodile, or that a bear would kill him. Then there would be one less bastard hunting them.

In London, the parlormaid at Duncan MacKenzie's Mayfair home was so agitated that she scarcely knew what she was doing. She looked at the post that she held in her hand, and then she scurried into Mr. MacKenzie's study and shoved it into a drawer of his desk, in such trembling-handed haste that she didn't notice that one of the letters shot to the back of the drawer and fell through the opening, to be hidden from sight, as well concealed as if she had hidden it on purpose.

Bessie Scroggins' steps took her from the study to the kitchen belowstairs. "Mrs. Bates, I'm going now. My mum's took bad, she is, and I've gotta go to her."

The cook's face showed disapproval. "You have no right to go without getting leave from the mistress."

"How can I get leave from her, when she's away? She and the master both, and they won't be back for a week so they won't miss me, and by that time my mum might be dead. You can get along without me, there's no need for a parlormaid when nobody's using the parlor! I'll come back when my mum's better, and not before."

"You'll come back to find you've been sacked, then," Mrs. Bates said. As if Mrs. MacKenzie, and Mr. MacKenzie too, didn't have enough trouble without Bessie running off! They hadn't been the same, either of them, since they'd had word from America that Donal MacKenzie was dead, killed in some horrible accident in an outlandish place called Georgia. All of them, Donal's sisters, Clara and Ann, as well as their mother and father, had been all but overcome by grief, and now Mr. MacKenzie had packed them all off to the country to stay with friends, hoping that the change of scene would do them good.

"Then I'll be sacked. My mum is more important than a post as a parlormaid, no matter what a good post it's been. And Mrs. MacKenzie won't sack me anyway, she's too kind and understanding to do such a thing, she'll know I had to go to my mum."

"Don't say I didn't warn you, then," Mrs. Bates said. But then her face softened. "Just take along this cake with you. It's seed cake, and invalids do seem to relish it."

"'alf of it," Bessie said. "We won't be able to tuck away more than 'alf of it. And thank you kindly. I put the post in Mr. MacKenzie's desk drawer. You can tell him if they get back before I do."

If Bessie had been able to read, she might have noticed that one of the letters she'd placed in the desk drawer had been addressed and readdressed in different hands, until it had finally reached its

Heaven's Horizon

destination. As it was, there was no thought of a letter that had come at last after many delays, and much less thought that it might have come all the way from a place called Florida, in America. Her best bonnet on her head and her bundle in one hand and half of the seed cake in the other, the cherries on her bonnet bobbing from her haste, Bessie left the house, with no thought of the morning post in her head at all.

Chapter Sixteen

Cordelia sat at the foot of Carlos DeHerrera's table, listening to the conversation of the gentlemen with one ear while her eyes missed no detail of the service to her guests. As Carlos's niece and hostess, it was her duty to see that everything was perfect. Wryly, more than a little amused, she reflected that only part of the reason that Carlos had brought her to Solopi Heni had been his sense of responsibility for a white girl in her unfortunate circumstances, so that his conscience had demanded that he rescue her. A good part of the reason was that Carlos had needed an attractive woman of breeding to run his household and act as his hostess.

Even more amused, she thought that if any of the gentlemen who were sitting at the table this evening had ever seen her in her Seminole clothing, with her skin darkened by the sun and her hands roughened by her labor among the Indians, they wouldn't have recognized her as the same woman. And if any of the ladies, although the table was ill-balanced with only three wives of the male guests present, had known that three years ago the girl they thought was Señor DeHerrera's widowed niece had lived as a squaw, had given birth to a son in a Seminole istihapo, they would have been so shocked that they would undoubtedly have swooned and had to be revived with smelling salts.

Even to Cordelia, that other life seemed a little unreal now. Her complexion had resumed its magnolialike creaminess, her gown was the latest fashion, brought to the territory by coastal schooner as were all of her gowns. Carlos was generous in the matter of her apparel, so generous that the wardrobe in her room was overflowing and a second one that he had ordered and had installed was already in danger of being as filled as the first.

The Empire gown became her. She had the figure to carry it off to its best advantage. Shorter, plumper women looked ludicrous in the high-waisted, low neckline dresses, with the ribbon sash just under the bosom and the skirt falling straight and round to the floor. The one she was wearing tonight was cream-colored, the deep cream that was so becoming to her dark eyes and hair. Her satin slippers, so delicate that they were virtually useless as foot protection, were of the same cream satin, the ribbons that held them on enhancing her high-arched feet and delicate ankles every time they were glimpsed as she moved around a room or sat gracefully in a chair.

Cordelia looked exactly what she was, a highborn lady of breeding. Her hair had been cut short and arranged in curls to frame her face, after the latest fashion. Her hands were smooth and white, the nails perfect ovals as pink as the inside of a seashell. She wore no rings except her wedding ring—all of Carlos's insistence couldn't move her to wear any other ring—but a pearl necklace encircled her throat and pearl earrings dangled from her earlobes. And upstairs, in a jewel chest on her dressing table, there were diamonds and emeralds and rubies. It amused Carlos to deck her out as the lady she was, to pass her off as his niece-by-marriage, to make her the showpiece of this plantation house that was itself the showplace of all of northwestern Florida.

Carlos could afford it. Cordelia had been astonished at her first glimpse of Solopi Heni, the Seminole word for heaven. Having achieved such a magnificent plantation, it had been his conceit to give it that name, even though few white men knew what it meant.

Heaven's Horizon

The plantation was vast, running for miles along the Apalachicola River. An army of slaves worked the untold acres, growing cotton, corn, sugarcane, even rice in low-lying fields. There were pine forests for lumber to be cut and shipped, there was a thriving industry in turpentine from those same pine trees, and there was a sugar mill. During the season the heavy, cloying smell of molasses pervaded the air. After having been familiar only with the cotton-growing plantations of Georgia, Solopi Heni seemed to Cordelia to be an empire in its own right, self-sufficient and enormously profitable.

The house was built of whitewashed brick, with deep verandas to provide shade and keep the interior cool even on the hottest days. The upper story boasted wrought-iron balconies like those found in New Orleans and even nearer, in Saint Augustine, far to the north, where the Spanish influence still prevailed. Cordelia was even yet unable to name all the different trees and shrubs and flowers that grew around the house, their deep green and flamboyant colors delightful to the eye.

There were warehouses, a blacksmith's shop, a cotton gin, the sugar factory, a boot and harness shop, a repair depot and a turpentine mill all on the plantation. The rows of slave cabins were whitewashed and kept in good repair. Carlos's slaves were allowed to grow garden patches of their own and keep all that they grew for their own use. Older slaves, no longer strong enough for a full day's work in the fields, kept the garden patches tended and the slave compound in order.

None of Solopi Heni's slaves was overworked or abused in any way, and not one of them had any desire to escape, even to the relative freedom of a Seminole village. Cordelia knew that Carlos had given at least half a dozen of his slaves permission to go—strong, virile men, some with their wives, who had yearned for the Seminole way of life. They hadn't had to run away, they had gone with his blessing. But not one of his slaves knew that Carlos himself was half Seminole, that his regard for their happiness and welfare, his genuine fondness for them, came from his Seminole heritage.

To his neighbors and peers, Carlos was pure Spanish, the grandson of an aristocrat who had made his home in New Orleans and who had left him enough to start this plantation. And that was true as far as it went.

Cordelia knew the entire story, and she found it a fascinating one. One of the patriarch DeHerrera's four sons had settled in Saint Augustine, and in his wanderings he had fallen in love with a Seminole girl and married her. But Spanish society being what it was, Morning Cloud had continued to live at her native *istihapo*, while his father had maintained his home in Saint Augustine, spending a good deal of time with his Seminole wife.

"And then my mother died," Carlos had told Cordelia. "She died of a lung congestion, an infection that my father had brought her from Saint Augustine. I was thirteen years old at the time, and although I was fond of my father, I knew even at that age that he wasn't exactly a paragon of a man. He was the black sheep of the family, and his father had disowned him for daring to marry a Seminole woman.

"But for all his imperfections, my father had a conscience buried inside him somewhere, because he grieved over my mother's death, blaming himself for having brought her the sickness that killed her, to such an extent that he tried to drown himself in a bottle. He died when I was fourteen, as a result of trying to chastise a Spanish gentleman who was abusing a Seminole girl who worked in a tavern and whose employer forced her to extend her favors to his patrons. My father being inebriated at the time, his reflexes slowed by alcohol, he was killed in the resulting duel.

"When my Spanish grandfather learned of my father's death, either his conscience or simply curiosity moved him to send for me, with a view to having me educated if I proved to be acceptable, and that is how I acquired my taste for the better things in life. I didn't live at the *hacienda*, naturally. That would have been unthinkable! But I was sent to school, and I visited my grandfather at the *hacienda* often, passed off as the orphaned son of a distant acquaintance, whom he had made a sort of protégé.

"When the old gentleman died, when I was nineteen, no one was more astonished than I when he left me enough so that I could establish myself in some other sort of life instead of going back to my istihapo and reverting to being a Seminole. It was no great fortune, he had his legitimate sons and grandsons to provide for, but it was enough to give me a start. And so here I am, neither fish nor fowl, passing myself off as a Spanish gentleman of pure blood, because that is the only way I could have achieved what I want from life. I had found that I liked the life of an aristocrat, you see. It was probably born in me, my inheritance from my grandfather even though the other half of my blood was too red to be acceptable in a white world."

"Doesn't your own conscience ever bother you? Don't you feel any remorse or shame at all, for leaving your mother's people? After all, as a Seminole, you belonged to her family, to her tribe."

"Certainly I feel qualms of conscience. But as you must have realized by now, I am not entirely an admirable character. Having had a taste of the good life, I had no desire to become a Seminole brave. Especially as Seminole braves have a regrettable habit of getting themselves killed in battle. A man could get hurt that way! I happen to be fond of fine food and wine, I have a greed for fine houses and fine furniture, and all of the things that being a wealthy Spanish gentleman can give me."

"And enough loyalty to your Seminole heritage to make you visit them regularly and revert to being Seminole while you're at the istihapo, even at the risk of being discovered."

"The risk is small. And now, my sneaky little niece, you've gotten away with keeping me talking about something else as long as you're going to get away with it. It's time for your Spanish lesson, and if you ask me even one more question you'd better ask it in Spanish or the lesson will be extended for another full hour!"

"Carlos, don't you ever want to marry? It isn't natural that you should spend your entire life single, without a wife or children."

"My dear and very naive Mrs. MacKenzie, marrying is a complication with which I have no desire to contend. You, Mrs. MacKenzie, are a devious little minx! You tricked me, but no more, not even one more question! ¿*Comprende*?"

Laughing, but saddened at the same time because it still didn't seem right that Carlos should have to remain single or risk losing everything he had built up for himself, Cordelia applied herself to her lesson.

Cordelia no longer felt that she was an object of charity. Although his wealth gave him almost unlimited resources, Carlos was sorely in need of a mistress for his plantation. A house such as this needed a mistress, and the running of it was a full-time job and she knew that she earned her keep.

Her hand moved so that her fingers touched the pearls she was wearing for this dinner party. Her keep was one thing, but the jewels Carlos lavished on her were something else again. She hadn't wanted to accept them, but he had swept all of her objections aside with an imperious wave of his hand.

"As a DeHerrera and my niece, it will be expected that you have jewels. And think what a pity it would be if those particular jewels had ended up adorning a woman who couldn't provide a perfect setting for them! You are the picture, the jewels are only the frame, and the frame must be worthy of you. Take the baubles, Cordelia. It gives me as much pleasure to see you wearing them as it does for me to confound those who would despise me if they knew the truth about me."

There was no doubt that Carlos enjoyed hoodwinking his peers. There was always surpressed laughter in his eyes when he came into contact with them. Cordelia watched, and joined in his silent laughter. There was something immensely satisfying about playing this game, about fooling people who would think they were head and shoulders above Carlos if they knew of his Seminole heritage, when all the time Carlos was head and shoulders better than they were! As for the planters among Carlos's friends, Cordelia dissolved into laughter every time she thought of how shocked they would be if they knew that she was the runaway daughter of another planter, and that she had run away with a slave who had still not been found.

It saddened her, though, that Runt had adamantly refused to come to Solopi Heni with her.

"Not me, I ain't goin'! I likes it fine right where I am. I don't care how kind Señor DeHerrera would be to me, the Seminoles are my friends, and I'm free here. It ain't as if you need me anymore,

Heaven's Horizon

Miss Cordelia. Even Zoe would know that you don' need me now. So if you ain't mindin', I'll stay put."

Cordelia hadn't argued with him. She knew how he felt, and she was glad that he was happy. If only Zoe could know how happy he was, and of the good fortune that had befallen Cordelia when Señor DeHerrera had discovered her!

In spite of the usual custom that gentlemen never discussed anything of a serious nature in the presence of ladies, the talk around the dinner table this evening had all been of the Fort Gibson treaty. Cordelia had become familiar with the Seminole names that fell so easily from the tongues of their guests.

Jumper, Fuch-a-lus-to-had-jo, Charley Emanthler, Coi-had-jo, Holati Emanthler, Ya-ha-had-jo, Sam Jones. And Abraham, the former slave of Micanopy, who acted as the Seminoles' interpreter. These few Seminoles, along with Abraham, had undertaken the long journey to Arkansas to inspect the lands that the government of the United States had set aside for them. They had been accompanied by Major Phagan. And in March of 1833 they had signed the supplementary treaty at Fort Gibson, and there was jubilation among the whites throughout the territory of Florida.

Listening to the gentlemen, Cordelia couldn't help but think that she knew a good deal more about the situation as a whole than they did. Carlos had talked of little else for months, until she was thoroughly grounded in the subject.

One thing she knew for certain. The Seminoles weren't being removed for their own benefit, but for the benefit of the whites. For years, land speculators had been buying up every parcel of land they could lay their hands on, at prices that were ridiculously low, and now they stood to reap fortunes when land-hungry settlers poured in. These same speculators had aided and abetted every hostile encounter between Seminoles and whites, because every incident of that sort had frightened poorer settlers into selling out and running for safety. Every ambush, every burned cabin, had added to more land for the speculators.

They had made rum available to the Seminoles, to give them false courage and arrogance, to make their tempers flare at every insult to their kind. Carlos's ravings about the speculators' manipulations had turned the air blue, and Cordelia had listened to words she'd never known before and that would have turned Zoe's black skin white.

"Once the Seminoles are cleared out, once the removal has been effected in its entirety, there's no telling how far this territory will go!" Marcus Meade, a portly Saint Augustine importer said, his face and voice so pompous that Cordelia felt like slapping him. "It was nothing less than a crime against the Almighty Himself to let that vermin hold so much valuable land that white people would put to good and profitable use! But now that's all over. There are fortunes to be made, gentlemen, now that the treaty has been signed at last and the Indians will be swept right off the face of Florida!"

Cordelia's heart twisted as she realized what the effort to keep quiet must be costing Carlos. His hands must be aching to take that fat throat between them and squeeze the superciliousness out of him. How he must be wishing that he could throw the contents of his wineglass into that smirking face! Her own hands trembled with the desire to do just that, so that she folded them in her lap for fear that if she didn't keep them under rigid control, she would actually do it.

"Yes-sirree! Good times are coming, and all our waiting for it to happen has finally paid off! Florida is going to be a heaven on earth once those Seminoles are cleared out, and all of those other Indians who've wandered down here, taking up room that belongs to us! I was in despair that it would never happen, the way our government dragged its feet, but now the treaty's been confirmed and there's no way those red savages can wriggle out of it. I don't mind telling you that I stand to make a profit myself, not only from the increased shipping that's bound to come once the territory's properly settled, but because I've invested in a bit of land, and I trust that all you gentlemen did the same."

"I'm content to be a planter and keep only what I have," Carlos said, his voice mild.

"Then you aren't as astute as I thought you were. Man, you should have seen this coming, and prepared to take advantage of it!"

Only Cordelia noticed the tightening at the corners of Carlos's

Heaven's Horizon

mouth, the cold fury that had replaced the usual humor in his eyes. Her hands tightened their clasp of each other in her lap, and she felt sudden nausea as she thought of Weleka and Hilolo, of Wacassa and Sam Brent, of Stillipika and all the others at the istihapo who would be ordered, so soon now, to pack whatever belongings they could carry with them and allow themselves to be moved to Arkansas, away from their own land and the land where the bones of their fathers lay at rest, away from their hunting grounds and their fields and the happy, abundant life that they had believed to be their right.

The Fort Gibson treaty, that dreadful treaty! Every time Cordelia thought of it, and there was no way she could forget it with Carlos's constant raving against it, she felt frustrated and physically ill.

The Seminole delegation hadn't known what they were signing. It had been winter, they had suffered agonies enduring the freezing blizzards of Arkansas, so different from their Eden-like Florida. But Major Phagan had told them over and over how lush the land would be in the summer, how their crops would prosper and how happy they would be with the exchange.

Still the Seminole delegation had held out against him, demurring, until Major Phagan, losing his patience, had invited them inside the fort and given them rum, a great deal of rum, to warm them, he said, and because he was their friend. And the more rum he had given them, the more they had come to believe that what he said was true, that the land might be satisfactory after all. Winter could not last forever, this weather was unusual, there would be all of the warm, balmy summers and springs and falls to grow their crops and gain in prosperity.

And so they had made their marks on the piece of paper, the new treaty that had been drawn up to replace the older one.

"The original treaty, the one they were led to believe was the same as this new one, clearly stated that the delegation was to inspect the new land and report to the Seminole people and tell them what they had found, and that then the Seminole people would decide," Carlos told Cordelia. "But this new draft stated that if the delegation signed, it bound the Seminole people as a whole, with no voice in the matter, to honor the treaty.

Lydia Lancaster

"The delegation didn't understand. Abraham, who is a good man, didn't notice the change that had been made in the wording. The Seminoles have been tricked, Cordelia, and the tricking was deliberate." Carlos's rage was beyond description. "Tricked, tricked! Why God doesn't strike such liars and cheaters dead is more than a poor ignorant half-Seminole like me can understand!"

It was more than Cordelia could understand too, and she was sick at heart.

"Isn't there anything they can do? If they didn't understand what they were signing, how can it be legal?"

"They'll be held to it, you can depend on that. And the only thing they can do is fight."

"Carlos, do you think it will come to that?" He had been warning her for so long, ever since he had first discovered her at the istihapo, but it hadn't happened yet and she had begun to hope that it never would.

"A few of the older chiefs will want to honor the treaty and leave. They have no heart for fighting, all they want is to live out the rest of their lives in peace even though they must do it in an alien land. But the younger men will fight. They are so angry at the white man's duplicity that they're willing to lay down their lives in the cause of justice."

"Wildcat, Osceola," Cordelia murmured. She had seen the two young braves only once, but she had never forgotten them. Recalling them vividly, she couldn't imagine them giving in to such trickery. Carlos was right, they would fight, and so would others like them.

"What does Micanopy say?" she wanted to know.

Carlos snorted. "Micanopy! He'll go whichever way the wind blows. He's willing to be removed from Florida if he can keep his slaves. He has no stomach for fighting. He's as incompetent as he is lazy. But Osceola, in particular, will incite the young men to fight, and Wildcat will side with Osceola."

Carlos's words came back to her now, and as though to echo her thoughts, Peter Breckenridge, the youngest among their guests that evening, asked Carlos a question.

"Señor DeHerrera, do you suppose that there will be trouble? Is there any possibility that the Seminoles will resist being removed?"

"Certainly there will be trouble. Unless a miracle intervenes, there will be a wholesale war."

Marcus Meade snorted. "If you will forgive me, Señor DeHerrera, that is the purest balderdash! The Indians won't dare resist! How could even such ignorant savages believe that they would have any chance against the army of the United States? They'll go peacefully, because they have no choice."

Peter Breckenridge's gaze came to rest on Cordelia's face, and he frowned. "Gentlemen, I think we should change the subject, which must be distressing to the ladies." Cordelia hoped that the flush she felt rise to her cheeks wasn't apparent to anyone else at the table. Peter had seen that she was upset, and as always, he had taken immediate steps to protect her.

A solidly built man just short of thirty, Peter had sandy hair and one of those open, good-natured faces that won him friends wherever he went. He was an attractive man, well educated and well spoken, with a natural sympathy for the human race and a lively interest in everything that went on around him. His plantation lay eighteen miles downriver from Solopi Heni, considerably smaller than Carlos's but still prosperous and promising to expand until he would end up as one of the most prosperous and respected men in Florida. The younger son of a Carolina planter, he had struck out on his own, seeking the adventure of carving out his own empire in the Florida wilderness.

Still unmarried, Peter was considered a prime catch for any lady in need of a husband, and Cordelia had run into more than a little poorly concealed dislike from the unmarried young ladies who were vying for his attention, because Peter had evinced so much interest in the beautiful young widow who was much too lovely to spend the rest of her life without a man.

Peter was in love with her, but that wasn't the real trouble. The real trouble was that Cordelia was attracted to him, very attracted to him. Being human and young, she could hardly help but be. It had nothing to do with the love she'd had for Donal. She still loved

Donal and she would always love him, there was no way she could forget him and the wild, short-lived happiness she'd known with him.

But Donal was dead, and she was very much alive, and every drop of blood in her body called out for a mate, someone she could be happy with and who could fill both her physical and emotional needs. Even now, after all this time, she spent most of her nights in an agony of longing after she had gone to bed in the lovely room that Carlos had furnished for her, bringing in furniture and bric-a-brac by coastal schooner after having ascertained her tastes down to the last detail.

It was the most luxurious bedchamber imaginable, the tester bed with its mosquito bar, standing on a raised dais, large enough for half a dozen girls of her size. The dressing table and the chaise longue and the side chairs and tables were of gilt, inlaid with mother-of-pearl, the hangings were a delicate shell pink. The flowered carpet was of shades of pink and rose, the dressing table accounterments were of sterling silver, the fireplace of Italian marble. In spite of Cordelia's simpler tastes, acquired at the Reynards' in Boston, Carlos had pounced on her remark about the bedchambers of the French nobility before the people had risen up against their monarchs and turned all of France into a bloodbath. Miss Virginia Baker, who thoroughly disapproved of the favored few trampling the impoverished masses under their feet, still had an appreciation for beauty, and she had described such chambers to her students in great detail.

So from being a fugitive, living the life of a Seminole woman in a Seminole village, Cordelia had been transformed into a princess, and although her new friends knew nothing of her Seminole life, it wasn't to be wondered at that they were a little jealous of all the luxury that her "uncle" lavished on her.

Looking at her full-length reflection in the cheval glass that stood in one corner, Cordelia sometimes had the sensation that she didn't know where she was. Once she'd been a school girl in Boston, attending Miss Virginia Baker's Academy for Young Ladies, and the Reynards' protégée. Then she had been Mrs. Donal MacKenzie, the

Heaven's Horizon

happiest bride since the day God had created the earth. After that she had been a Seminole, with a little son she adored. And now she was Carlos's niece, the most desirable young lady, and the most fortunate, in the territory of Florida.

It was confusing, and if she sometimes felt disoriented it wasn't to be wondered at. She still missed Donal Frederick intensely, aching for him until she thought she couldn't bear it. When Carlos had decided that it was too dangerous to bring her son with her to Solopi Heni, she had rebelled against coming without him until Carlos had had to virtually bring her by force.

"We can get away with claiming that you're my niece, but a niece of Cordelia MacKenzie's age and appearance, with a son the age that Cordelia Leyland MacKenzie's child would be if she had survived, would be an open invitation to disaster. Don't think for a moment that your father has given over his search for you. And consider Little Coacoochee, Cordelia. He's safe where he is, and he's happy. He has Little Thunder for his constant playmate, he thinks of him as his brother, as well as the other children of the village. Weleka and Wacassa consider him as their second son, and Hilolo adores him. He has two mothers at the istihapo, and two grandmothers, Little Acorn and Stillipika, and Runt and Sam Brent are his doting uncles. He has his place in the world and he knows who he is.

"But here at Solopi Heni, he would have only the slave children for playmates, and no matter how he would accept them as his equals, they would know that he was the young master, and it wouldn't be the same. And how could we expect that a child of his age would never mention the istihapo, that he must never mention his friends there or let it drop that you're his mother? It would be impossible, and you know it. Think with your head instead of your heart. It isn't as if you won't see him often. I'll take you to visit the istihapo often, to spend several days. Bringing him here would not only be dangerous, until he's old enough to understand, but it would be a disservice to him. In a few years, we will give out that he is your sister's child, an orphan, and what would be more natural than for us to give him a home? He'll be old enough to understand then, and the danger will be minimal."

"If I can't have him with me at your plantation, then I'll stay here with him! The life isn't that bad, I've come to love everyone here and Weleka and Hilolo are my sisters. It isn't the life I would have chosen for us if I'd had a choice, but as long as Donal is dead I can be content with it."

"And the men your father has searching for you will return to the istihapo again and again, and one day they'll appear without warning, and see you and Donal Frederick together, and come to the right conclusion. But if you are here, you will be my niece, and if Donal Frederick is there, he will be just another small Seminole boy, indistinguishable from any other Seminole boy. It isn't as if you're losing him. We're buying time, time for him to mature and make your having him with you safe."

"It isn't right! It isn't fair! He's my son and I want him, I can't live without him!"

"You must learn to live without him. Only you won't be living without him any more than any mother of the privileged class in England, whose children are tended by nursemaids and later sent away to school."

"He won't even remember how to speak English!" Cordelia railed.

"All the better. He'll pick it up again soon enough, when the time comes. You aren't deserting him, Cordelia, you're protecting him!"

In the end, Cordelia had accepted Carlos's logic, and had come to Solopi Heni without Donal Frederick. The situation was bad enough as it stood, but now there was Peter Breckenridge to complicate it even more. Peter, no more than anyone else, had no idea that she was not only a widow but a mother, that she had a walking, talking son growing up as a Seminole child in a Seminole village.

Even if she could trust Peter to understand, and something told her that she could, Peter deserved more than a secondhand woman and a secondhand child. How would she feel, when Peter was making love to her, and the memory of Donal's lovemaking swept over her with poignant, aching agony? How could she keep from

Heaven's Horizon

feeling that pain and keep Peter from knowing that she felt it? It would be unfair to him, when he could have the choice of a dozen girls who had never loved any other man and who would not bring him another man's son whom he must accept as his own? What of the other children that they might have? She'd love any child she bore him, but always, Donal Frederick would be first in her heart.

It was impossible. She'd have to let Peter know that there was no hope for him, and if she had to tell him the entire truth about herself to make him accept it, then she'd tell him and that would be the end of it. She couldn't bear much more of this, she'd go mad.

Peter was still looking at her, with so much love in his eyes that it was all she could do to sit there smiling as if all was right with her world. She'd tell him tonight. There was no use in putting it off any longer, it would only prolong the agony for both of them.

But when the opportunity came to tell him, it hurt so much more than she had thought it would that she was almost undone.

They were in the garden that she had spent so many hours helping to plan, a flower garden so filled with scent and color that it made the senses reel. The fertile Florida soil and the unequaled climate made every sort of plant and flower thrive, so that almost anything the mind might conceive could be carried out. The gardens she'd known in Boston paled into insignificance in comparison, and the memory of her mother's ruined garden, abandoned after her death, made her want to weep.

Peter's face glowed with joy when she suggested that they walk in the garden after the meal was finished and the gentlemen had had their brandy and cigars. They had no sooner moved out of the sight of the windows than Peter gathered her into his arms, and she could feel him tremble with the insistence of his need, and her own body caught his trembling until her legs felt weak, as if they couldn't bear the weight of her body.

"Jennifer, you've put me off long enough! It's been so long, it seems like eons! I know that you had to have time, that you loved your husband and that it would take a good deal of time for your grief for him to heal. But you can't live all the rest of your life alone, it isn't natural, any more than it would be for me. You know how much I love you, you know I'll do everything in my power to make you happy! You need me as much as I need you, and it's time we did something about it before I go stark-raving mad."

His mouth came down over hers, and something inside of her broke. She pressed herself against him, returning his kiss with such ardor that Peter's blood burst into flame and his heart leaped with wild exultation.

"Oh, God, Jennifer, I've waited so long for this! We'll be happy, I swear that I'll make you happy!"

It was his use of the name that Carlos had chosen for her when she'd come to live at Solopi Heni that had brought her to her senses. She wasn't Jennifer DeHerrera, she was Cordelia MacKenzie, and she had no right to feel this longing, no right to even dream of finding happiness with Peter. She must live out the rest of her life as only half a woman, because anything else would be even more of a lie than the one she was living now.

She remembered, with a stab of physical pain, the last time she had visited Donal Frederick, when she and Carlos had been ready to leave.

"Mama, when will you come again? I don't want you to go, I want you to stay here with me. Don't go, Mama, please don't go!"

The memory tore through her, and Peter sensed the change in her. In the starlight, the stars so close and bright that the night seemed almost like day, she saw his mouth tighten and his face tense with the old, familiar hurt.

"Peter, I'm sorry. I'm so sorry! I want to say yes, you know I do, but I can't! Forgive me, I never wanted to hurt you."

Where was her recent resolution, arrived at less than an hour ago, to tell him everything? It was gone as if it had never existed. There was no point in telling him. He would only tell her that it was all right, that he accepted her for what she was and that he'd accept her son as well. But she couldn't marry him, she was Donal Frederick's mother first and a woman after that. She'd promised Donal, when Donal Frederick was born, that she'd take him to England, that she would see that he got the heritage that was his by rights. She'd promised herself as well, and she still had to do it, no matter how

Heaven's Horizon

long it took, and Peter could have no part in her plans, no part in her life.

Her face soaked with the tears that she couldn't hold back, she tore herself out of Peter's arms and left him standing there, his face pale and bleak with disappointment. She didn't sleep all that night. She couldn't bear any more of this. She had to get away, she had to be with Donal Frederick, to try to get her life into some kind of perspective.

When Carlos saw her pallor, the circles under her eyes in the morning, he agreed without hesitation to take her to visit her son. Seeing Cordelia unhappy was the one thing he couldn't bear.

Coming to the istihapo was like reentering another world. Weleka and Hilolo ran to embrace her, their faces shining with welcome and love. And then Donal Frederick saw her from where he was playing a game with long pointed poles with Little Thunder. They were thrusting the poles at an angle, the thrusts hard and vicious, and Cordelia shuddered, realizing what game it was they were playing. They were killing alligators in the Seminole way, by thrusting the pointed poles down their throats.

Donal Frederick dropped his pole and raced to throw himself into her arms. "Mama, have you come to stay? This time are you going to stay?"

She held him close, as if she could never let him go. He was her life, he was her world. Donal's son, all she had left of Donal. He had first claim on her life and no personal needs or longings could change it.

They stayed for three days, and before they left Cordelia had made up her mind. She'd return to Solopi Heni just this one more time. She couldn't simply disappear from the face of Florida's white world without questions being asked. But after she and Carlos made it known that she was leaving to make her home with a cousin in the northeast, a lady in her late sixties who needed her, she would come back to the istihapo and never leave it again until she and Donal could leave it together to go to England.

Carlos argued with her, bringing every argument he could think of to bear and searching for still more. It was mad for her to bury herself alive, it was mad for her to take such chances. Carlos roared and Carlos ended up by cursing.

"There's no reasoning with a woman! I always knew it and this only proves it. You're denying life itself, and ruining Peter's life in the bargain. It'll serve you right when Donal Frederick grows up and leaves you and his wife shuts you out of his life entirely! And you'll be stuck in England alone, in all that cold and damp and rain, and you'll remember Florida and Peter and know what you threw away!"

Nothing he said made any difference. Cordelia would do what she had to do, even if she regretted it all the rest of her life. She would always be grateful to Carlos for what he had already done for her, but she had to make her own decisions. Nothing that Carlos threw at her all during their journey back moved her. It was something that had happened at Solopi Heni while they were away that made her change her mind about returning to the istihapo until Carlos found out that it was safe at last for her to take Donal Frederick back to England.

A man had been there, a white man, a stranger. He'd asked a lot of questions about a young white woman with a small child, a young woman with dark hair and brown eyes who had run away from Georgia to make her home among the Seminoles. He had asked about a slave named Runt, a short man, but abnormally strong.

"I didn't tell him anything, Señor DeHerrera," Daniel, who had served as Carlos's majordomo ever since Solopi Heni's beginnings, told them. "None of us told him one little thing. We knew that you wouldn't want us to talk to a man like that even if we knew about such a young woman and such a child."

None of Carlos's house slaves spoke as ordinary black slaves spoke, their English was perfect, as befitted their dignity and intelligence. Some of Carlos's friends raised their eyebrows about it but Carlos ignored them.

"What did he look like, this man who came here?" Carlos asked.

"He's a sly-looking man, well dressed but he didn't speak like a gentleman. I don't believe he's known around these parts, Señor DeHerrera."

There was no doubt about it. Andrew Leyland hadn't given up his

Heaven's Horizon

search for Cordelia and her child. Going back to the istihapo to live, reunited with Donal Frederick, would be far too dangerous. If this latest agent of Andrew's had got this far, he'd search every istihapo in Florida, and there was no way that Cordelia dared to be where she could be spotted as Donal Frederick's mother, a white woman with a child who was also white no matter how fluently he spoke Seminole.

Chapter Seventeen

Marguerite Flemming MacKenzie looked at Donal across the breakfast table, and although her usual bright smile was on her face, her heart was heavy.

Marguerite had changed little over the years. Although by all standards she should be considered a middle-aged woman, her hair was still silvery blond, showing only a few strands of white. The lines around her eyes were virtually indiscernible; the mild, damp English climate had been kind to her complexion, and her skin was smooth and had that rosy look of youth that British women are blessed with. She was still slender, and when she walked she moved with the effortless grace of a girl.

All of Marguerite's movements were graceful, and Duncan MacKenzie's eyes lighted up with appreciation as she rose to take Duncan's cup to the sideboard and refill it with tea. He was a fortunate man indeed, blessed with this beautiful wife whose acceptance of him, a man many years her senior, still made him feel a deep and abiding gratitude.

Lydia Lancaster

The daughters she had given him were lovely, intelligent girls. Clara was already married to a rising young barrister, and Ann was all but engaged to the eldest son of a substantial country squire. And no man could have asked for a more satisfactory son than Donal, who had been a real son to him ever since he had been a toddler.

The house in Mayfair seemed quiet without the girls. Ann, who had always been the livelier of the two, was in the country visiting her young man's family. Duncan suppressed a sigh as he thought how different it would have been if Donal's wife, Cordelia, were with them now, and the child whom Donal had learned she had been pregnant with at the time of her disappearance.

It was a pity that Donal couldn't seem to form an interest in any other young lady. To Duncan's mind, which was as acute today as it had been thirty years ago, there wasn't a doubt in the world that Cordelia was dead, lost somewhere in the wilderness along with the slave with whom she had run away from her father. Donal's descriptions of that wilderness, with its hardships and dangers, left no room for doubt that the girl had perished. How could any gently bred girl survive such a wilderness, with nothing but the clothes on her back and the help of a slave who had no more experience in wilderness survival than she had?

All these years, Duncan thought. And still Donal remembered her, and couldn't bring himself to fall in love again and remarry. Two or three times, it had been a near thing, when Donal had taken an interest in some extraordinarily pretty and intelligent young lady. Both Duncan and Marguerite had crossed their fingers and hoped that this would be the one, that at last Donal would make the move that would allow him to live out his life as a happy and contented man, with the wife and children that he deserved to have.

But Donal's interest had always been brief. Mentally shaking his head, Duncan could almost wish that once Donal had been convinced that Cordelia was dead, he would have brought that extraordinary creature, the backwoods girl he'd gone through some outlandish wedding ceremony with when his memory had been lost, back

Heaven's Horizon

with him to England. From Donal's accounts of her, she had been quite intelligent in spite of her deplorable lack of background and education. Those lacks could have been remedied, the rough edges polished until the girl would have been acceptable in English society. Certainly she would have been capable of producing children.

"There you are. It's still nice and hot," Marguerite told her husband as she placed the cup beside him. "Donal, what are your plans for today? Surely you aren't going in to the office on a lovely day like this? Haven't any of your friends asked you to spend the weekend with them? You should have gone to the country with Ann, they especially asked you, and you like Jonathan." It was a blessing that Donal and Ann's young man hit it off so well, because long weekends in the country were just what Donal needed to lift him out of these dark moods that came over him every so often, the same kind of mood he was in this morning. Ann could always cajole a smile out of him, and Jonathan would have contrived to keep him busy so that his thoughts wouldn't dwell on the past.

"I'm afraid that I am going in to the office, Mother." Donal's smile was rueful as he saw how disappointed Marguerite was with his answer to her question. "I need to do some research on a case that's coming up, I'm sure there's a precedent somewhere if only I can lay my hands on it." Now that Duncan was getting on in years, Donal was taking over more and more of the practice that provided them with such a comfortable living. He wished now that Frederick Reynard were sitting at the breakfast table with him. Frederick's mind was so keen that he'd probably put his finger on the crux of the matter in an instant.

It was true that he needed to consult the tomes that lined Duncan's office, but it wasn't true that the matter was so urgent that it couldn't be put off until the first of the week. Donal felt a compulsion to keep busy, always to have some case or other in the uppermost part of his mind. Working, having to turn his entire attention to what he was doing, was his salvation, as bitter and unsatisfactory as it was.

Bessie Scroggins entered the dining room unobtrusively, as she always did, to lay the salver that held the morning post beside Duncan's place at the table. "It just arrived, sir," she said, bobbing.

Duncan sorted the letters with deliberate slowness, as he did everything in these later years of his life. At first it seemed as if there were nothing of importance. There was a letter to Marguerite from Lady Blanch, inviting her, no doubt, to help with a church jumble sale, and a statement from Duncan's tobacconist. Duncan totted that up, and reminded himself that he must cut down on smoking. The pipe tobacco he favored was out of sight these days, and although Duncan's financial position was such that he could afford anything he wanted for the rest of his life, it was foolish to throw money away on something that wasn't good for him.

The last letter was for Donal, and he handed it to his stepson with a little frown between his eyes. It was natural that Donal should keep up a correspondence with Frederick Reynard. The American lawyer had a personal liking for Donal that Donal reciprocated. But on the other hand, Mr. Reynard's missives always contained the news that he'd heard nothing of Cordelia, and Donal's face still tightened and an almost shamefaced hope leaped into his eyes every time one of them arrived.

It was the same today. Marguerite bit her lower lip as Donal broke the seal, aware that Donal's hands were trembling as he straightened the letter paper out so that he could read it. Like Duncan, she half wished that the correspondence between her son and Frederick Reynard would peter out, because the letters always left Donal despondent.

It was the same this morning. Donal's eyes raced over the words before he returned to the beginning to read more slowly, his face already bleak with disappointment.

There had been no news of Cordelia, and Frederick was sorry to have to tell him the same thing yet again. He and Lucy were delighted with their third grandchild, and Emery Haskwell was still proving to be an exemplary husband for Nadine and a satisfactory son-in-law, diligent in furthering the prosperity of his father's shipping company. Miss Virginia Baker was still well and vigorous and wanted Frederick to convey her appreciation for writing to her, although she herself had sent him a letter no more than three months ago in reply to his.

Donal refolded the letter. There was no need to read it a third time. Pushing back his chair, he walked around the table to plant a kiss on his mother's cheek. "I'll be off," he said. "Don't get into any mischief while I'm gone."

"You'll be back for dinner?" Marguerite asked. She almost wished that he would say he wouldn't. It would be better for him to seek the company of other young men of his age, even if it meant what she thought of as roistering in less than savory places, or spending hours in one of the coffee shops where young radicals were fond of tearing the government down and building it up all over again according to their own views.

"I'll be home. Don't throw my dessert away if I'm a trifle late," Donal teased her. That had been Marguerite's way of punishing him when he'd been a boy and come late to the dinner table. She'd never sent him to bed supperless or with only bread and milk, but desserts were expendable, not needed to build strong healthy bodies.

"You'd better not be late, then, or you may have an unpleasant surprise!" Marguerite bantered back, her eyes merry although they clouded again with pity for him as soon as he turned away. "Mrs. Bates has promised us a trifle, and it would be a shame to have to do without it, wouldn't it?"

Outside the house, it was a fine day, just as his mother had mentioned. There was no hint of rain, the sky was a clear blue, and a slight breeze had done much to dissipate the odors of coal and wood smoke that usually plagued London. Donal decided to walk. He needed the exercise, a long, brisk walk would help to alleviate the disappointment that was still roiling inside of him.

Cordelia is dead! he railed at himself. Why can't you face the fact, and accept it? She's been dead for years. If she hadn't already been dead somewhere in the wilderness, you'd have found her because God knows you left no inch of Florida unturned! Not only you, but Andrew Leyland.

The memory of his long and fruitless search still haunted him whenever his guard was down. The savagery of the Florida wilderness, the endless miles of brush that had had to be chopped through before he could clear a way for his mount, the huge stretches of swampland, the mosquitoes and other insects a torment, the heat of summer sucking the last drop of energy from his body, the chill of cold winter rains freezing him as he huddled in makeshift shelters at night. The wild animals, some of them extremely dangerous, so that even he, well-armed and a dead shot, had had more than one close call. How could Cordelia have survived, with only one unarmed slave to protect her? Survive afoot, facing hardships and dangers that a strong man could barely endure, let alone a gently reared girl, who was pregnant in the bargain!

His initial search had lasted for months. Gaunt, hardened, not recognizing himself on the rare occasions when he came face to face with a mirror in some settlement where he put up for a night or two to renew his strength and ask his endless questions, he had refused to give up, he had been determined that Cordelia was still alive and that if he searched for her long enough he'd find her.

He'd learned to eat the hearts of cabbage palms, to skin and gut rabbits and squirrels and roast them over a tiny, smokeless fire, to do without salt when he ran out of that precious commodity, to live off the land and to do without food when there was none to be had. He'd learned to have eyes in the back of his head, to recognize every least sound that could mean danger, to find his way through trackless stretches with only his sense of direction and the stars to guide him at night and the position of the sun by day. He had lost his last resemblance to an English gentleman and become a woods runner, indistinguishable from others of that breed.

He woke in the middle of a rain-drenched night and cursed himself for a fool. Cordelia wasn't in Florida, of that he was certain by now. And so it followed that if she were still alive, she must be somewhere else.

He set out for Saint Augustine that morning, as soon as it was light enough to see. The ancient walled town held little interest for him in spite of the fact that under normal circumstances he would have been enthralled by it. The buildings were made of coquina, a

Heaven's Horizon

mixture of shells and coral; old Spanish-built houses were frosted with lacelike iron balconies; the streets were extremely narrow because the town had been built before wheeled vehicles had become common. The brooding fort reminded everyone of the past as well as the present necessity of maintaining armed troops to keep the peace.

At the fort, he talked with General Wiley Thompson, who was the Indian agent as well as the commander of the fort. Surely, if Cordelia had ever been in Florida, word of it would have gotten to the agent. But although Donal took a liking to Thompson, who carried out his duties efficiently as well as having the best interests of the Indians at heart, wanting to do the best he could for them, the man had heard nothing of the girl Donal sought.

"I'll tell you frankly, Mr. MacKenzie, I think that your quest is a futile one. The chances are almost infinitesimal that your wife survived her flight from Georgia, but even if she had arrived in Florida and taken refuge with one of the tribes, if the Seminoles were determined that you shouldn't find her, you wouldn't have any chance at all. Personally, I think that she perished before she ever reached this territory. But of course I'll make inquiries, and let you know if there is the least word of her, if you'll keep me informed as to your whereabouts."

"I'm going to Boston on the first available coastal schooner," Donal told him. "Cordelia has friends there, people who would help her if she could get to them. It's a slim possibility, but one I can't afford not to investigate. I'll be at the Liberty Arms while I'm there."

"Mr. MacKenzie, may I suggest that if you find no trace of your wife in Boston, you return home to England? You can't spend all the rest of your life in the wilderness, searching for a girl who is undoubted dead. It would be a waste, and serve no purpose. The main part of your life is still ahead of you, and it would be foolish to waste it over something that can't be helped. In any case, I wish you the best of luck."

General Thompson's handclasp was firm, and Donal wished that he had more time to spend with him, perhaps to become friends. But his search in Florida was ended, and he must get to Boston and check out that last, faint possibility.

In Saint Augustine he rested, ate civilized meals in civilized surroundings, looking once again like a civilized gentleman with a clean-shaven face and new clothing. He walked the streets, admiring the masses of Cherokee roses that climbed over the balconies, breathing deep of the clean, salt air. How Cordelia would have enjoyed this historical town! The thought sent him back to his inn, heartsick.

His voyage to Boston was an agony. By some cruel circumstance, the coastal schooner was the *Sea Sprite*, the same one that had brought him to Savannah with his heart almost bursting with joy at the prospect of marrying Cordelia.

After a great deal of thought, he broke his journey at Savannah, and went to Leyland's Landing. He knew it would be a fool's errand, that Andrew Leyland would tell him nothing even if he had learned anything about his daughter, but what if by some impossible stretch of the imagination Andrew had found Cordelia, and she was at the plantation, still being held prisoner by her father?

By all rights he should lodge a formal complaint against Andrew, but once again he decided that it would be pointless and only delay the completion of his journey. Even killing Andrew would hold little satisfaction. If Cordelia was dead, nothing mattered, and Andrew would have to live out the rest of his already twisted and bitter life in even more bitterness. Death, Donal thought grimly, was too good for the man, because it would release him from his torment.

As he had before, he approached the plantation under cover of darkness, and he had a sense of *déjà vu* when he found Andrew again in his study, with the same window opened, so that he could catapult himself into the room before Andrew was aware that he had an unwanted visitor.

Andrew stiffened as Donal's feet hit the floor, and as he had on that other night so long ago, his hand darted to the desk drawer where he kept a loaded pistol, only to freeze at the sight of Donal's pistol aimed directly between his eyes.

"You! I thought I'd seen the last of you!" Andrew's voice was

Heaven's Horizon

without a trace of fear, and his eyes burned with hatred and the frustration of knowing that Donal had the upper hand and that there was no way he could finish the job he thought he had finished when he had shot his son-in-law and left him for dead in the bog.

"Have you heard anything of Cordelia? Anything at all, even a rumor?"

Donal's heart felt like lead at Andrew's answer, because there was no doubt that the man was telling the truth.

"I still have agents searching for her, but I've heard nothing. I believe she's dead, there is nothing else to believe. But as long as I can afford to have a watch out for her, I will continue doing so, because even a grain of possibility that she might still be living must not be ignored."

As he had before, Donal bound Andrew and left him in his study and went in search of Zoe. Having learned a great deal about the black slaves of the South, he thought it possible that Zoe might have heard something where Andrew had not. The grapevine between the blacks, even widely separated blacks, was beyond understanding but Donal knew that it existed and that Runt might have got word to his mother.

Zoe was in her lean-to room off the kitchen house, no longer locked in but as effectively a prisoner as she had been before. There was no place for her to run, no way she could escape. An old woman, growing more frail with each passing month, Andrew had no need to keep a guard over her.

But Zoe had heard nothing. She wept, her shoulders shaking, her face a mask of tragedy and grief. "They's dead, Master Donal. My head tells me that even if my heart won't accept it. They's dead, but I go on prayin' just the same. Now that you're back without findin' them, there just ain't no hope left."

Donal's arms were gentle as he held her to him. "Don't say that. Go on praying, Zoe. I'm going to Boston, she may be there or have sent some word. Is there anything you need, anything I can do for you?"

"I don't need nothin'. All I need is my Miss Cordelia an' my

Runt, an' if I can't have them or at least know they's safe there ain't nothin' left for me to want."

Going to the McCabes' holding was a duty that Donal would much rather have avoided, but his conscience made him do it. He had to assure himself that they were all right, he had to find out if there was anything he could do for them to help make up for what he had done.

Nate, coming home with a brace of rabbits he'd snared, was the first one Donal saw as their paths met. He had grown so tall that for a moment Donal didn't recognize him. His mouth dropped open as he gaped at Donal, his face filled with astonishment.

"Climb up," Donal invited. The horse he had rented in Savannah shied at the smell of him, at the smell of the dead rabbits, but Nate vaulted up behind the saddle without hesitation.

"You come back to stay?" Nate wanted to know.

"No, Nate. Not to stay. How are you, and the rest of the family?"

"We're all right. We're still here, anyways."

"And Becky?"

"She'll be mighty glad to see you, I reckon. But not so glad iffen you ain't goin' to stay."

Groaning inwardly, Donal thought that that was exactly what he was afraid of.

Donal had to stoop to enter the cabin, and the motion, that came so automatically after all the time he had lived there, made him wince. Eben was sitting by the fireplace, whittling something from a block of wood. A new bowl, Donal thought. Eben spent a great deal of time whittling, which was a deal easier on the back and the feet than working.

Etta was mixing corn pone to bake on the hearth, and the kettle of stew hung over the embers, waiting for the rabbits that Nate had caught. Rufe huddled on the floor in his favorite corner, his knees drawn up to his chin and his arms wrapped around them as he watched his father's knife send curls of wood shavings to the floor, his face wistful as he wished that he had a knife and could whittle like his father did. He could do it, iffen he only had him a knife, and he'd keep it sharp, too, just like his pa did, and he wouldn't go a-losin' it.

"We got company," Nate, who'd entered the cabin before Donal, announced. "Lookee who's here."

Eben and Etta had barely had time to start with surprise when Becky came in from the other cabin, which was now her own private domain. By all rights she should have a man to share it with her, and she'd almost done it, too, missing Donal like she did and cussing herself to sleep every night while her body ached for him till it hurt like blazes. She'd let Mort Hadley court her, and she'd let him do a sight more than that, once, but while her body had been satisfied she'd known that she could never marry him because he wouldn't ever be able to satisfy her mind and her heart, no matter how much he loved her and begged her to marry up with him. So she'd sent him packing, even though she'd called herself a fool for doing it because Mort was strong and a good worker. But although two or three other men, more or less as acceptable as Mort, had come courting her, she'd never seen one who could hold a candle to Donal. And until she did, she reckoned she'd just have to stay single.

Becky screamed, and then she was all over Donal, her arms wrapped around his neck, her body pressed against his as though she were determined to get right inside of him.

"You come back! I knowed you would, I knowed it! You just had to come back!"

Donal felt like a cur as he pushed her away from him. "I'm sorry, Becky. I'm glad to see you, glad that you're well, but I haven't come back to stay. I'm on my way to Boston and I only stopped in to see if everything is all right here."

"It ain't all right! How kin it be all right, without you? Damn you, John Martin! You're my man, and you belong here with me!"

"Becky, I'm not John Martin. I'm Donal MacKenzie, and I'm married to another woman."

"She's dead! We done heared about it, Pa heared when he was to town. Run off, she did, and wasn't never no trace of her, for all her pa had a dozen men a-searchin' fer her. And as long's she's dead,

Lydia Lancaster

you're my husband, there ain't no two ways about it. An' as long as you ain't John Martin an' nobody's a-huntin' you, we kin get hitched in town an' do it right this time, so's there won't be no mistake."

"Becky, I have no proof that she's dead, and as long as I have no proof there's no way I can marry you. And I still love her, I'd never be able to give you the love you deserve even if I did know for sure that she was dead."

Becky threw herself at him again, and this time she kissed him, her tongue darting out so that Donal felt sweat beading his forehead and a flush of heat like fever envelop his body.

"You love me enough! I could make you forgit her, I know I could! Don't go a-leavin' me agin, I couldn't stand it!"

Once again, Donal extricated himself from her embrace. "It wouldn't do, Becky. You'll just have to accept that." He wished he were a thousand miles away, anywhere but here. To ease the situation, he turned to Eben. "How are things with you, Eben? Is everything going all right?"

"Old mule died," Eben remarked, as though he was unaware of the drama that was being enacted before his eyes. "Old Stubborn just laid him down an' died."

"Corn crop weren't good. Won't hardly hev enough fer plantin' come next spring," Etta remarked. "Likely we'll hev to depend on Nate's trapline an' huntin' to make it through."

Donal reached into his pocket. "I can give you enough to buy another mule, a good, strong animal. And seed corn, and something extra to get whatever you might need. Rufe, what would you like?"

"Kin I hev me a knife, a good sharp un like Pa's?" Rufe's face was so bright and shining that Donal swallowed. He looked at Etta for her approval, and Etta nodded.

"Like as not Rufe could handle him a knife. Lord knows he's been a-wantin' one long enough, we just couldn't never scrape it out."

"And material for clothes for you and Becky, and shoes," Donal said. "And snuff, and something for Nate and Eben." He handed her the money, she would be the one to decide how every dollar of it would be spent. She accepted it in the spirit it was given. It wasn't like it would make them beholdin' to Donal. Donal had been Becky's husband for a spell, an' they'd done for him when he'd needed it, so now it was all right that he should do for them.

"I don't want no new dress, I want you!" Becky stormed. She was still beautiful, vibrant, radiating sexual appeal that would draw any man to her.

"Becky, it ain't fittin', carryin' on like that. You'll set an' eat with us, Donal?"

"No, I have to be going." He was hungry, but he couldn't face taking a meal here, having Becky going at him. "I only wanted to thank you again for all you did for me, and make sure that you were all right."

He left the cabin, anxious to put as long a distance between it and himself in as short a time as possible. But Becky followed him, clinging to him, her eyes streaming tears that drenched her face. "Don't you dast go! Don't you dast!" she screamed. Donal had to fight her off to remount his wildly prancing horse, frightened by her screaming and the struggle that was taking place under its feet.

Even then Becky followed him, running after him, calling for him to wait. Donal's face was set and grim as he resisted the urge to turn and look at her. He touched the horse with his heel and set it into a fast trot and then a canter. When he did look back, after Becky's voice had become faint from the distance he'd put between them, she was still running. Cursing under his breath, he urged his mount to an even faster pace, until he could no longer see or hear her.

He felt as if he had been whipped. But Boston lay ahead of him, and the sooner he got there, the sooner he would learn whether Cordelia had managed to get there or to get a message either to the Reynards or to Virginia Baker. It was the only hope he had left.

It was a hope that was dashed on his arrival in Boston. The Reynards were shocked to learn Cordelia's story and his own, but they had heard nothing. Lucy and Nadine both wept. Virginia Baker didn't weep, but her eyes were dark with sorrow. She felt a personal responsibility, because she had had a large part in bringing the two young people together.

Lydia Lancaster

Donal did not remain long in Boston. He remembered General Thompson's advice, and he knew that for his own sake and the sake of his mother and father he should follow it. The Reynards' kindness to him only made him feel more alone, Nadine's happiness with Emery Haskwell, whom she had married, only made him feel more desolate.

He returned to England late in 1832. He had spent well over two years in his search for Cordelia. And now, in the autumn of 1835, he still remembered her, and the memory hurt as unbearably as it had when he had first admitted to himself that further search was useless. Cordelia was dead, she had been dead for years, and unless he wanted to spend the rest of his life in sterile solitude, and break his parents' heart in the bargain, he must decide what he was to do with the rest of his life, he must settle on some woman to marry, someone who wouldn't remind him of Cordelia, who was as different from Cordelia as it was possible to be.

At home, Duncan had gone into his study to go over some papers, more for something to do than because it needed to be done. His semiretirement irked him, he'd only entered into it because Donal needed more to do, and although he was glad that running the law office kept Donal busy and contributed to saving his sanity, Duncan himself was hard pressed to fill up his days.

Impatiently, he yanked at the drawer where the papers were that he wanted, and it came out too fast, and fell to the floor. Scowling with still more annoyance, Duncan knelt to gather the papers up, with the intent of sorting them immediately and putting them back more neatly so that the drawer wouldn't jam again.

Some papers had made their way down behind the drawer, in that annoying way that papers had, and he reached in and extracted them, glancing at them first. And then his hands froze as he saw that one of them was a letter that still had an unbroken seal and he broke the seal and opened it, and the blood left his face as he read what was written there.

Cordelia was alive, or she had been alive when this letter from a Señor DeHerrera, who lived in Florida, had been written to him. Alive and safe in some Seminole village, and Señor DeHerrera

Heaven's Horizon

intended to befriend her and see that no harm came to her until such time as he could safely send her to England.

Shaking, Duncan shouted for Bessie to run and fetch him a cab. He must get to the office at once, without a moment's delay, and place this letter in Donal's hand.

Chapter Eighteen

Cordelia was a little annoyed when Daniel rapped at her bedroom door with the message that Carlos wanted to see her in the library immediately.

"Miss Jennifer can't come right now. You go and tell Master Carlos that she's busy and she'll come as soon as she can." Delores, the ladies' maid Carlos had spent a fortune for in Saint Augustine, offering such a price for her that her master had overridden his wife's protests and sold her, informed Daniel. No matter what price Carlos had paid for her, Delores was worth every penny and more, Cordelia said, and thought, that the thirty-five-year-old woman, who was both an expert seamstress and a genius at dressing hair, was worth her weight in gold.

Even more than for her services to Cordelia, Cordelia valued Delores as a friend, as mother, sister, and aunt all rolled into one. Delores was always cheerful, her pleasant face always wore a smile, and her patience was without parallel, so that she was always ready to listen to Cordelia's problems and offer the best advice she could.

"Master Carlos says that he wants to see Miss Jennifer now. *Right* now!" Daniel insisted.

Cordelia turned from the cheval glass where she had been inspecting herself in the gown she was going to wear for this evening's festivities, and sudden alarm made her slip the dress from her shoulders and reach for a dressing robe. If it was that urgent, something must have happened, and motherlike, her mind flew to Donal Frederick.

"Your slippers!" Delores exclaimed. "Miss Jennifer, put on your slippers, you can't go running around the house in your bare feet!"

"Bother my slippers! Something's happened to Donnie!" Cordelia's face was white as she sped from the room and passed Daniel on the staircase, almost toppling him over in her hurry to find out what was the matter. Behind her in the bedroom, Delores shook her head and picked up the discarded gown, inspecting it with an eagle eye for the least trace of dust before she hung it away. Delores wasn't one to look at the dark side of things. It wasn't possible that there could be bad news on the afternoon of Christmas Eve with the house filled with guests and Miss Jennifer already in a dither about being a credit to Master Carlos, and everything going as smoothly as it should in a well-run household.

Carlos was sitting behind his desk, a massive piece of furniture made of mahogany and polished to such a sheen that his reflection showed in it when Cordelia burst into the room, her hair disheveled and her eyes filled with alarm. This room, with its book-lined walls—and Carlos had read nearly every one of the books—and its deep maroon hangings, reflected both Carlos's taste and his love for the good things in life. The decanter on the desk was of Irish crystal, the paintings on the walls were a sampling of the old masters, the carpet a priceless oriental.

"What happened to him?" Cordelia demanded even before she came to a halt in front of the desk.

"May I ask what the devil you're talking about?" Carlos wanted to know. "What happened to whom? And how should I know what happened to him when I don't know who 'he' is?"

"It isn't Donnie, then? Nothing's happened to Donnie?"

Heaven's Horizon

"Women!" The word was inflected with exasperation. How could anything possibly happen to Donal Frederick, with Weleka and Wacassa looking after him, with Hilolo and Sam Brent fighting for the privilege of keeping an eye on him, and Stillipika always hovering near him, every inch a protective grandmother? "He's the best-protected boy in the istihapo, as you know perfectly well, never out of the eyesight of one or all of them. I want to talk to you about Peter."

Now that her first fright had abated, Cordelia's heart gradually slowed down to a reasonable rate of beating. "Peter? What about Peter, Carlos?"

"You know perfectly well what about Peter. Cordelia Leyland MacKenzie, you are without a doubt the most stupid woman it has even been my misfortune to know! How long do you think you can go on dangling him on a string without his turning to another woman, or several other women?"

Cordelia was completely taken aback. For some unknown reason, unless she was as stupid as Carlos had just said she was, such a thought had never crossed her mind. It was true that Peter kept coming to Solopi Heni even though she had told him that she couldn't marry him, but he was Carlos's friend, and she thought that he was hers as well. Her astonishment was evident in her face as she stared at Carlos, nonplussed.

"And not women you would care to know," Carlos told her, his face more serious than she had ever seen it. He was in no mood to be gentle. This had gone on entirely too long and his patience was at an end, even if Peter still had a little left. "Peter isn't the sort to dally with any decent woman when he has no intention of marrying her. But there are women, one after another, and sooner or later he's going to be hurt."

"But, Carlos, how could it hurt him?" Cordelia wanted to know, even as she struggled with an emotion that she had never dreamed that she would feel in connection with Peter Breckenridge. It was jealousy—plain, unadulterated green-eyed jealousy—and it surprised her so much that it was difficult for her to recognize it for what it was. "I mean, don't gentlemen do that? In the South, that is. I'm not sure that many of them in the North indulge themselves in that manner although I know that some of them do. I'm not a complete innocent."

Carlos threw back his head and laughed. "My dear Cordelia, you're as innocent as a newborn infant! How could it hurt him, you ask! Let me tell you a few of the more unpleasant things of life. Women of the sort Peter is consorting with are apt to have diseases that are not in the least pleasant and that are impossible to cure. And sooner or later Peter is going to come into intimate contact with such a woman, with a very good possibility of becoming sterile at the least, or of going blind, or of rotting away as more than one king of England and Europe did, back in former times, although I doubt that any history Miss Virginia Baker taught you included such unsavory facts. Insanity is one of the lesser evils that can result from contracting such diseases. At least if a man goes insane, he might not mind so much about the other things that are happening to him."

Cordelia was appalled. She had never before heard as much as a whisper of such things as Carlos was telling her. It made her ill, and it made her conscience hurt her until she couldn't bear it. If such a thing were to happen to Peter, it would be her fault. Dear, good Peter, whose temper sometimes exploded until she was afraid he'd strike her or even take her by force when she said no to him yet once again, but who would never allow himself to do such a thing no matter the provocation.

No, he hadn't struck her, or taken her by force, although by all rights she wouldn't have been able to blame him if he had. He'd remained faithful to her, refusing to give up, when she'd flirted with and had brief romantic episodes with half a dozen other men in her efforts to discourage him. But instead of helping the situation, according to Carlos, it had only driven Peter to other women, the kind of women Carlos was telling her about, to find relief from his physical and mental torment.

She couldn't go on doing this to Peter, in all conscience she couldn't. Besides, the thought of even such casual contact with other women, even though they could mean nothing to him, made her

Heaven's Horizon

tremble again with that jealousy that she had only this moment discovered she was capable of feeling.

"I'll say it again," Carlos told her, with no hint of his normal good humor on his face. "You are a fool! You're throwing away one of the best men who ever walked the face of the earth, and for a ghost! You can't go to bed with a ghost, and it's time you realized it. A ghost can't warm you on a cold night, or offer you a shoulder to lean on when you need it, or give you the extra children that you need if you're ever to be a complete woman. Peter can give you all that, and the assurance that you will never be alone or lonely again, and still you go on dangling him as if you had all the years in the world to make up your mind. When in reality they're slipping away from you at a pace that one of these mornings you'll wake up and realize that you've thrown away everything that would have made your life worth living."

It was true, every word of it was true, but there were obstacles. "There's Donal Frederick," she said, her voice shaking. "What about Donal Frederick?"

"Tell him about Donal Frederick. Tell him the whole story. If Peter's the man I think he is, he'll accept it, and love you all the more for it. Donal Frederick needs a father, and he couldn't find a better one if he searched the world over. So tell him, and get it over with, and for the love of all that's holy, marry him! If you don't, you're going to be sorry all the rest of your life. You'll watch yourself growing old, alone, and watch Peter's body and his mind disintegrate from one of those diseases I told you about, and your grief and your regret and your guilt will be more than such a slender pair of shoulders can bear."

Carlos was being brutal, but Cordelia knew that he was being brutal for her own good. She thought about what he had told her after she returned to her room, she thought about it deeply and long.

Peter had been patience itself, he'd had the patience of a saint, but he was very far from being a saint, he was very much a flesh and blood man with the needs of any healthy male, needs that had to be satisfied because nature itself demands it.

And she had her own needs, as strong as Peter's although a

woman wasn't supposed to admit the existence of such needs. Admit them or not, they were there, and they were getting worse instead of better and, in the meantime, just as Carlos had said, her life was slipping away from her. In a few more years she'd be middle-aged, her life behind her and nothing to look forward to.

Donal was dead. No amount of weeping and longing could bring him back to her. And she was alive and she had to go on living because of her son, if for no other reason, and she couldn't go on living alone much longer or she would crack into a million pieces.

There was Carlos to be considered as well. It wasn't fair to him. Not being either blind or a fool, Cordelia knew that Carlos too was a man, with a man's needs and desires. And she was a woman, a beautiful and desirable woman, and living a celibate life as he did, her presence under his roof throughout the months and years, the knowledge that she was sleeping in a room just down the hallway from his, must be a torment to him.

Carlos could laugh off his single state and his desire to go on in his single state all he wanted to, but Cordelia knew that he must spend countless sleepless nights thinking of how near she was, and fighting against his natural impulses. As grateful as she was to him, owing him as much as she did, she might very well have gone into his arms, not only because of her gratitude but because she was so genuinely fond of him and because of her own needs that cried out, endlessly, to be fulfilled.

It was time it came to a stop. Carlos was right. Either she must accept Peter now, or suffer the consequences when everything that made life worth living fell apart.

"Miss Jennifer, are you going to sit in front of that mirror staring at yourself all the rest of the afternoon, or are you going to get yourself ready for this evening?" Delores demanded. "It's time to stop mooning, or I won't have time to do your hair properly, so get up and get yourself in that bath that's been ready for you for fifteen minutes before the water gets stone cold!"

When they were alone, Delores talked to Cordelia in a manner she wouldn't have dreamed talking to her in the presence of other people, even the other slaves. To Delores, Cordelia was the daughter

Heaven's Horizon

she had never had, the daughter that her own pride had refused to let her bear. She was a mulatto, the result of a liaison between her mother and one of her mother's master's friends. Her mother had been beautiful, and her mother had been sold away, forced to leave Delores behind when the master's wife had decided that her mother was too much temptation not only to her husband's friends, whose wives were her own friends, but to her husband himself.

Delores had not inherited her mother's beauty, and the lack was something she had thanked God for every day since she'd been old enough to understand such things. By no means unattractive, still, as a young girl, she'd made herself as inconspicuous as she could. Her gentle manner and her being so quick to learn had caused her mistress to single her out, to bring her into the plantation house to help first with the sewing and mending and, as her skill had improved, to being a seamstress. She had learned to do her mistress's hair when her mistress's personal maid had been ill, and until her mistress had died, when Delores was seventeen, she had been well protected.

By that time, Delores had been able to protect herself, her determination not to be forced to bear a child to be raised as a slave giving her the strength to fight off the amorous advances of the three different male slaves her master had tried to mate her with. At last, Delores had been sold to be the personal maid of a vain middle-aged wife of a successful merchant in Sant Augustine. Safe now from the fear that she might bear a daughter who would be as beautiful as her mother had been, a daughter who would have been singled out and forced to live a life of shame as the plaything of some white master, she had been the best ladies' maid in Saint Augustine, so far above the others that other ladies coveted her and often tried to buy her. But all such offers had been refused until Carlos DeHerrera had offered her mistress's husband such a figure for her that the man hadn't been able to refuse.

At Cordelia's instigation, Carlos had offered Delores her freedom, but she had refused.

"I'm better off as I am, if you don't mind. Here, I know I'm safe and protected, but who knows what might happen to me if I were free? Even if I could set myself up as a dressmaker, there would always be danger. Bounty hunters don't always bother to check into papers if they see a chance for a quick profit. A black person alone is easy game. Thank you kindly, but no. I'll stay where I am. I'm content here, more content than most slaves can ever expect to be."

Slave she might be in name, but not in fact, and so she dared to order Cordelia around as if Cordelia had actually been the daughter she had always wanted to have. And of all the slaves at Solopi Heni, of all the people in Florida who knew her, Delores was, with the exception only of Carlos himself, the only one who knew Cordelia's whole story. Delores was Cordelia's friend, her confidante, her second mother.

"Up, up! It's getting late, the ladies will be getting up from their naps and your other guests will be arriving and you won't be ready. Don't worry about what's going on downstairs. Daniel and I have checked everything, all you have to do is make yourself beautiful."

Bathed and dressed at last, her shell pink gown fashioned of soft cut velvet from France, Cordelia was so breathtakingly lovely that even Delores could not wish for more. Pearls adorned her throat and ears, and Delores handed her a fan fashioned from pink-dyed egret feathers. She needed no other ornaments. As Carlos had once told her, she was the masterpiece, everything else was merely the frame.

"You can wear that Empire gown, you have the perfect figure for it. Some of the other ladies look like pork-barrels with a ribbon tied near the top! Now you get yourself downstairs and let all the gentlemen eat their hearts out. The ladies will hate you, but that will be our triumph. And don't you go drinking too much of that bubbly wine Master Carlos got in, that packs a wallop and it won't do for you to get giggly. I'll know if you take too much, and you'll hear from me in the morning, when your head's splitting, and you won't get any sympathy, either."

"Delores, you know I never overindulge!" Cordelia protested.

"Humph! That depends on what you mean by overindulging. Seems to me that I remember laying cold cloths on your forehead not a month past, when you didn't overindulge! And all because you felt so bad because you'd had to turn Peter Breckenridge down

Heaven's Horizon

again, and you'd best take Master Carlos's advice and put the man out of his misery tonight. It's my advice too, darling. Now run along. You're as beautiful as I can make you, and nobody could ask for more than that."

Cordelia was beautiful, and she knew it. The knowledge radiated from her, gave her confidence and poise. And it was reflected in the eyes of all of the gentlemen as she greeted them, standing beside Carlos as his niece and hostess, but most of all in Peter Breckenridge's eyes.

It was a small gathering, as such gala occasions go. Carlos was always careful never to invite anyone to Solopi Heni whom he did not know well, any recent acquaintance who might conceivably carry the story of Cordelia's beauty to other ears, from where it might conceivably reach Andrew Leyland's ears and set him to speculating. On the few occasions when Carlos took Cordelia to Saint Augustine to shop and to enjoy the fine restaurants and the company of his good acquaintances there, or to Pensacola during the season to see the horse races, he kept her close within his own small group, shielded from the prying eyes of strangers, although by now she was so well established as his niece that there was little danger.

On this Christmas Eve there were twenty-two guests, so that there were twenty-four around the table. The house was festive with trailing ivy and pine branches, there were flowers everywhere, and a clump of mistletoe hung from the crystal chandelier in the drawing room to tempt gentlemen to maneuver ladies under it for a stolen kiss, and ladies to maneuver themselves under it by calculated accident if no gentleman took the initiative.

Cordelia had no such problem, as every gentleman present strove to entice her to the desired position, while Carlos looked on with amusement and Peter with grim-faced resignation. Flushed with excitement, her eyes shining with the happiness of having at last made up her mind that she was going to accept Peter, Cordelia was happier than she had ever dreamed she could be after Donal's death.

"You're as hard to capture and hold on to as a sunbeam!" Peter accused her when at last he had her in his arms and they were waltzing in the ballroom, which glittered with the reflections of

Lydia Lancaster

hundreds of candles in the crystal chandeliers, all reflected back from the mirror-lined walls. "And now that I have you, for a moment, there isn't a sprig of mistletoe in this whole room! Whose oversight was that?"

"It wasn't an oversight," Cordelia teased him. "I thought it would result in chaos to have mistletoe in here. Couples would be colliding all over the place, trying to get under it while they dance. You should have claimed your opportunity in the drawing room, before the dancing started."

"And have to fight for the privilege? No, thank you. If I can't have you all to myself, I have no desire to have you at all." His face still glum, he pulled her closer into his arms, and Cordelia saw that his jaw was clenched.

How many women had he known, had he been with in the Biblical sense? The thought came unbidden into her mind, and as it had before, it filled her with furious jealousy. Tonight would be the end of it, because she wasn't going to give him another opportunity for as long as he lived! As she gave herself up to the joy of waltzing in his arms and the anticipation of telling him, later, when she would take him out into the garden, that she was going to marry him, she had no idea that at Fort King, and in another place leading to the fort, dramas were about to be acted out that would change the course of every living soul in Florida.

They danced until midnight. Cordelia's slippers were worn through so that she as well as some of the other ladies had to excuse themselves to change into the spare pairs they had provided themselves with for this occasion. Kneeling to lace the ribbons around Cordelia's ankles, Delores admired the foot she held in her hands.

"If I'd been dancing all evening, my feet and ankles would be swollen up till I couldn't get into another pair of slippers! But look at yours, nobody would even know that you've been on your feet for hours. That's the joy of being young, child. Appreciate it while you can."

"And I'm going to dance for hours more!" Cordelia caroled. "But first, before the midnight supper, I'm going to kidnap Mr. Peter Breckenridge and take him into the garden, and the next time you see me I'll be an engaged woman! Oh, Delores, what a shame that I can't be married in white! A bridal gown seems so much more like a wedding. But widows can't, we won't even be able to have the huge wedding that Peter deserves, it wouldn't be in good taste as this will be my second marriage. I'll have been cheated out of a big, beautiful wedding twice!"

"You can have a big party afterward, a real celebration ball, to make up for it," Delores told her complacently. "And the wedding will be so beautiful that it'll make up for not being big. I've been planning that wedding for months. You'll wear a cream-colored gown, that's close enough to white, and you'll be the most beautiful bride the world has ever seen. Master Carlos is going to give you a string of pearls so long that I can wind it in your hair, and you'll wear your saphires to contrast with your dress. You'll be lucky if Master Peter doesn't die from joy when he sees you walking toward him. Stop your fretting and get back downstairs and take Master Peter out into that garden and let him know what a lucky man he is. Go on, scat!"

Cordelia scatted. She seemed to float down the staircase, her newly slippered feet scarcely touching the treads. She wasn't surprised to see Peter waiting for her at the foot, it was as though this moment had been ordained.

"No, not to the ballroom. I'm overheated, I want to walk in the garden for a few moments," Cordelia said as Peter started leading her back to the dancing.

His face lighted up. "May I take the mistletoe from the drawing room with me?"

"You won't need it, you goose."

Still feeling as though she were floating, Cordelia slipped through a side door directly into the garden. The winter evening was chilly, but not cold. People who lived in Florida, she thought, couldn't conceive of the cold of a severe Boston winter, of the snow and ice and sleet, of the bitter winds that chilled even heavily clothed bodies to the bone. She didn't even bother to take a shawl. Her excitement, her happiness, was more than enough to keep her warm in her short-sleeved dress, and if they weren't, then Peter's arms would.

"Now?" Peter asked, stopping under an arbor.

"Now," Cordelia said. She didn't wait for him to make the first move, she stood on tiptoe and wrapped her arms around his neck and kissed him, so hard and so long and with such fire that Peter gasped as if from pain.

"Damn it, Jennifer, you don't know what you're doing to me!"

"I'm just preparing you for a story I'm going to tell you. It's a long story, so you'll need at least that kiss for fortification. And I want you to listen, without interrupting, will you promise me that you will?"

"Of course I will. You know that I'll do anything you want."

"All right. In the first place, my name isn't Jennifer DeHerrera. My name is Cordelia Leyland MacKenzie. Shhh! Remember your promise!" Her fingers pressed against his lips silenced his astonished exclamation. "And now I'll tell you the rest of it."

It took a long time to tell it. Peter kept his promise not to interrupt, but it cost him an effort. He couldn't help making sounds of dismay and distress as Cordelia's story went on to the end, but he uttered no word. He only held her closer when she faltered, his cheek pressed against her hair.

"Good Lord," he said at last. "Good merciful Lord! Jennifer..."

"Cordelia," Cordelia corrected him. "Only you mustn't call me Cordelia."

"Jennifer, Cordelia, I had no idea! My poor darling, my dearest darling!"

Cordelia's face glowed with joy as she raised it to meet his eyes. "I'm still your dearest darling?"

"You'll always be my darling! Now, more than ever, a hundred times more than ever!"

"Then I'll give you your Christmas present right now. Peter, I'm ready to marry you. I've made up my mind. I love you and I want you and..."

That was all she was allowed to say. For a moment, she thought that the strength of Peter's arms around her was going to break her in two. His mouth was like fire against hers, bruising, filling her with rapture. How was she going to wait until after they were married to consummate her love for this man? And if it would be hard for her, how much harder it would be for him! Especially, she thought mischievously, since she meant to give him no opportunity to relieve his aching needs with any other woman! No more of that, not now or ever. Peter was hers, and she wasn't the kind of woman who would share her man!

She didn't know how long they stayed in the garden. It wasn't until a chill breeze brought gooseflesh to her bare arms that she realized that they had left the others far beyond the the dictates of decency. Her guests would be raising their eyebrows, speculating, giving each other knowing looks.

"We must go back in, or you'll be a ravished bridegroom before we're married!" she laughed at last.

"Give me a moment or two, or I'll disgrace myself, because my happiness has gone straight to a vital spot of my anatomy and everyone would notice the bulge. No, don't kiss me again, for God's sake! We'll just walk for a moment, and I'd appreciate it if you didn't even hold my hand."

Cordelia broke into peals of laughter that doubled her over and hurt her stomach. She couldn't help it. Putting her hands behind her back and clasping them together firmly, so that they wouldn't stray toward him of their own accord, she finally managed to fall into step with him, still giggling to think that in one respect women were more fortunate than men, because no such outward manifestation could cause them embarrassment.

But although Peter was fully in control when they returned to the ballroom, Carlos knew, the moment his eyes fell on them, that Cordelia had taken his advice. At last! His face lighted up, filled with the joyous anticipation of announcing the engagement of his niece and Mr. Peter Breckenridge at the midnight supper, which had already been delayed well past midnight because these two inconsiderate people had stayed in the garden for so long!

And it was just about time, Carlos thought, although no hint of his emotions was discernible on his face. His endurance, these last few months, had been rapidly running out. Cordelia had been little more than a child when he had found her in the Seminole village, a young, frightened child who had cried out for someone to defend her. Her body too thin except for where it had been swollen with pregnancy, her face pinched and her eyes still dark and hollow with grief even though the Seminoles had treated her with kindness and Weleka and Hilolo and Stillipika had been her special friends, she had exuded no sexual appeal for him but had only aroused his compassion.

She had still been little more than a child when he'd brought her to Solopi Heni, even though she had been a mother. Hardened by the work she had insisted on doing at the istihapo to earn her keep, browned by the sun, dressed in a shapeless Seminole dress, and still grieving over Donal MacKenzie, she had still excited no sexual response in him, but only a determination to succor and protect her.

But a change had taken place since she had come to live at this plantation. Her life of luxury, her exotic environment, had transformed her until just the sight of her was enough to make him ache with love for her, ache with wanting her. He, years too old for her, a half-breed, a man who could never take a wife or sire a child without complicating all of their lives so badly that he had put the idea away from him years before! Cordelia was his niece, he had made her his niece, and that was the way it was, but it would be a heartfelt relief to see her married to Peter and out of his house.

He'd miss her. *Madre de Dios*, how he'd miss her! His house would be no more than an empty shell without her, devoid of her laughter, of her light footsteps, of her gaily teasing voice. Devoid of the beauty that he adored, of the companionship that meant so much to him. And unlike Peter, he couldn't relieve his emotions and his needs with a woman of bad repute, because he had sworn that he would take no chances of bringing a bastard child into the world, a child who would have no place or sense of identity.

It was time for the midnight supper. And after the happy announcement had been made, they would dance again, until even the most avid reveler would be forced to stop from sheer exhaustion. This was Christmas Eve, or rather, Christmas Day, and all unpleasant thoughts must be banished. It was a time for joy, not for dark thoughts and musings.

But Carlos knew, there was scarcely a man in the territory who did not know, that underneath the peaceful surface of Florida there was a seething volcano ready to erupt. Carlos was afraid that the seeds of that eruption had already been sown at the conference between the Seminole chiefs and the army, when the chiefs had been called upon to honor the treaty that their representatives had signed without knowing what it was that they had signed.

Some of the chiefs had agreed, some had demurred. Those who had demurred had been ordered to sign the treaty, they had been reviled, told that they were not men of their word, told that their disgrace would go down in history and that all men would turn their backs on them. In the face of this railing, some of those who had demurred changed their minds. Dishonor was something they could not tolerate.

But Osceola, who wasn't a chief at all, had responded in his own way when he was ordered to sign the paper agreeing that the Seminoles would allow themselves to be removed from Florida, as the delegation to Arkansas had agreed when they had signed the false treaty at Fort Gibson. Drawing his hunting knife, he had plunged it through the paper deep into the wood of the table on which the paper lay. That had been his answer before he had stalked from the conference, with Wildcat and more than one other young chief and brave following after him, to disappear into the surrounding forest before the startled army officials could order that they be stopped. By the time the white men's wits had returned to them, there had been no sign of the defiant Osceola and his followers, the forest had swallowed them without a trace.

There had been incidents after that meeting, ugly incidents, so ugly that Carlos didn't like thinking about them although he knew that they had to be thought about. An isolated cabin burned here, its occupants slain, scalped, mutilated. Seminoles alone, or in twos or threes, who were surprised by white men, were beaten or shot down with no chance to defend themselves. Fields were burned, cattle driven off, and some of the settlers were already taking to their heels to get out of Florida before every white person in the territory was massacred, while others determined to stand their ground and fight it out until the Seminoles were exterminated.

Lydia Lancaster

The volcano was simmering, seething, just below the surface, and every thinking man knew it. Osceola had called the chiefs who had agreed to honor the treaty traitors, and condemned them to death if he could lay his hands on them. Osceola would not leave Florida, and neither would Wildcat, or Alligator, or any number of other chiefs and braves who listened to his words and believed them as they quietly bought up powder and shot in whatever small quantities the traders would sell to them, storing it for future use, a future that was growing closer with every passing day.

But this was Christmas, and Cordelia and Peter were engaged, and this celebration must not be marred by thoughts of what was to come. Smiling, Carlos led his guests to the dining room, his heart warmed for this moment by the happiness on Cordelia's face.

Cordelia was studying her reflection in the mirror again, while Delores looked on with tolerant amusement. Peter had come to Solopi Heni yesterday, and stayed until the middle of the evening, and the results of his visit were still visible on her face.

There was no doubt about it. Her mouth was as swollen as if it had been stung by a bee. And slipping the neckline of her dress off her shoulders, she touched the bruises placed on her arms and breasts gingerly but tenderly, smiling with dreamy eyes as she remembered every detail of the moment when Peter had inflicted them on her.

He hadn't meant to hurt her, or to leave her mouth bruised and swollen. He'd simply been carried away by his passion, as the reality of their engagement got through to him and his impatience for their marriage reached its limits. And Cordelia hadn't objected because her own body had been anesthetized by the desire that had flamed through her, until she had clung to him shamelessly while she fretted against the months that would have to pass before they could satisfy their flaming needs.

More than once, they had been tempted to jump the gun, as Delores put it. But Peter managed to hold back at the last moment, unwilling to do anything that might cause Cordelia pain later, and Cordelia had remembered Delores's warning in time.

Heaven's Horizon

"Don't you go jumping the gun, young lady! I don't want you having to get married in a Mother Hubbard to hide your condition, and you're ripe, Jennifer, you're as ripe as they come. You'd get pregnant if you sat in a chair a man had just got up out of! So you be careful, because I don't want you shamed, and I don't want Master Carlos shamed, and I don't want all of Solopi Heni shamed and I don't want to be shamed myself. To say nothing of that little son of yours. Maybe he's too young to know what it's all about now, but when he gets older he might take a notion to go comparing dates and see that there's a discrepancy between the time you were married to his new daddy and the time there should have been before his little brother or sister was born. And take my word for it, boys are more unforgiving than girls when it comes to their mothers! A boy puts his mother on a pedestal, only a little lower than an angel, and they can't handle it if they find out their mother isn't an angel or a saint."

Cordelia had remembered, but obeying Delores's injunctions hadn't been easy and she had a feeling that it wasn't going to become any easier as the days both dragged and flew by. Peter was coming again tomorrow night. That Peter! If he didn't stop spending half of his time at Solopi Heni his own plantation would begin to deteriorate before they were married.

"You look like a tabby cat that's lapped up the cream," Delores told her. "You haven't lost your good sense, have you?"

"No, I didn't forget, darn you! I wish I had! It would be easier to bear today!" Cordelia told her, as irritable as she could ever be with Delores. "Oh, Delores, it's so long until we can be married, why do people have to wait so long after they fall in love? Drat people and their mean, suspicious minds anyway! Sometimes I think that civilization is more trouble than it's worth! If I could just walk between you and Carlos tomorrow, to stand by Peter's side and that would make us married, it would be a whole lot more civilized than having to go through all this torture!"

"You can't go flinging yourself in the face of custom. You'll just have to wait the best you can."

Delores broke off as they both heard the sound of pounding hoofbeats. A horse was being ridden faster than any other horse had ever been ridden up the long, winding drive to the plantation house. Cordelia jumped up from her dressing table and ran to the window to see who it could be. Carlos was away. Two days after Christmas, he had taken a wagon and a handful of slaves to the nearest trading post of any size, whose proprietor had sent him a message that a load of goods he'd ordered had arrived, including three cases of the finest French cognac. Restless after the quiet that had followed the Christmas festivities, he'd welcomed the chance at something to fill his time.

Cordelia's face paled as she saw that the rider was Carlos, that Black Fire, his prize stallion, was lathered and near exhaustion, and that Carlos carried a small boy in front of him.

Donal Frederick! Oh, God, what had happened? As pale as death, her heart pounding with terror, she sped down the stairs and out through the front door just as Carlos reined to a stop and handed her son down to her.

"What is it, what has happened? Don't just sit there on that horse, tell me!"

"All hell has broken loose," Carlos told her, his face so grim that it made her feel faint. "On December twenty-eighth, Micanopy and Wildcat and a large war party intercepted and ambushed a large column of soldiers marching for Fort King. Colonel Dade and his entire command, except for two or three who managed to get away, were massacred."

He paused to wipe the sweat from his forehead, and his face was as pale as Cordelia's. "And to top it off, Osceola and another small party of warriors jumped General Wiley Thompson and his aide when they were taking a walk after their dinner, only a few yards from the post! Jumped them and murdered them, and went on to murder the sutler and his family for good measure!"

Cordelia held her wildly struggling son close to her pounding heart. "Oh, Carlos, no!"

"I wish it were no," Carlos said, his eyes bleak. "It's come, Cordelia. It's war. There won't be any stopping it now. This whole territory is going to go up in smoke. The istihapo is already virtually deserted, only the old are still there. Hololo and Sam Brent only stayed behind to keep Donal Frederick safe until I came for him. The others are gone, into the forests and swamps, the warriors, the women and children.

"They'll fight, and run and hide and fight again, and no one can even guess how long it will go on. For myself, I think that it will go on for as long as Osceola can draw breath. The others listen when he speaks, and they follow him, and he has determined to drive every white man out of Florida so that his people can keep the land that rightfully belongs to them."

Cordelia held Donnie even tighter, her heart breaking for Carlos, for Weleka and Wacassa and their son Little Thunder, for Hilolo and Sam Brent, for Little Acorn and Stillipika, who had gone with the younger Seminoles in spite of their age, to help any way they could. How many of them would live to see the end of this war, how many of them would she ever see again? And Carlos was torn apart. Half Seminole, half white, his life was with the whites but his heart was with his mother's people.

Cordelia didn't ask him what he was going to do. He probably didn't know himself, yet. But holding Donal Frederick close, safe in her arms, her heart broke and broke again.

Chapter Nineteen

By the time Donal disembarked from the coastal schooner at Saint Augustine he was frantic. He'd heard rumors about the Seminole war in Florida ever since he had reached America. The Indians, the story went, were being troublesome, but what could anyone expect of savages? They'd broken their treaty with the United States and were running amok, murdering white settlers right and left so that no one was safe outside of walled forts, and even then their safety was doubtful.

Not that the rebellion would last long. What chance could a handful of savages, a few thousand at the most, have against the army of the United States? Troops had been sent in to reinforce those already there, and the whole thing would be over with in a matter of weeks.

Donal was told that he would have been wise to postpone his visit for a month or two, until the uprising was quelled. As long as he was already here, he'd best stay in Saint Augustine. Searching for his wife, was he? Like as not she was already safe behind fortified walls, or she'd already been murdered by the savages. In any case, it wouldn't do to go looking for her, it would only be throwing his life away for no purpose.

Saint Augustine was in turmoil when Donal left the schooner. The town was filled with refugees who had fled to find shelter there. Whole families occupied one room, and tents and hastily erected shacks had been thrown up out of any material that came to hand. Food was scarce, and fear was rampant.

Donal went immediately to the fort, to inquire about Cordelia. He was shocked to hear of Wiley Thompson's death. Surely the Indians had made a mistake when they had murdered him, because Donal had had the impression that Thompson had had the best interests of the Seminoles at heart and had been determined to do his best to see that they were not mistreated or cheated.

The officer who talked with him shook his head, making it obvious that he had no time to waste on such a request. He'd never heard of Cordelia Leyland MacKenzie being located by the agents Andrew MacKenzie had sent searching for her, and although he had heard of Señor DeHerrera, it would be the worst kind of folly for Donal to try to make his way to Señor DeHerrera's plantation, because to reach Solopi Heni he would have to cross through hostile territory, where the chances of reaching his destination were almost nil. The officer had heard rumors that Señor DeHerrera had a niece living with him, but he had never seen the young lady and it was virtually impossible that she could be Donal's wife.

Disheartened, Donal explored every nook and cranny of the refugee camps. He talked to everyone he saw. Cordelia Leyland MacKenzie? Young, beautiful, with black hair and brown eyes, and possibly with a child who would be six years old by now?

"Mister, you know where we kin git some victuals? My young'uns is hongry, my woman's starvin' herself so's they kin hev more of what little we kin come by." The men who made that request were starving themselves, by the look of it, their faces gaunt and their eyes hopeless. There were only a few men of fighting age among them. The younger, stronger men were out hunting Seminoles and the other Indians from other tribes who had made their homes in Florida who had joined them.

Heaven's Horizon

"Ain't no use of your lookin', iffen she hain't here. It'ud be like lookin' fer a needle in a haystack. Mister, iffen I'd come from England, I'd of stayed there! Leastwise there you wasn't in no danger of gittin' yer scalp lifted."

"My wife took refuge with the Seminoles more than six years ago," Donal told them. "I have good evidence that she reached them and that they took her in."

"Then she's daid, mister. Ain't no way she ain't daid. She's white, ain't she? They'd of kilt her fust off, once they decided to go killin' an scalpin' every white pusson in Floridy, man, woman an chile. Iffen I wuz you, I'd git back on the fustest ship I could find and hightail it back where I come from."

"She was befriended by a plantation owner, a Señor DeHerrera, he wrote my family that she was well and being cared for. But with all this going on, he might have come here for refuge."

"He ain't here, as I know on. DeHerrera, you say? I heered tell of him. Big place he's got, livin' high on the hog. Ain't never seed it myself, but I've heered tell of it. It's a far piece away, mister. Ain't no way you kin git there, things bein' the way they are. Them redskins is all over the place, just waitin to jump out at anybody foolish enough to try to travel around."

"Can you tell me exactly where it is?"

"Not rightly. You'll hev to ask around. Somebody'll know, I reckon. You sure you don't know where I can lay my hands on some victuals? My young'uns are mighty hongry."

Heartsick, Donal gave the man a few dollars, although what he could buy with it was doubtful. Even in circumstances like these, he had to convince the man that what information he had been able to give was helpful enough to be worth the price. The pride of these people, so like the McCabes, always astonished him. Such, he thought, is the backbone of a nation.

From what he'd seen here in Saint Augustine, he was glad that Cordelia wasn't among the refugees. The thought of her living in such primitive, filthy conditions, crowded, hungry, was unbearable. Disease was bound to raise its ugly head before much more time had passed, as well. Still, he went on searching doggedly until he was

319

convinced that she wasn't here and that the only thing for him to do was to go in search of Señor Carlos DeHerrera at the plantation that was called Solopi Heni. Unlike the men he had questioned, Donal knew the meaning of the name. He had picked up a smattering of the Seminole language during his first futile search for Cordelia, when he had been in almost constant company with one guide or another. A fanciful name for a plantation, he thought, and he hoped that it lived up to its name and was indeed a heaven as well as a haven for his wife.

The directions he was given for reaching the place were precise enough, he knew that he wouldn't have any trouble finding it. The time he had spent in the wilderness searching for Cordelia had given him an unfailing sense of direction. But he found that there wasn't a horse to be had in all of Saint Augustine. Every creature that was fit to be ridden was already in the hands of men who were out fighting the Seminoles.

"You're insane!" he was told at the fort, where he'd gone as a last resort in search of any kind of mount, no matter how poor. "To set out on such a journey alone is nothing less than suicide! I've half a mind to lock you up until you come to your senses. If you weren't a foreigner, I would. All the same, any able-bodied man in Florida now has no business searching for a woman who's obviously dead, but should be out helping us to round up the Seminoles so that Florida will stop being a slaughterhouse!"

Donal winced. The slur against his moral sense cut deep, but he had to think of Cordelia first. This wasn't his country, nor was it his fight. But Cordelia was very much his concern, and the child that he might or might not have. It hadn't been born when Señor DeHerrera had written to his parents, the letter had been lost for so long that it had cost Donal precious years. The child might have been stillborn, or died later. But he would not believe that Cordelia wasn't alive. And now, with this brutal war, she needed him more than ever, and he had to find her and if he had to walk to Solopi Heni, then he'd walk.

He walked. The men who watched him leave shook their heads

Heaven's Horizon

and told each other that he was insane, and speculated on whether or not all Englishmen were as crazy as this one.

"It's kind of a pity, at that," they agreed. "He was a likable feller, fer all he wuz an Englishman." They were already referring to him in the past tense even though he was scarcely out of their sight.

Donal blessed the time he had spent in the wilderness, and the hardness and the ability to survive its hardships that it had given him. If it hadn't been for that, he wouldn't have had a chance of making it to Señor DeHerrera's plantation alone and on foot, traveling through stretches of country so wild that even native Floridians might quail at it. Every sense had to be razor-keen as he traversed forestland, his ears as well as his eyes and his intuition as he fought his way through underbrush, as he strained for the least indication that there were Seminoles in the vicinity. His only weapons were his pistol and a hunting knife; like horses, rifles had been unavailable to sell to a man who was walking into death, on a wild-goose chase.

Hunger was his constant companion, gnawing at him day and night. What rations he'd packed with him, slung over his shoulder in a leather pouch, were soon gone, and he had to live off the land. Most of the small settlements and trading posts he passed were deserted, their inhabitants fled to safer places, even though the main area of the war was farther to the south. He didn't dare to use his pistol to bring down small game, both because of the danger of the shots being heard by savage ears and because he might later have desperate need for the few bullets he had. The snares he set out at night, before he slept, netted him an occasional rabbit, and the fish he managed to catch kept him from starvation, as well as such edible roots and berries as he could find.

He had not only to be constantly alert for Seminoles but to take the greatest care not to leave signs of his own passage through this wild country. He built no fires at night, not even the tiny smokeless star-fires he'd learned to build on that other search, for fear that the light would be seen by alien eyes, and he fumed at the delay that having to stop to cook his game in the daytime caused him.

Lydia Lancaster

On his third day out, his never-faltering alertness paid off. A small war party trotted past his hiding place in a thick clump of brush, where he crouched not even daring to breathe.

As prepared as he had been for such an encounter, he was still appalled at the sight of the Seminoles. Gone were the tunics and leggings of their traditional dress. Clad in nothing but breechclouts and long stripes of red and white and green and orange war paint on their bodies, and with their faces splotched with circles and designs, the hideously transformed warriors seemed to have no relationship to the civilized and gentle people he had known in the past. They trotted their horses in single file, their eyes moving from right to left, and Donal fought down nausea as he saw the scalps that dangled from their belts. It was fortunate for him that they were in a hurry, otherwise there would have been a very good chance that they would have discovered him.

He didn't dare to move for an hour after the Seminoles had passed. When he crawled out of his hiding place, his knees felt weak and his legs were trembling. By all rights his own scalp should have been hanging from one of the Seminoles' belts at this moment, and if he wasn't extraordinarily cautious and extraordinarily lucky it would probably adorn some other Seminole belt before long.

A few miles farther on, he smelled smoke. Crouching low, moving with the utmost caution, he crept forward to discover its source. It wasn't smoke from a campfire, although the sickening smell of charred meat hung heavy in the air.

At the edge of a clearing he stopped, frozen to the spot. There had been a cabin there, but now all that was left standing was part of the chimney. He saw the remains of a butchered cow, scattered feathers, the corn patch that had been trampled and ruined. But it was the bodies that made his stomach churn and the acrid vomit rise in his throat.

There was a man and a woman, both scalped. The man's genitals had been cut off and stuffed into his mouth. The woman was worse. A stake had been driven into her body between her legs. Lying at the base of a tree, a child of three or four, a boy, spilled his brains out onto the ground where his head had been shattered against the trunk.

And a short distance away, a little girl, no more than six or seven, had been butchered. It was the first time Donal had known that people's faces sagged down in thick wrinkles when their scalps were gone, no longer giving support to skin and facial muscles.

Going gingerly to the ruins of the burned cabin, he saw what remained of a cradle, and that was the source of the smell of burned meat. The infant, what was left of it, was so charred that there was no way to tell whether it had been a boy or a girl.

Buzzards were circling overhead, drawn to their grisly feast. What little Donal had eaten that day came up, in long, convulsive shudders, until he felt as if his insides were being torn apart.

His retching stopped when his ears picked up a noise even though the sound of his sickness almost drowned it out. Instinctively, he flung himself behind the nearest tree and cocked his pistol.

But this was no war party. The men who came into view were militia, making enough noise so that any Seminole party within miles of them would have located and been able to track them down. There were about twenty of them, led by a baby-faced lieutenant who must be fresh from his training and who looked bewildered and totally unable to cope with this unheard of kind of warfare that hadn't been covered by any of the books or drills that had made up his training.

"Will you be kind enough to hold your fire? I'm a white man," Donal called before he stepped out from behind the tree. His precaution had been a wise one, because a dozen rifles were aimed at his midsection and even with his warning it was pure luck that more than one finger didn't squeeze a trigger.

"What the devil are you doing here?" the lieutenant demanded before his face turned the color of putty at the sight that had already cost Donal so much agony.

"I'm on my way to a plantation called Solopi Heni. I had a close brush with the war party that did this."

"Dirty, savage beasts!" the lieutenant choked. "How far ahead are they, do we have any hope of catching up with them? We've missed them at every turn, the devils melt into thin air just when we're sure we have them at last!"

"Not a prayer, if you go barging ahead making enough noise to be heard clear to the Okeechobee, and all afoot. Haven't you any horses?"

"Back there. Not that they haven't been more hindrance than help, in this abominable country! We've had to hack out passage for them more than once, and it held us up until we lost those savages entirely and it gave them a chance to do this! Bates, Simmons, take a detail and bury these poor souls. It's all we can do for them now."

Seeing the buzzards still circling, hoping that these live people would soon leave, the lieutenant drew his pistol and his face whitened with astonished fury as Donal slapped down the hand that held it before he could take aim and fire. "Just what the devil do you mean!" he exploded.

"I mean that you ought to save your ammunition, and not advertise your presence to any other Seminoles who might be within hearing distance, if they haven't already heard you with all the racket you've been making!" Donal's voice was sharp. "There's a chance we might come up with the war party that did this. I know what direction they were headed." Sick at heart, he wished he didn't know. The Seminoles were headed in the same direction he was taking, and although he had been told that the fighting hadn't spread that far to the northwest, how could he be certain that they wouldn't go on to attack Solopi Heni?

"If you think you can move without making enough commotion to be heard back at Fort King, I'll guide you," he said.

"You tell him, mister!" a lanky man of near middle age, his teeth stained by tobacco juice, said, a grin splitting his bearded face. "I done been tryin' to tell him ever since I jined up, but he thinks he knows more'n a ignorant cracker 'cause he's had book eddication. But you're a gentleman, even if you do appear to hev more sense tham most of 'em, so mebbe he'll listen to you."

"That's enough, Pettigrew!" the lieutenant said sharply before he turned back to Donal. "You're a guide? We lost our guide. Either he's been killed, or he's run away. More likely he ran away."

"I'm not a guide, but I can make a stab at it. I've had experience in the wilderness. Have you seen much like this?"

The youthful look was gone from the lieutenant's face now, and he looked older than his years. "Yes. Too often." He held out his hand. "Cary Bullfinch. And I'm grateful for your offer of help, Mr.—?"

"MacKenzie, Donal MacKenzie."

"You're an Englishman? What are you doing in Florida, alone out here, when there's a war going on?"

"It's a long story. Right now we'd better get these people buried, and push on. The war party that did this already has too much of a head start."

Loads were shifted on the packhorses to free one of them so that Donal would have a mount. The animal wasn't used to being ridden, it was balky and it had a gait that jolted Donal's spine every time it took a step. He was grateful that he had to dismount and walk so much of the time to make sure that they were still on the right track. His eyes, keen and accustomed to looking for sign, had no difficulty in telling him that they were following the Seminoles even if they might not overtake them.

"Make sure that all of your men are ready to go into action at an instant's notice," Donal told young Bullfinch. "Don't believe for a moment that we'll be given any warning, once they know we're on their track. They'll either melt into the wilderness without a trace, as you already know, or jump us before we have any idea that we're within miles of them. And don't believe for a moment, either, that they won't know we're trailing them."

Cary Bullfinch's face and voice were as grim as Donal's.

"We'll be ready, Mr. MacKenzie."

They pushed the horses as fast as the terrain would allow, every man filled with bloodlust as the scene they had left behind them refused to erase itself from their minds. If they could kill even a few of the marauding devils, it would be balm to their hearts. It was maddening to come across scenes like that and never be able to lay a hand or even an eye on the Indians who had perpetrated them. Most of the men were of the opinion that if they had known it would be like this, they never would have joined the militia.

Ten miles from the burned cabin and the newly buried bodies, all trace of the Seminoles' passage disappeared. They knew that their presence had been discovered, and they had vanished.

Donal felt like cursing as heartily as the enlisted men. There was no point in going on this afternoon, it was near sunset, and even Donal couldn't search for sign in the dark. They stopped to make camp and prepare their evening meal, still cursing.

"Put out that fire!" Donal demanded. "Now! Don't any of you know how to make a smokeless fire?"

They didn't then, but they did the next morning, after Donal had shown them.

"You'll stay with us?" Cary Bullfinch asked, wolfing down his portion of cornmeal and bacon gone rancid.

"As long as you're headed in my direction. And if we come across any Seminoles on the way, I won't take it amiss. But wherever you head when our paths part, I'm going on to Solopi Heni."

He winced as the man Bullfinch had called Pettigrew took out a comb and began combing a scalp that Donal had noticed hanging from his belt the evening before. "Do you allow your men to take scalps?" he demanded.

"Certainly not. But it isn't that easy to stop them, when they have the opportunity, as few and far between as opportunities are. Sometimes I have a little trouble with my eyes and I don't see all that I should see." It was as good an answer as any.

"Why did they, the Seminoles, do that to the woman at the burned cabin?" Donal asked, not sure that he wanted to know. "Wasn't just killing her and scalping her enough, without that?"

"It's so the woman cain't hev no more white babies even in the beyond," Pettigrew drawled, taking care to untangle every snarl in the scalp. "Makes sense, in a way, even if it is downright uncivilized. Me, I'm satisfied with a scalp."

Donal shuddered. Those dark-skinned men, whom he had known to be civilized and gentle when he had been here before, were capable of brutal savagery that he wouldn't have been able to imagine even a week ago. He prayed that the woman had been dead before they had impaled her. The thought of her suffering made his mind turn black. He tried not to think about what the refugees back in Saint Augustine had told him, that if Cordelia had still been with the Seminoles when this war had broken out, they would have killed her. His mind screamed through the blackness as he fought down the image of Cordelia being murdered and scalped and mutilated as had the woman who had lived in the burned cabin.

"Clem over there..." Pettigrew nodded in the direction of another man much like himself, "...likes to take a woman's scalp 'cause they's purtier, longer-like, but it sort o' turns my stomach to scalp a female even if it be an Injun. Never did scalp no youngster, either."

"Women and children!" Donal's breath exploded from his mouth with the words. "Surely no white man would scalp women and children!"

"Some do, iffen the wimmin an' chillern are fightin', and there's times they do. When a batch of 'em's cornered, the wimmin fight alongside their men, an' they fight near as good, to boot. Strong critters they be, most on 'em, an' fierce as ary warrior. This here be a war, Englishman, an' we cain't allers pick who we want to fight, we take it like it comes."

"But the children aren't killed! Surely not the children!"

"Sometimes they git in the way, seems like. Tryin' to stick a knife in our bellies iffen they cain't reach no higher. I had me one sink his teeth in my leg a spell ago, hung on like one o' them pit bulls they use in dog-fightin' at fairs. I done thought I never would shake him off afore he hamstrung me!"

Donal felt forced to ask the question. "Did you kill him, this little boy?"

"Nope. We had 'em licked. Sent 'em back to Saint Augustine under guard, to be held for removal. Two, three, o' the wimmin was kilt afore they decided to quit fightin', and some o' the warriors got clean away, disappeared like they do even when yer eyes is fastened plumb on 'em. That boy was still a-hollerin' at me, his face all screwed up with hate, when he wuz marched away with his ma. We found two dead babies, too young to walk, arterwards, but none o' us did that, their own mas done it so's they wouldn't hamper 'em in the runnin' an' fightin'."

Donal looked at the cold coffee that remained in his mug, and felt bile rise up into his throat. He emptied the coffee onto the ground. He was glad that he hadn't eaten much. Mothers killing their own babies! What a fierce determination they must have, not to be forced to leave their land! It seemed as if there should have been some other way, that whites and Indians could have reached a compromise so that they could live side by side in peace. Surely this territory was large enough for both!

He could remain silent, and as a stranger in this country he supposed that he ought to, but he felt compelled to make his sentiments known.

"Couldn't enough land have been found for the Seminoles, well out of the way, so that they could have stayed here, seeing that they feel so strongly about it?"

"Might could be. But this here's our land, Englishman. Ain't no sense lettin' Injuns take up space we need. Iffen they'd druther stay an' fight till they's all kilt off, that's their decision, not ourn."

The subject seemed to be closed. Wearily, Donal followed the other men's example and found a place to lie down and get what sleep he could before he took his turn at sentry duty in the small hours of the morning, the most dangerous time, when his wilderness-keen senses would be of the most value.

They moved on in the morning, grim, determined, but there was no sign of the Seminoles. They couldn't even pick up any signs of the war party that they had been pursuing. The Indians had simply vanished.

Donal lost count of the days. One day was like the day that had gone before, march, eat, rest, and march again. They passed two or three other burned-out holdings, pitiful evidence of the war that was raging farther to the south as marauding parties of Seminoles struck toward the north in their determination to wipe all the whites from the face of Florida. But they found no more slain bodies. Ray Pettigrew told him that the chances were that the cabins' owners had fled before the savages had struck.

"Only a few stubborn ones insist on stayin' put, thinkin' they'll be lucky an' not git hit at all, or they'll be able to fight off the varmints iffen they are hit. Most on 'em's long gone, an' they won't come back an' build their cabins agin an' start over till this here war is ended. A lot of 'em won't never come back, they've hed a bellyful, but there'll be ten to take the place of every one that skedaddles fer safer places, once we've cleared Floridy of the Injuns. I wisht I'd hed me the cash money to buy up a passel o' land, so's I could be a rich man when the new settlers come pourin' in. Them land speculators, they's the ones goin' come out of this rich." He spat to the side of the trail, shifted his rifle to a more comfortable position, and squinted his eyes against the sun.

And so it had been since the beginning of time, Donal reflected. The backbone of a country, the common, honest, hardworking man who toiled with his hands and his heart, took the brunt of the wars, while the scoundrels reaped a fortune from their misfortunes. There was nothing to be done about it, except to hope that in future generations things would be different.

"Iffen you find yer woman, I reckon you'll be hightailin' it out o' here," Ray Pettigrew said.

"I expect I will. England is my home, my family and my work is there."

Donal changed his mind two days later, when they came upon the ruins of another burned-out homestead. This had been a larger, more prosperous holding than the first one Donal had seen laid to waste. From the looks of the cleared land, its crops destroyed, the livestock either slain or driven off, it appeared to have been on its way to becoming a small plantation.

Now all of the buildings, including what had been a modest house instead of a cabin, were burned to the ground. The remains of bodies were everywhere, some picked clean by the buzzards, others with remnants of rotten flesh still clinging to the bones. Adults and children, the clothing they'd been wearing stiff with dried blood that had turned black in the sun and air. Two men who had been full grown and white, from what they could piece together from what their sickened eyes saw. Three women, and eleven children. All of them had been scalped, and there was evidence that all of them had been mutilated as had the bodies Donal had first discovered. One of the men and two of the children had been black. This particular slave must have chosen to fight beside his masters, and the two half-grown black boys with him.

There was nothing left that was usable. There had been two slave cabins, as far as Donal could make it out; the other slaves had undoubtedly chosen to cast their lots with the Indians, because there was no trace of them. All of the guns, the knives, the axes and other tools had been carried off.

Their faces white and sick, their eyes filled with shock in spite of having seen such things before, the men shook their heads as they went about burying what was left of the victims. There was no way that they could spare the time to dig individual graves. All were gathered together, to be decently covered by the earth for which they had given their lives.

"Hark! What was that?"

Ray Pettigrew, whose ears were even more keen than Donal's, cocked his head as his eyes went to a clump of brush some distance from the homesite.

Donal's eyes followed the direction Ray's had taken, and he strained his own ears. Ray hadn't been mistaken. There was the faintest of rustlings in the center of the brush, before all was still again.

"Alert! Rifles at the ready!" Donal barked before Lieutenant Bullfinch was aware of the danger. Seminoles? It didn't seem likely, but it was possible. In any case, they must not take chances.

"Come out of there!" Donal commanded. "Whoever you are, show yourself!"

There was no response. The lieutenant, his pistol in his hand, flanked by two wary-eyed militiamen, started toward the bushes. Donal hurried to lay a hand on his arm. "Not you," he said. "If anyone is in there it wouldn't do for you to get yourself killed."

"An' not you," Ray grasped Donal's arm and swung him aside. "Jist in case that wife o' yourn is still alive, it better be somebody else."

Heaven's Horizon

Covered by every rifle in the company, Ray walked forward, his own rifle at the ready. Breaths were held as he reached the clump of bushes, and even the chirping of the birds seemed to be stilled.

Cautiously, his rifle poking ahead of him, Ray forced his way into the brush, and an instant later his voice came back to them clearly, filled with disbelieving astonishment. "I'll be dogged!"

He came out, leading a child by the hand. It was a girl, probably eleven or twelve years old. Her dress hung on her skeleton-thin frame, her face and arms and legs were covered with scratches and bruises, some of them old and half healed, others still fresh. Her almost colorless hair hung in tangles around her shoulders, and her face was deathly pale as she let Ray lead her. But it was her eyes that brought expelled breaths of disbelief and pity from every man there.

Her eyes were dead. They could see, but they were pools of emptiness.

Somehow, no one would ever know how it had come about, this child had managed to escape the massacre that had wiped out every other member of her family. The mystery of how she had kept herself alive until now was another one that would never be solved. Roots, bark, grass, whatever she had found to eat had had so little substance that there didn't seem to be any flesh between her skin and her bones at all.

Now a sound made the hair of every man rise on the back of his neck and his flesh creep. It was a sound so alien to them, never heard before, that it took them a moment to realize that it was coming from the child. It was a high keening, without meaning, heartrending. It went on and on until Ray clapped his hand over her mouth.

"Reckon she's about hed it," Ray said. "From the looks o' her, it mighta been more merciful iffen she'd died with the others."

They petted her, they soothed her. Her eyes remained blank, and whenever she got her breath back after breaking off she began her keening again. It was eerie, and the men exchanged uneasy glances. They didn't blame her. They could see that her mind was gone, wiped out from the shock of seeing her family butchered.

They fed her. She was ravenous, tearing at the food like a wild animal, which in retrospect she was. Donal tried to stop her from wolfing the food so fast but he was too late, and it came up again.

This time Donal fed her, a morsel at a time, with spaces in between. Her eyes were fixed on his face, but without understanding, and she opened her mouth for each morsel like a baby bird, snapping and gulping. When she had taken all Donal dared give her, she began to keen again.

It was Ray who stopped it. "Mebbe she'll understand this," he said. Shamefaced, but desperate to try anything, no matter how outlandish, he took the Seminole scalp from his belt and put it into her hands.

"Injun," he said. "Seminole. Dead Seminole."

The girl held the scalp in her hands. Slowly, with a grace that seemed ludicrous in such a situation, she sat down on the ground as a grimace of such hatred and fury crossed her face that Donal's heart contracted. She began to beat the scalp, beating it against the ground.

"Wal, there's somethin' still left in that mind o' hern," Ray said. "She knows how to hate Injuns."

"What in God's name are we going to do with her?" Donal asked, sick at heart.

"We'll have to take her with us," Bullfinch answered. "It's been in my mind for the last two days that we're wasting our time in this section. The Seminoles have cleared out. I'll have to take these men back to the fort and get another assignment where we might have more luck. There'll be some family that will take her in."

And maybe, with a woman's arms around her, with a woman's voice to soothe her, this child might regain her sanity. Donal had to tell himself that he believed that she would. But he wasn't so sure that regaining her sanity would be the merciful thing. Sick in every millimeter of his being, he clenched his jaw and knew that he wouldn't hightail it back to England once he'd found Cordelia and his child.

This must not be allowed to go on. England was Donal's home, but his conscience told him that if he didn't remain in Florida and

Heaven's Horizon

help to put an end to this nightmare, to this wholesale slaughter of both whites and Seminoles, he would never be able to live with himself again.

When he found Cordelia, when he had taken her to a safe place where she could be in no possible danger, he would offer his services in whatever capacity the army chose to use him. If his doing so would bring this bloodbath to a stop even one day sooner than it otherwise might, it would be well worth it.

Chapter Twenty

He was challenged before he even knew that he had stepped across the boundaries of Solopi Heni. For the past several days he had been well out of the path of the war that was raging farther to the south. Here, the country through which he passed had seemed free of the red marauders, and the two small settlements he had stopped at had not been evacuated, with the inhabitants fleeing for the safety of walled encampments or forts.

This was the country that the Seminoles had given up in a former treaty, when they had been led to believe that the lands farther to the south, in mid-Florida, were to be theirs.

He'd been given precise directions at the last settlement, a place of one short main street and a few shacks and cabins, with a trading post as its principal reason for being. No Indians had been sitting against the walls of the trading post or looking with stolid faces at the wares that they couldn't afford to buy once they had exchanged their furs and hides or alligator skins or other commodities for the things that they needed the most. In Donal's former wanderings, he had noted that the ones who lingered at the posts had been of the baser sort, eager for rum. The others, the large majority, left the posts as soon as their business had been transacted, and returned to their villages to go about their lives of dignity and producing the crops and doing the hunting that had assured them of a happy and bountiful life.

"Made themselves scarce," the proprietor of the trading post, a man named Isaac Jones, for whom the settlement had been named, had told him. "Disappeared overnight, seemed like, else they'd have been rounded up and held for removal. They might have been drunk, but they weren't too addled to know that, and they lit out for parts unknown. We've been lucky here, the war hasn't spread this far north, it's the lands they thought of as their own that they're fighting for."

"Do you know a plantation called Solopi Heni?"

"Certain sure. Ain't far from here. You head northwest and you'll come on it tomorrow if you step right along. Where are you from, mister? Englishman, aren't you? I thought I recognized the accent."

"I came from Saint Augustine. It's been a long journey."

"Saint Augustine!" Jones's eyes widened with astonishment. "Alone, and on foot? Mister, you must have a guardian angel, else you'd have been dead two days after you started!"

"I wasn't alone the entire time. I met a detachment of militia a few days out, and joined up with them for a while, while we were trying to run down a band of marauding Seminoles who'd burned out a homestead and murdered a farmer and his family."

"Didn't catch them, of course. You never had a prayer, if they had any head start at all. You've earned yourself a free drink. Any man who could make his way all that distance, alone and on foot, has earned himself a drink."

It wasn't the raw rum that was kept for trading with the Seminoles that Isaac Jones offered him, but brandy, of a quality good enough to surprise him. "Keep it for my own use, and for such plantation people as trade with me," Jones explained. "Drink up, Mr. MacKenzie. Now that you're almost home free, you deserve to celebrate."

Donal accepted the brandy with gratitude, but he declined to stay long enough to celebrate. He only asked permission to clean up, to

Heaven's Horizon

bathe and comb the tangles from his hair and the short beard that had already grown since he had set out from Saint Augustine, and to buy a new set of buckskins to replace the old, travel-stained ones that he was wearing. He didn't want his rancid odor to announce him before he arrived in person. If Cordelia were at Solopi Heni, and he refused to allow himself to think that she was not, or that at least Señor DeHerrera could tell him where he could find her, he had to be presentable. And then he set out again, covering the ground with the long, bent-kneed, loping stride of the woodsman, a skill he had acquired on that other long journey through Florida and that he had picked up again almost immediately he had begun this search.

When he was challenged, he froze. Whoever it was spoke in English. With his hands in the air, Donal identified himself and stated his destination.

The branches of a large tree a few paces away swayed as his challenger came down. It was a black man, grave and alert. A black man, armed with a rifle! Donal's heart sank. Was it possible that this was a slave who had gone to the Seminoles after he'd run away from his master, that he had been captured when he was this near to his goal?

"I'll have to ask you for your pistol and your hunting knife." The voice was apologetic but firm. "You are in no danger between here and the plantation house, sir, and they will be returned to you when Master Carlos gives the word."

Silently, Donal handed them over. "Do you belong to Señor DeHerrera?"

"I do." There was pride in the face of the stalwart young black. "You are on Solopi Heni land now." The voice had scarcely a trace of the usual black accent, although Donal thought he detected a lilting quality in it that spoke of the islands, pleasing to hear. "Just keep on going down this road, and you'll arrive at the house before dark."

Donal was challenged again before he got to the house, by a shorter, smaller sentry, and this one put a horn to his lips and blew three long blasts. "If you will wait here, sir, someone will come to escort you the rest of the way." Donal was impressed. Señor

DeHerrera believed in taking no chances, and it was obvious that his slaves were so trustworthy that he didn't hesitate to arm them.

The wait was not long, less than an hour. The black man asked for news of the war to the south, and told Donal in return that Señor DeHerrera had a niece living with him, but that he had never heard of a young white lady named Cordelia MacKenzie. Donal's heart sank, but he still refused to despair. If Señor DeHerrera was not sheltering Cordelia here, he would know where she was.

A rider approached, leading another horse. The rider was black, but that did not surprise Donal. "If you will mount and come with me, I will take you to the house," he was told. Also armed, with both a pistol and a rifle, the man was as courteous as the other two had been.

There were signs of activity all around him now. Fields stretched out in every direction, with slaves working in them. Black people came and went on whatever business they were about. White smiles flashed in black faces, and the dark eyes regarded him with friendly interest. Here on Solopi Heni land, one unarmed white man posed no threat even if he were a hated slave hunter. No bounty hunter, to their certain knowledge, had ever been successful in removing as much as a single slave from Solopi Heni, even though a handful of them were runaways from plantations to the north.

At his first sight of the plantation house, Donal reined to a stop, mesmerized by its magnificence. He'd realized that Señor DeHerrera was a wealthy man, but he hadn't expected anything like this. It was a mansion, its wide wings giving it a grace and beauty that he had never expected to find in this still-raw frontier land.

He was admitted by a liveried black man and left to wait in a small anteroom, furnished with authentic Louis XV pieces. Donal was grateful that he'd exchanged his filthy buckskins for this new set, or else he wouldn't have dared to sit in one of the chairs.

Actually, he didn't quite make contact with the seat, because he caught the sound of a female voice coming from an open door somewhere else on the ground floor. It was as though an electric current had passed through his body, sending it rigid with shock.

Heaven's Horizon

That was Cordelia's voice! Instantly, he was on his feet again, following the direction from which it had come.

The magnificence of the drawing room was lost on him as he saw nothing but Cordelia, his Cordelia, his *wife*, in the arms of a young, handsome man who was holding her closely and tenderly even as his mouth came down over hers in a kiss that she was certainly and without a shadow of a doubt returning with as much ardor as it was given.

"Cordelia!" His voice sounded like thunder as he crossed the room in three long strides and grasped the man by his shoulder and flung him away from her.

"What the devil!" The exclamation was torn from Peter Breckenridge, as his face went blank with astonishment that was immediately replaced with fury. "Just what is the meaning of this? I don't believe that I know you, sir!"

"But it's obvious that you have the pleasure of knowing my wife!" Donal's face was as thick with fury as Peter's. "And I'm the one who should ask just what is the meaning of this! Cordelia, who the devil is this man, and what the devil were you doing in his arms?"

Cordelia was frozen in her spot, her body as immobile as a marble statue, and her face had gone white. Only her dark eyes showed any life, and they were filled with bewilderment and shock and a dawning recognition that her mind was incapable of accepting.

"It isn't." Her whisper was strangled. "It isn't, it can't be, you're dead, you've been dead for years!" Her agonized voice tore at him, and then he moved to catch her in his arms as she swayed and would have fallen if he hadn't moved so fast.

"You leave my mother alone, damn you! Leave her be, I say! What are you doing to my mother?"

A pint-sized fury launched itself from a corner by a window where a set of wooden blocks had been fashioned into a fort, with tin soldiers scattered around the blocks to be deployed when the structure was finished. "You take your hands off my mother! Peter, make him stop!"

Some of the words Donal understood, but some he did not,

because Donal Frederick, in his fury, had lapsed half into Seminole, the language that he still understood better than English even though Uncle Runt and Sam Brent had talked to him in English every day when he had lived at the istihapo, to make sure that he didn't forget his own language.

But if Donal missed the meaning of some of the words, the fists that were pounding his midsection and the feet that were kicking viciously at his shins were a universal language that needed no interpreting.

"Let her go! Leave her be!" The eyes that glared up at him were completely hostile for all that they were the same soft brown as Cordelia's. There was very little resemblance to Donal except in the set of his shoulders and something about the jawline, and yet Donal knew, instinctively, that this was his son, the son Cordelia had borne him in some Seminole village. He opened his mouth to speak to the lad, to his son, and he realized, blankly, that he didn't know his name.

"Donnie, stop that." Cordelia's voice was faint, but it was clear. She wasn't going to faint after all, although she still needed the support of Donal's arm to keep from falling. "Stop that this minute!"

"Jennifer, Cordelia, do you know this man? My God, he called you his wife!" A second ago Peter had been ready to lay this interloper, whom he had never laid eyes on before, to the ground, to beat him to a pulp for this inexcusable intrusion into his and Cordelia's private lives, but now he was held immobile by shock.

Still as white as marble, her eyes dark with her own incomprehension and shock, Cordelia's voice was a little stronger. "He is, I think he might be, I think he is only he can't be, oh, *Donal*!"

The last word was a scream, and Cordelia's arms were around him, clinging, and she sobbed convulsively, shaking so hard that she still would have fallen if Donal hadn't been holding her up. "Donal, Donal! I can feel you, you're solid, you aren't a ghost, but how? Hold me, oh, God, hold me, don't let me go, I couldn't bear it again, I could never bear it again!"

Donal's reply was a resounding "Ouch!" as Donal Frederick's

Heaven's Horizon

toe caught him on his calf, the kick delivered so vigorously that he nearly dropped the wife he had just found again.

It was Peter who grabbed Donal Frederick's arm and dragged him off. Peter's face was as white as Cordelia's. "Easy, son. I think we might have made a mistake. I think that there's a remote possibility that this man is your father."

"I don't got no father. You're gonna be my father. You said you were gonna be! Uncle Carlos is my uncle and you're gonna be my father an' I ain't got no other father!"

Cordelia's eyes were staring into Donal's. "But you're dead! My father killed you and threw your body into the bog and you're dead! How, Donal? How can you be alive, and here?"

"It's a long story. I'm here, and that's all that matters. The important thing right now is, who is this man?"

He wouldn't have thought it possible, but Cordelia's face turned even paler than it had been before. "Donal, may I introduce Mr. Peter Breckenridge, my fiancé?" As she realized what she had said, her mouth opened in an O of dismay. "I mean, I thought he was my fiancé, he was my fiancé before you came back, we're engaged..."

The electric moment was relieved when Carlos strode into the room, his face alight with curiosity at seeing a stranger in his drawing room. He had been at the far east field, involved with a planting problem, when the horn that had announced an arrival at Solopi Heni had sounded, and he had spent a few more moments discussing the solution of the problem with his overseer before he had ridden in to see who was visiting them. He looked first at Cordelia, then at Peter, and last of all at Donal, who for some unknown reason was holding Cordelia in his arms. Surely the Reynards, in faraway Boston, hadn't managed to track Cordelia down, and this was Frederick Reynard? But no, Mr. Reynard must be a much older man, so who the devil could it be?

Donal managed a small bow in spite of its awkwardness. "I am Donal MacKenzie, Cordelia's husband. It's taken me a long time to find her."

Carlos's pause was all but imperceptible. "Are you indeed? Welcome to Solopi Heni, Mr. MacKenzie. I had never thought to have the pleasure of meeting you, as it was my impression that you were dead."

"You're Señor DeHerrera." Even in this emotionally charged moment, Donal's eyes evaluated this man and he liked what he saw. "Thank you for befriending my wife. I've been given to understand that the Seminoles would have killed her if you hadn't brought her here out of harm's way."

"That's outrageous!" Cordelia gasped, her face flaming with the indignation that was in her voice. "Kill me, indeed! Donal, the Seminoles are my friends! They would no more have killed me than they would have killed Hilolo or Weleka or Stillipika! But I wasn't at the istihapo when this horrible, senseless war broke out, I've been here at Solopi Heni for years. Only Donal Frederick was still at the istihapo, and they wouldn't have killed him either, he was one of them, Wildcat considers himself his godfather!"

"You left my son with the Seminoles while you came to live with Señor DeHerrera?" Now Donal's voice rose in anger. "How could you have done such a thing, how could you have deserted your own son?"

"I didn't desert him! You don't understand!"

"There is apparently a great deal that I don't understand, and I'm beginning to wonder if I want to!" Donal's voice was thick now, as he glared from one to another of the people in this room. His first, overwhelming joy at hearing Cordelia's voice, at knowing that she was alive, had been spoiled. Cordelia, living here with Señor DeHerrera for years, and Carlos DeHerrera was by no means old enough to make such an arrangement feasible unless he had a wife, and if he had a wife, where was she? To say nothing of finding *his* wife in the arms of another man, this Peter Breckenridge, with the announcement that he was her fiancé!

Carlos held up his hand in a comical, depreciating gesture. "I believe it's time to call a truce. We'll have a drink while we attempt to bring our emotions under control. I can recommend the cognac, Mr. MacKenzie. Cordelia, you shall have some as well, rather than your usual sherry, I believe that this occasion calls for something stronger than sherry to restore your strength."

"Make it a big one!" Cordelia said. Her arms were still around Donal's neck, and she pressed herself against him as if she had every intention of crawling inside of him so that she could never lose him again. "And a bigger one for Peter. Oh, Peter!" Her voice was anguished. "Peter, I'm so sorry! I haven't even had a chance to think what this must be doing to you! I wouldn't have had it happen for anything!"

She released one of her arms from around Donal's neck to clap her hand over her mouth, her eyes wide. "What am I saying! Of course I'd have had it happen, it's what I would have prayed for every moment of every day and every night if only I'd known, but I do love you, Peter..."

She was making it worse instead of better. Carlos placed a glass of brandy in her hand. "Cordelia, I suggest that you shut up long enough to drink this," he said, his tone mild. "And you'd better sit down if you can't stand up under your own power. Your husband must be tired of holding you up, and besides he needs at least one of his own hands to hold his brandy glass. Here you are, Peter. Let's all of us sit down. No, Donal Frederick! I didn't include you in the invitation to have some cognac!" A lightning-fast movement of his hand removed a glass that Donal Frederick had appropriated for himself and filled to the brim from the decanter that stood on a side table. "Brandy is not for young braves."

"Why isn't it? It isn't rum!" Donal Frederick wanted to know. "And I don't want this man for a father, I want Peter to be my father!"

"I'm sorry, Coacoochee, I am afraid that there's been a change of plans." Carlos's voice was as grave as if he had been speaking to an adult. "If you will be patient with such obtuse grown-ups, we will attempt to explain it to you so that you'll understand in good time."

His eyes smoldering, every inch of his body radiating hostility, Donal Frederick gave Donal one scathing glance and sat down in a chair, refusing to look at him again. Donal's son, and he hated him! The knot that was already in Donal's stomach because of finding the wife he'd searched for for so long in another man's arms tightened.

He tore his eyes from Donal Frederick and looked at Peter

Breckenridge again. Cordelia had said that she loved him, and the way she'd been responding to his kiss only a moment ago certainly bore that out. And yet in the same breath she had told Donal that she loved him! It was too much. His legs felt as if they wouldn't hold him as he took the chair that Carlos DeHerrera indicated.

It seemed that everybody in the room, with the exception of Donal Frederick, who had been forbidden to speak, was at a loss for words. Carlos rescued them by taking the initiative after he had taken a deep swallow of his own brandy. It was at times like this that he was thankful that he hadn't inherited the Indians' intolerance for alcohol, but had taken after his paternal grandfather, with the Spanish capacity for consuming as much as he wanted without ill effects.

"I think we had better start with you, Mr. MacKenzie. After I have welcomed you to my house, of course, and expressed my delight that you are alive after all these years we have believed that you were dead. How does it happen that you're alive, and here?"

"I'm here because I was looking for Cordelia. And I'm alive because Andrew Leyland's bullets didn't finish the job he set out to do. He shot me, twice, as a matter of fact. You can see the results of one of those shots here." He touched his fingers to his forehead, where the scar left by the grazing bullet had left its mark. "Andrew had every reason to believe that I was dead when he rolled me into a bottomless bog somewhere in the wilds of Georgia. Fortunately for me and unfortunately for him, he was mistaken."

"But, Donal, how did you get out, if you were so desperately wounded? Surely you must have been unconscious, if my father thought you were dead!" With a glance of mute apology, Cordelia rose from her chair and went to squeeze herself in beside Donal's in his, unwilling to be any farther away from him than that. She still needed physical contact to persuade herself that this wasn't just another dream, that she wouldn't awaken in a moment feeling the desolation that was so unbearable sweep over her as she had after so many of her other dreams.

"Providence must have been looking after me that day," Donal said. "It was the merest chance that two members of a homesteading family happened along in time to see your father shoot me and put me into the bog. Andrew heard them coming, and left the scene before I had been completely drawn under. The homesteaders dragged me out and cared for me until I recovered from my wounds."

"But, Donal, why didn't you send word to me! Didn't you know how I must have suffered? You could have managed to send word, I would have come immediately, we wouldn't have been separated for all these years!"

"I couldn't send word. You see, I was unconscious for a long time, for weeks. And when I finally regained my senses, I had no memory. The bullet that so narrowly missed entering my brain was responsible for that. I had no idea in the world who I was or any inkling of my past life."

"Dear God!" Cordelia closed her eyes and put her arms around him again, managing to spill what was left of the contents of her brandy glass on him in the process. "Donal, it must have been dreadful! I should think that you'd have lost your mind!"

The ridiculousness of what she had just said struck her, and she began to laugh, near hysteria. "Of course you'd lost your mind! Don't pay any attention to me, darling. Just tell me everything. When did you remember, and didn't you go back to Leyland's Landing to try to find me when you did remember?"

"It was months before I remembered. I stayed on with the McCabes. They were kind to me, and they needed my help on their homestead as I regained my strength, and I owed them my life, after all. Not knowing who I was or where I could go, I felt that I owed it to them to repay them insofar as I could."

"The McCabes? I don't believe I ever heard of them."

"It isn't likely that you would have. They are what you people in Georgia call crackers, they would hardly have moved in your social circle."

"I had no social circle," Cordelia reminded him. "Oh, dear, I've spilled my brandy all over you!" Her voice was almost a wail, as if such a trivial thing could matter now. "Never mind, Delores will clean the stains for you, she's very good at such things, you won't even be able to tell where the brandy was spilled."

"Delores is Señor DeHerrera's wife? Or his niece? I believe someone told me that he has a niece."

"Oh, no! Carlos doesn't have either a wife or a niece. I'm his niece."

Things were making less and less sense. Cordelia called Señor DeHerrera Carlos, rather than addressing him, with proper formality, by his title. And Señor DeHerrera had no niece, but Cordelia was his niece?

"The small deception was necessary, in order to protect Cordelia's good name," Carlos offered mildly. "I could hardly have brought her here to live unless I'd invented such a fiction. It served very well, by the way. No one yet has an inkling of Cordie's true identity, except, of course, for Peter. Cordelia had to tell him her entire story when she consented to marry him."

"You came here, posing as Señor DeHerrera's niece, and left our son with the Seminoles?" Donal demanded, glaring at his wife, outrage plain in his voice.

"Mr. MacKenzie, if you please. It was necessary. It was possible for me to invent a niece and bring her here so she could enjoy my protection and have a fuller and more comfortable life than she could lead at the istihapo, but the sudden advent of a young lady of Cordelia's age and description, along with an infant of the right age to be Cordelia Leyland MacKenzie's child, could hardly have escaped her father's notice. Your son was a good deal safer where he was, and he was happy there. I might add that he was so happy there, among the people he'd known from his birth, people who loved and cared for him as if he were one of their own, that when I was forced to bring him here when the people of the istihapo fled to the swamps in order to escape being rounded up and removed from Florida, he protested violently. He wanted his mother to live with him at the istihapo, but he had no desire to be separated from the people he regarded as his real family."

"You wrote to my parents to tell them that she was safe. I haven't thanked you for that. But you failed to state her exact whereabouts."

"I considered the omission necessary. Andrew Leyland had spies everywhere; certainly he had someone watching your parents' home. It was possible that my letter might fall into the wrong hands. As a matter of fact, both Cordelia and I were convinced that it had, especially when agents of Mr. Leyland showed up here at Solopi Heni, searching for her. And the letter was never answered, so it was natural that we thought either that it hadn't been received, or that your parents had decided not to answer it, that they wanted nothing to do with your wife and child. After all, Cordelia had explained to me that you had married her rather than the girl you had come to America to court, and they might not have been willing to accept the substitute."

"The letter was mislaid before my parents saw it, and it wasn't discovered until last autumn. I'd already spent more than a year in Florida before I returned to England, searching for Cordie. I swear I must have visited every istihapo in the territory! I'll never understand how I missed finding her!"

"She would have been hidden. You weren't the only one searching for her, you know. Andrew Leyland's agents had already visited the istihapo more than once. The Seminoles would have made sure that you caught no glimpse of her, or of Runt. They'd have known of your approach long before you reached the village."

"And I gave up, and returned to England! And now when I've finally found my wife, I find her betrothed to another man, a man she loves!"

"Donal, no! I mean, yes, of course I'm engaged to Peter, or rather I was, until you walked in a few moments ago! I thought you were dead, I thought you'd been dead for years! I grieved for you for so long, you'll never know how much I grieved, and how long! But Peter loved me, and I knew that I could be happy with him, and I was very fond of him, I still am, how could I help but be? Don't glare at me like that! He's the one who's being hurt! He's everything that's good, and kind, and he's going to go and fight the Seminoles although I don't like that at all, I don't like anybody fighting them and trying to take their lands away from them. He might be killed..."

"I'm going to fight the Seminoles, as well," Donal told her. "After the things I've seen on my journey here, I have no choice."

"No! I won't let you! I won't have it!" Cordelia cried, her face white again, but this time it was with rage as well as from shock. "Not you, Donal! You have no reason, and how could I bear it if I thought that your hand was the one that struck down Wacassa, or Sam Brent!'

"It's just as likely that their hands will be the ones to strike me down," Donal pointed out to her.

"Enough!" Carlos's voice was sharp. "It would be ridiculous for you two to start your own full-scale war within minutes of being reunited. We don't have to discuss such things now. Mr. MacKenzie must rest, and regain his strength after his journey, and you must both have time to become acquainted again. Do you realize that you're virtual strangers? Peter, you'll stay for dinner, of course. This concerns you as much as it does Cordelia and her husband, and you have the right to know everything."

"I think not," Peter's voice was stiff, although his manner was correct. He held out his hand to Donal. "Mr. MacKenzie, I won't—" he broke off painfully, glancing at Cordelia. "By the way, you must remember to call her Jennifer here, that is the name she is known by and it's taken me weeks to get used to calling her by her real name."

Cordelia, Jennifer. They were indeed strangers!

Cordelia ran to hold both of her hands out to Peter, and Donal felt a surge of jealousy that astonished him. He'd never thought himself capable of feeling such jealousy for any other human being.

"Peter, I'm so sorry! I'm so dreadfully sorry that you're being hurt! I hope we can still be friends. I'll always love you, you know that, don't you?"

"Of course we'll still be friends. It could hardly be otherwise." Peter's voice started out being formal, but at the end it cracked, and he turned on his heel and almost bolted out of the room. "I'll show myself out, I know the way."

"Don't you dast go killin' any Seminoles!" Donal Frederick

screamed after him, goaded into ignoring Carlos's orders to be quiet. "Don't you dast, or I won't want you for my father neither!"

He turned then to Donal, his legs planted apart, his face screwed up in a ferocious scowl. "And don't you dast! Iffen you do, I'll hate you forever, I'll kill you, I will!"

Carlos swooped him up into his arms. "You have a right to your opinion, but you don't have the right to shout it out in that manner, and to a guest who also happens to be your father," he admonished the boy. "You and I are going for a gallop among the fields until your head cools, my lad, so that your mother and father can have an opportunity to get to know each other again."

In spite of the boy's wild struggles, Carlos bore him from the room. "I'll tell Daniel to lay out some of my clothes for you, Mr. MacKenzie, and have a bath prepared."

"And have him shave off that beard!" Cordelia put in. "I don't know you anymore, Donal! You never wore a beard, you look like a stranger."

"I think it's rather becoming, myself," Carlos grinned. "But, then, I'm not a lady. I'll see you at dinner, Mr. MacKenzie. In the meantime, *mi casa es su casa*."

My house is your house. Donal knew enough Spanish to understand Carlos's words. But Carlos's house was also Cordelia's house, and what had the two of them been doing in it, all alone except for house slaves, in all the time before Peter Breckenridge had come on the scene? Señor DeHerrera wasn't exactly a handsome man, but he was without any doubt far from past his prime, and virile. That jealousy was there again, directed now against the man who had befriended his wife, and Donal felt suddenly tired and sick and unable to cope.

"Donal!" Cordelia's voice butted into his thoughts as she threw her arms around him again. "You're here, you're really here!" She drew back her head to look at him, and her face was aghast. "And you haven't even kissed me yet!"

Her mouth was soft and hot and throbbing under his as the breath was crushed from her body. Now she was sure that Donal was alive, that he had come back to her. But even then she managed to spoil the moment, because with the first clear breath she was allowed to draw she cried, "That damned beard! Go and shave it off, darling. I don't think I like being kissed by a bear!"

"And I'm not all that bloody sure that I like kissing another man's fiancée!" Donal snarled back at her. With that, his emotions threatening to undo him, he followed Daniel, who had appeared to pause discreetly in the doorway to lead him to Cordelia's room, where a bath had already been prepared for him in anticipation of Carlos's orders. Cordelia's eyes stung with tears, and then she blinked them away and squared her shoulders. Everything was going to be all right. If this first meeting after so long a separation hadn't been exactly the stuff that fairy tales were made of, there was still tonight. Tonight, she'd sleep in Donal's arms, but not, she hoped, for a long, long time after they had gone to bed.

When Donal reappeared downstairs, he had been transformed from a bearded, woods-running stranger into the husband that Cordelia remembered. Carlos's perfectly tailored clothing was almost an exact fit, and with his hair trimmed and his beard shaved off Cordelia's breath caught in her throat.

The dinner was such as Donal hadn't enjoyed since he had left England on this second stage of his search for Cordelia. Some of the dishes were unfamiliar, an aromatic gumbo and a rice dish so hotly spiced that it burned the inside of Donal's mouth even while he savored it, but the quality of everything was excellent. It was difficult for him to believe that any slave could be capable of producing such food.

The wine that was served with the meal had been imported from France, the table sparkled with crystal and silver. Cordelia certainly hadn't been suffering all these years! She'd been living in the lap of luxury, as her low-necked gown and the jewels at her throat and ears attested, every inch the lady of this *hacienda*.

She was beautiful, God, but she was beautiful! When Donal had first fallen in love with her he had thought that she was the most beautiful girl in the world. But she wasn't a girl now, she was a woman, and her fresh young beauty had ripened and come into full bloom. Her gown was that shell pink that was so becoming to her,

Heaven's Horizon

and Donal realized that the pearls she wore were genuine and priceless.

He couldn't help but wonder why Carlos had given her such costly clothing, such costly jewels. The man was obviously as wealthy as a nabob; perhaps such gifts were so trifling to him that he thought nothing of the giving. But on the other hand, a man doesn't ordinarily give such gifts to a woman unless she means a great deal to him, unless there was something of a serious personal nature between them. The jealousy that he had barely managed to fight down while he'd bathed and dressed and submitted to Daniel's razor and scissors reared its head again, and he felt bile rising in his throat to spoil the flavor of the food he had been enjoying so much just a moment ago.

Carlos's eyes were sardonic, as though he guessed what was going through Donal's mind. But his naturally sympathetic nature demanded that he put Donal's mind at rest.

"You are admiring your wife. I agree with you that she carries off her gown and her jewels to perfection. It was necessary for me to provide her with the things that would be expected as my niece, and it was my pleasure to do so. People would have wondered if I had not. As the mistress of my house, as my hostess and my niece, she had to look the part as well as play it."

"Carlos has been far too generous! I tried to stop him from giving me so much. I think he enjoys spending money so much that he's never happy unless he's throwing it away," Cordelia told Donal. "Frederick Reynard would have a heart attack at such extravagance, and so would any other man in Boston. Get him in a shop, and he's like a little boy with his money burning a hole in his pocket."

"I resent that! To what possible better use could money be put than to adorn a beautiful lady? And Cordelia has repaid me many times over. A house without a mistress, without a hostess, is only a house and not a home. I had a wish to become the most celebrated host in Florida, and without Cordelia this could not have been achieved. What was good for one of us was good for the other. As a confirmed bachelor, there was no other way I could have attained my wish, but Cordelia posing as my niece made it all possible."

They talked long after the dessert dishes had been removed from the table, the men smoking Havana cigars and sipping brandy, Cordelia refusing to remove herself to the drawing room, but sitting on with them, toying with a glass of sherry. There was so much to be caught up on, so many things that they were frantic to know about each other! But at last Carlos stood up.

"We can't talk all night, as pleasant as it is. As a planter I have to rise early, and Donal must be tired. Good night."

Delores left Cordelia's room as soon as they entered, only holding out her hand to Donal for a firm, welcoming handclasp while she told him that she was delighted that he had found her mistress at last. She liked him, she approved of him. And then they were alone.

It was like their wedding night all over again, only much more poignant. Donal realized, half amused and half with an aching sadness, that Cordelia was actually shy of removing her clothing in front of him! But the shyness disappeared in a wave of overpowering passion as he slipped her gown from her shoulders and his hands found her breasts.

And then it wasn't like their wedding night after all, because although Cordelia had been perfectly satisfactory on their wedding night, now she was a full woman, able to give him and to take from him all that love could ask. They made love to each other not once, but twice, the first time so wildly that it was over much too soon, the second time slowly, savoring every second, every inch of each other's bodies. Donal felt more married, more in possession of his wife now than he ever had before Andrew Leyland had shattered their lives with his act of treachery.

Exhausted, content, they lay in each other's arms, and Donal fell asleep first, as was only to be expected. He had come a long way, most of it on foot, through wild and dangerous territory. It was a miracle that he had lived to reach Solopi Heni at all.

But he was alive, and he was here, his arms were still around her, her head was resting on his shoulder as Cordelia was still unwilling to move an inch farther away from him, needing the constant, close contact to reassure herself that she would never lose him again.

It was almost wicked to be this happy. But Donal was her

husband, she was his wife, and so it wasn't wicked at all. Groping for his hand on the moon-drenched bed under the mosquito bar, Cordelia raised it to her lips, gently so as not to disturb him.

It did disturb him, but not enough to wake him. He muttered something in his sleep. For a moment, Cordelia didn't credit her ears, she must be half asleep herself, and imagined that he'd said what he'd said.

"Becky, not again! I love you, but aren't you ever satisfied? Have a little mercy, you've exhausted me!"

For another moment, while she realized that Donal had actually said those words, Cordelia lay rigid with shock. The next moment, both of her hands were on Donal's shoulders and she was shaking him with fury.

Donal's eyes flew open, filled with bewilderment as he struggled to remember where he was and who was shaking him.

"Who's Becky? Tell me, who is Becky?"

Still befuddled by his sleep of exhaustion, Donal said, "I thought she was my wife."

Chapter Twenty-one

Carlos was exasperated. The battle had been raging off and on for days, and it seemed to him that it was more often on than off.

"Was she pretty? She must have been very pretty."

"She was all right. She was just a girl." His defenses up, Donal was wary of telling Cordelia more than the bare facts, because each additional bit of information could aggravate a situation that was already far from comfortable.

"But a girl like that, completely ignorant, uneducated, a backwoods girl! Even without your memory, you must have realized that she wasn't suitable for you, unless she was so beautiful that her background didn't matter."

"Since when have you become a snob, Cordelia? I never saw any trace of it in you before."

"I never had to contend with an unknown rival before."

"She isn't your rival. I'm married to you. I'll never see her again. It's done, over with, why can't you let it rest at that?"

And for a little while, for a day or two days, Cordelia would let it rest at that, ecstatic that Donal was alive, that she had him back again, that she was the only one he loved. But then her nagging curiosity would get the better of her again.

"What did she look like, really? Was she tall, short, thin, plump? What color were her hair and her eyes?"

"Blue. She had blue eyes."

Like Nadine's, Cordelia thought. Nadine had blue eyes, and Nadine was beautiful, so beautiful that Donal had come all the way from England to court her because he hadn't been able to forget her beauty.

"You didn't tell me about her hair. Was it fair, like Nadine's?"

"It was red. Dark red, the shade that's called auburn. It is red. Stop speaking of her in the past tense, Cordie! Becky's still alive. You don't have to consign her to her grave just because our paths happened to cross."

"From what I already know, they did a lot more than cross! She was, I mean she is, beautiful, then. How tall did you say she was?"

"Medium, I suppose. About your height. Cordelia, let's drop the subject! I'm not only tired of it, but I have more important things to think about. Getting you away from here, for instance, to somewhere where you and Donal Frederick will be safe."

"We're safe here. We couldn't possibly be in a safer place!"

"That may be so. It seems safe enough at the moment, but who can tell how the tide might turn? In any case, Solopi Heni is too far from the fighting for me to be able to get back to see you, once I offer my services against the Seminoles. I want you in Saint Augustine, where you'll be really safe with the fort to protect you, and where I'll be able to see you once in a while."

"You might not be able to see me even then. And this war can't go on much longer. It wouldn't have to go on at all, if the white people would just admit that they're wrong, and leave the Indians alone."

"They aren't going to leave them alone. I've talked to enough men to realize that. The whites won't be satisfied until every Indian in Florida has been removed, so far away that they'll never be able to come back."

"So they go out murdering every Seminole they can find! That's removing them all right, to where they certainly will never be able to come back!"

"I didn't start this war. I didn't have a thing to do with it. There's no point in yelling at me."

"But you're going to fight in it, when there's no need! You yourself just said that you didn't have anything to do with it, so you're contradicting yourself."

"I am not contradicting myself! I didn't have anything to do with starting it, but if you'd seen the things I've seen, and I pray to God that you never will, you'd understand why I have to help to put a stop to it."

"By killing my friends? By killing the kindest, most gentle people who ever lived?"

Kind, gentle? Donal remembered the mutilated bodies, and he shuddered. In his anger, he almost blurted it all out to Cordelia, but he stopped himself in time. It wasn't the sort of thing one told a woman, no matter how unreasonable she was, so unreasonable that you felt like shaking her until her teeth rattled. Donal almost wished that the old colonial laws were still in effect, so that he'd be justified in beating his wife with a stick no larger around than his thumb.

If it wasn't Cordelia and Donal arguing and fighting about Becky and about the Seminoles, it was Donal Frederick. The passing days brought no change in the boy's attitude toward his father. To put it bluntly, Donal Frederick didn't like Donal.

"Son, I'm going out riding. Why don't you come with me, act as my guide? I'd like to see more of the plantation while I have the chance, and you know all about it."

Donal Frederick was not deceived by Donal's ploy. Let this man offer him his false friendship all he wanted, but Donal Frederick wasn't about to give an inch.

"My name is Coacoochee."

"Is that what they called you, in the Seminole village?"

"It's an istihapo, not a village. Villages are for white people."

"Doesn't Coacoochee mean Wildcat? How does it happen that you have such a name?"

Donal Frederick drew himself up to his full height, and his face was suffused with pride.

"Wildcat is a warrior, a chief. He's the greatest warrior who ever lived. He's stronger and braver than any other warrior in the world, and my name is Coacoochee too. Wildcat said I could have his name, he gave it to me himself."

Coacoochee, Wildcat, was Donal Frederick's idol. The young chief had visited the istihapo often before the war had started. Wacassa was one of his particular friends, the two of them had grown up together until Wildcat, who was older, had married into another village. Wacassa had tried to be like his older friend in every way; they had hunted together, fished and wrestled and gone swimming together, they had slain alligators together with sharpened poles. At the Green Corn Dance, Wacassa had tried to consume as much of the Black Drink as his hero.

Donal Frederick had never lost his babyhood adoration of the young chief, who had never failed to toss him into the air, to play with him and make a fuss over him, as he had grown from babyhood to boyhood. To Donal Frederick, the claw marks on Wildcat's face and shoulders were beautiful, the marks of bravery and honor. And now that this war had come, Wildcat was the bravest warrior of all the Seminoles.

Donal Frederick admired Osceola, Wildcat's friend whose name was on everyone's lips these days, but Osceola had killed only Wiley Thompson, while Wildcat had ambushed and massacred the entire of Major Dade's column, a feat that had struck fear and trembling into the entire white population of Florida. If Donal Frederick were old enough, he'd join Wildcat, and then this war would be over in a hurry, and the whites wouldn't win it, either, he and Wildcat would drive every white man in Florida back to where he'd come from, with the exception of Uncle Carlos and perhaps of Peter Breckenridge. And this man who had come to Solopi Heni and who fought with his mother all the time would be the first one that they'd drive out.

If a man couldn't find peace in his own house, things had come to a pretty pass, Carlos thought. And although he was convinced that

Heaven's Horizon

Cordelia and Donal Frederick were safe here, as safe as they'd be in Saint Augustine and a good deal more comfortable, he was beginning to think that it would be a good idea to follow Donal's wishes.

It was more than a good idea, as a matter of fact, because although Cordelia was trustworthy, because she would thoroughly approve of what he planned to do and what he was already doing on a small scale, still a wife will confide in her husband and she might tell Donal things that Carlos had no wish for Donal to know.

With his vast plantation, with his almost unlimited commodities and resources, Carlos wanted to place everything he could at the Seminoles' disposal. Moving around as they were, always on the run, not being able to stay in one place long enough to raise and harvest a crop, the Seminoles were in desperate need of food. And of guns, and ammunition, of things that Carlos could supply them if no white man's eyes were around to see.

As recently as last night, when Donal Frederick had been safely asleep, when Donal and Cordelia had slept at last after another of their interminable arguments, Carlos had overseen the loading of a wagon of supplies and escorted it miles on its way as it was driven by two of his most trusted slaves. He'd been compelled to turn back well before dawn, to push Black Fire to his limit in order to be back at Solopi Heni before Donal arose in the morning, to ask questions about his absence that Carlos would have found difficulty in answering.

So now he threw his own weight behind Donal's opinion that Cordelia and Donal Frederick should be taken to Saint Augustine, because then Donal would have no more reason to visit Solopi Heni, where his keen eyes and his trained sense of observation might lead him to the correct conclusions. Not only would Carlos's life be at stake if he were discovered, but his usefulness to the Seminoles would come to an end. Playing a double role, skulking behind two identities, did not sit well with Carlos. There was something shameful about it, almost as though he were a spy betraying his own people. But there it was again: he was two people, a white and a Seminole, and he had to choose, and there was no way that he could not choose that which he thought was right.

Although by inclination he would have rather come out into the open and joined with the Seminoles within every man's eyesight, to do so would be to sacrifice his greatest usefulness to the Indians' cause. His plantation would be confiscated, divided up among squabbling whites quarreling over the spoils. There would be no more supplies from Solopi Heni diverted to the hungry Seminoles, no more powder and shot that he, as Carlos DeHerrera, could procure where the Seminoles could not. His slaves, those loyal people who looked to him for protection, would belong to someone else who might not treat them as fairly as Carlos did, or who might resell them into who knew what sort of a situation.

So in order to be of the greatest use and to protect his slaves, he was forced into the dual role that was so distasteful. But with Donal at Solopi Heni, the role was difficult to maintain. That being the case, the sooner Donal could be removed, the better.

Donal himself was worried, more than worried. "It was difficult enough for me, a man alone and knowing the wilderness, to cross through country where the fighting is raging without being caught. Even when I joined with the company of militiamen there was danger enough. As much as I'd like to get Cordie and my son to Saint Augustine, I can't fathom how it's to be done."

"You'll have help," Carlos reminded him. "I myself will accompany you, with as large a body of armed men as I can spare from the plantation. It's doubtful that the Seminoles would attack such a party even if they were to discover us."

Donal wasn't inclined to think that it was all that doubtful. He had no way of knowing, after all, that the chances of Carlos DeHerrera's party being ambushed were infinitesimal. The Seminoles knew him, knew him to be on their side, and they knew Cordelia as well, and all knew of Donal Frederick, whom Coacoochee held under his personal protection. But there was no way that Carlos could allay Donal's apprehension by telling him how little danger there would be.

"I agree with you entirely that Cordelia and Donal Frederick must take shelter in Saint Augustine. There's no way of knowing whether the war will spread this way, and if it were to do that, it would be too late to remove your wife and son to safety."

So Donal was torn one way and then the other, but in the end, it was Peter Breckenridge who tipped the scales in favor of setting out despite the danger.

Peter had stayed away from Solopi Heni for the first few days after Donal's astounding reappearance from the dead, but then his love for Cordelia had compelled him to start visiting again to make sure that she was happy and that Donal would go on making her happy.

What he had seen and heard on his first visit had filled him with doubts, as he had happened to arrive just when Cordelia was in the middle of one of her fits of jealousy. He heard her raised voice, he heard some of her accusations and Donal's evasive or angry replies, and in spite of the immorality of even thinking of such a thing, to come between a husband and his wife, a spark of hope was kindled in his heart. Divorce was almost unheard of, but it did exist, and certainly Cordelia had grounds. Her husband had cohabited with another woman, had lived with her in flagrant adultery, had committed bigamy! And so if Donal would not or could not make Cordelia as happy as he knew that he himself could and would, then he was justified in trying to get her back.

Therefore Peter continued his visits, and used every opportunity to bring home to Cordelia that he loved her and her alone, that he would always be faithful to her and never think of another woman. Donal seethed every time he saw Peter coming, and went on seething after he had left, and there were more quarrels, with Cordelia defending Peter and throwing Donal's liaison with Becky in his face when Donal accused her of encouraging his rival.

And Carlos was quick to turn the situation to his own advantage. Peter, even more than Donal, was a danger to him, because Peter, being plantation-wise, might spot the nefarious activities going on at Solopi Heni where Donal might miss them.

"It's plain to see that there will be no peace between you and Cordelia until you've taken her away. Peter Breckenridge is a determined man, and with Cordelia's suspicions about you and this Becky, with the hurt you dealt her, however unknowingly, she might turn to him simply out of her rage and heartbreak."

Donal was forced to agree.

"It's settled, then," Carlos said one evening as dinner was drawing to its conclusion. He raised his wineglass in a salute. "To our safe journey! We will start in three days' time, as soon as I can complete the necessary arrangements."

At his place at the table, Donal Frederick's heart froze. The thought of going to Saint Augustine, of being forced to be on the side of the whites, was more than the boy could bear. Too young to reason, his emotions were as strong as those of a full-grown man.

He wouldn't go! He wouldn't, and they couldn't make him, because he'd be gone. He knew the direction to take to reach the istihapo, and once he reached it someone there would tell him where he could find Coacoochee. He'd join Wildcat and fight by his side. He and Little Thunder would both fight, Little Thunder, his brother! Little Thunder was probably already fighting and Donal Frederick was being left out of it, but no longer. He would go tonight, after all of the grown-ups were asleep.

"Donal Frederick, finish your supper," Cordelia told him. "Eat the rest of your turkey, I know you like it. Don't you want to grow up to be big and strong like your father?"

Donal Frederick felt like gagging, but he ate the turkey that remained on his plate. He was going to grow up to be bigger and stronger than this man they said was his father! So much bigger and stronger that after he and Wildcat and Little Thunder had driven all of the white men from Florida, he could take his mother back away from his father, and he and his mother would live at the istihapo again and they'd be happy for as long as they lived, and at Donal Frederick's age, that was forever.

He went to bed that night without any of his usual protests, protests that had barely escaped being violent because he hated to leave his mother alone with his father. He was astute enough to notice the glances of relief that all three of the adults exchanged when he left the drawing room to go upstairs without putting up an argument, and he laughed inside even though something else inside of him kept trying to tell him that he was frightened. That part of the something else inside of him mustn't be listened to. No warrior would listen to it. Certainly Wildcat himself had never felt such a shameful thing. So Donal Frederick giggled to himself to shut out what he didn't want to admit was there, and steeled his determination even further.

Cordelia and Donal quarreled, or near-quarreled, again that night. Cordelia didn't want to go to Saint Augustine and she couldn't understand why Carlos had taken Donal's side in the matter. She was happy where she was, and as long as she stayed here Donal would stay and then he would neither be in danger of getting himself killed by the Seminoles, or be out killing her friends.

The quarrel ended, as they so often did, with Cordelia and Donal in each other's arms. Having each other again after all of those years was still so new to them that they couldn't get enough of each other. Even when their tempers were the most heated, just being close was enough to break down the barriers that separated them and they would reach out to each other, to cling together with fast-beating hearts and the determination that nothing must ever come between them again.

It was late before they slept. Their lovemaking had been both passionate and violent after this latest quarrel, and they were so exhausted that they slept until nearly nine the next morning. It was almost eleven before it dawned on Cordelia that she hadn't seen Donal Frederick around the house. It didn't particularly worry her. She assumed that he was out on the plantation somewhere with Carlos as he so often was.

But when Carlos came in for the midday meal, Donal Frederick wasn't with him.

Delores hadn't seen him. None of the other slaves had seen him. A search was instituted, the meal forgotten as the search spread to cover not only every inch of the house, but the immediate grounds, every place that the boy might be.

It was Daniel, who had gone to question the field slaves, who returned to the house with his face so grave that Cordelia's heart leaped into her throat.

"Donal Frederick's pony is missing," Daniel told them. "And no one saw him take it this morning."

They looked at each other, dismay in their eyes. Carlos, who knew Donal Frederick even better than his mother did, was the first to come to the right conclusion.

"The little devil's run away. It's more than likely that he's headed for the istihapo. Daniel, have our horses saddled, Black Fire and Fox Fire."

"Have Star Fire saddled too! I'm going with you!" Cordelia cried.

"No. It's out of the question. I know how well you ride, but you have to stay here in case the boy comes back on his own. I'll have my best men searching every inch of the plantation in the meantime, and if he hasn't headed for the istihapo, he may have met with an accident and he'll be found and brought back to the house and he'll need you."

Cordelia watched them ride out, Carlos and Donal, their faces grim as they urged their mounts into ground-covering lopes down the long avenue. Every drop of blood in her body cried out in protest at being left behind, but she knew that Carlos was right. She wasn't needed to help find Donal Frederick if he was headed for the istihapo, but she might be needed here.

What none of them knew, or even suspected, was that Donal Frederick hadn't set out this morning, after daylight, before anyone else on the plantation was stirring, but that he had set out the night before, while Cordelia and Donal had still been quarreling in their room and Carlos had shut himself into the library with a bottle of cognac and a book to try to ignore the shattering of his peace. How could any of them have guessed that the boy who was more Seminole than white had no fear at all about setting out at night, his sense of direction infallible, his war games with his Seminole friends enabling him to make his way past all of Carlos's sentries without them being aware that anyone was within miles of them. While he was still on Solopi Heni land, he had nothing to fear, and he had refused to allow himself to think beyond that. As a Seminole, he would cope with it when the time came.

"You must eat something," Delores told Cordelia, her voice firm and brooking no argument. "It isn't going to help anything for you to go hungry, and you might need your strength later. I'm going to watch to see that you clean this plate."

Cordelia ate, although she had little idea of what went into her mouth. Wherever he was right now, Donal Frederick was probably hungry, and it seemed wicked to be filling her own stomach.

"Now drink your coffee, and then we'll go through Donal Frederick's clothes, to see what needs mending and what's past mending. That boy can tear up clothes faster than any other boy I ever knew. After we've sorted them we'll start patching and mending."

"Delores, you know that Donnie doesn't need to wear patched clothes! Carlos would never allow it!"

"Master Carlos is a generous man, but if Donal Frederick can't wear what we mend and patch, there are other boys on the plantation who can. The best thing you can do while you're waiting is to keep yourself busy."

Donal had thought that he was a good woodsman, but watching Carlos made him realize that no matter how good he was he had to take a backseat as far as Carlos was concerned. Where Donal would have had to dismount to look for signs of a pony's passing, Carlos spotted Little Fire's tracks from the saddle without seeming to have to look.

"He's headed for the istihapo, all right, in a beeline. And he started a lot earlier than we thought, Donal. If I'm not losing my touch, the little devil hauled out of here early last night. That's going to make it take longer before we catch up with him."

"At night!" Donal was aghast. "A boy of that age, riding alone through this vast, empty country at night? Surely he would have gone only a little way, and then stopped to sleep! Or maybe he's already come to his senses and is headed back and we'll meet him, unless he's lost."

"He won't be lost, and he won't have headed back. And Little Fire is as tough as Donal Frederick is, he can keep going indefinitely. Unfortunately in this case, I insisted that his pony be as good a piece of horseflesh as any at Solopi Heni, and Little Fire is good, he's fast and he's tough and he's tireless."

"But the danger! Good Lord, what if some stray band of Seminoles were to come across him?" For a moment, Donal's stomach heaved, and he quailed at the thought of the little lad he'd seen, whose brains had been dashed out against the trunk of a tree.

"It's highly unlikely that that would happen. Even if it did, Donal Frederick would call out to them in their own language, and they'd stay their hands long enough to find out who he is, and then they wouldn't harm him. You can consider yourself fortunate that Coacoochee is so fond of that boy of yours. Even a renegade band would realize that Coacoochee would exact a horrible vengeance on them if any harm came to him."

They pushed on as fast as they could without tiring their horses. Even in his agitation, Donal was amused at the names Carlos had given his best mounts, Black Fire, Star Fire, Fox Fire and Little Fire. The names were appropriate, because the horses were fiery, the best that could be had. Donal had ridden nothing better in England, even when he had been fox hunting on great country estates.

The afternoon wore on and the shadows lengthened. How far ahead could one small boy on a pony be? Donal Frederick had had so many hours' start, they weren't even sure how many. Carlos didn't lose the track, his keen eyes saw the most minute of signs, some of which Donal spotted at once and some that he did not. They kept on until the last light was gone from the sky, when Carlos called a halt.

"As long as we know that Donal Frederick is headed for the istihapo, we might as well stop for the night. I don't believe in abusing my horses. He will have stopped as well. I've trained him too well for him to push Little Fire too hard."

As much as his mind protested, Donal's common sense made him agree. Carlos fell asleep immediately after they had eaten from the provisions they had brought with them, but Donal wasn't able to drop off as easily. What would he be able to say to Cordelia if they were forced to return to Solopi Heni empty-handed, without her little boy? His little boy, his son whom he hardly knew! How would she be able to bear her grief? And he himself, how would he be able to bear it? He'd never forgive himself, he should have realized that

Heaven's Horizon

Donal Frederick might do something like this, he should have been more watchful, more aware of the boy and what he was thinking instead of trying to cope with Cordelia's fits of jealousy and their quarreling and making up with wild, sweet lovemaking only to quarrel again.

They set out again as soon as it was light. They found where Donal Frederick had rested, where Little Fire had grazed. For such a young lad, Donnie had done a remarkable job of erasing all traces of his camping place. No crumb remained to show that he had eaten, the place where he had curled up had been brushed over, Little Fire's droppings had been covered with dirt and leaves.

"He's played at this game since he could walk. Remember, he spent all but the last few months of his life as a Seminole. If he hadn't been as careful and skillful, I'd whale the daylights out of him when we come up with him," Carlos said. "His education as a Seminole will stand him in good stead all of his life, Donal, if we don't let him forget it. You've had experience in the wilderness in survival yourself. See that you keep on instructing the boy and keep his senses sharp, even after you take him to England."

"I intend to." Donal's voice was grim. And something else stirred in him, a sense of pride. This son whom he scarcely knew, this small lad who was so cunning, so wilderness-wise, was his, his own flesh and blood, the seed of his loins! It was then that Donal knew that he loved Donal Frederick as much as he could have loved him if he'd been with him since the moment of his birth. He'd find his son, and he'd never lose him again, if he had to search to the ends of the earth.

The sun was in its last leg of its journey before setting when they heard a horse approaching them. They both reined to a halt, and Donal's pistol was in his hand even before the rider came into view. Only it wasn't a horse, it was a pony, a more red than brown pony with a blaze on its forehead and one white stocking. Beside the pony, an Indian was leading it, while with his other hand he kept a firm grip on the arm of the boy who rode it.

Donal's first reaction was rage. Donnie had been captured, and after the things he'd seen and the things he'd heard, he had no thought but to put a bullet between the Seminole's eyes.

In the next instant Carlos knocked the hand that was holding the pistol up, so that the reflex made his finger tighten on the trigger and the ball passed harmlessly over the Seminole's head.

"It's Holati, you ass!" Carlos said. "Can't you see that he's an old man, and that he's bringing Donal Frederick back?"

Now that the first haze of anger had left Donal's eyes, he thanked his Maker that Carlos's reaction had been so fast. The Seminole who held Donnie in such a relentless grip was so old that he was bent with his years and his legs moved stiffly. The eyes in his seamed face looked at Donal impassively, quite as if Donal hadn't just tried to shoot him.

"Holati." Carlos spoke the name with deference and respect, ignoring Donal Frederick, who was struggling to break free of the old man's grasp. "You are far from your istihapo."

"I come to return Little Coacoochee. He was brought to the new camp where all of the old men of the istihapo who could not follow the warriors have gone to hide from the white men's soldiers."

Carlos dismounted and took food from his saddlebag. "*Hum-box-chay*," he said. It was an invitation to eat. "You have come a long way and you are hungry. Donal, close your mouth and make yourself useful. We'll camp here for the night and start back in the morning." For the first time, he looked at Donal Frederick. "Why are you riding, and allowing an old man to walk?"

"We took turns," Donal Frederick told him, his face flaming with resentful pride. "I wanted him to ride all the time but he wouldn't, he said my legs are too short and it would take too long and he's heavier than I am and it would tire Little Fire. But I walked most of the time."

The explanation satisfied Carlos. "Very well. If you will not give me your word that you will not sneak off again while we're sleeping, I'll tie you up for the night, is that understood?"

"Yes, sir." Donal Frederick's lower lip thrust out. "But iffen I hadn't been took, I'd of got to Coacoochee, I woulda!"

"That only proves that you aren't clever enough, and capable enough, not to be taken, that you aren't old enough to fight by Coacoochee's side. You will have to wait a little longer. You're fortunate that Seminoles do not carry tales, because if word of your being taken so easily got back to Coacoochee, he would be disappointed in you."

Defeated and knowing that he was defeated, Donal Frederick accepted his fate, and sat silently while the three men talked after they had eaten. Carlos interpreted for Donal as the old man told how it was with those who hadn't been able to go with the warriors in their war against the whites.

"There is no hope among us. We are hungry and ragged, and we have no heart left. All we ask is to stay on the land of our fathers and to die here so that our bones may lie beside theirs. We hear little of how the war is going, but what strength we have left is spent in praying that Osceola and Wildcat and the others will succeed where we old ones have failed. We are old for hunting, and food is scarce. Charley Jones, who caught this small Wildcat, came back with only rabbits from his snares, he could not bring down a deer. We wait to die, that is all that is left for us now."

"I will see that you have food," Carlos promised him. "I will send it by slaves."

"We thank you, but it will be food wasted. Better that you should send it to the warriors who are doing some good, than to nourish bodies that are useless."

They had switched to Seminole for this last exchange, and although Donal asked Donal Frederick what they were saying the boy's mouth clamped shut and he refused to answer.

Before they slept, Carlos looked at Donal with wry, sad humor. "This is one of the savages whom you are about to fight. So savage, so treacherous, that an old man whose bones give him agony when he walks set out without hesitation to return your son to you. Not only your son, but a pony that would have fed the ones remaining for days, because it was not their pony but ours. Just so, the Seminoles' honor has made any Seminole in time remembered return to his village to be put to death, after he had been condemned for some sin, after he had been allowed ample time to go wherever he wished to set his affairs in order before the sentence was carried out. It might give you something to think about, Donal. It certainly gives me a great deal to think about.''

Donal thought about it for a long time before his body demanded that he sleep. This was another face of the Seminole. His conscience raged and protested, he was torn from one mind to another, but in the end he decided, all over again, that for the sake of these Seminoles as well as for the whites, this war must be brought to a close as soon as possible. If the Seminoles were removed from Florida, they would be fed, clothed, allowed to live in peace, and there would be no more tragedies like this of a handful of aged men waiting alone in their hiding place to die.

But he knew, with a conviction that would never leave him, that if it fell his way that he had to kill a Seminole or a number of Seminoles, he would regret the killing as deeply as he regretted their killing of whites. This war should never have happened, it was greed that had caused it, the greed of white men eager to take what was not theirs. But as there was no way to stem the white man's greed, the only thing to do was to end the war as quickly as it could be ended, so that the senseless killing would stop, and what remained of the Seminole people could begin to build a new life in a new land, and pray God that this time the white men would keep their word.

Chapter Twenty-two

The journey to Saint Augustine was accomplished without incident, in spite of Donal's misgivings. As a matter of fact, he had come very near to changing his mind about taking Cordelia and Donal Frederick there at all, after the incident of Donnie's running away and Holati's bringing him home. To Donal, it seemed to be reasonable assurance that the Seminoles would not attack Solopi Heni as long as Cordelia and Donal Frederick were there.

But Carlos disagreed with Donal. "We can't be that sure. It is too much of a risk. Cordelia and Donal Frederick will be better off in Saint Augustine. Even if Solopi Heni escapes being attacked, there would be the constant worry for you while you're off playing at being a knight errant, intent on curing the ills of the world single-handed."

"But if Saint Augustine is so overcrowded with other refugees, where will Donal Frederick and I stay? It doesn't seem right that we should add to the problem when we're perfectly safe here!" Cordelia argued. "Honestly, you men aren't thinking straight!"

"All the same, it's my decision to make, mine and Donal's,"

Carlos reminded her. "And you will be able to make yourself useful, Cordie. From all I've heard, the refugee camps are in chaos. Most of the settlers who took refuge there are uneducated, without any sense of organization, but the way you took over running this house proves that you could help them. You could organize the town ladies, for one thing. Having a lady of your class take the lead would set an example for all of them."

"I'm to help the settlers' families while their men are out killing my friends!" Cordelia protested, her face flushed with anger.

"Cordelia, it isn't the women's fault that this war has disrupted their lives. They had no choice but to follow their husbands to this territory, to suffer hardship and deprivation while their men tried to wrest a living from their holdings. Don't forget that many of them have lost husbands and children to the Seminoles. Of course you will help, you will do everything you can."

"Of course I will. But who is there to help the Seminole women, who is there to help Weleka and Hilolo and Stillipika, and all the others? They've lost husbands and children too, and their lives are just as disrupted and they're just as frightened."

"You can't help the Seminole women, but you can help the settlers' women. Cordelia, don't make it harder for me than you have to," Donal begged her.

With both men against her, Cordelia could do nothing but capitulate. They were right, anyway, no matter how much she would have liked to deny it. If she could be of any help at all, then she must go.

There was still the problem of Delores, and that was even more difficult.

"If you think that I'm going to let Miss Cordelia face that journey without me, and stay in that overcrowded, pestilent city without me to take care of her, you'd better think again!" Delores stormed. "I'm going, and that's all there is to it."

"You are not going. In the first place, you can't ride well enough to keep up with us. And in the second place, with me gone for such a long period of time, I need you here. You will be in complete authority after Daniel, and your nursing skills are needed in case of sickness or injury among the slaves."

Heaven's Horizon

For a while, Carlos was afraid that he would have to keep Delores locked up for twenty-four hours after they had departed, to make sure that she wouldn't try to follow them. But in the end she, like Cordelia, capitulated. No one else on the plantation could nurse a sick child as she could, bring down a fever or tend to cuts and gashes so that they wouldn't fester and cause possible death.

They took only a reasonably strong party of slaves with them when they set out, as a small party could travel faster and without attracting as much attention. The slaves they took were picked men, every one of them above average in intelligence and well versed in handling firearms. Carlos and Donal and Benjamin, the best of the slaves, took turns keeping watch every night, just in case some raiding party, driven to near-madness by their lust for revenge against all whites, might not be as wary of Wildcat's wrath as most of the Seminoles if anything should happen to his namesake.

If Donal was apprehensive about the journey, the way Cordelia and Donal Frederick kept up was a revelation to him. What gently bred Englishwoman of his acquaintance would have been able to keep to the saddle during most of the daylight hours, untiring and uncomplaining? What other boy of Donal's age would be able to ride as well and as tirelessly as a man?

They subsisted on the coarsest of food, as no wagon had been brought along to slow them up. Often a way had to be hacked through underbrush so that the horses could pass. They were plagued by mosquitoes and swarms of gnats, and soaked from torrential rains. But still they pressed on, keeping as well as they could out of the way of any fighting that Carlos knew of.

"Your face is dirty," Donal told Cordelia teasingly. "Miss Virginia Baker would be horrified."

"And you're growing that blasted beard again!" Cordelia snapped. "It's just as well that we haven't any privacy at night, because I don't think I could tolerate making love to a shaggy bear! Besides, you stink."

"We all stink," Donal told her, his smile so cheerful that Cordelia felt like slapping him. "I'm sorry, but we didn't think to pack a bathtub. And if I wanted you to make love to me you'd make love to me. I'm the lord and master, remember. It's your duty to do as I wish, without complaint."

"You'll just find out about that, if you try!" Cordelia warned him, her eyes flashing and her face pink with fury. "Lord and master indeed! I'm no man's slave or servant, and don't you forget it!"

Listening to them, Carlos smiled. The bickering was healthful, and besides it was nothing like the outright battles those two had indulged in when they were at Solopi Heni. And Donal Frederick, thankfully, had settled in, the adventure of the wilderness trip keeping him content. How he would behave himself when he was confined in Saint Augustine was something that remained to be seen, but that wasn't Carlos's worry. Cordelia would just have to cope with him without help.

They arrived in Saint Augustine dirty, unkempt and bone-weary, but they arrived whole and in good health. And here the power of money and influence was brought home to Donal forcefully. In a town where no lodgings were to be had, by nightfall Cordelia and Donal Frederick were settled with the family of a merchant who was only too happy to make room for them in his house in order to gain Carlos's favor, and if Bertram Nettleton's main motive was the profit he hoped to gain from Carlos's patronage after this war was over, Eunice Nettleton was beside herself with joy at the privilege of having a lady of Cordelia's social standing as her guest. Their two boys were doubled up in an attic room to free their own, and Eunice spent agonizing hours with her cook trying to contrive menus that were grand enough for the niece of Señor DeHerrera, the wife of such a distinguished English gentleman.

Carlos felt, and Donal agreed, that there was little danger to Cordelia from Andrew Leyland's agents here in Saint Augustine now that the Indian war was raging. No bounty hunter would risk his life remaining in the territory unless he was there to try to claim the slaves of the Seminoles after the Indians were subdued. Men whose only business here had been to find Cordie would have hightailed it to safety long before this. And if Donal was to be able to visit Cordelia at the Nettletons and spend nights with her whenever it was possible, they could hardly pretend that they were not married.

Heaven's Horizon

Donal appreciated Carlos's influence and the Nettletons' hospitality, more relieved than he would have been willing to admit, but with Cordelia and Donal Frederick having to share a bedroom there was still no privacy. Frustrated at the prospect of not being able to make love to his own wife when they were on the brink of being separated again, he reported to the fort immediately to offer his services in whatever capacity he could be used.

"You're in an all-fired hurry to get away from me!" Cordelia accused him, her eyes burning with combined hurt and fury.

"Cordelia, be reasonable! What good would it do me to hang around Saint Augustine when we can never have a moment alone? I don't like leaving you any more than you like having me go, but that's the way things are and there's nothing we can do to change it. But Donal Frederick will have to sleep in the attic room with the Nettleton boys tonight, even if he has to sleep on the floor!" As if sleeping on the floor would be any hardship for a boy who had just traveled from Solopi Heni to Saint Augustine!

"You just can't wait to take a few Seminole scalps!' Cordelia wasn't in the mood to be reasonable. "It'll give you something to brag about when you're back in England!"

She knew that Donal wouldn't take scalps. The very idea of him scalping a Seminole was ludicrous. But there was a very good chance that his own scalp might be taken, and her worry about him took this means of letting itself out.

Angry and disgruntled, Donal left for the fort, leaving Cordelia to stew in her own juices. It wasn't fair! What was fair about a world that would let them be separated for so many years only to tear them apart again almost as soon as they had found each other? And it wasn't fair that her emotions had to be torn to shreds because her husband felt compelled to go out killing the people who were her friends, and it wasn't fair that her friends would have the same compulsion to kill her husband. Donal was under no protection from Wildcat or any other Seminole. A white man with a rifle was their enemy, no matter whose husband and father he was.

Donal remained in Saint Augustine less than a week. The army had jumped at the chance to procure the services of an experienced wilderness guide, even though he had to act as a civilian adviser, not being trained in military matters. And then he was gone, with Carlos leaving a day later, and Cordelia was left to wait out the end of the war alone, with only her son and Eunice Nettleton for company.

She had no intention of waiting in idleness. The first thing she did after Donal left was to visit the refugee camps. She was appalled at what she found. She nursed the sick, she held fretful babies and rocked them to sleep so that their exhausted mothers could get some rest. She cornered what men were there and raised the question of sanitation, of the necessity of improving their tents and hovels. "I don't care how much work it is, the privies must have deeper holes dug, and be insect-proof so that flies won't breed! You can find something to patch up those cracks to keep the flies out! And any garbage must be burned or buried."

"Ain't no garbage, missus. Not even a bone. Iffen there wuz any garbage, we'd eat it."

Cordelia spent the whole of one endless night helping a settler's wife bring a new life into the world. She ripped up one of her own petticoats for diapers, and the next day she went from house to house begging any usable clothing for all of the refugees.

"I wouldn't dare do what you're doing," Eunice breathed, her eyes wide. "How do you know what disease you might pick up, rubbing elbows with that kind of people? Glory, you might even pick up lice! Let me look to make sure, we can't have lice infesting the children, whatever would we do."

Picking up lice was the least of Cordelia's worries.

The officers at the fort grew to know Cordelia all too well as she demanded admittance again and again and railed at them for not arranging for more assistance for the unfortunates.

"My dear Mrs. MacKenzie, we have done and are doing everything that is in our power to do," Lieutenant Larkin, whose unhappy duty it was to placate her, said.

"Then find the power to do more, because what you're doing isn't enough!" Cordelia stormed. If the lieutenant was frustrated, she was even more frustrated. She had little idea where Donal was. For all she knew he might have been engaged in a major battle, it was

Heaven's Horizon

distinctly possible that at this very moment his scalp was dangling from the belt of a Seminole warrior whom only a short time ago she would have held as one of her friends.

The days were long and hard, but the nights were longer. While Donal Frederick slept in a trundle bed, Cordelia lay awake, fighting to keep from tossing so much that it would disturb his rest. Her first worries that Donal Frederick was too young to hold his tongue and not blurt out that he was a Seminole at heart, that both he and his mother had lived with the Seminoles and loved them, had abated now. Donnie might be only a little boy, but his mind was sharp and he realized that to let it slip would be to jeopardize their position in Saint Augustine. Cordelia had explained to him, and he had understood, that if the authorities were to find out how closely attached they had been to the Seminoles, Cordelia could very well be questioned, commanded to tell them everything she knew of their habits and where she thought bands of them might be right now, and that if she refused to answer their questions she would be treated as an enemy, or even as a spy. Seminole-lovers were not highly thought of in Saint Augustine, and at the very least it would hamper her efforts to solicit clothing and food for the refugees.

So Donal Frederick kept his secrets locked inside of him and no one, not even George and Ben Nettleton, his constant companions, suspected that he was more Seminole than white. It was only when he was alone with his mother that he exploded.

"Iffen I have to keep my mouth shut much longer, when they go sayin' bad things about our friends, I'm just gonna have to pop them one! I'll have to knock out their teeth! Ben's front teeth is already out, but I can knock out George's, hissen have grown back in again."

"I know it's hard, darling, but it's necessary. You wouldn't want to put Uncle Carlos in danger, would you? If anyone found out he'd taken us from the istihapo, they might go poking around and find out that he's half Seminole and that would be dreadful for him, they'd take away his plantation, maybe, and they'd certainly watch him so that he couldn't help the Seminoles any more. We know he's doing it even if he never told us."

Lydia Lancaster

Alone at night, after Donal Frederick was asleep, she lay aching for Donal, longing for him, her longing an actual physical pain.

Why had she been so mean to him, so unreasonable, so jealous? She must have been out of her mind to let her jealousy of the girl Becky McCabe show as much as she had, nagging and prying and accusing until Donal had been driven to distraction. She must have been insane to rail at him about wanting to help to bring this war to an end. Donal was what he was, and no amount of railing on her part would change him. She'd spoiled the short time they'd had together, and now she would give five years of her life to undo it. If only she could see him, only for a moment, to tell him that she was sorry! If only they could be in each other's arms again, then nothing else would matter. She'd never let herself think about Becky again, she'd bite her tongue off before she'd mention her name. She'd never accuse him of wanting to murder her friends.

But Donal wasn't here, and there was no telling how long it would be before she would see him again. Or if she would ever see him again! Heartbroken, worrying, she prayed for the nights to end so that she could at least keep so busy the following day that she wouldn't have time to think.

It was at the refugee camp that she found Carrie White, the young girl Donal and the militiamen he had been with had found at the site of a burned-out holding. Cordelia had taken particular notice of the Appleton family. Julia and Seth Appleton had lost everything, their cabin, their crops, and most of all their hopes.

But Julia was one of those raw-boned, plain-faced pioneer women whose courage could not be destroyed even though everything around her went up in flames. Seth was lame, he walked with a limp because a tree fell on him while he'd been felling logs to raise his cabin, and his unshaven face was gaunt and his eyes had that lost look that Cordelia had seen so often since she had started visiting the camp. Julia was the strength of the family, and it was a mercy that she had that strength.

It was the Appletons who had taken Carrie in, in spite of their own desperate circumstances, when Lieutenant Cary Bullfinch and his men had returned to the fort after Donal had left them to go on to

Heaven's Horizon

Solopi Heni. Julia had taken one look at the girl's face and held out her arms and Carrie had gone into them. "One more to look out fer won't matter," Julia had said. "We-uns got to stick together. Poor, orphaned young'un! I'll do fer her, you just leave her with me."

She'd done for Carrie ever since, giving her the same love and care that she gave her own children, two boys of nine and twelve and a girl of six. Shy, timid, afraid of everything, Carrie clung to Julia like a shadow. The girl never talked, even now, except to give her name.

"It takes time," Julia told Cordelia. "It'll take a deal of time. But she's gittin' better. Reckon she don't look it to you, but you should of seen her when she first come to us. We-un's haulin' out of Floridy as soon's this war is over. Seth, he's got no heart to start over here. But I got some folks back in Georgia, they's dirt poor like us but it's fambly and we'll make out. I'm strong, and the boys is gettin' up to where they kin help. Only I wisht I hed somethin' decent to put on Carrie's back. I patched up the dress she was wearin' when she come to us as good as I could but it's about to fall apart an' leave her naked."

Julia's own clothing was ragged, her children's in even worse state, but still Julia yearned for something decent for the orphaned girl to wear. Her face set with determination, Cordelia had gone back to the Nettleton house and ripped up one of the few dresses she'd managed to bring with her, to cut down to fit Carrie. And she'd made her rounds of more fortunate families even once again, cajoling, begging, charming the ladies of the house to give her anything at all that they could spare.

Today Cordelia had something else for Carrie and little Effie. She'd spent hours making two rag dolls and dressing them. Carrie's had hair fashioned from yellow yarn to resemble her own flaxen hair, and Effie's from brown.

Now she kissed Carrie's cheek. "I have something for you, a surprise."

Carrie hung her head and fingered the one possession of her own, the Seminole scalp that no one, even Julia, had been able to get away from her. Cordelia had seen the girl shake it, throw it on the ground and stamp on it, beat it with a stick. The scalp was only a tattered remnant of its former self by now, and Julia's eyes were sad when she told Cordelia that she didn't know what Carrie would do when it finally fell apart.

"It cain't be good fer her, clingin' to it like she does. It's like she's got to take her hate out on it. She likes to go crazy when I try to take it away from her but how kin she start forgettin' as long as she has it to remind her?"

It had to be taken away, but Cordelia realized that something must be provided to take its place, and that was why she'd made the dolls. Carrie was a little old for dolls, but it was all Cordelia could think of.

Now Carrie's face changed, hardened, suffused with fury as she threw the scalp onto the ground and picked up a stick, squatting down to beat the scalp methodically, her blows falling in a perfect rhythm of mindless hatred.

Cordelia knelt in front of her, careless of her skirt. "Carrie, look at this. It's for you. What are you going to name her? Dolls should have names, don't you think?"

For a moment Carrie didn't look up from her beating of the scalp. When she did, her glance was oblique, and for a moment Cordelia was afraid that all of her work had been for no purpose.

Slowly, Carrie laid the stick aside. Slowly, she stretched out both hands and grasped the doll, and then she hugged it fiercely to her chest.

"Amanda!" she said. "Her name is Amanda."

Cordelia's eyes filled with tears. "Amanda is a nice name. I think it suits her. I have a doll for Effie too. Maybe you can help Effie think of a name for hers."

"No. Hers is hers, she kin name it. Amanda is mine."

Julia's work-worn hand rested on Cordelia's shoulder. "Say 'Thankee'," she told Carrie.

Carrie mumbled the word, rocking the doll. She touched its hair, she fingered its dress.

"I think she musta hed a rag dollie, afore her cabin was burnt an' everythin' in it," Julia said. "It's a blessin' you thought to bring her this one, Miz MacKenzie. She's done talkin'! God bless you, Miz MacKenzie."

Cordelia picked up the stick that Carrie had laid aside, and, gingerly, picked up the scalp with the end of it. "I'll just take this away," she said. "We'll hope that she doesn't need it any more."

"Burn it!" Julia said. "Don't leave no ash of it!"

But Cordelia didn't burn it. She had no idea of what Seminole warrior had given it up to Ray Pettigrew, or of how many white people he had slain. But this war wasn't the fault of the Seminoles, and she couldn't forget that no matter how many tales of horror she was told. The warrior had died in battle, and his scalp deserved a decent burial. And so she buried it, in the Nettletons' backyard, before she went in to endure an hour of very good tea and very boring conversation with Eunice, who still thought that talk of the latest fashions and the latest gossip was more interesting than what was going on all around her in Florida.

"My dear Mrs. MacKenzie! How ever did you get your hands so dirty?"

Cordelia suppressed a sigh. She'd hoped to reach the sanctuary of her room and wash before Eunice saw her.

"I am a little dirtier than usual," she admitted. "But it won't take me a moment to wash and change. And I'll be grateful for a cup of tea, Mrs. Nettleton. I've been looking forward to it all day."

The flattery made Eunice forget her question, and that was a blessing.

Cordelia was at the fort when four Seminole prisoners were brought in. For a moment, the sky seemed to turn dark as she recognized them. Only two of them were adults, the other two were small children, a boy and a girl. Hilolo and Sam Brent, and their children!

Sam's hands were bound behind his back, and he was limping badly. Hilolo's face was a mask of grief and terror. The children clung to her skirts, wide-eyed with bewilderment. They were thin to the point of emaciation, all four of them. Cordelia's heart twisted and she couldn't hold back her cry of protest.

Hilolo's eyes flashed with recognition, but she said nothing. Even now, captured and hopeless, she would not betray Cordelia. Sam also held his tongue, but only stood there, his head high, too proud to show fear.

"How were they taken?" Cordelia demanded. "How did it happen that they were alone, and where they could be discovered?"

"Mrs. MacKenzie, will you please go home? This is no place for you."

"Lieutenant Nelson, I asked how it happened!" Cordelia wanted to run to Hilolo, to gather her into her arms, to speak to her in Seminole so that these soldiers wouldn't know what they were saying, but she was forced to stand there and demand an answer from Hugh Nelson.

"It seems that the slave was wounded and that he couldn't move on with the others after they left their camp, and that this woman, his wife, and the children, stayed on with him. These misguided runaway slaves fight right beside their Seminole masters, as I'm sure you already know. We didn't manage to catch up with the main body, but we found the slave and his Indian wife and children in the camp they had abandoned."

"What's to be done with them?"

Hugh Nelson sighed. "The slave will be held to be returned to his rightful master as soon as it can be determined who it is. The slave hunters have lists, it won't be difficult to find out where he belongs. The woman will be held until she can be removed from Florida with other captured or surrendered Seminoles."

"You're going to separate them! But they're married, you can't do that, they belong together!"

"They do not belong together. The man is a slave, the woman is a Seminole. I didn't make the rules, Mrs. MacKenzie. There's no use in shouting at me. They'll be humanely treated. You shouldn't be wasting your sympathy on them, there are enough white people for you to expend your sympathy on."

Two soldiers took Sam's arms and led him away. Hilolo cried out and wrenched free from the one who was holding her and ran after

Heaven's Horizon

him. If the soldiers couldn't understand what she was saying, Cordelia could, and her heart was lacerated.

Hilolo wanted to go with Sam. If Sam had to be returned to his former owner, then she would go with him and she would also be a slave, so that they would not be separated.

She was overtaken and dragged back. Hugh Nelson shook his head. "It's a pitiful case, I grant you. But there's nothing to be done about it. There's no way they can stay together. Under her own Seminole law, she and her children belong to her tribe."

"Don't try to explain Seminole law to me!" Cordelia wanted to scream. "I know more Seminole law that you've ever dreamed of!" It was a blessing that these stupid soldiers didn't try to claim that the children were slaves as well, because their father was black, but it wasn't only Seminole law that protected them. Their value would be so little, at their age, that Sam's master wouldn't want them.

"Good-bye, Hilolo. Don' you cry. Be brave," Sam called back as he was led away. "Take care of our children. I love you, Hilolo. I love you."

Hilolo didn't answer. The look on her face was answer enough. Her life was over, because Sam was her life.

Sam called something else, and for the briefest second hope flared in Hilolo's eyes. He called it in Seminole, so that the soldiers couldn't understand.

"I'll git away, don' you fret about that. I'll git away, and I'll come back and git you an' the children away too. The white men aren't going to win this war, and when we have 'em licked, we'll be together again."

"What was that you said?" Lieutenant Nelson demanded.

Sam's mouth clamped shut. Lieutenant Nelson realized that it would do no good to question him further. He turned back, and was just in time to see Cordelia make some kind of sign to the Seminole woman. It was a sign filled with sympathy and love.

Women! Hugh thought with disgust. And he turned to follow Sam and his escort into the fort, never knowing that at that moment, Cordelia would as soon have killed any white soldier as look at him.

Chapter Twenty-three

On the few occasions when Donal got to Saint Augustine, Cordelia thought that they were almost as much strangers as they'd been when Donal had found her at Solopi Heni, long after he'd given her up for dead, after she'd gone through years of torment thinking that he was dead.

Donal was haggard on those visits, his eyes hollow with all he'd seen and all he'd endured. And Cordelia's eyes were almost as hollow from worrying about it, and she was almost as haggard from her constant driving of herself to do all she could for the refugees.

"Really, Mr. MacKenzie, you should put a stop to it! Dear Cordelia exhausts herself, her health is bound to suffer, and after all, as your wife and Donal Frederick's mother, her first duty is to her husband and son. You should forbid her to go on with it." Eunice Nettleton was so used to Cordelia's presence in her house now that she ventured to call Cordelia by her first name.

"Mrs. Nettleton, I doubt that the Lord Himself would be able to forbid Cordelia to do what she wants to do, and have her obey Him." Donal, ordinarily the most polite of men, was too exhausted to be tactful, but Eunice's gasp of shock wasn't lost on him. More gently, he added, "Thank you for your concern, but Cordelia will insist on doing what she thinks is right, and nothing I could say would stop her."

With the greatest of tact, Eunice moved Donal Frederick in with her own two boys for the few days Donal was ever able to spend at Saint Augustine, so that he and Cordelia could have her room to themselves. As tired as they were, as low as their spirits were as this war dragged on and on with no decisive victory on either side, but only more senseless killing, their lovemaking was fierce and sweet, leaving them both drained and elated. But, inevitably, the questions were raised, as Cordelia demanded, "How much longer is it going to go on? When is our wonderful army going to give up and let the Seminoles stay where they belong, where they have every right to be?"

"Cordelia, they aren't going to give up. You know that as well as I do. Every burned cabin, every scalped and mutilated settler, only adds fuel to the fire. It's the Seminoles' choice to go on fighting, not the army's."

"They had no business coming here and persecuting the Indians in the first place. You ought to tell them that. You're a gentleman and they might listen to you."

"I'm also an Englishman and my opinion wouldn't carry a great deal of weight. Just because I'm doing what I see as my duty doesn't give me the right to tell your country how to run its affairs. The Seminoles can stop fighting any time they choose. If they don't choose, it's none of my doing and I'll have to go on doing what I have to do."

"How many Seminoles have you killed?" Cordelia could have bitten her tongue off the moment the question was out, but it was too late. Her heart constricted with almost unbearable grief when Donal turned away without answering, his shoulders sagging. He didn't want to kill Seminoles, he didn't want to kill anyone, he only wanted this war to end, and it gave no indication that it was ever going to end.

"Donal, I'm sorry. I had no right to say such a thing. But I keep thinking of Hilolo and Sam Brent and their children, and it breaks my heart. Sam was killed, Donal! He escaped from his captors and tried to make his way back to the Seminoles so he could go on fighting, but he was caught up with and shot, and he died. And Hilolo and her children have been sent to Tampa Bay to wait for removal. I don't even know where Weleka and Wacassa and Runt and Stillipika are, whether they've been killed, or captured, or whether they're still fighting. Sometimes it seems as if I can't bear it any longer."

Donal drew her close, and she pressed herself against him, finding comfort in his closeness. She loved him, she loved him so much! What if he was killed, as Sam had been killed? What would she and Donal Frederick do then? Ashamed, she realized how much more fortunate she would be even then than Hilolo was. Carlos would still protect her and see that she lacked for nothing, and she would go to England and make her home with Donal's family, loved and protected there as well, and knowing that her son would have the heritage to which he was entitled. But Hilolo had no place to go but into exile, her children would never inherit the land that should have been their birthright.

"Don't, darling, don't cry. It can't go on forever. From all accounts, the Seminoles are hard pressed, they can't hold out much longer."

Cordelia knew that. It was on every lip, the stories of how hard pressed the Seminoles were after all this time of fighting, of failed crops, of having to move on before whatever they could plant in the swamps became ripe enough to harvest. They were near starvation. Wherever she was, Weleka was hungry, her children were hungry, Wacassa and Runt were hungry, in rags, footsore from running and hiding and fighting and running again.

"Someday all of this will seem like a bad dream. When you're sitting in my mother's garden in London, you'll find it hard to believe that it happened. It's so peaceful there, Cordie! You'll be happy there, I know you'll be happy because I'll spend all the rest of my life making sure that you're happy."

But England was so far away, and there was no telling when

they'd get there, or if they'd ever get there. Donal was leaving again tomorrow, and this time he might not come back.

No! Cordelia clung to him convulsively, trying to merge her body into his. She mustn't think like that, she must be grateful that he was here now, that he still loved her even when she was bitchy and unreasonable. Now, this moment, was all that she had, she couldn't afford to think of a future that was so uncertain.

They made love. As tired as they were, as heartsick, they were drawn together as though this might be the last time. It was almost indecent, Cordelia thought, as they came together yet again after the first time, and her face burned as she wondered what Eunice must be thinking of all the hours that she and Donal remained behind their closed and locked door. Eunice would undoubtedly think it was a scandal.

Donal Frederick regarded his father warily on Donal's visits. He accepted the fact, now, that Donal was his father and that he had to behave in a reasonable filial manner toward him. Uncle Carlos had told him that he must and he never questioned Uncle Carlos, who knew everything. All the same, whenever Donal came, Donal Frederick wished that it was Uncle Carlos instead. If Mama had to marry anybody, it would have been so much nicer if it had been Uncle Carlos! Then Donal Frederick would get to stay in Florida, right at Solopi Heni, which he had come to love as much as he had loved the istihapo. He could visit back and forth, and it would be perfect. He didn't want to go to England and go to some silly old school just because his father had gone there, and he had no desire to learn to be a gentleman. It was better to be a Seminole and a plantation boy.

If only he were a little older, maybe nine or ten! Then he'd run away again and help the Seminoles. Brooding, he reflected that the way the war was dragging on, it might still be raging when he was old enough to join Coacoochee. So he bided his time, and treated Donal with the minimum, required amount of respect, and dreamed of great deeds that he would perform when he was a warrior and helped to drive the whites out of Florida.

His dreams were crushed on that day in 1837 when full accounts of the new treaty between the Seminoles and the whites found its way to Saint Augustine. There had been rumors that it was going to happen, but Donal Frederick hadn't allowed himself to believe them because they couldn't be true, but when Donal came back after this last time that he'd left, exhausted but jubilant, even Donal Frederick had to believe it.

Things had been going from bad to worse with the Seminoles this year. They were near actual starvation, and all but the most determined of them realized that to go on fighting would end with their complete extermination except for those who had already turned themselves in or been captured.

Abraham, Micanopy's black interpreter, came and went freely between the Seminoles and the army. Both sides trusted him because he was doing his best to bring about a reconciliation of terms that would end the war. And now at last Abraham had persuaded General Jesup to make a great concession. If the Seminoles were to give up, if they would consent to go peacefully to Arkansas, they would be allowed to keep all of their slaves.

There were howls of outrage from white slave owners, but Jesup had agreed to the terms. This war must end, and allowing the Seminoles to keep their slaves was a small price to pay. The white slave owners would just have to accept their losses, for the good of thousands of settlers who wanted to get back to their business of homesteading, both those who were already in the territory and those who were poised to swarm into Florida the moment the war was over and it would be safe.

The final treaty was drawn up at Camp Dade. Jumper, old and broken, came in and signed it. Hola-too-chee came to sign for Micanopy, who sent word that he was too ill to come. And the Seminoles who came in with the chiefs were gathered together and sent to Tampa Bay to await loading on steamers to be taken on to New Orleans and then up the Mississippi to their new reservation.

Micanopy, along with seven hundred Seminoles, came in as soon as he was well enough to travel. At Tampa Bay, the Indians were set up in two encampments, while Jesup waited for the rest of the Seminoles to come in and surrender. All of them were supposed to sail by April 10, but to Jesup's chagrin, the straggling remnants who were supposed to obey the Pond Chief delayed and delayed again. They sent excuses. Some were out hunting and had not returned. Others were preparing to come and would come at any time.

What neither Jesup nor any of the other whites knew was that the Seminoles who hadn't come in, Coacoochee and Osceola among them, were waiting to see if Jesup would keep his promise about the slaves. Donal Frederick know nothing of that, either, he only knew that his hero Coacoochee hadn't surrendered.

"It ain't over! They'll go on fightin', you just wait an' see!" Donal Frederick shrilled, his hands balled into fists as he glared at his father. "They won't never give up, not Coacoochee, he won't, nor Osceola neither!"

"Son, I admire your loyalty to your friends. Loyalty is a wonderful thing, a man isn't a decent man without it. But in this case, you'll have to resign yourself to the fact that even Coacoochee and Osceola will have to give up. They can't go on fighting alone, and when the others come in, it will be over."

"It won't, it won't!" Donal Frederick insisted. "Uncle Carlos, tell him that it won't! Nobody can lick Wildcat an' he ain't about to quit!"

Carlos had arrived two days after Donal had. Immaculate, perfectly groomed, he gave no appearance that he had been fighting at the side of the Seminoles, as well as supplying them, at considerable risk, with everything that Solopi Heni could furnish. His face was as bland as ever as he puffed on a Havana cigar and savored the excellent brandy that he himself had brought with him in case Bertram Nettleton's cellar wasn't all that it should be.

"I'm sorry, Donal Frederick, but your father is right. It's all but over. The Seminoles have lost the war."

He looked at Donal Frederick's face. He tried to soften the blow for the boy he had come to love as though he were his own son. "But look at the bright side. We'll be going back to Solopi Heni now. You'll stay there until it's sure that the Seminoles will all surrender. You'll like that, won't you?"

Next to having Coacoochee and Osceola win the war, there was nothing that Donal Frederick would like better. The longer the delay before he had to go to England, the better.

"I'm afraid we won't be staying at Solopi Heni very long," Donal said. "I must get back to England. I've been away for too long. And your grandmother can hardly wait to see you, son. It's hard for a woman to have a grandson she's never seen."

"Stillipika is my grandmother, and Little Acorn is my grandmother. I don't need another grandmother." Donal Frederick was not to be placated. Only Cordelia noticed the bleakness in Carlos's eyes. He had told her, but not Donal Frederick, that Little Acorn was dead, that even her strength and determination hadn't been enough to allow her to withstand the hardships and starvation that the Seminoles had been forced to endure. Cordelia knew that Carlos's grief would live with him all the rest of his life, and her own heart ached for him as much as it ached for the woman she had loved both as friend and grandmother.

"Nevertheless, you have another grandmother, and she loves you very much. Now run along, Señor DeHerrera and I have things to discuss."

The things they had to discuss were not for Donal Frederick's ears, because they wanted to keep some knowledge of his maternal grandfather from him. It would be cruel to remind him that Andrew Leyland had wanted him dead, and that Donal wanted to return to Leyland's Landing as soon as Cordelia had had time to rest and to pack her ridiculously large wardrobe, to settle with his father-in-law once and for all, to charge him with attempted murder and make sure that he could never again be a threat either to Cordelia or to Donal Frederick. Cordelia would stay in Savannah with their son while Donal took care of it, and once it had been taken care of they would be free to sail for England.

Their journey back to Solopi Heni began a week later. Cordelia had found an opportunity to talk with Carlos alone, her heart aching for him although she tried to lighten the occasion by teasing banter.

"So the intrepid half-Seminole warrior isn't going to immigrate with his mother's people, he's going to stay right here in Florida on his plantation."

"That's right. I may be a stupid Indian, but I'm not that stupid! I like my comforts, as you know perfectly well. I never did claim to be a hero."

"You are a reprobate, Carlos DeHerrera. But I love you anyway."

"Thank you. I love you too, even when you're being a bitch. Cordie, it wouldn't do the Seminoles a particle of good if I called up my Seminole pride and cast my lot with them. My plantation would be forfeit, given over to the greedy whites who started this war. My slaves would go to other masters. I have a responsibility to them, and to the few Seminoles who will manage to slip through the white man's net and take refuge in the swamps. I can be of use to them, where I'd be of no use to anyone in Arkansas, an impoverished man with no influence and no means of helping anyone at all. I wouldn't make a good martyr, Cordelia. But I'm a damned good businessman and a damned good plantation manager so I'm staying where I am. It's just my good luck that staying is where I'll be able to be of some use."

Cordelia put her hand on his big brown one, and her touch was tender. "You don't have to explain yourself to me, Carlos. You did all you could, you did more than almost any other man in your position would have done, so you will never have any reason to be ashamed."

"There's no shame in me," Carlos said lightly, but Cordelia detected a slight mistiness in his eyes. "You ought to know that by now. I'm just a lazy, luxury-loving half-breed and that's all I'll ever be."

Carlos was in a fever of impatience to get back to Solopi Heni, to take the reins firmly into his own hands again no matter how capable Jupiter, his black overseer, was. Donal Frederick was just as impatient. They had been more than fortunate that Black Fire and Fox Fire had come through the campaigns unscathed, and Cordelia's Star Fire was as eager to go as Donal Frederick's Little Fire.

"I'm going to take Little Fire with me to England. I'm not going without him. If he can't go, then I won't go either." Horses, Donal Frederick thought, couldn't go on a ship to England, and so this was a good reason for him to stay in Florida.

Heaven's Horizon

"I'll manage it for you, Little Coacoochee," Carlos assured him, reaching out to ruffle his hair. "Where you go, your pony goes, and that's a promise."

Disgruntled, even though he was delighted that if, by some dreadful turn of fate, he was actually compelled to go to England, Little Fire could go with him, the boy jabbed his heels into the pony's sides and lifted him into a gallop. For a few wildly exhilarating moments he thought that he was going to outrun them all, before Black Fire overtook him and Carlos reached for Little Fire's reins to bring him to a stop.

"No more of that, and that's an order. We don't want you taking a spill, or getting lost."

"Wouldn't fall off, an' wouldn't get lost, you know that." Disgusted, Donal Frederick chafed because the grown-ups were so poky. At this rate, it would take them forever to get to Solopi Heni.

There was no need on this return journey for them to plunge through the worst of the wilderness, avoiding beaten trails in order to elude Seminole war parties, and so they stopped at whatever settlements and trading posts were along their way. It was at one of these that they came upon a slave hunter with five black men, their hands shackled, whom the slaver was herding toward the north so that he could turn them over to their former owners and collect the rewards that had been posted for them.

Cordelia's hand went to her throat as she gasped, "Runt! Runt's with them, he's been taken!"

Carlos reined Black Fire directly in the path of the desolate party with their captor. There was one other white man with them, but he was obviously of less importance, someone who merely helped to guard the slaves.

"What is the meaning of this?" Carlos demanded. "Haven't you heard of the treaty? And that's one of my niggers you have there, the small one. Turn him over to me and let the others go."

"I don't know about that. How do I know this here one's your nigger? And them others, I got no proof that they're Seminole slaves. It's my duty to take them to where their status can be established. As far as I can see, you got no cause to interfere."

"You, there," Carlos looked at Runt. "Look at me! What the devil do you mean, running off? And who are these other blacks with you?"

"They's Seminole slaves, Massa," Runt said, rolling his eyes. He was favoring his right foot, which was swollen and obviously badly hurt. "They done tole me they was. They was took before I was, but they tole me they's Seminole slaves."

"Turn them all over to me," Carlos ordered the slave hunter. "I'll see to it personally that they're returned to their Seminole masters, as the treaty states."

"You look here, if you want the little one, you can have him, but I want my reward. I found him and I'm entitled to it."

"No reward was posted. He wasn't worth posting a reward for." Cordelia made a strangling sound in her throat and controlled it quickly. Runt's eyes gleamed with fury, but he also held his tongue. "But he belongs to me, and I mean to have him. Turn them loose."

The slave hunter made no move to obey. On the porch of the trading post, several men were watching the drama unfolding in front of them with interest, but they made no move to interfere. The owner of the post knew Carlos, and he almost felt sorry for the slave hunter.

"Mister, I don't like to disaccommodate you, but I'm about to shoot right where you're standing." Carlos's hand had moved so fast that even Donal was amazed to see his pistol leveled at the slave hunter's head. "If I were you, I'd move. Getting on your horse and getting out of here would be the smartest move."

The slave hunter's face paled. Even he could see that he didn't have a chance. Behind Carlos, Donal also had drawn his pistol, and all of the blacks in the party held rifles at the ready. Armed black men! This white man must be insane, the slave hunter thought, and who could deal with an insane man in a situation like this?

The slave hunter mounted his horse and wheeled it around. "You owe me!" he shouted. "You haven't heard the last of this!" But it was an empty threat as he and his helper made haste to put all the distance they could between themselves and Carlos and his armed party.

Carlos scowled at Runt. "How did it happen that you were damned fool enough to get caught?"

"Couldn't help it. I was on my way to Solopi Heni, to see about getting a wagonload of supplies for them of us as hasn't surrendered. I got careless. I let a 'gator take a chunk outa my foot."

"And now you have one hell of an infection. I'm going to have to cut it away, and cauterize it. It's going to hurt."

"I reckon it is. You go ahead an' do what you gotta do, but don't call me nigger, you half-breed! Miss Cordelia, Weleka and Wacassa will be mighty glad I seen you, when I git back."

"You've been with them?" Cordelia held out her hands to him, grasping his, "Tell me, Runt! How are they, are they all right? They haven't surrendered, gone to turn themselves in for removal?"

Runt shook his head, his grin stretching from ear to ear. "Not them. They aren't about to get themselves removed. They still have faith in Wildcat and Osceola. And they ain't the only ones. There's more, waitin' to see what's goin' to happen, an' ready to fight again the minute Osceola or Wildcat gives the word."

"And I suppose you're going to be with them, instead of staying at Solopi Heni where you'd be safe and living off the fat of the land," Carlos said.

"You suppose right. As soon as I can walk again I'll be on my way. I ain't your nigger, Mister DeHerrera, and you'd best not take it into your head to try to stop me when it's time for me to go."

"I wouldn't dream of it. Climb up behind one of my men, and we'll get you far enough away from this settlement so that you won't break everybody's eardrums with your screaming when I start to work on you. There are enough curious ears trying to overhear our conversation right now."

Carlos was right. Four bestubbled men and the trader were on the porch of the trading post, their eyes filled with curiosity, but the trader had recognized Carlos and had kept his distance from the altercation with the slave hunter out of respect, just as the other men had kept their distance out of discretion. "I'll ride back in later to pick up what we need. You other men, you had better come with us. You'll be free to go wherever you wish as soon as we can be sure that your recent captors aren't lurking in the vicinity, or you may stay on at Solopi Heni, working for me, whichever you prefer."

They rode until they came to a pleasant glade far enough away from the trading post to suit Carlos. Carlos looked at Cordelia. "You'd better ride on ahead for at least half a mile. I'll send two men with you. This isn't going to be anything for a woman to see or hear, or a boy, either, so take Donal Frederick with you."

"I'm going to hold Runt's hands," Cordelia said firmly. "It will give him something to hang on to."

"And I'll help hold his leg. He's my Uncle Runt, an' I got the right to help him," Donal Frederick put in, his face a stubborn mask that showed that he meant what he said.

Carlos nodded. To send Donal Frederick away would be an insult to his adopted Seminole blood, and to attempt to send Cordelia away would be a waste of breath.

Runt's teeth went clean through his lower lip as Carlos began cutting. His back arched and he jerked spasmodically, and two of the other slaves had to help Donal Frederick hold him down. Still Runt didn't cry out and, unfortunately, he didn't faint. His eyes were wild, starting out of his head, as Carlos finished cutting the infection away and held the knife blade in the flames of the small fire that had been built for the purpose. Cordelia closed her eyes and began to pray. The stench of burned flesh filled her nostrils and made her gag, but she still held tightly to Runt's hands. "Help him, give him the strength to bear it," she begged.

"You done now, half-breed?" Runt's voice was filled with venom.

"I'm done, nigger."

Cordelia was convinced that she would never again hear such a world of respect and affection in any other voices. And, then, at last, she turned away and retched.

Chapter Twenty-four

The white people in Florida thought that the war was over, that nothing remained but for the rest of the Indians to come in so that their entire body could be placed aboard the ships to be removed from the land for which they had fought so ferociously. At Tampa Bay, in June of that year of 1837, General Jesup was losing his patience. The Seminoles had been scheduled to be removed in April, and here half of the year was gone, and still all of the Seminoles hadn't come in. And to make it worse, a good many of the slaves in the two camps of seven hundred Seminoles had slipped away in the night, not convinced that the white people were going to keep their word about letting them go with their Seminole masters.

To add to Jesup's problems, slave hunters kept at him constantly, demanding the right to go into the camps to take slaves who were known to have run away from their white masters. Seething, frustrated, Jesup finally allowed two of them to search the camps.

Seminoles and blacks were equally stunned. Once again, the white man had broken his word, the treaty they had signed meant nothing. In his hiding place, Wildcat heard of the seizures, and his heart was filled with fury. He'd warned the chiefs, he'd warned them over and over, but they hadn't heeded his word.

Filled with the anger that all but consumed him, he set out, alone, across country, to find Osceola where he was camped somewhere near Lake Monroe. The journey was grueling. He went on foot, keeping up a pace that would have killed any other man, around lakes, across barrens, and through danger-ridden swamps. The journey ordinarily would have taken a month. Wildcat arrived at his destination in three days.

Osceola's eyes flamed when Wildcat told him that slaves had been taken from the camps. He himself had had no intention of surrendering, he'd have spent the rest of his life hidden in the swamps where no man could find him.

Osceola sent runners, immediately, to contact all of the Seminole warriors who had not yet turned themselves in for deportation. Some of those who were still free had every intention of abiding by the treaty, but this act of treachery would draw them together and they would stand by Osceola and Coacoochee.

At Tampa Bay, Jesup had come to the last shred of his patience. Not only blacks were slipping away, but a Seminole warrior here, an entire family there. His conscience nagged at him. He'd bent the treaty, if not broken it, and it wasn't an easy thing to live with. Now he must take definite action, and he gave orders for his officers to go into the camps and count every living person in them and give them instructions to pack and be ready to be loaded aboard the ships that were riding at anchor in the bay.

The mounted officers cantered to the encampments, and drew rein, their eyes wide with disbelief. No campfire was burning, there was no one to be seen.

Dismounting, they made their way among the lodges. All they found were the dogs that had been left behind, dogs that had made no outcry to warn of what was going on for the simple reason that every one of them had had its neck broken. Outside of the dead dogs, not a scrap of evidence of the Seminoles was left. Osceola and Wildcat had come in the night, creeping unseen and unheard from one lodge to anothar, taking Micanopy prisoner first and then convincing the others that they should go with them and continue fighting, because they now had their final proof that the white man's word was worth less than the paper that the words of his treaty had been written on.

It was impossible, but it had been done. The entire encampment, more than seven hundred people—men, women and children—had disappeared into thin air right under the noses of the army that was there to guard them.

Abraham, his face drawn and his shoulders sagging, reported to General Jesup after the interpreter had located Osceola and Wildcat. Pacing, his face livid, Jesup exploded. "Micanopy was my hostage, he gave his word! Lying, cheating Seminoles! I should have kept him under guard, I should have known that he couldn't be trusted!"

"General, it was not Micanopy's fault. Osceola and Coacoochee brought two hundred warriors with them. Micanopy was taken prisoner first, he was kidnapped, he had no choice in the matter. If he hadn't agreed, they would have killed him. He wouldn't be the first chief they have killed for wanting to surrender. Osceola sent you a message. He says that the treaty has been broken, that the white men broke it and that it is no longer valid."

The two men looked at each other, with something near despair in their eyes. They had both done evarything in their power to bring this war to an end, and now it was all undone.

"We'll have to run them down," Jesup said, his voice heavy.

"General, they're in the Everglades, and summer is settling down."

Reluctantly, Jesup nodded. There was no way he could take an army of white men into the Everglades in the summer. The rainy season had already begun. His men would suffer, they would sicken and die as their boots rotted from their feet and their uniforms disintegrated. They would have to wait until fall, when cool weather would allow them to march. And then, the flames of war that they had thought they had extinguished would spring up again, and set all Florida ablaze, and the war would go on for a third year, if not longer. It wasn't a bright prospect.

* * *

At Solopi Heni, Cordelia's face was white with anger as she faced Donal.

"You don't have to go! Haven't you risked your life often enough, haven't you done more than any other man in your place would have done? This time you might be killed!"

"Cordelia, they sent for me. Tracking Osceola and Wildcat down isn't going to be an easy task. Plans must be made, strategy worked out, and I can't turn my back on this situation no matter how much I want to stay with you."

"It isn't your war! If I were a man, which I thank God that I am not, it would be my war, after the Seminoles took me in and treated me as one of them, but you don't have any such excuse!"

"I'm not looking for an excuse. All I want is to help resolve this vicious, senseless conflict before every last one of your friends is killed, to say nothing of an untold number of innocent settlers, including women and children!" There was an edge of exasperation in Donal's voice. "Why can't you understand that, Cordelia? I don't want any more people killed if it can possibly be helped, it's as simple as that. Carlos is my friend, I don't want to be safe in England and hear that Solopi Heni has been burned to the ground and he's been massacred. If my services, as small as they are, can help bring this war to a close one day sooner than it otherwise would be, then it's worthwhile."

"I understand, but that doesn't mean that I have to like it! Oh, Donal, how am I going to bear it? Do you realize that we've been married for eight years, and we haven't spent six consecutive months together in all that time? It's too much, it isn't fair!"

"Darling, it can't possibly go on much longer. Even Osceola and Wildcat will realize that there's no point to going on resisting. They're intelligent men, they realize that going on fighting can only end in disaster for their entire nation."

"Then you don't know Coacoochee and Osceola! They won't give up, they won't ever give up!" Cordelia cried.

There was no reasoning with her, so Donal tried to comfort her in the only other way he knew by taking her into his arms and holding her close and kissing her. He could feel how she was trembling, and it hurt him to the core. The last thing he wanted was to cause her any more distress, after all she had already been through. It seemed as if they must have been born under some crossed star, destined to suffer through separation after separation, and he could only pray that it would all end soon and that at last they could be together.

He wouldn't dwell on the possibility that he might not come back, this time. He would come back, anything else was unthinkable. And the next time he returned to her, it would be permanent.

Cordelia was stiff and unyielding in his arms for a moment, but then he felt her begin to relax as his kisses drew some of the tenseness out of her. But the moment was shattered as Donal Frederick burst into their bedroom, his eyes filled with belligerence.

"Delores said you're goin' this morning. It won't do you any good, you ain't never going to catch Coacoochee nor Osceloa! Nobody kin catch 'em! I knew the war wasn't over, I knew it 'ud never be over as long as Coacoochee wasn't catched!"

"Yes, I'm going. A man has to do his duty, son. I hope that that's something you'll understand, when you grow up."

Donal Frederick's face was filled with scorn. "I know it now. All Seminoles have to do their duty, no matter how much they don't want to or how much it hurts. Do you think I'm a baby?"

Donal sighed. "Of course I don't think you're a baby. You're extremely grown-up for your age. I suppose it's because of your upbringing and your natural intelligence, although your grammar is something to be deplored. It will be a good thing when you're in school in England, but in the meantime I hope that your mother will work on your speech habits so that you won't find yourself disgraced among your peers when we get there. You will want to fit in. Being a misfit isn't a comfortable thing."

"I'm glad you're goin' away!" Donal Frederick told him. "Wildcat's gonna go on fightin' anyhow, an' now we won't have to go to England so soon."

"Our journey will be delayed, certainly. But I'd advise you to resign yourself to going to England, Donal Frederick." Donal the elder grimaced. "Darn it, Cordie, we must do something about that name! Why don't we just call him Freddie? It would save a lot of confusion. I'll be damned if I'll have him called Junior, and Donal Frederick is too cumbersome."

Cordelia couldn't help laughing even in her present state. "Why don't we call him D.F.?" she suggested. "That would solve the problem."

"Call me Coacoochee!" Donal Frederick said, his face scarlet with indignation. "That's really my name, anyway, not just dumb initials!"

"I think D.F. would be better, although the boys you will know in England will probably call you Freddie. I'm afraid that Coacoochee would be too much of a mouthful for them."

"Then they're stupid," Donal Frederick said flatly.

"That's enough, D.F." Cordelia spoke sternly. "Say good-bye to your father now, and it wouldn't really hurt you to wish him a safe return."

"All right, but I ain't gonna wish him good luck in catchin' Coacoochee! It's all right if he comes back without gettin' himself kilt. You like him." For such an ungracious statement, it brought a great deal of satisfaction to his parents, because it was the closest he had ever come to accepting Donal as his father. Not that he'd had much chance, with all the separations, but it was a beginning.

"Thank you," Donal said gravely. He held out his hand, one man to another. "I'll see you when I get back, then. And don't attempt to run away again to join your Seminole friends, no matter what kind of reports filter back to the plantation. I want your word on that. Your mother has enough to worry about without having to worry about you."

Reluctantly, Donal Frederick nodded. He wouldn't break his promise. Cultured English gentleman or untutored Seminole, a man's word, once given, was not to be broken. There wasn't so much difference between them after all.

Cordelia stood at the head of the drive, her arm around Donal Frederick, to watch her husband ride away from her once again. Fox Fire was well rested and eager to go, and Donal sat the saddle as if he'd been born to it. She thought that her heart would break when he turned to look at her once last time before he turned his face forward again, going toward what he felt compelled to do.

"Don't you cry. Don't you dast cry!" Donal Frederick commanded her.

"I'm not going to cry. At least, not right this minute."

"All right, then. Let's go ride the fields, Mother. With Uncle Carlos away, we ought to make sure everything is all right. You don't have to come if you don't want to, you can just come if you want to."

Cordelia looked down at him, at his straight back and the shoulders that were already showing signs that they would be as broad as Donal's when he had attained his growth. His sense of responsibility in wanting to ride the fields and see if everything was all right was another trait that she was proud of. Jupiter was perfectly capable of running things, but a white man was supposed to supervise no matter how capable his superintendent was.

"All right. But this evening, we're going to study! I want to surprise your father with how much you've learned when he comes back. He's right, you've picked up too much of the idiom of the plantation boys. Not that I don't approve of you playing with them, darling. The more you know about other people, the better you will understand them and the better you'll get along with them. But there is another world, and you must be prepared for that as well."

Helping Donal Frederick with his studies would take her mind off other things that she didn't want to think about. When this war was over, one side would have lost and one side would have won, and she knew which side would win no matter how unjust it was.

But there was nothing she could do for the Seminoles, nothing she could do for uprooted, bereaved Hilolo and her children, for Weleka and Wacassa and all the others. Even Runt, who had left Solopi Heni as soon as his foot had been fit to travel on, mounted on one of the plantation horses carrying a paper that stated that he belonged to Carlos and that he was on Carlos's business, in case he should be unfortunate enough to run into slave hunters again, or the army. By this time Runt would be back with Coacoochee and Osceola, as much a Seminole as they were and with as much to lose once the Seminoles had met their final defeat. He had said that he would not return to Solopi Heni, that he would live in the Everglades with the other Indians who managed to escape the final roundup.

"Come on!" Donal Frederick tugged at her hand. "I'll race you to the stable, and if you win because your legs are longer I'll race you to the east field, 'cause Star Fire can't beat Little Fire, I'll bet you anything she can't!"

"You're on. It's a bet. If I win, you will study for an extra hour this evening!"

Cordelia filled every day to the brim with activity, but still the hours dragged. With both men gone, virtually nobody visited the plantation, and there was a dearth of news. The long summer had passed, and she had received only two letters from Donal, both of them as cheerful as he could make them but holding out little hope that this second phase of the war would soon be over.

The plantation ran like clockwork. When Carlos returned he would find his holdings in as good and prosperous a condition as he had left them.

Cordelia and Donal Frederick rode the fields every day. It helped fill up the time, and Donal Frederick loved pretending that he was in charge as the only white man in residence. Jupiter, concealing his amusement, deferred to him, and managed in the process to teach the boy a great deal about plantation management, not by correcting him, but by saying, "Yes, I see your point, but I had it in mind that we might do it this other way. We'd better think about it and decide which would be best, don't you think?"

So they thought about it aloud, both faces filled with concentration, until Donal Frederick made the final decision, to do it Jupiter's way. Donal Frederick gave the orders and Jupiter carried them out and Donal Frederick was filled with enormous satisfaction that he was doing a good job of management for Uncel Carlos. The other slaves followed Jupiter's lead, calling Donal Frederick Master Donal, their voices filled with affection because the boy was never arrogant with them, as he so often was with Carlos and his father. He would be able to handle men when he grew up, to win their respect and their liking.

A handful of the strongest, youngest slaves slipped away in the night, to go and find the Seminoles and join them, filled with the sense of injustice that they knew so well no matter how fortunate they themselves were to be owned by Señor DeHerrera. Jupiter and Donal Frederick discussed it, and decided that as long as Carlos had let any slave go who was determined to leave to seek a life of freedom among the Seminoles, they would continue the policy and close their eyes to the disappearances, giving orders to the sentries to let the "escaping" men pass. The slaves who remained worked a little harder to make up for the loss of manpower, and Solopi Heni didn't suffer.

Peter Breckenridge came to visit one afternoon. He had been south, where the fighting raged on and off as the army attempted, with indifferent success, to find and force a decisive battle. Cordelia stifled her gasp of dismay when she entered the drawing room where he was waiting for her. He was thinner than she had ever seen him, and his face showed the strain and horror of the things he had seen. Like Donal, he too had offered his services in order to help bring the war to an end.

"I hope my visit isn't inconvenient, Mrs. MacKenzie," he said, stiff and formal.

"Peter, you stop that! You know perfectly well that no visit from you could ever be inconvenient. And if you call me Mrs. MacKenzie again, I'll snap your head off. I've missed you. Outside of Carlos, you're the best friend I have in Florida."

The expression on Peter's face tore at her heart. "And I've missed you. I came because I have news of your husband, and I knew that you'd want to know what I've learned no matter how little it is. The last I heard, he's still all right. He's acting as a scout, as he did before. All that time he spent searching for you, before he gave you up for dead and returned to England, is invaluable now. His Seminole guides taught him well. He's a fine man, Cordelia. If I had to lose you, I'm glad that it was to him."

"Has he been in any fighting?"

"Skirmishes only. It seems that that's all the army can manage. The Seminoles still strike and disappear. Damn Osceola, and Wildcat as well! I would never have believed that any savage could have their intelligence, their brilliance at doing the most damage with the least losses to themselves. With so few of them left, and ill-armed and starving, it's phenomenal how they manage to go on."

Cordelia's throat felt tight. Crushed at losing her, still Peter was gentleman enough, and man enough, to bring her news of her husband. He would have made a wonderful father for Donal, and he would have made a wonderful husband for her. She hated it that he'd had to be hurt. Why did someone always have to be hurt? If there were any sense to the scheme of things, Peter's plantation would have been so far from Solopi Heni that she would never have met him, and then he wouldn't have fallen in love with her only to lose her when Donal had reappeared. He could have been married by now, had a wife he loved and children of his own.

But there wasn't any sense to things, and human beings had to take what was handed to them and make the best of it. She told herself that Peter was still young, that after she had gone to England he'd fine some girl who had been waiting all her life for him, and find his own happiness. All the same, it wasn't fair, because none of this should have happened in the first place.

In spite of his protestations, Peter was so exhausted that he was forced to accept Cordelia's insistence that he stay for dinner and for the night. If he'd set out after dinner to make the long ride to his own plantation, he might have fallen off his horse simply because he was too tired to go on sitting the saddle.

Cordelia slept poorly that night. She was too aware of Peter sleeping in a room just down the hallway from her. If things had turned out differently, she might have been sharing his bed. She ached for him, hating the longing she knew he must be suffering, just as she ached for Donal, and suffered because Donal wasn't with her now.

She was up at daybreak, in spite of having slept so poorly, but Peter was up even before she was, ready to leave after a hasty breakfast. They stood together in the doorway while his horse was brought around, their hands clasped together.

"Cordelia, this is a hard thing for me to say. You know that I don't wish any harm to Donal, but if it should happen, if by some unthinkable circumstance Donal doesn't come back, would you think about marrying me? I still love you, and I know that you're fond of me. We could make it work, we could build a happy life together, and Donal Frederick would accept me, there would be no problem there."

Cordelia swallowed through her clogged throat. "If Donal didn't come back, I'd want to die. But I wouldn't die. I wouldn't be allowed to die, because of Donal Frederick. And Donal would want me to go on, and to find all the happiness I could. Yes, Peter, I would think about it. I'd think about it very hard. But promise me that you'll look for someone else."

"It's a pact, then," Peter said. He managed to smile, his smile filled with a tenderness that almost undid her. "Or would an adopted Seminole like you call it a treaty?"

"Not a treaty. Treaties seem made to be broken," Cordelia did her best to smile too. "Just call it a promise, and remember yours to me, that you'll start looking for someone else. There are so many girls who would be delighted to accept you! And one of them would be right for you, I know it."

Neither of them had intended it. It simply happened, in Peter's case because he loved her so much, in hers because she was so genuinely fond of him. His mouth came down over hers in a kiss that broke both their hearts, and then Peter put her gently away from him and strode out to where a groom was holding his horse.

"Send word if you hear from Donal," Peter said. "And I'll do the same. I think it would be better if I didn't call on you again, unless I come to bid you and Donal good-bye before you leave for England."

Cordelia was so torn after Peter left that she couldn't bear to stay in the house. She didn't want to ride the fields, she needed to be alone. What she needed was exercise, hard, punishing exercise, to clear her mind and take it off Peter, and the possibility that was always in the back of her mind that Donal might not be so lucky this time, that this time he might not come back. He didn't have a charmed life, and she knew that he was in constant danger.

A few minutes later she was in a riding habit, and Donal Frederick, regretfully, was explaining to her that he couldn't ride with her to Jonestown, the trading post nearest to Solopi Heni, the same one where Donal had been given his final directions for finding Carlos's plantation. "Jupiter an' I have to have a conference. And besides, there ain't anything to do at the trading post 'cept hang around while you look at everything in the store an' gossip with Mrs. Jones. An' Isaac's sons are stupid, likely I'd crack one of 'em right in the mouth iffen he said something against the Seminoles."

"Like as not you would, and so it's a good idea for you not to come," Cordelia agreed. Her journey would be safe enough. Jupiter would assign, through Donal Frederick of course, two well-armed guards to accompany her, and there was no fighting in this vicinity.

The journey by horseback would take up the first half of the day and leave her plenty of time to look at what wares Isaac had to offer and to hear whatever news he'd heard of the war, and still get back to Solopi Heni only a little after dark.

Almost as soon as she had started, she knew that this journey had been a good idea. The weather was cool and the air was clear and sweet, and once they had left the cleared land and plunged into a stretch of pine forest the peace and quiet soothed her nerves. Tom and Sam, the guards Jupiter had assigned her, were in high spirits because this was a holiday for them. Grinning, they reined their mounts from one side of the trail to the other, making a great show of their alertness.

"All clear ahead. Ain' nothin' to one side or the other. Hain't laid eyes on a Seminole yet," Tom, who was in the lead, called back.

"You keep that rifle ready anyhow, don't pay to take chances!" Sam called back. Both slaves patted and stroked the horses they were riding. In the southern states, it was unheard of for a slave to ride a horse. If they had to be mounted, it was on mules, but no such rule prevailed at Solopi Heni. Carlos said that if there was any reason for a slave to be mounted, then he should be mounted on a good piece of horseflesh so they'd be of some use if an emergency arose. Tom and Sam would be as proud as kings as they rode into the settlement mounted on such fine animals, and armed, every inch Carlos DeHerrera's men, which set them head and shoulders above any other slave. And favored slaves at that, to be entrusted with guarding the mistress herself!

The scent of pine needles was so clean that Cordelia could taste it, and the rhythm of Star Fire's movements and the clip-clop of hooves lulled her and set her mind to wandering. For some reason, she began to think of the Reynards, of Nadine and Lucy and Frederick, of Caleb and Matthew and David and Mark. Caleb would be a man now, he must be twenty! And her darling Mark, her six-year-old Mark, would be fourteen.

Was Nadine happy with Emery Haskwell, was she able to love him as much as she had thought she'd loved Donal? She'd be a good wife, and there was no doubt that Emery would be a good husband to her, if Nadine could stand his overbearing manner, so sure he knew better than anyone else. And what about Miss Virginia Baker? Was she still running her academy for young ladies, did she ever think of Cordelia?

Lost in her dreams, Cordelia was jerked back to the present by the sudden urgency in Tom's voice, so low that she nearly didn't hear it at all.

"Hist! There's someone, or somethin', up ahead there and off to the right. There, in them bushes, I saw them move. Sam, you stay back with that rifle ready to shoot, hear me? I'll have me a look."

Cordelia and Sam were far enough behind, and around a little bend in the trail, so that Cordelia couldn't see where Tom had pointed. But her curiosity got the better of her and she slid from her saddle and tossed Sam the reins and crept forward until she could see. There couldn't be any real danger. If it was an Indian, he wouldn't harm them, and if it was an animal Tom would take care of it.

She reached the bend in the trail and strained her eyes. Afoot, his rifle at the ready, Tom was advancing on the clump of bushes when they parted. The figure ran toward a swift-running branch of the

Lydia Lancaster

Apalachicola, half carrying, half dragging a shorter figure and carrying a burden in its other arm.

"Stop!" Tom shouted. "Stop or I'll shoot!"

The figure paused at the bank of the river, and, then, as Cordelia's blood froze, it released the smaller figure and its hands moved to the throat of what Cordelia now saw was a baby.

"Tom, don't! Don't shoot! Weleka, no! For the love of God, no! It's me!"

Weleka's face turned toward the sound of her voice, and her hands stayed their dreadful task. Running, her heart pounding as if it were trying to burst out of her breast, Cordelia was crying as she raced toward her friend, who held a tiny baby in her arms, while Little Thunder stood there, tottering on legs that could hardly hold him up.

Weleka was thin, drawn, starved to skin and bones. Her clothing, what remained of it, was in shreds. As thin as his mother, Little Thunder was obviously ill, very ill. However they had come here, Cordelia knew that Weleka, in order to save the boy who was already half grown into a warrior, had been going to slay her tiny infant so that she could support Little Thunder when they plunged into the river to escape being taken. If Little Thunder had been well enough to swim on his own, Weleka would have swum the river with one arm, holding the baby over her head with the other. Cordelia had seen other Seminole women do the same.

Now she had Weleka in her arms. "I can't believe it! Weleka, I simply can't believe it! What are you doing here, so far from your people?"

Weleka was weeping too, as she clung to Cordelia, great sobs tearing at her body.

"I was coming to you, to Carlos's plantation. Little Thunder is sick, he has a fever, nothing I could do, any of us could do, could help him. The swamps made him sick, I knew he would die if I didn't get him away. And the soldiers were hunting us, the others had to run, to find another hiding place. My only chance to save Little Thunder was to get him to Solopi Heni, where he could be cared for until he is well. Carlos has told us how Delores is wise in

Heaven's Horizon

the ways of illness. I hoped to get there before my time came, but it took a very long time. Wacassa saw that I had a horse, although it couldn't be spared. We rode double but still we covered a great distance every day. But four days ago, the horse fell, and its leg was broken, and I had to kill it. The next day, while we were walking, my time came upon me, and my daughter was born."

A daughter, a little girl. The baby's black eyes looked at Cordelia, unblinking, unaware that in order to save her older brother, her mother would have had to sacrifice her.

Alone, weak and starving, pregnant, Weleka had managed to cover all that distance to reach her goal. After the horse had died she'd had to help support Little Thunder when he was too weak to walk. It was no wonder that she had given birth ahead of time, it was a miracle that she, that any of them, had survived at all.

Tom already had Little Thunder in his arms, the boy's emaciation making him so light that lifting him was nothing at all. Tenderly, he placed Little Thunder on his horse and then remounted and held him with one arm so that he wouldn't fall off. And Sam, without being told, lifted Weleka and placed her on his horse, mounting behind her to hold her steady while Cordelia handed her her baby.

Delores herself met them at the door of the plantation house, having hurried to see who was coming when she had heard the sentry's horn. With an exclamation of dismay, her arms received Weleka as Sam handed her down. Cordelia supported Little Thunder up the few steps and through the door into the entrance hall.

Donal Frederick appeared at the top of the staircase, a book in his hand. He'd been going to surprise his mother by studying his next English lesson and knowing it before she got home. The book dropped to the floor as he raced down, his feet flying.

The eyes of the two boys met, and together they sank to the floor, clinging to each other, not saying a word but just holding each other as if no power in the world could ever make them let go. Donal Frederick's brother was here, he had his brother, and his heart swelled with such joy that he felt that his whole body was singing.

Chapter Twenty-five

Donal squatted on his heels in the first cool of the evening. All around him the patrol was setting up camp for the night. The smell of meat roasting over campfires filled the air, and he grimaced. In spite of all his protests, the lieutenant in charge had allowed the fires so that they could cook the deer that Donal himself had brought down that afternoon, far enough away from the patrol that if any Seminole had heard the shot the soldiers would not be put into any danger.

The lieutenant was probably right, he told himself. There weren't any Seminoles to see the fires or to smell the roasting venison within miles, they were on another wild-goose chase. They'd found the remnants of an encmapment, in one of the swamps, yesterday, but the Indians had abandoned it several days before, leaving so little trace of their presence that if Donal hadn't been so well versed in using his eyes to detect the slightest sign the patrol wouldn't have realized that the Seminoles had been there at all.

One of the soldiers approached him, carrying a pole with the handles of small buckets of coffee looped over it. The coffee was strong and bitter, but it was satisfying and Donal drank it gratefully. As soon as the venison was done, he'd fill his stomach, and then he'd catch a few hours' sleep before he took the most dangerous watch of the night, the one that came before dawn, when men's eyes were filled with sand and their heads were apt to nod as their bodies demanded sleep at the proper hours for sleeping.

There was very little point for them to be out on this patrol anyway. King Philip, Coacoochee's father, had been captured, and Donal had heard that the old chief had sent for his son, who would be allowed safe passage to see him with a view of bringing the war to a close. The Seminoles' backs were against the wall, they were running out of places to hide and strike and run and hide again.

The Indians were never safe in one place for long enough to harvest a crop, they were living on the hearts of cabbage palm and on flour made from pounding coontie roots, they were starving. Even a firebrand like Wildcat must realize that their only hope of surviving was to surrender and allow themselves to be taken to their new lands in Arkansas. If Wildcat reported to Osceola that he could also come in under a flag of truce to discuss terms, then this war would come to an end at last. King Philip was old and tired and ill, he had given up, he had seen the wisdom of surrender, and his word carried weight. In a matter of a few weeks Donal could be back at Solopi Heni at last, reunited with Cordelia and Donal Frederick.

Rolled in his blanket, Donal slept, while his stomach told him that it was grateful for the full meal even as his mind told him that he might have to pay for that meal in a very unpleasant way. But the night passed without incident, and he told himself that he was turning into an old woman, jumping at shadows where no shadows existed.

They marched again the next day. Donal couldn't for the life of him figure out what they were supposed to do if they did come upon any Seminoles. With Wildcat scheduled to talk to King Philip with a view to ending the bloodshed, a battle with the Indians now hardly seemed appropriate.

Viciously, he swatted a mosquito that landed on his neck. Damn this war anyway! What was he, Donal MacKenzie, an Englishman

Heaven's Horizon

by birth, doing in the Florida wilderness being eaten alive by insects? He'd had enough insect bites to last him for two lifetimes. He didn't know which was worse, fighting Indians or enduring swarms of flying, blood-thirsty bugs.

He needed new moccasins. Swamps played the devil with clothing. The common soldiers suffered even more than he did, in their inappropriate woolen uniforms, in their heavy boots. You'd think that any fool would know that men should be equipped according to the climate and the terrain they had to fight in. When all this was over, and he was back in England, he never wanted to come within shouting distance of an army again.

He ranged ahead, every sense alert, eyes, ears, sense of smell. Even his pores seemed to be alert. He wondered if he'd ever again, as long as he lived, be able to sleep through an entire night, or make a journey of any sort, even down a Mayfair street, without that wariness he'd learned could make the difference between living another day, or dying right now.

Another thought, and one that he didn't welcome, kept intruding into his mind. He was here, while Cordelia was at Solopi Heni, within easy traveling distance of Peter Breckenridge's plantation. And he knew that Peter had been going home, and there was no doubt that Peter still loved Cordelia. The question was, did he love her enough to do his damnedest to betray Donal while Donal was away? And lonesome, heartsick, frightened, would Cordelia turn to Peter for comfort?

Donal was ashamed of himself. Peter Breckenridge was an honorable man, and it was an insult to Cordelia to let himself imagine that she would succumb to her loneliness so far as to go into Peter's arms. All the same, he wished that Peter was any place on earth but at his plantation, too near to Cordelia for Donal's comfort.

Even as Donal was thinking dark thoughts, Coacoochee was riding into Saint Augustine to meet General Jesup and his father. Wildcat was dressed in his finest for the occasion. He was not here as a prisoner or as a beggar, but as a chief to be contended with, one who demanded respect and intended to have it.

The people of Saint Augustine lined the streets to see the officers escorting Wildcat ride by with the Seminole chief in their midst. Wildcat sat as tall as his slight stature allowed him, dressed in bright red leggings and a tunic made of the softest, palest skins. He wore a turban bound with silver and set off with a white feather. There was an intricately beaded belt around his waist, and he wore bands of silver on his arms. The citizens of Saint Augustine gaped and cheered, and if the cheering wasn't for him, then it only showed the ignorance of the white people. All the same, he knew that his appearance impressed them, and there was a gleam of satisfaction in his eyes. Let them realize that they were dealing with a warrior, with a great chief, and not a defeated enemy come to beg for mercy.

The procession wended its way to the northern edge of town. Fort Marion was built of stone, erected by the Spanish, who had called it the Castillo de San Marcos. It looked like nothing less than a castle that had been kept in ill repair, with its battlements and a forty-foot moat that was filled with muddy water. Once the proud defender of Saint Augustine, the fort was now used by the army as a prison.

Wildcat rode across the drawbridge into a great, central square, its flagstones broken by weeds that had split some of the stone in their battle for life. Here was where Philip and the thirty or so men, women and children who had been taken prisoner with him were allowed to exercise and to build fires to cook their food.

Wildcat waited, his face impassive, while a heavy door was unlocked and his father, followed by his people, came out. King Philip was a pitiful sight, and Wildcat's heart wept. His father, that proud, unconquerable man, was a walking skeleton, his shoulders stooped, his face heavily lined. Defeat had broken him, and there was no hope left in him.

"There is no course left for us except total surrender. If our nation is to survive at all, it must be in exile," Philip told his son. "Go to Osceola, tell him to come in, tell Alligator and Jumper and Micanopy and all of the others who still resist that it is no use, that I, Philip, say this."

Coacoochee's heart burned, and he wanted nothing more than to tell his father that he would never surrender, that Osceola would never surrender. But he knew that his father was right. Even exile, as bitter as it was, was better than total extinction.

"I will talk to Osceola," he promised. "He must be the one to negotiate with the whites, he is the one with the gift of words that will win us the most favorable terms, if he will agree to come."

The conference between father and son was brief. Wildcat was taken immediately to General Jesup's office. Jesup sat behind his desk, and General J. M. Hernandez, who had been the one to capture Philip, stood behind him. A black interpreter was also there, to translate what was said.

Jesup was curt to the point of being insulting. "The fighting is over. Even the most recalcitrant among the chiefs realize that. I will give you two weeks, no more, to find Osceola and give him my ultimatum. By the end of the two weeks you are to return here with Osceola's answer, because you are as of this moment my prisoner."

It was all Wildcat could do to contain his anger. He burned to leap at Jesup and fasten his hands around his throat and squeeze the life out of him. But his father's instructions weighed heavily on him, and he must do as he had been told.

"I will return at the appointed time," he said, his words as still as his face.

Fourteen days later he was back, bearing a beaded pipe and a white plume, gifts to Jesup from Osceola, the symbols of peace.

"Osceola has agreed to talk with you. He and his warriors will meet you five days from this day. The meeting place will be at Fort Peyton, under a flag of truce, on the understanding that they will come as free men, not as a defeated enemy."

Jesup bit back his sharp retort. Damn these Seminoles and their pride! For the sake of the peace that was so essential, with Washington leaning heavily on his neck demanding to know why he hadn't brought the war to a close, why he had let a handful of savage, ignorant people hold him at a standstill, it would be the height of foolishness to say anything that would ruffle this savage's feathers now.

"I wish to stay here for the five intervening days, to be near my father," Wildcat went on, laying down his own terms as if he fully expected them to be met. "At the end of the five days, I will attend the parley between you and Osceola."

Once again Jesup choked on his bile. Let Wildcat have his way, it would make no difference in the end.

With a look filled with contempt, Wildcat stalked out of the room, as proud as though the Seminole cause had not been lost. Even hating and distrusting the white man's word as he did, Wildcat would have found it hard to believe the conversation that was taking place between Jesup and Hernandez even as he stepped into the cell where his father was held and the door was locked behind him.

"President Van Buren wants this war ended, and he wants it ended now. My own officers are grumbling, and my patience is at an end. Enough! When Osceola comes to Fort Peyton, he is to be taken prisoner, along with every savage who accompanies him, and that will put an end to it once and for all."

Hernandez's face expressed his shock. "But, General Jesup, they're coming to Fort Peyton under a flag of truce! You can't do that, it would be beyond all honor!"

"Honor!" Jesup snorted. "Don't talk to me about honor! I know Osceola, I know him like a book! He'll talk, using that cursed golden tongue of his, and all of his words will mean less than nothing. And when the talks have finished, he and his warriors will fade back into the forest and the war will go on. No! It's to end now, and the only way to end it is to take him, flag of truce or no flag of truce. You are to head the delegation and you are to take the man and his warriors prisoner on the spot. That is an order!"

His face white, Hernandez reluctantly nodded.

Osceola, keeping his own word, was gathering his people. He sent droves of cattle to Saint Augustine, and a number of slaves. Five days later, he was at Fort Peyton with his people, seventy or so warriors and women and children, to meet the white general as he had agreed.

Osceola's heart was heavy as he stood beside the pole that had been thrust into the ground and that bore the white flag of truce that waved in the mild October breeze. He no longer believed that he and the Seminoles could win against the whites, but he still hoped to win

Heaven's Horizon

more favorable terms than exile to Arkansas. There was a possibility, one that he meant to fight for with every ounce of his strength, that he could force the whites to grant the Seminoles a reservation in the Everglades, rather than removing them entirely from Florida. No white man coveted Everglades land, no white man could or would live there. The Great Spirit knew that it was little enough to ask, room to live in the swamps that no white man wanted.

General Hernandez, with two hundred men, was prompt in keeping the appointment. Filled with shame for what he was being forced to do, Hernandez began the talks by demanding to know why some obscure Indian chief had not sent in his slaves as he had promised.

Osceola was bewildered. He knew nothing of the matter, and the matter had nothing to do with these talks, and he said so.

"I have never heard of this chief you mention. I am here in good faith, to discuss terms of peace between our peoples."

"You haven't answered my question! There can be no talk of terms until you have answered it," Hernandez snapped, his hatred of what he was doing making him sharp. There had to be some excuse for his actions, and this was the one that had been agreed upon.

Osceola turned to a warrior who stood beside him. "Words fail me, my throat closes over them in the face of this treachery. Speak for me."

Too late, he realized that he had walked into a trap. The soldiers were already deploying, circling the band of Seminoles, and there was no escape. Almost before the full realization of what was taking place got through to him, every Indian was seized by two soldiers, even the women and children. Mounted near Hernandez, Wildcat shouted with fury.

"Treachery! What treachery is this? I persuaded Osceola to come to this meeting in good faith, and once again the white man has broken his word, his word means nothing!"

It was too late for escape, Wildcat was as much a prisoner as Osceola and all of the rest. His face a mask of hatred, Coacoochee dismounted and fought his way to Osceola's side. Together, side by side, they walked the seven miles to Fort Marion, looking neither to the right nor to the left, their faces betraying nothing of their emotions at this final, unbelievable piece of treachery against them.

Osceola and Wildcat and several others were locked in a cell in the southwest part of the prison. Altogether there were about a hundred and fifty Seminoles at Fort Marion, made up of other small bands that had been taken over a period of time.

While Wildcat paced and raved, Osceola sat impassive, saying little. Osceola was ill. No one had known of it, and even now he made no mention of it, but he had been ill for months, and he knew that his illness was one that would take his life. If it hadn't been for his illness, he would not have considered the peace talk that had ended in this disaster.

"The white eyes won't hold me, no prison will hold me!" Wildcat raged. "I'll get out, and I'll make them pay. I, Wildcat, will exact such vengeance on them for their treachery that they'll wish they had never set foot in Florida!"

But there was no way to escape. The walls of the prison were thick, they were heavily guarded. Their cell had only one window, a narrow slot set so high in the wall that no man could reach it and even if he could, no man could get through it, it was simply too small. And outside of the prison, directly underneath its walls, was the moat.

Wildcat studied the opening high in the wall. And that evening, he refused food, and the next morning he refused food. Half a dozen of the other warriors, inspired by his example, also refused to eat.

Osceola ate what was given to him. He was too ill, too near the end of his strength, to make an attempt at escape, and his frame was too large in any case, there was no way that even total starvation would shrink his bones so that his body could pass through that window.

Doggedly, at night, under cover of darkness, the Seminoles ripped blankets into strips, hiding their work under other, whole blankets during the day. And still Wildcat fasted, and the handful of others with him.

At night, one of the striplings, more agile than the others, steadied himself on the shoulders of a warrior and drove the blade of a knife

Heaven's Horizon

into the stone wall. Pulling himself up by the handle, he reached the narrow ledge that was under the window and with another knife, he worked crumbling bit by crumbling bit to loosen the stone and plaster that held the rusted bars in place. There were two bars, and he loosened only one of them until it could be lifted out. The loosened bits of plaster and stone were concealed with the strips of blanket. And at last, Wildcat was ready to lead the others who had starved with him in their bid for freedom.

"I grieve that you cannot come with us." he told Osceola. "You are the leader we need, you are the one our people will follow."

"There is no way I can go with you. You must go alone. Go to Arpeika, who has not come in with his people. Tell him that I, Osceola, ask him to take up arms again against the white people. He will heed your words."

The two lifelong friends looked at each other for a long moment before Wildcat turned away, his heart heavy with grief. He was certain that he would never see Osceola again. This was their final farewell.

Donal listened with stunned disbelief as the exhausted scout delivered his message. Sprawled on the ground, holding a bucket of coffee with both hands, the scout gave vent to his feelings without regard for army etiquette.

"You left a trail a blind, hundred-year-old Seminole could follow! I didn't hev no trouble findin' you, it just took time. Squattin' here like a bunch o' sittin' ducks, that's what you are. You got some real desire to git yerselves massacred, or is it you just don't know no better?"

"I am unaware that there is any danger," Lieutenant Price told him, his face stiff. "We are on our way back to Saint Augustine. There is a truce on."

"Truce in a pig's eye! That's what I'm here to tell you, if you'll wash that West Point pride outa yer ears an' listen! There ain't no truce, there ain't no treaty, all hell's about to bust loose agin. Wildcat come in all right, an' he talked to Osceola like King Philip tolt him, an' Osceola an' his people met General Hernandez and two hundred troops at Fort Peyton. But Jesup had done give Hernandez orders to take the lot of them prisoner an' throw them in cells at Fort Marion, an' that's just what Hernandez done."

"Under a flag of truce!" Lieutenant Price's face showed every ounce of his shock and disbelief. "That is impossible, Simmons. No officer of the United States Army would violate a flag of truce!"

"They wouldn't, huh? Well, they done did! Took 'em by surprise without a shot fired, an' throwed them in prison. Only they didn't stay there, leastways not some on 'um. That there Wildcat done the impossible. He done starved hisself, an' some others along with him, till they could slither outa a openin' no more'n eight inches wide! It couldn't be done but they done it, an' they hightailed fer Arpeika's town an' Wildcat talked Arpeika into goin' on fightin', an' every other Seminole still loose is helpin' 'em. The war's still on, an it's still hot an' it's gonna git hotter, an' you better keep yer eyes peeled iffen you want to keep yer scalps."

Colonel Zachary Taylor was a competent man, and one who had every intention of carrying out General Jesup's orders to pursue the Seminoles into the Everglades and defeat them so soundly that they would be forced to surrender. Disgraced by his action in violating Osceola's flag of truce, the whole country raising outcries of outrage against him, attacked by the press, it behooved Jesup to get this business over with in order to salvage what he could of his reputation.

With more than a thousand men, with hundreds of horses, with supply wagons carrying food and ammunition, Taylor set about carrying out his orders. For once, the high command hadn't stinted.

Abraham, the interpreter, was with them as were a few Delawares. Heart-weary, his heart all but broken, Abraham still had hope that the war could be ended without the loss of any more lives, if only the Seminoles could be persuaded to listen to reason.

With Taylor's hard-won permission, Abraham set out with four Delawares to search for and find Seminole villages in the swamp, to try to persuade them to surrender. It took them several days of traveling through incredibly hostile terrain before they located Wildcat's village, situated on one of the broad hammocks that were the only places in the Everglades where people could attempt to wrest out a living.

Abraham's heart sank as Wildcat derided the offers Abraham had brought. "Promises!" Wildcat said. "Do the white men think I'm a fool? Go back to that man Taylor, and tell him that Coacoochee will never listen to more promises, that Coacoochee will fight and go on fighting."

There was no moving him. Even with the few people he had left, he was determined to carry on the war. Abraham had no choice but to leave without accomplishing his mission.

But there were other hidden villages, handfuls of other scattered Seminoles, who might listen to him, and he sought them out, and many of them, starving as Wildcat and his village were starving, agreed to surrender. As the days passed small groups of them made their way to Taylor's camp, until nearly five hundred had come in, both Seminoles and blacks, along with whatever cattle they had left. They were sent north under heavy guard, to wait for schooners that would start them on their journey of exile. And then Taylor marched. He had had reports that Wildcat was now camped near Lake Okeechobee, with two thousand people, including more than two hundred able-bodied warriors who were still in condition to fight.

Fighting his way with the others through saw grass that was almost impossible to penetrate, Donal steeled himself to endurance. God grant that they'd find the camp, and that the battle would be decisive.

He put one foot in front of the other, his hands were cut and bleeding in a dozen places from hacking at the saw grass, his ears strained to hear that first, dread sound that would herald the battle that lay ahead of him, the *yo-ho-ee-hee* of the Seminole war cry. He'd heard it before, often enough so that the very thought of it could make the hair on the nape of his neck stand up and his pores run with cold sweat. It haunted his dreams, and he thought, in his blacker moments, that it would haunt his dreams until the day he died, even when he was safe in his own bed in London.

It was Christmas Day. At Solopi Heni, Carlos would be making it as festive for Cordelia and Donal Frederick as he could. There would be gifts, there would probably be a party, with families from neighboring plantations invited. The plantation house would be filled with the scent of pine boughs, mistletoe would hang from the chandelier in the drawing room, Cordelia would dance until dawn in other men's arms.

"*Yo-ho-ee-hee!*"

Every drop of blood in Donal's blood froze as the cry rent the air, and then his blood began to race, hot and fast. The waiting was over, the searching was over, they had found the enemy but the enemy had been waiting for them. The hammock ahead of them had been cleared of brush to make a battlefield. Beyond the cleared place was a forest of cypress, where the Seminoles were concealed.

Bullets ripped the air around him, sped past his face with the sound of angry bees. The first line of troops was advancing, and Donal saw Colonel Gentry, in the lead, fall, and an untold number of his men. But Zachary Taylor was shouting for others to fill the ranks, orders were obeyed. And then Donal didn't have time to think anymore, he was too busy fighting for his own life.

The troops surged forward, into the deadly fire from the Seminoles. Wildcat handled his warriors like the wily, seasoned general he was, ordering them to move back, and back again, and to gather up their wounded and leave none to the mercy of the soldiers. With rifles empty, red men and white met in individual, hand-to-hand combat, using their weapons as clubs, slashing with knives and tomahawks. Even in the heat of battle, Donal marveled that a handful of Seminole warriors, two hundred against a thousand of Zachary Taylor's troops, could fight with such brilliance and such deadly effect even as they retreated.

The main tide of the battle had gone through the cypress forest now, and gained the beach of Lake Okeechobee. Donal, who had been carried off to the side, still in the trees, grasped his rifle barrel and faced a painted warrior who was springing at him with a knife. The warrior was short, but his shoulders and arms were powerful, and for a moment Donal thought that this was where he was going to die.

And, then, another warrior appeared and struck down the shorter warrior's knife. Donal's eyes widened as his mind flooded with disbelief. It was Carlos. Carlos DeHerrera, dressed in breechclout and painted with war paint, fighting on the side of the Seminoles! And the short warrior wasn't a Seminole at all, it was Runt, Donal would know him anywhere now that he had a chance to dash the sweat from his eyes.

The Seminoles were losing, there was no way they could win against such odds. But Runt, with a scream of frenzied rage, turned to search for another victim.

Donal's eyes and Carlos's met and locked. "Get him out of here!" Donal said, his voice hoarse. "Get him to hell out of here! It's all over, do you want him taken and sent back into slavery?"

Carlos nodded. An instant later, his long strides caught up with Runt, his hand raised and fell with perfect precision, and Runt crumpled to the ground. Carlos swept him up into his arms and disappeared among the trees.

Carlos! Señor DeHerrera, here, fighting for Wildcat, fighting against his own kind! Donal was stunned. He'd had no idea, he hadn't even come close to guessing, but then, he thought wryly, neither had any other white man in Florida.

His seconds of reflection were his undoing. He whirled barely in time to see a tomahawk descending toward his head, wielded by an arm so powerful that he knew it would cleave his skull in two. In the same split instant, he saw Peter Breckenridge, his rifle hanging muzzle-down toward the ground as Peter saw what was happening and made no move.

This is it, Donal thought. This, then, is the time and the place, in this hammock in the Everglades in the territory of Florida, and I will never see Cordelia again, I will never see England again.

And then Peter raised his rifle and fired, and the Seminole fell, the blade of the tomahawk missing Donal's skull by a fraction of an inch.

If I don't make it out of this battle alive, marry Cordelia, Donal thought. You've earned the right, and I'll try not to begrudge it to you.

It was the last thought he had as a bullet from another direction tore into his shoulder, the force like a sledgehammer as it knocked him off his feet. The battle still raged around him and on the beach, but he knew nothing of that. Soldiers were being killed, Seminoles were being killed, twenty-six soldiers with more than a hundred wounded, and the Seminoles suffered even more casualties before they at last broke and fled.

Chapter Twenty-six

Donal remembered little of the aftermath of the battle, and he thought it was probably a good thing, because his brief periods of consciousness had been filled with pain that was so unendurable that he was glad when unconsciousness overtook him again.

He remembered that he had been carried on a litter back to where the supply wagons waited, that Peter had supervised every step of the journey. He knew that Peter had ridden beside the wagon that had transported him all the way to Saint Augustine, cursing every jolt that threatened to set his wound bleeding again. He knew that he'd lost so much blood that it was nothing less than a miracle that he had survived the journey at all. And he remembered, filled with deep shame, screaming when a doctor had probed for the bullet that was still lodged in his broken shoulder, before he had fainted and remained unconscious for so many days that hope for his life was given up.

The doctor who was caring for him here in Saint Augustine was named Bryant. A harried, tense man, he took more than an ordinary interest in Donal's care.

Lydia Lancaster

"You must lead a charmed life. I see where you nearly cashed in your chips at least once before," Bryant told Donal when Donal was capable of making sense out of spoken words. "How you ever survived that one is something I'll never understand. And why you're still alive now is also something I'll never understand. It can't have been any doctor's ministrations, you were too near death for that."

"I had reason to live. Two reasons, a wife and a son."

"Then that's what saved you."

"How soon can I travel? I have to get back to Solopi Heni, Cordelia is waiting for me, she'll be frantic."

"Not for a good while yet. Do you want to undo all my work? A journey like that would kill you. Not to mention the fact that nobody knows where Wildcat and those devils of his will strike next. How the man manages to hang on is something else I'll never know. We'll get a message to your wife. You aren't getting out of that bed if I have to tie you to it, so you might as well be patient and let nature finish my work for me."

Patient! How could Bryant know the frustration that the very word caused? More than eight years, and in all that time, he'd hardly been with Cordelia at all, he'd spent most of those years believing that she was dead and his unborn child with her. And the miracle of finding her again had been shattered all too soon, when he'd found her only to leave her again so soon after their reunion. There must be something seriously wrong with his head to have let his conscience force him to take part in a war that was none of his own, and yet he knew that if he hadn't tried to help, he would have regretted it all his life.

"Peter Breckenridge," he said. "Do you know where he is, if he's still all right?"

"I know where he is, but his being all right is a matter of opinion. He went off chasing after the Seminoles again as soon as he knew that you had a fighting chance, and he didn't come out unscathed this time. He took a gash in his left leg that I had a devil of a time stitching up. Luckily someone on the field knew how to apply a tourniquet to control the bleeding. Señor DeHerrera took him to his plantation. Foolish thing to do, but Breckenridge wanted to go and Señor DeHerrera had him carted on a litter, I understand.''

Donal lay digesting that bit of news. He was glad that Peter was alive, but he wasn't at all sure of his emotions about Peter being at Solopi Heni, with Cordelia nursing him, in constant company with him.

"If he could go on a litter, why can't I?"

"Don't be a damned fool, man! The cases are entirely different. Your shoulder has to knit, and you're still so weak from loss of blood that you'd undoubtedly die the first day out. Look at you, you're exhausted just from talking for this little while! And I have work to do. Go to sleep. If I had a chance to sleep for twenty hours a day for the next month or so, I'd be eternally grateful! Grab a couple of hours of sleep for me, ha ha."

Fuming with impatience, Donal had no choice but to follow Bryant's advice. Carlos wasn't here to organize a safe passage through the wilderness in any case. Carlos! Donal still couldn't get over his shock at finding out that the man he had so admired was a turncoat, a traitor. No wonder he hadn't been worried about bringing Cordelia to Saint Augustine, no wonder he dared to travel wherever he wished, whenever he wished, without fear! Donal knew that Carlos was half Seminole, Cordelia had told him, but he'd never dreamed that Carlos's Seminole blood would prompt him to throw in his lot with his mother's people, knowing full well that there was no way the Seminoles could win and that if he were discovered he would lose everything, his plantation, his slaves, the way of life that meant so much to him.

He heard the talk that went on around him, as well as the talk of other wounded men who were ambulatory and who came to discuss the war with him. For all of Wildcat's continued defiance, with Osceola imprisoned and with the larger part of the Seminole nation gathered and awaiting removal, the war was all but over. No decisive battle was possible, all Wildcat could do was strike isolated cabins and settlements, ambush small parties of soldiers, and then fade away into the swamps to lick his wounds until he could strike and run again, each time suffering losses that could not be made up.

Lydia Lancaster

* * *

When he was allowed, at last, to try to stand on his feet, Donal was appalled by his weakness. It was all he could do to stagger on leaden legs to the nearest chair, sweat streaming from every pore on his body while waves of nausea swept over him.

"Still think you're fit to travel?" Bryant asked him, his mouth curved with wry humor. "To hear you talk, I thought you'd head right out the door the minute I allowed you to get up, and be halfway to the DeHerrera plantation before I could stop you."

"Very funny." Donal's voice was vicious.

"Mr. MacKenzie, you'll gain strength very rapidly now. I only caution you not to push your luck. Give it a week or two at the least, and you'll be fit to travel if you're foolish enough to try to make it all that distance when you might very well fall into one of Wildcat's traps. It could be you as well as anybody else."

Almost as though Donal's wishing had made it come true, Carlos appeared at his bedside less than a week after Donal's initial attempt at walking. Donal was still shaky on his feet, subject to fatigue greater than any he had ever known, but his determination to get back to Cordelia made him throw common sense to the winds.

"Get me back to Solopi Heni. I'm going out of my mind here."

"You were out of your mind to be here in the first place. You could have been back in England. You're all right where you are."

"Try me! I'll sit a horse if I have to tie myself to the saddle, but I'm going whether you help me or not. You took Peter, so why can't you take me?"

"I was prepared to take Peter. I'm not prepared to take you, I didn't bring that large a party with me. I made a fast trip just because Cordelia's fretting to have firsthand word of you."

"Peter had to be carried on a litter. I can ride."

Carlos sighed and then he shrugged, a purely Latin gesture bf reisgnation. "Very well, then. The day after tomorrow. I might have known you'd get out of your bed hell-bent to get back as soon as you knew I'd left Cordelia alone with Peter. Don't you trust your wife, Donal?"

"Don't push our friendship too far!" Donal snarled at him.

Carlos only grinned at him, and that made Donal angrier than ever, for no sane reason that he could think of.

If Carlos was philosophical about Donal's determination to return to Solopi Heni, Bryant's anger could hardly be contained.

"You're insane! It's one thing for a man like Señor DeHerrera to make the journey, knowing the country as he does, and in the best of health, but hampered by an invalid neither of you will have any chance at all! You'll be taking both of your lives in your hands. I have a good mind to order you placed under arrest so that you can't do such a damned-fool thing."

"I'm a civilian, Doctor. You can't place me under arrest. And Señor DeHerrera is far too smart to be caught in an ambush." What would Bryant think, Donal wondered, what would he do, if he knew the truth about Carlos, that Carlos was half Seminole, and that he had chosen to fight on the side of the Seminoles? But he would never know, because Donal had no intention of telling him or anyone else. God knew that the man must have gone through hell before he came to his decision, and that he must still be going through hell knowing that his mother's people would soon be exiled forever.

"I'll send my condolences to your widow!" Bryant snapped. "I should have operated on your brain as well as your shoulder!"

Donal had thought that he was strong enough, that his determination to get to Cordelia would carry him through, but the first few hours in the saddle proved him wrong. By noon of the first day he was reeling, his face drawn and white and his shoulder throbbing with every jolt. Carlos regarded him with detachment, almost as though it held no interest for him.

"We can camp the rest of today and take you back to Saint Augustine tomorrow."

"No! I'm all right. If I can just lie down for an hour I'll be able to go on."

"Have it your way." Laughter sparked from Carlos's eyes. "If we were actually in any danger from the Seminoles, it would be the disaster Bryant predicted it would be. A fat lot of help you'd be!"

They rested for two hours, not one. Somehow, he never knew how, Donal managed to remain in the saddle for four more hours that afternoon. He could scarcely swallow the food Carlos pushed at him that evening. His shoulder felt as though it were on fire, and the rest of his body was numb, as heavy as lead.

"It isn't too late. We can still turn back in the morning," Carlos told him.

Donal closed his eyes, not bothering to answer. He wasn't going back. He'd be all right in the morning, all he needed was a good night's sleep.

They made even slower time the next day. After the noon stopover, Donal had to be helped back on his horse. By the time the sun was sinking in the west, Carlos's eyes were narrowed to thoughtful slits as he looked at him.

"I was insane to let you come. The journey's going to take a great deal longer than you bargained for, Donal. Get all the rest you can tonight, because we're veering south in the morning."

"Not going directly to Solopi Heni!" Donal was jolted out of his aching fatigue. "What the devil are you up to now, Carlos?"

"How does the idea of spending a little time in a Seminole camp strike you? We'll be catching up with packhorses loaded with supplies, that I sent from Solopi Heni, along the way. It's time you learned how the other side lives, if you don't go dying on me on the way."

His words, so casually spoken, stunned Donal to the core. "A Seminole camp? Are you entirely insane, then?"

"Temper, temper!" Carlos chided him. "John, here, has a notion that he'd like to drop out of our party when we get there, and throw his weight into the fight."

"Now I know you're mad! You'd let one of your best men throw his life away, when all you have to do is forbid him? He's your slave, he has no choice but to obey you."

"No man is my slave, in that sense of the word. My people stay with me of their own choice. Any man among them is free to leave any time he chooses. Now close your mouth and save your strength, because the going will be rough and we have a long way to go."

"You can't even find a Seminole camp!" Donal protested. "They're so well hidden that the whole United States Army has only been able to find a handful of them!"

Carlos laughed. "You forget who I am, Donal. I can find the one I'm looking for. But it won't be necessary, even if the camp has moved, because we'll be found before we can fine them. Now, do as I say and go to sleep."

No one who didn't know the terrain as though a map of it were etched on his brain could have followed the tortuous trail, indiscernible even to Donal's practiced eyes, that Carlos followed with such confidence. Far from any beaten path, far from any human habitation, Carlos kept on, meeting the packhorses and his slaves whom he'd sent out from Solopi Heni, just as he had told Donal he would. Supplies for the Seminoles, sent at a risk that made Donal's blood run cold.

They went on and on, always south, into wilder and wilder territory. When Donal's strength gave out, he was carried on a litter. When he could ride, he rode. The journey took on the quality of a nightmare. What was he doing here, going to a rendezvous with the Seminoles, when a short time ago he had been fighting them? What was he doing here, when Cordelia and Solopi Heni were in the opposite direction?

The unseen track seemed to go on forever. Donal felt lightheaded. Grimly, he gripped the reins more tightly with his left hand, and twisted his right into his horse's mane. He'd be damned if he'd black out and fall!

The shape materialized out of the darkness after they had camped for the night. Half asleep, Donal jerked awake when he saw that it was Runt. Carlos flashed Donal a sardonic grin. "I'm afraid you'll have to get up again, Donal. Our guide is here," he said, with laughter in his voice.

They came on the camp so suddenly that one moment everything around them was blackness, and the next there was a dimly glowing campfire. Donal had no idea where they were. He'd given over keeping track days ago, knowing that he had no choice but to follow Carlos. He attempted to dismount as the others were doing, but he would have fallen if another figure hadn't materialized beside his horse and steadied him. And then Runt was beside him, grinning as widely as Carlos had when Runt had found them.

"Lean on me, Master Donal. We don't want you fallin' flat on your face, there's some here might think it was funny."

"Then they have a peculiar sense of humor," Donal told him. "I'm glad you're still alive, Runt. Cordelia will be glad as well, if Carlos ever decides to get us back to Solopi Heni."

"I'm considerable more alive than you are, right at the moment," Runt told him. "Over here. We better git you settled down, Miss Cordelia would be mightily upset if we didn't take good care of you. By rights I ought to drop you, for telling Señor DeHerrera to knock me head over ass back at Lake Okeechobee, to git me out of the fightin', but I reckon you did it in good faith, to keep me from gittin' taken or kilt. My jaw ached for a week. I'll pay that half-breed back someday, when I git the chance, just to let him find out how it feels to have a friend turn on you like he did on me."

It was the poorest sort of camp. It was obvious that the handful of people here had no intention of staying once they had received the supplies that they so sorely needed. There were no chikees, only ragged blankets spread on the ground. The Seminoles were in rags and obviously on the point of starvation. There were no children here, and Donal could make out only three or four women. Nothing remained of their former glory except their fierce pride and the determination not to be driven from their homeland.

As little as the Seminoles had, the visitors were invited to eat. The food was unpalatable, nothing like the savory food, in limitless quantity, that had been offered Donal at the istihapos he had visited during his first search for Cordelia. But he ate it, with expressions of satisfaction.

A slight, graceful black woman, tiny and scarcely more than a girl, with the gentlest face Donal had ever seen, came out of the shadows to stand at Runt's side. Her pregnancy was obvious, she must have been four or five months along.

"Marilu," Runt told Donal, his face filled with pride. "She's my wife."

Heaven's Horizon

Donal was set back on his heels. He'd had no idea that Runt had married, that he was to become a father.

"Congratulations, Runt. Your wife is lovely. Cordelia will be happy when I tell her."

Another woman came from the shadows to stand beside Marilu. This was a Seminole woman, the tallest, strongest woman Donal had ever seen, towering over Runt and the tiny Marilu. She was many years older than Marilu, probably in her thirties, her face carved of sharp planes and having nothing of beauty except for its pride. This woman was also pregnant, further advanced than Runt's wife.

The grin on Runt's face widened. "Gentle Doe," he said. "She's my wife."

For a moment Donal couldn't speak at all, it was as if he had lost command of his vocal cords. Two wives! He knew that the Seminoles often had more than one wife, Osceola himself had two, but for Runt, who had remained single all these years, to suddenly appear with two wives was more than he could assimilate. And such a wife as this second one was!

Then he had to fight to keep his face expressionless, because of the incongruity of Gentle Doe's name. Gentle Doe indeed! She looked as fierce as any warrior.

"Again, congratulations. You're a fortunate man, Runt. Cordelia will be delighted. But tell me"— his curiosity was so great that he was forced to step over the bounds of propriety —"how do your two wives get along together?"

"They get along just fine. They love each other like sisters." And Donal saw that it was true. There was no jealousy here, no ill feeling between the two women. Gentle Doe put her arm around Marilu and murmured something to her, and then led her away.

"She wants Marilu to get her rest, to go back to bed. She looks after her like a mother hen with one chick. I don't have to do much worryin', when I'm off huntin' or fightin', because I know Gentle Doe will take care of her better than I could. If something should happen to me, Gentle Doe would take care of her, they'd have each other and the children."

Donal had to agree with him. How shocked most white people

would be, but wasn't this still another manifestation of the Seminoles' highly civilized way of life, of their gentle natures? Everything Cordelia had told him about them had been true, and it gave him a great deal to think about. Only when they were pushed and betrayed further than the limits of endurance did they show fierceness and cruelty.

A brave came to sit, with his legs crossed, in front of Donal, his black, unblinking eyes studying Donal's face. Donal tried not to appear uncomfortable under the scrutiny.

"You are Donal, the husband of Cordelia, who is my sister and the sister of Weleka, my wife. I am Wacassa. I wish to send my gratitude to my sister for caring for Weleka and Little Thunder, my son, when Weleka took Little Thunder to Solopi Heni when Little Thunder was sick. Your woman Delores nursed my son back to health, and both they and my new daughter, who was born on Weleka's journey to Solopi Heni, are back with us safely. Your son, Little Coacoochee, gave the orders that they be escorted safely to us, with well-armed guards. Your son and my son are brothers."

And you should be my brother, just as Cordelia is your sister, Donal thought, his heart heavy. Only fate had decreed that it was not to be, because of the greed and inhumanity of the white men against the red.

He had known nothing of Weleka's journey, Carlos had not mentioned it. How could Weleka, a lone woman, burdened with a sick child, and pregnant, have made it all the way from the swamps to Solopi Heni? His admiration for the Seminole people deepened. No white woman could have done it, no white woman would have dared to try.

"Little Thunder will live to become a warrior," Wacassa said. "Weleka is sleeping, she was caring for a wounded man for days before we made this journey and she is tired and I do not wish to disturb her now, but she will thank you herself in the morning. She has a great desire to meet the husband of Cordelia."

Even in the midst of war and poverty and disaster, the Seminoles persisted. Donal felt humble. Carlos had been right. It had been time he learned how the "enemy" lived.

Heaven's Horizon

Runt led Donal to a blanket. Carlos was directing the off-loading of the packhorses for the night, horses that would beyond any doubt go with the Seminoles tomorrow when they started their perilous journey back to the Everglades.

Trembling with exhaustion, Donal lay down on the blanket and drifted off. The camp was quiet now, the others settling in for what was left of the night. He was asleep almost before his head touched the ground, confident that when he woke in the morning he would still be in possession of his scalp.

He woke to full sunlight, at a gentle touch on his forehead. A young Seminole woman stood there, her face filled with concern.

"I am Weleka," she said. She knew a little English, and with Donal's smattering of Seminole words, they could make themselves understood. "You have no fever, and that is good. My sister Cordelia would be sad if you did not return to her in good health."

There had been three girls, Donal remembered. Cordelia, and Weleka, and Hilolo. But Hilolo's husband, Sam Brent, was dead, a victim of this war, and Hilolo and her two children were captives. The same grief for Hilolo that Donal had seen in Cordelia's eyes was plain in Weleka's. There was a lump in Donal's throat.

"I am happy to meet you at last, Weleka. Cordelia will never forget you, she holds you fast in her heart."

Weleka smiled. "And I am happy to have met you, my sister's husband. I will bring you food now. Eat all you can."

Donal was just finishing when a small commotion in the camp brought him to his feet. The handful of inhabitants of the camp, only enough, he realized, to see to getting the supplies Carlos had brought back to the Everglades, were gathered around another figure he didn't recognize.

He walked toward them, and, then, with what amounted to pure intuition, he knew who this warrior was. Not a warrior, not a brave, but a chief, the prime motivator of this continuing war. It was Wildcat himself!

Donal studied the man as he approached the group. For such a powerful chief, he didn't look like much until you took into account his fierce eyes and the equally fierce expression on his face.

Wildcat, his once-wiry figure a little thickened now with full maturity, was still little more than skin and bones, faring no better than his followers, but there was something about him that sent a chill down Donal's spine. No man of any intelligence would make the mistake of underestimating him.

Wildcat looked at Donal as he approached, and his penetrating gaze made the short hairs on the back of Donal's neck prickle. For a few heart-stopping seconds, he wondered if Wildcat would give the order for him to be killed on the spot. And, then, incredibly, Wildcat smiled.

"You are the father of Little Coacoochee. Take my greetings to my namesake and tell him that I remember him well."

"I'll do that. Coacoochee. Donal Frederick, Little Coacoochee, has never forgotten you, to him you are the greatest warrior, and the greatest hero who ever lived. He will never forget you, and Cordelia and I will never do or say anything to diminish you in his eyes."

The black eyes remained fixed on him, but Wildcat said nothing more. Clearly, whatever the men were talking about, Donal was not to be included and his presence was not wanted until they had finished. Nodding at Wildcat, Donal turned and retraced his steps to help with the loading. He'd seen Wildcat, he'd talked to him! It was hard to believe, but it had happened. Back in Saint Augustine, no one would believe that he had been within touching distance of the man who had struck fear across the face of Florida, and walked away alive.

For a moment it bothered Donal that there was no way that he could get word to the army as to Wildcat's whereabouts. But the feeling passed. Even if he could tell them, by the time they could get here Wildcat would be gone, and all of his people with him. Donal had the feeling that this war was far from over. Having seen Coacoochee, he knew that the man was by no means ready to give up, that he would go on fighting as long as it was humanly possible.

Cordelia felt as if every drop of blood had been drained from her body, leaving her so weak that her feet wouldn't move even as she began to run, her skirts gathered up so that she wouldn't trip over them. John, one of the guards who watched the perimeter of Carlos's holdings, had galloped up only moments before to tell the household that Carlos was returning, that his party was in sight, and that Donal was with them, being carried on a litter.

She couldn't believe it, she wouldn't believe it until she had seen him with her own eyes, until she could hold him in her arms, living proof of flesh and blood that she could touch and hold and go on holding until her mind would accept the miracle that he was actually here.

It was true, there they were, she could see them now as her flying feet carried her to the end of the long, winding drive. But Donal wasn't on a litter, he'd insisted on remounting even though he'd had to be helped to do it. He was damned if he was going to arrive flat on his back and frighten Cordelia half to death. It was shameful enough that he had had to allow himself to be carried for the last two days, although Carlos had shown great restraint in not saying I told you so.

And then he was on his feet again, and Cordelia was in his arms, and he felt as though he could have ridden another hundred miles for the joy of this moment.

"Donal! You look awful, you look terrible! Carlos, why did you let him come? Men never did have a grain of sense! I swear that all the men in the world don't have as much sense as any single, lone woman! And that beard, that damned beard, that's got to go, even if it does help hide how thin your face is! Donal, if you hadn't come, I couldn't have borne it!"

Donal Frederick came racing toward them, his face alight. "They ain't caught Coacoochee yet!" he crowed. "He's still loose, an' still fightin', an' they ain't never gonna catch 'im! I know, 'cause Peter came over two days' ago and told us. I'm glad you're home, Father. Let me help you, you can lean on me."

Second place was better than none, Donal thought wryly as he ruffled his son's hair. A few months ago, Donal Frederick probably wouldn't have remembered to tell him that he was glad he was home. Supported on one side by Cordelia and the other by Donal Frederick, the long distance to the house was covered, but, then, to his humiliation, he found that the task of mounting the steps was too much for him and he had to submit to being lifted and carried by two of the slaves.

His recuperation took longer than he had expected. The journey had depleted his strength to a dangerous level. All the same, he didn't regret having come, he only fretted and fumed at the delay in setting out to deal with Andrew Leyland and then to take Cordelia and Donal Frederick, at last, home to England. Even he conceded that there was no longer any need for him to remain in Florida. There were more than enough scouts to go around now that Wildcat had so few fighting men left, now that the end was inevitable.

They were discussing his plans over dinner, now that he was well enough at last to set his plans in motion. So well, in fact, that last night Cordelia had almost sent him into a relapse again as she had lifted him to heights of ecstasy that had threatened to kill him. When he thought how alarmed he had been when he'd known that Peter Breckenridge was recuperating from his own wounds at Solopi Heni, how jealous he had been, he was torn between laughter and shame. Peter would find a woman of his own in good time, but Cordelia was his, and she never let a night go by without proving it to him beyond any doubt.

But now they were arguing again, an argument that threatened to develop into another of their full-scale battles. Donal wanted to make the journey to Leyland's Landing alone, and return for her after he had put an end to any threat from her father once and for all. Cordelia's eyes blazed as she faced him down.

"If you think I'm going to let you leave me behind, you'd better think again! There's no way I'm going to stay here. Besides, I want to tell my father just what I think of him! It's my right, and neither you or any other man in the world is going to stop me!"

"Carlos, can't you talk some sense into her head? I want her here, safe with you."

"But I'm not going to be here," Carlos said blandly. He took another puff of his Havana cigar, rolling the smoke in his mouth before he blew a perfect smoke ring, and then another, as though that were the most important thing on his mind at the moment. "I'm

Heaven's Horizon

going with you, of course. There's no telling what you'll run into at Leyland's Landing. That man is dangerous, Donal, as you have reason to know. And you aren't as able-bodied as you think you are. I'm going with you, and we're taking a dozen well-armed men with us, because I'm damned if I'm going to let you walk into a death trap after all the trouble I've gone through to get you and Cordelia together again. If anything happened to you at this stage of the game, she'd never forgive me, to say nothing of that fire-eating Scot, your stepfather. Duncan MacKenzie would probably make the voyage to America for the sole purpose of shooting me. And if he didn't, Cordelia would no doubt cut my head off some night while I'm sleeping."

"There, you see! I have to go with you! Or do you want me to stay here and have Peter come to visit me every day? I'd be in sore need of comforting, and I'm sure he'd be only too glad to supply it!"

Delores appeared in the doorway, smiling as she regarded her fiery charge. "Miss Cordelia, that isn't any way to talk. You know you'd never look at another man except your husband. And, Master Donal, you might as well give in. You know that Cordelia is going to go, you're only wasting your breath when you try to talk her out of it. I'm going too, in case you didn't know it. Master Carlos has said that I'm to go to England with you, and it would be foolish for you to have to come back here to pick me up after you've finished your business in Georgia. Master Carlos has already set me free, as long as I'm going to live all the rest of my life in England, so you can't order me around either, any more than you can your wife. We're going, and that's an end to it."

Donal threw his napkin on the table, and for a moment Cordelia thought that he was going to sweep the remaining dishes to the floor. But he controlled himself. In the face of Carlos and these two women, there wasn't a thing he could do and he knew it. And he admitted to himself, although he refused to admit it to any of them, that he was glad. Whatever the future held, he and Cordelia must face it together. There had been enough of separation, and they must never be separated again.

Chapter Twenty-seven

They arrived at the McCabe cabin in midafternoon, having made a wide detour around Leyland's Landing so that no word of their coming could possibly reach Andrew Leyland. Both Donal and Carlos had agreed that it was important to have Becky's and Nate's assurance that they would stand up in a court of law and testify that they'd seen Andrew shoot Donal in the back, and then drag him to the edge of the bottomless bog and roll him in, leaving him for dead when he'd heard their approach, certain that they hadn't seen anything that had transpired. Added to Donal's testimony, it was certain to bring a conviction, no matter how wealthy a landowner Andrew Leyland was.

Rufe saw them coming. A full-grown man now, he was in the corn patch, frowning with concentration as he made sure not to chop down any of the stalks that were thriving under the warm June sunlight. He was a giant of a man, his shoulders massive, but his face was still childlike in its innocence as he raised guileless eyes at their approach, eyes that widened with amazement and then with alarm when he saw two white strangers and a white lady and a dozen black men, all armed to the teeth, approach his cabin.

He didn't recognize Donal. It had been years since he had seen him, and if Donal hadn't seen his awkward movements and the utter concentration on his face as he performed his simple task, he would have thought that Becky had married again and that this must be her husband.

But it was Rufe, there was no doubt of it as he sprinted toward the cabin, his bare feet racing to its safety even as he shouted, "Maw, Paw, strangers a'comin'! Lots of 'em, an' they's all got guns!"

Donal urged Fox Fire forward. "Rufe, don't be afraid. It's me, and these are friends, we aren't going to hurt you."

If Rufe heard, he gave no indication of it as he grabbed up the ax that was stuck in a stump in the doorway, left there after Nate had chopped out some firewood. Holding the ax in both hands, his feet spread far apart, he turned to confront the invaders, ready to defend his home and family.

"Friendly cuss, isn't he?" Carlos said, his eyes smiling. "That will be the slow-witted one, I expect. God help us if he's the smart one!"

"Rufe's all right. He just doesn't know us." Even as Donal spoke, Etta stepped out of the cabin, shading her eyes against the sunlight after the dimness inside, and close on her heels Becky came out, holding Eben's shotgun pointed directly at them, her long, bright hair caught back by a string but as beautiful as Donal had remembered her. She was older but, like Cordelia, the years had not diminished her beauty, the backbreaking work of the clearing, the life of deprivation, had not yet taken their toll. Her curves were riper now, but her waist was still small and her legs, bare under the hem of her skirt, were slender and shapely.

From behind Donal and Carlos, Cordelia nudged Star Fire closer. Donal had wanted to leave her behind at the nearest settlement but she had insisted on coming. Nothing outside of an act of God was going to keep her from seeing the woman Donal had thought himself married to, the woman he had loved.

Her face paled a little when she saw how truly lovely Becky was,

Heaven's Horizon

and it was all she could do to fight that damnable tide of jealousy that rose in her, threatening to overwhelm her. She would *not* get off Star Fire and snatch that beautiful auburn hair right out of Becky's scalp, she would *not* claw that lovely face to ribbons. She would behave like a lady if it killed her. All the same, her fingers ached to do those very things, and she couldn't tear her eyes away from the girl who had had Donal for all those months, the girl who had shared not only his life but his bed.

Last of all, shuffling even in the face of Rufe's shouts that must have told him that there was an emergency, Eben came into view, squinting against the sunlight just as Etta was doing. Neither Etta nor Eben recognized Donal. Their faces were filled with fear and bewilderment. It was Becky who lowered the shotgun and snapped at Rufe to drop the ax.

"It's John!" she cried. She thrust the shotgun into her mother's hands and sped forward, her face alight with joy, only to come to a stop before she reached him, her face going white at the sight of Cordelia.

"You brought *her*!" Becky said, her voice filled with accusation. "It has to be her, she's your other wife!"

The agony in her eyes made Cordelia wince just as Donal was wincing. Impulsively, she slid off Star Fire and held out her hand. "I'm afraid I am, Becky," she said. "Not his other wife, but his only wife. I'm sorry, but I was married to him before he ever met you."

Becky's voice showed every grain of her despair. "How could he hev forgot you! Lord, I wish he'd never lost his memory! Only I ain't sorry, I ain't, 'cause I had him fer a little spell even iffen he did remember you finally, an' go off an' leave me, sayin' we wasn't married at all! I reckon I hate you, Cordelia Leyland MacKenzie." Her honesty somehow made it even harder to bear.

"I reckon I hate you a little, too," Cordelia answered. "But that's the way things are and nothing can change it, so we'll both just have to make the best of it."

"But you're the one that's got him!" Becky said. "We heered that you wuz dead. An' I hoped it wuz true, so's John, I mean

Lydia Lancaster

Donal, would come back to me, even iffen I knowed it wuz a sin to hope it. But he never did come back, he went off to England instead, and now he's here agin an' you're with him, and what in tarnation are the pack of you doin' here, with that stranger an' all them Nigras?"

"Becky, this is Señor DeHerrera, my friend. He was kind enough to come with us from Florida to make sure we got here safely and that I could settle with Andrew Leyland without danger to myself or Cordelia. And the lad is my son, Cordelia's and mine. His name is Donal Frederick," Donal told her. He was distinctly uncomfortable.

Thoroughly confused, Etta still remembered her manners. "Light down. I'll stir up some victuals, but I don't know how I'm gonna feed that passel of blacks."

"That won't be necessary, Mrs. McCabe." Carlos spoke for the first time, touched by this backwoods woman's dignity. "We have our own provisions, they can take care of themselves."

For the first time, Becky tore her eyes away from Donal and Cordelia, and they widened as she stared at Carlos. She had never seen a man like him before. Dressed in the softest, most costly buckskins, Carlos was an imposing figure, with his laughing eyes and black hair, with his startlingly blue eyes contrasting with his brown skin, with his crooked nose that hadn't healed properly, with his air of complete authority and of being a real gentleman in spite of his obvious foreignness. She couldn't take her eyes off him, and for a moment she didn't understand when Carlos went on to explain exactly why they were here, that he wanted her and Nate to testify against Andrew Leyland.

"Don't want Becky an' Nate gettin' mixed up in rich men's affairs," Eben said. "Don't want no rich men a'comin' to take revenge on us fer it. We mind our own business, all we want is to be left to ourselves, an' that's the truth of it."

"You'll be in no danger. That's why I'm here. When we're through with Andrew Leyland he'll be in no position to be a danger to anyone, I can promise you that."

Eben looked at Carlos, at his pistol, at his rifle, the likes of which he'd never own if he lived to be a hundred. He looked at the armed black men, every one of them tall and stalwart. "Still an' all, it ain't none of our affair an' I'd as lief we stayed out of it."

Carlos's eyes held Becky's. "But it's Miss McCabe who must give the final answer. She's of age, although she scarcely looks it, and it's her decision to make." Becky's face flamed, and she couldn't help preening a little. She knew she was comely, but she hadn't had a gentleman like Mr. DeHerrera tell her so before, only Donal, and a handful of backwoods louts whose opinion didn't matter anyhow.

Carlos pressed his advantage, not at all ashamed of the means he had used to get it. "I'm sure that Miss McCabe will do her duty, and from what I've heard of Nate, he'll also want to see justice served. You must realize that Donal and Cordelia will never be safe unless Andrew Leyland is settled with."

"He'll kill 'em fer sure?" Becky demanded.

"The first chance he gets. He'll leave no stone unturned to do them harm. So you see, I am convinced that you won't refuse."

"Reckon I won't," Becky said. "An' I reckon I kin speak fer Nate, too. He liked John, he wouldn't want to see him come to harm."

The inside of the cabin seemed even smaller and meaner than Donal had remembered it, but Carlos didn't seem to notice, he acted as though it was as fine a place as he was used to. His courtesy, his cultured voice, his genuine interest made themselves felt, so that even Etta relaxed and her hands stopped trembling as she mixed up a batch of cornbread to go with the ever-present kettle of stew.

"What can I do to help?" Cordelia wanted to know.

Becky looked at her, her eyes filled with scorn. "You'd dirty that fancy ridin' dress an' spoil yer pretty white hands," she said, her voice short.

"I didn't always wear a fancy riding habit. For more than a year I wore Seminole dresses, and my hands were rough and red from working. I pounded corn into meal, and sewed with a bone needle, and worked in the fields, weeding and hoeing, anything I could do to earn my keep among the Seminoles."

Becky's eyes widened, and she nearly dropped the bowls she was setting out. "You never! You lived with them savage Injuns, an' they didn't scalp you?"

"They were kind to me. They helped me when my son was born, and they treated me as one of their own. Two of them, just our age, were like my sisters, we still call ourselves sisters. I lived with them until Señor DeHerrera found me and took me to his plantation."

Becky's eyes went back to Carlos. "Is it a big place, his plantation?"

"Bigger than you can imagine. It's the biggest plantation I ever saw or even dreamed of."

"And he has slaves? More'n what he brung with him now?"

"He has almost too many to count! And he's kind to them, they're never mistreated, he even sets them free if their hearts are set on it. Carlos is the kindest man I've ever known."

"What's his house like?" In spite of her antagonism for Cordelia, Becky couldn't control her curiosity.

"It's a mansion." Seeing that Becky didn't understand, Cordelia explained, "It's big, Becky. You could set this cabin down in his drawing room . . . his sitting room . . . and lose it. His dining room can seat twenty-four people at the table without crowding. There are twenty rooms in all, and all of them are large, and the furniture is beautiful, priceless. Ther are paintings on the walls and lovely carpets on the floors, and the house is always filled with flowers, kinds you've never seen and couldn't believe unless you'd seen them."

Becky's expression was one of bemused amazement. "Lordy, he must be the richest man on earth!" Instantly Cordelia was making and rejecting plans having to do with Becky's future, and Carlos's. There were possibilities, there were difficulties, but . . .

But the men were outside, talking, keeping out from under foot while the women prepared the meal. Carlos was showing interest in Eben's corn, making suggestions as though this small clearing was as important as any man's plantation. Donal was both amused and impressed at the way Carlos put Eben at ease.

"I'd do better, iffen I hed some real help. Nate's a good hand in the corn patch, but he's allers off runnin' his traplines, a-huntin' an' fishin', an' it won't be long till he's courtin' to boot, an' then I'll see even less o' him. Rufe tries, an' he's strong, but he has to be watched."

"We owe you something for your cooperation. I'll leave you one of my blacks, one who is knowledgeable about farming, if that would be acceptable to you as payment. Or if one of my blacks doesn't want to stay, I will buy one for you. It's little enough to do, considering what your daughter and your son are doing for us."

"A slave? I don't know as I want no truck with a slave. Ain't never had one an' never expected to. 'Sides, it's too much, slaves cost a heap o' money."

"The way I look at it, Mr. McCabe, if Donal hadn't, in all innocence, married your daughter, she would have married someone else long before now, and you would have had a strong son-in-law to help you. The least we can do is see that you are recompensed for the loss by providing you with some help now. And you'd be doing God's work by accepting, because you would see that your slave was well cared for, you'd treat him right, like a human being. Any slave would be grateful for having you for a master."

"I reckon you're right about that part. I'll think on it. I won't say yes an' I won't say no till I've thought on it."

"He'd be an added protection for your family," Carlos pointed out. "And with him to help you keep an eye on Rufe, a lot more could get done. You could clear more land, grow a larger crop. On second thought, I believe a married slave would be better. A woman would help Mrs. McCabe with her work, and be company for her as well. I'll have my blacks put up a separate cabin before we leave, for them to live in, if it's agreeable to you. You have all the logs on hand, just waiting for the trees to be felled and stripped."

Eben's head was reeling. "I allow as how it might be done. More trees here than a man has need fer, need to git rid o' some on 'em."

"A married man, then. Yes, I think you're right, a married man would be better. Married men are more content, they work harder and are more grateful for good treatment."

Donal had to turn away and pretend to study a squirrel that was scampering up a nearby tree so that Eben wouldn't see the laughter bubbling in his eyes. By the time Carlos got through, Eben would think that this was all his own idea and that it was no more than he was entitled to. Donal fully intended to buy the two slaves himself, however.

Nate returned from his hunting, taller than Eben, nearly as tall as Donal. He had the lithe stature of a woodsman, the same keen eyes, the same noncommittal expression. But he was glad to see Donal, and he readily agreed that he would swear to what he had seen. After that, he scarcely said a word, scarcely seemed to realize that he was eating the meal that the women had prepared, as he never took his eyes off Cordelia's face. Cordelia had made a conquest, and Donal could only hope that seeing her wouldn't spoil all other girls for him.

"We'll set out for the nearest settlement where they have any law tomorrow morning, then. With you permission, Mr. McCabe, Rebecca and Nathan will go with us, to give their testimony so that a legal warrant can be sworn out for Andrew Leyland's arrest. It must all be accomplished legally, with whoever is in authority accompanying us to Leyland's Landing to place Mr. Leyland in custody," Carlos said. "Mrs. McCabe, that was a fine meal, I've seldom had a finer. I thank you for your kindness, it was a treat to have a home-cooked meal after so long a time traveling in the wilderness."

Becky's face flushed. "I don't hev nothin' fitten to wear to a town, to talk to law people. Cain't Nate go without me?"

"I'm afraid he can't. It would be better if you both went." Carlos frowned, and then looked at Cordelia. "But Mrs. MacKenzie can lend you something."

Cordelia bit down on her lower lip. It wasn't enough that this girl, this disturbingly lovely backwoods girl, had taken Donal from her, had shared his bed, had passed herself off as his wife, but now she must lend her her own clothing! Immediately, she felt ashamed of herself. Becky had so little, and she'd been robbed of the most important thing of all, of Donal and Donal's love.

"I have a green riding habit that will be perfect with your hair," she told Becky. "And anything else you might need. I'll be happy to give them to you, if you'll accept them."

Heaven's Horizon

"Lendin' will be fine. I don't need them give to me," Becky retorted, her eyes flashing. "Won't never hev no use fer a ridin' habit arter you've gone nohow." But that was before she saw the riding habit, before Cordelia shook it out and she touched the soft cut velvet, drank in the beauty of the cut and color. Her heart was in her eyes even though she fought to hold on to her refusal of charity.

"Of course you must have it. It will become you better than it does me," Cordelia said. "And look, here's a dress you can wear in town, and you must keep that too, Carlos has been far too generous with me. We'll go through everything and find what will look best on you and you shall have them, as an expression of my gratitude for saving Donal's life."

"I never saved him fer you," Becky muttered. "I saved him fer myself. I took one look at him an' I knowed I hed to hev him." She met Cordelia's eyes, and her own were honest. "I lied my head off, makin' up stories so's he'd think he didn't hev nobody, that there wasn't no reason he shouldn't stay with me. An' I went on a-lyin'. cause I couldn't stand it iffen he left."

It cost her a lot to make that admission, and Cordelia knew it. "But he did remember." She took a breath and made her voice gentle. "In your place I might have done the same thing. I can't blame you for loving him. I love him too."

And it cost Cordelia something to say that. Inside, she was still disturbed that Becky should wear her things. Why couldn't she learn human kindness, human compassion! How ashamed Miss Virginia Baker would be of her! She added still another dress, and riding boots and slippers, and underclothing as well. Let them help Becky catch another man! And there was no doubt that they would, because she would be entrancing in them. She'd just better not be so entrancing that Donal would notice how lovely she was!

Turning away from the trunk she had been rummaging through, she caught Carlos's laughing eyes on her face. Drat the man! He knew what she was thinking. She glared at him, and then smiled her sweetest smile.

"We'll buy some things for your mother while we're in town, as well. She was kind to Donal too, and she deserves some nice things." And she'd let Carlos pay for them, and she'd pick out the most expensive, and it would serve him right! Not that he would care. It would give him pleasure to pay for anything she chose, there just wasn't any way a woman could get back at a man like Carlos.

She had no way of knowing what Becky was thinking, and she would have found it hard to believe if she had. Becky's first impulse had been to throw all of these lovely things right back in Cordelia's face, to tell her that she wasn't about to accept her charity, she'd go to town ragged and barefoot first.

But then Becky caught sight of Carlos, and she wondered what he would think when he saw her in this riding habit, with her hair freshly washed and shining like the sun had set it on fire, and what he would think when he saw her in that dimity dress, with the satin ribbon hitched close right under her breasts to show them off as they all but spilled out of that indecent neckline!

Carlos fascinated her. Yesterday, she would have sworn that no man could ever take her fancy as Donal had done, but now she couldn't keep either her mind or her eyes off this man who was so different from any other she had ever seen. She couldn't help wondering what kind of lover he'd be, and just thinking it made hot desire flood through her body, too long starved for the love of a man.

She knew that she'd never stand a chance with a man like Carlos DeHerrera. What an outlandish name! Unlettered, ragged, barefoot, she must seem as strange to him as he was to her. But with clothes like these, and if she watched the way she talked, if she tried to talk like Cordelia did, he might look at her. She knew she was pretty enough for any man, if the way men looked at her didn't prove it, the jealousy in Cordelia's eyes proved it without any doubt. Being a woman, Becky knew what other women were thinking, and she knew that she was pretty enough to have set Cordelia right back on her heels.

So she gave in, even if it was grudgingly. "All right, then. Guess I got no choice. I wouldn't want to be disgracin' you, not lookin' right. If you'll excuse me, I'm goin' down to the creek an' wash my hair." And all over as well, she was going to be clean as spring rain before she put on any of these clothes, and if Carlos DeHerrera didn't look at her then, she'd just figure that there was something wrong with him and she wouldn't be missing much if he didn't look at her.

She looked fresh and radiant when she returned, so radiant that Cordelia felt jealousy flooding over her again. No wonder Donal had loved her, no wonder he'd gone through a form of marriage with her! How often did he still think of her, how often, when he smiled in his sleep, was he dreaming of her? And now that he'd seen her again, seen her like this, bright and shining, with sexual allure simply flowing from her body, how often would he think of her again?

Etta was mentally arranging sleeping places for them. "You and John, I mean you and Mr. MacKenzie, it's still hard for me to think of him as anythin' but John, kin take Becky's room. Becky kin make do in the loft tonight."

Cordelia's face flamed. Sleep in the bed that Donal and Becky had shared, in the second cabin Donal had built for them? And across the cabin, Becky's face was just as hot. She didn't want Cordelia in her bed any more than Cordelia wanted to be in it.

"That isn't necessary. We have everything we need, and we're used to sleeping out. We've done it all the way from Solopi Heni. Donal, it's time we were settling in for the night, if we're to make an early start tomorrow," Cordelia said.

Donal's face, too, was red with embarrassment, and he rose with alacrity. "D.F., come along, you'll see Nate again in the morning." For the past two hours, Donal Frederick had stuck to Nate like a shadow, fascinated by Nate's accounts of his life as a woods runner. Too shy to talk to the others, too enthralled by Cordelia's beauty, Nate had taken refuge in Donal Frederick's company so that he could ignore Donal and Cordelia.

Donal Frederick understood only a little of what was going on. Cordelia and Donal had debated on leaving him at the settlement in Delores's care, where the black woman had been persuaded to rest in a real room, with a real bed, while the others went on to the McCabes. Delores had borne up well under the rigors of the long journey, but she herself was quick to admit that it had been just a little more than she had bargained for. Not an experienced rider, she'd taken to one of the two wagons for the better part of the trip, and every bone in her body felt as if it had been dislodged from all the jolting.

But in the end, Donal and Cordelia had decided that Donal Frederick should see how backwoods people lived, and that anything he heard would only be what he was entitled to know. He was an intelligent boy, and he could handle it, and wondering what it was all about could do him more harm than knowing the truth.

Rolled up in their blankets a discreet distance from the rest of their party, with the memory of Carlos's amused smile still fresh in their minds, Cordelia turned her back on Donal and didn't speak once they were settled.

"Cordie, don't be like that! I wouldn't have come here at all if we didn't need Becky and Nate to testify. You know that, you know Becky doesn't mean a thing to me!"

"But she did mean something to you, she meant a whole lot, she meant so much to you that you married her! And you still mean something to her, a blind person could see that!"

"Women!" Donal said, baffled. And he too turned his back, too disgruntled to sleep for another hour. Women were the very devil. He couldn't help it if Becky was still beautiful, could he? Wouldn't Cordie ever forget what had happened during those months when he'd had no memory, was she going to hold it against him all the rest of his life?

All the same, it was astonishing how Becky had kept her attractiveness, living the life she did. He supposed he couldn't blame Cordelia for being jealous. He'd have to watch his step until this was over with, or the fur would fly. From what he'd seen, both women were ready to scratch each other's eyes out, and if there was anything he didn't need it was that.

And if Carlos grins once more, he thought, I'm going to punch him right in the teeth!

Andrew Leyland turned his horse toward the house when he heard the bell ring, announcing a visitor. It had been so long since he'd

Heaven's Horizon

heard the bell that summoned the master to the house that for a moment he was bemused, not remembering what it meant. But he had to answer its summons. It must be important, or Selma, who did both the cooking and what housework there was to be done these days, wouldn't have dared to ring it.

The fields were a sorry sight this year. He didn't have enough slaves left to cultivate them properly. In spite of being known as a wealthy man, Andrew was all but impoverished, barely eking out from one crop to the next, and each crop was smaller and of poorer quality than the last.

It wasn't unusual for planters to be short of cash between crops. It was their way of life. But Andrew had spent all he had, much more than he could afford, in his frenzied efforts to locate his daughter. All those agents, forever watching the ports, the agent he'd posted in England to keep watch on the MacKenzies' home, had cost him far more than he could spare. He'd sold off acreage to get the cash to continue his search, he'd sold off a good many of his slaves, until there were so few left that there was no way Leyland's Landing could go except downhill.

Now, he no longer cared. Cordelia was dead, he was convinced of that, she'd been dead for years, and although Donal had escaped with his life, by the ironic twist of fate that had allowed those cracker children to find him and pull him from the bog, at least no blood of Donal's would ever taint his own bloodline.

The empire he'd been intent on building was dust in his mouth. He had no children to inherit and carry it on. And so he lived in self-imposed exile from his fellowmen, he lived with his bitter memories and his constant physical pain, and he would welcome death when it came rather than fear it.

He rode slowly, easing himself in the saddle, squinting his eyes against the late afternoon sunlight when he came within sight of the house. Then he drew his horse to a stop, his back stiffening, as he saw that his yard was filled with horses, that a dozen or more black men had dismounted and were deployed at vantage point, all of them cradling rifles in their arms. Slaves, armed with rifles!

There were four white men with the party of blacks, their own eyes narrowed, their hands near their pistols. He knew one of them, it was Michael Towndson, from Greenleigh, the nearest settlement of any size. Towndson was assistant to the marshal, but what the devil was he doing here, with a body of armed blacks, when it was against every law for any black man to be armed?

With a feeling of fate closing in on him, he recognized another of the white men. It was Donal MacKenzie, there was no doubt about it, that face was etched in his memory so that even acid couldn't erase it. Donal MacKenzie, come for his final retribution! The armed men, the very way they were looking at him, told him that.

There was no place to run even if he had had the chance; crippled as he was, he wouldn't have got a quarter of a mile before they overtook him. And there was no point in running, even if his pride would have permitted it. Donal had no proof, only his own word against Andrew's.

Towndson stepped forward, his face showing his discomfort. "Mr. Leyland? I'm sorry to have to tell you that you are under arrest and you will have to accompany me to Greenleigh to await trial for attempted murder."

"You have a proper warrant?" Andrew's voice held contempt.

"I do, Mr. Leyland. Charges have been entered against you, all legal and in order. Two eyewitnesses have signed their names, as well as Mr. MacKenzie."

With a feeling of despair, Andrew realized who one of the other men must be, the cracker boy, grown into a man, who with his sister had saved Donal's life. For a brief instant, he contemplated going for his pistol.

"I wouldn't do it, Mr. Leyland. My pistol is aimed right between your eyes, and I haven't missed an easy shot like this since I was eight years old." The voice was offhand, amused, but Andrew did not make the mistake of taking it lightly because the fourth man in the party meant exactly what he said.

"I suggest that you drop your pistol, and then dismount so that Mr. Towndson can show you the warrant, and then we will ask you to come with us so that we can get this over with." Carlos's voice was still soft, but Andrew heard the steel underneath the softness.

Heaven's Horizon

He did as he had been told. It was difficult for him to dismount, and he was more angry at having to show his weakness to these men than he was at being taken in such an ignominious fashion. His face tight to hide his pain, he walked toward them, his hands in the air.

"There are a few things I would like to take with me, if you will permit me to enter my office and get them."

"Permission granted. Every exit will be covered." Carlos made a signal with his hand, and his black men deployed, surrounding the house on all sides. Towndson was mightily glad that this Señor DeHerrera was with him, and just as glad that no white man in the county would ever know that he had been in charge of a band of armed slaves to take a white planter. He'd be run not only out of the county but out of the state, no matter how guilty Andrew Leyland was. All the same, Carlos DeHerrera was a good man to have on your side.

Carlos went on speaking in a conversational tone. "You needn't worry about your plantation while you're absent. I will leave one of my men, an experienced overseer, to manage it until after your trial, and at that time Mr. MacKenzie will arrange to have it properly managed in case you live long enough, in prison, to return. I have no doubt that you will find it in better condition than you left it."

It was over, and oddly it brought Andrew a sense of relief, a relief that was shattered when Donal spoke for the first time.

"You have the right to know that I found Cordelia. And that she is here, in town, along with our son."

For a moment the shock of Donal's words held Andrew immobile. Then he nodded, an almost imperceptible gesture. He had a grandson, and the blood of his enemy flowed in the boy's veins.

"I will not be long," he said. "If you will excuse me, gentlemen?"

He entered his house for the last time, careful not to brush against the black man who guarded his door. He walked into his office and stood there for a moment, and then he crossed to his desk, where he always kept an extra, loaded pistol.

Slowly, but without any trembling of his hand, he took the pistol from the drawer. Slowly, he raised it to his head and pulled the trigger. For Andrew Leyland there would be no public trial, no public disgrace, there would be only the oblivion that was all he had left to long for.

Chapter Twenty-eight

Cordelia rose from her knees, her eyes filled with the tears she had shed but with a feeling of peace in her heart. Zoe's grave, the last of the graves in the place allotted to the slaves, was covered with flowers, every weed had been removed under her own careful supervision. She'd pulled some of them herself, wanting to do this last thing for the woman who had been a second mother to her.

Footsteps were approaching, and she turned and forced a smile as she saw Donal approaching her, his face filled with concern.

"I'm all right, darling. She knows I'm here. I feel that she knows it, and that she's happy."

Her first grief when she'd learned that Zoe hadn't lived to see her return was abated now. What was done was done and there was no way to change it. At least she knew that Zoe had spent her last years in comfort, that her father had no longer locked her up at night, or interfered with her in any way. The fact that he simply hadn't cared anymore didn't detract from Zoe's peaceful life, sitting in the kitchen with Selma, well fed and well cared for because Selma had loved the old woman.

Lydia Lancaster

Donal reached out to gather her in his arms, but he couldn't resist saying, "Did you tell her about Runt's two wives, if you're so sure she heard you talking to her up there in heaven?"

"Of course I did! Only she knew already. I'm sure she knows. Zoe was special, she knew things that other people didn't know. And she was so filled with love. Love like that doesn't die, Donal. It can't. I just know that she knows about Runt, and that she's happy that he has two wives he cares for and that he's a father."

They talked about Runt often. They knew that he would never give up the fight until Wildcat surrendered, and Coacoochee had as yet shown no signs that he was ready to give up. Carlos had told them that if Wildcat ever did capitulate and allow himself to be exiled, Weleka and Wacassa would follow him, but that Runt and a handful of others would elude the net and go on living in the Everglades, unmolested because no one would want that land and there would be too few of them to pose any danger to the whites. Runt's fierce heart would never allow him to accept exile or to live in any kind of slavery. Donal had already made out emancipation papers for him, to be entrusted to Carlos, who would see that he got the proof of his freedom when the time came that he might need it. Now that Andrew Leyland was dead, the plantation belonged to Donal, along with all the slaves that Andrew had owned, and that included Runt.

Cordelia had been furious when Donal and Carlos had refused to allow her to accompany them to Leyland's Landing to confront her father. Now she was glad that she had not been here. The shock of her father's suicide had been severe, leaving her somehow feeling empty and cold. She had not loved him, she had never loved him because even when she'd been a child he had been distant and cold, but still there was a feeling of emptiness when your father died, no matter how much you had come to hate him.

She had stood dry-eyed during Andrew's funeral, conducted here at Leyland's Landing. It seemed a desecration to lay him beside Lorelei, whom he had caused so much grief, but conventions must be observed and her mother would have wanted it that way, her mother had loved him.

Heaven's Horizon

And strangely, after her father's funeral, the bitterness she'd felt toward him had abated. He had looked old and shrunken in his casket, his once jet black hair had turned almost entirely gray, and in death the harsh lines of his face had softened. She remembered what her mother and Zoe had told her about him when he had been young, that he had been handsome and gay, always laughing, loved by his family and friends alike. And she pitied him for the man he had become, filled with the agonizing pain that had blighted his life and twisted it.

She and Donal walked back to the house hand in hand, where Carlos was having a conference with Tom, the experienced, dependable slave he was leaving in charge of Leyland's Landing until the agent he'd appointed in Greenleigh had sold the place. Seven of the remaining slaves at the plantation had elected to go to Florida with him, jubilant at the prospect of belonging to a man who had already earned their respect. One of them, a young man of twenty, had accepted Carlos's offer of freedom. The others, older men, had chosen to stay, trusting that their new master would be kind. There were only a few female slaves. In these later years Andrew had culled them out, selling them off to raise the money he so desperately needed. A man in his thirties, strong and intelligent, with his wife and a boy of ten, had agreed to take his family and live with the McCabes, glad to accept the challenge of helping to a small holding on its feet.

Becky was also at the house, ready to ride back to town with Cordelia and Donal while Carlos stayed on until nightfall, making sure that everything was in order. Cordelia and Delores and Becky had attacked the house like a whirlwind, making the men look at them with something akin to awe, as they had made sure that every window sparkled, every floor was polished, restoring it as far as possible to the condition that Lorelei had kept it. "Mama would be ashamed to have prospective buyers see it the way we found it," Cordelia had told Donal. "I'm doing it for her."

It was a caution how Cordelia and Becky got along these days. For a while there, he'd been afraid that they'd end up clawing and scratching like two cats fighting over the same mouse. To see them now, you'd think that they were the best of friends, and this unfathomable wife of his had insisted on keeping Becky with her until they should leave for Savannah to board a coastal schooner that would take them to Boston, as neither he nor Cordelia could bear to go on to England without seeing the Reynards and Miss Virginia Baker, people to whom they owed so much.

Now that the house was in order, there was nothing further to delay their departure. Cordelia had chosen the few things from the house that she wanted to take with her, a miniature of her mother, sweet-faced and done when she had been sixteen, a crystal vase she had brought from her home in Virginia, Zoe's dog-eared Bible, worn from much handling even though Zoe hadn't been able to read it, and tearstained now after Cordelia had wept over it.

Donal Frederick came racing to meet them. "Hey, I'm not ridin' in with you, I'm stayin' with Uncle Carlos!" he shouted.

They smiled and nodded that he might. They both knew how hard it was going to be for their son to say good-bye to Carlos. But on the other hand, Carlos painted brilliantly colored word pictures of England to him, talking as if he'd been there himself and knew just how it would be.

"You'll be a hero among the boys there, their eyes will bug out when you tell them how you were born in a Seminole istihapo, and how Wildcat himself gave you his own name, Coacoochee. You won't have time to miss Florida. You'll like school. You'll shine at sports, and be the best rider in your class, and the best at handling firearms. And what boy among them will ever have helped skin an alligator?"

Little by little Donal Frederick had come to believe him. All the same, he wanted to spend every remaining moment with Carlos.

Donal's breath caught when Becky stepped from the house. Lord, but she was beautiful in that green riding habit that Cordelia had given her. In the three weeks that had passed after Andrew Leyland's suicide, Becky had undergone a transformation. She'd always been lovely, but this new Becky was a creature of Cordelia's creation, as Delores taught her how to pile her hair on top of her head in intricate swirls, how to walk and stand and sit properly, as Cordelia worked

Heaven's Horizon

on her grammar. At first glance, anyone would take her for a lady, and here was Cordelia, looking like a cat that had lapped up a forbidden bowl of cream, and what was going on in her mind he didn't know and he wasn't sure that he wanted to.

Now, to his additonal chagrin and bewilderment, Cordelia went directly with Becky to Becky's room at the inn. "Find yourself something to do, darling. Becky and I are going to be busy until dinnertime. Make sure that the innkeeper prepares something special."

He would have been even more bemused if he could have heard the conversation that went on behind Becky's closed door, as Becky turned around and around, preening herself in the green-sprigged dress that Cordelia had given her and that Becky was going to wear to dinner tonight as soon as Carlos arrived.

Becky's face was flushed with excitement as she smoothed the dress over her hips. Lands, it was downright indecent, the neckline was so low she was spilling right out of it but she wouldn't have taken it off for all the tea in China. She'd never known she could look like this, and it was hard for her to believe it now.

"You're sure you're sure?" Becky asked Cordelia.

"I'm sure I'm sure. More than three months along, I expect. I've had a time of it, I can tell you, holding back my morning sickness so Donal wouldn't guess. He'd never have let me come if he'd known, he'd have insisted that I stay at Solopi Heni, coddled and pampered. Men just don't realize how tough women are!"

Becky grinned. "For certain they don't. They'll stand right there and watch a woman seven months' gone splittin' wood, an' still think she'd weak an' helpless an' couldn't get along without them. But it's about time you had another young'un, with Donal Frederick already half growed. You'll hev...have...to make up for lost time. Tell me more about Señor DeHerrera's plantation. What in tunket does he need with all those rooms?"

"Well, when he has a party, a lot of people have to stay overnight or even for several days, so there are a good dozen bedrooms. And there's a library and the drawing room, and a small sitting room for the lady of the house, and Carlos's office, and a ballroom, and the formal dining room and a small dining room for when there aren't any guests. All of the rooms get used, there aren't really too many."

"And you're sure he doesn't have a woman, one you might not know about, even? Doesn't seem natural, fer...for...a man like him not to have a woman."

"I can't say about that. I don't know what goes on when he goes to Saint Augustine alone, or to Tallahassee, or other places. I only know there isn't any special woman because he's a confirmed bachelor, and it's a pity because he'd make some woman a wonderful husband."

Wouldn't he just! Becky thought. She liked that funny face of his, and that crooked nose, and the way his eyes crinkled up when he laughed. She liked everything about him, and she couldn't care less if he was half Seminole Indian. He was a real man, and it didn't hurt a mite that he was rich, too. But she would have liked him even if he wasn't rich. A man like that, who laughed a lot, who was kind and considerate and sure of himself, would be worth having if he was as poor as Pa.

"You're sure this neckline isn't too low?" Becky twisted, trying to get the full effect.

"I'm sure. It's the way they're being worn. You look lovely, Becky. The men's eyes will pop right out of their heads when they see you."

"I know Ma's would. Likely she'd take a stick of kindlin' wood to my backside for all I'm a woman growed. Grown," she corrected herself, touching her earlobes tenderly. They still hurt, but she didn't care. Delores had pierced them for her last week, stuck a needle right through them and then stuck in little gold earrings so's the holes wouldn't close up again. Pierced ears! Ma would fall over when she found out. "Do you think I've healed up enough so's I kin borrow those purty green earrings fer...for...tonight? They'd go right pretty with this dress."

Pretty green earrings! Cordelia bit back her laughter. Well, emeralds were pretty, and it was just as well that Becky didn't know that they were worth a fortune or she would refuse to borrow them. "I'm sure they have. I'll get them now, you won't have any trouble. We want to be our most beautiful, this last night we'll be together."

She paused at the door, and her eyes were laughing. "Go get him, Becky! Don't take no for an answer. Carlos doesn't know what's good for him, but we do, and you're it. I wish you luck!"

"I'm gonna do my darndest," Becky said. Cordelia had an idea that this time Carlos DeHerrera had met his match, and if she had anything to do with it she was going to push them into each other's arms. Becky would be a good wife for Carlos, she was intelligent as well as beautiful, a woman he could be proud of.

But all of their scheming came to nothing. Carlos was clearly bemused by Becky, his eyes seldom left her face and there was a longing in them that made Cordelia's heart contract with hope, but even after she had spirited Donal out for a walk after dinner and Delores had swept Donal Frederick off to her own room despite his protests, Carlos was too wary to be caught in such a trap. He was so close to doing something foolish, like asking this enchanting creature to marry him, that he determined to wind up his business here in Florida and set out for Florida the day after Donal, Cordelia and Donal Frederick boarded the coastal schooner for Boston.

"Dang him!" Becky exploded to Cordelia. "He was right on the point of askin' me, an' then he changed his mind! All the same, I'm not a-gonna give up. He's fixin' to pull out an' hightail it fer home, but he ain't gonna git away with it! Do you think you could let me have a horse? There's still some at Leyland's Landin'."

"You aren't thinking of following him! He'd only send you back."

"Not me, he won't. I don't aim to let him know I'm a-followin' him till it'll be too late fer him to send me back! A party that size, I could follow their track with my eyes closed!"

Donal had entered their room unheard, just in time to hear that last.

"Now just what is all this? Becky, you are out of your mind! It would be dangerous, there's no way I could allow you to set off alone to try to catch up with Carlos."

"Nonsense," Cordelia said, perfectly calm. "Of course we'll let

Lydia Lancaster

her have a horse. And we'll send a slave with her. I'll talk to one of the ones who's agreed to go with Carlos, I'll have him say he changed his mind, and we'll see that both he and Becky are armed. If it doesn't work, if Carlos still sends her back, nothing will be lost, but we aren't going to give up without trying!"

"I won't enter into such a nefarious scheme. I think both of you have taken leave of your senses."

Cordelia looked at him, her eyes filling. She began to cry, and then she cried harder, her shoulders shaking, her tears giving way to a hysteria that Donal had no way of knowing wasn't genuine.

"Now look what you've done!" Becky screamed at him, going to put her arms around Cordelia. "It'll be all your fault if she loses her baby! Ain't that right, Delores? It ain't good fer her to cry like this, the condition she's in!"

"It certainly isn't. Mr. Donal, you'd better give in. If you don't, Miss Cordelia will be upset all the way to Boston and I couldn't answer to the consequences." The little minx, Delores thought, suppressing her laughter. Upset, indeed!

Donal's face turned such an alarming shade of red that for a moment all three women thought they had gone too far. "You're pregnant?" he demanded of Cordelia. "You're pregnant, and you didn't tell me? I ought to shake your teeth loose! What if you'd lost the baby on the trail? You had no business making such a journey!"

"You keep on like that, an' she will lose it! Ain't that right, Delores?"

"That's right. Go on, shoo yourself out of here and let Becky and me get her calmed down. You can make yourself useful by doing what Miss Cordelia wants while you're gone. See about a horse for Becky, and talk to that slave. And don't you go telling Señor DeHerrera any of this, you hear? That would really upset Miss Cordie, and it would be your fault if anything happened!"

Donal left, seething, wishing that he dared to refuse. Women! He already knew that he was beaten. Poor Carlos!

And then he grinned. Poor Carlos, my eye! Lucky Carlos, was more like it. Becky would make him one heck of a wife. She'd have her horse, and the slave to escort her, and if Carlos wriggled out of this one, then he was a better man than Donal thought he was.

Ten days later, as Becky knelt to cup her hands in a stream and raise them to her lips, drinking greedily, she screamed and nearly choked as a hand clamped on her shoulder.

"If you aren't a pretty sight!" Carlos said. "Look at the riding habit, all spattered with mud! And your hair has burrs in it."

"Dang you! You scairt me outa a year's growth! How'd you sneak up on us without us hearin' you, anyhow? How'd you know I was followin' you?"

"I've known for days," Carlos told her, his eyes filled with amusement. "You forget, I'm half Seminole."

"If you knowed, then why didn't you do somethin' about it? Why'd you let me go on makin' a fool of myself? I oughta claw your eyes out, that's what I oughta do!"

"Watch your grammar. Cordelia would be disappointed if she could hear how you've reverted. I didn't let you know because I wanted to see just how stubborn you are. No white girl who would turn back when the going got rough would make a suitable squaw. But we're getting into more dangerous territory now, so I thought it was time our little game came to an end."

"I ain't goin' back. There ain't no way you kin make me. I'd just set out again, and I'd find that Solopi Heni of yourn alone, iffen I hed to!"

"I think you would at that. But it won't be necessary. I've come to the conclusion that I'm going to make either the biggest mistake, or the best decision, of my life, and marry you. Cato, you rascal, get on up ahead. We're camped five miles down the trail, you can find it. I ought to cut your back to ribbons for lending yourself to this scheme, and if Donal MacKenzie were here I'd loosen a few of his teeth because he had to be the one who let you have those horses, I'll be bound."

"That's all you know! It was Cordelia talked him into it. And Cato didn't heve no druthers, he belongs to Donal an' he had to do as Donal tolt him, didn't he? Carlos, you said you wuz gonna marry up with me!"

As strong as he was, Carlos was almost knocked off his feet as Becky launched herself at him, her arms wrapped around his neck and her face so radiant that Carlos felt his heart constrict.

"You don't have to strangle me! Behave yourself." He swatted her posterior, hard enough to make her yelp, but Becky went right on clinging to him.

"I'll behave myself after I've learned to be a fine lady. Right now I'm only a woman who's finally caught her man."

She was a woman, there was no doubt of that. Carlos's blood turned to fire as her body pressed against his, as her lush mouth met his eagerly seeking one, as Cato scrambled back onto his horse and made tracks away from there, assured that he wouldn't be beaten because he already knew that Carlos never beat his slaves. Besides, his new master was going to be so busy for a spell that he wouldn't have time to think of punishing him, even if he would have. He was powerfully thankful that this part of the journey was over.

"You're out of your mind, you know that, don't you? I'm a half-breed, I never intended to marry."

"So our young-uns will hev just enough Seminole in them to give them some spice!" Becky said. "An' won't they be handsome! We'll be fightin' off girls who want to latch on to the boys, an' fightin' off boys who want to latch onto the girls, and it'll be right interestin'."

"To put it mildly, yes. Stop talking. Right at the moment I don't give a hang about anything that far in the future." He stopped her mouth in the most effective way he knew, with his own.

At the camp up ahead, the slaves waited patiently, and for a long time, before their master and their new mistress appeared. They were content, almost as content as Carlos and Becky were. If Carlos had felt a little shame-faced an hour ago at letting this woman change his mind about remaining a bachelor, that feeling was gone now, evaporated into thin air after the glory of their lovemaking. She was his woman, and he thanked whatever fate had led Cordelia to the istihapo where he had found her, a fate that had been directing him toward this time and this place as surely as if the stars had ordained it.

Heaven's Horizon

* * *

Nadine was still so beautiful that Cordelia's breath caught. She was a little more plump, but only enough to become her. Her hair was still like spun gold, her skin peaches and cream, her eyes as blue as sapphires.

She had three children, two boys, Emery and Frederick, and a fairy-child of a girl, the youngest, who looked exactly like her mother, while one of the boys was the image of Emery and the other the image of Frederick, although their names should have been reversed.

Emery was as self-satisfied, as smugly overbearing, as he had been when he had pursed Cordelia all those years ago. But Nadine obviously adored him, respecting him and looking up to him as the most intelligent, the most remarkable man in Boston. Emery was a wealthy man, an important man here on the East Coast, and Nadine was Boston's reigning queen among the young married element in their social circle.

"To think that you lived among the Indians! To think that you suffered all those hardships, while I was living in luxury! Cordie, I nearly died when Donal came to Boston and told us that you were lost, that he thought you were dead. It's unbelievable that so much could have happened to you, and that you survived it all!"

"That's because I'm a survivor," Cordelia told her, and Frederick Reynard smiled at her, nodding. Indeed she was, and he was as glad that she had survived as if she had been his own daughter.

"And now that it's all over, I wouldn't have missed it for the world," Cordelia went on. "I learned so much, it will always stay with me, and I can appreciate what I have now so much more. If I hadn't lost Donal for so long, I never would have known how much I love him, how lucky I am to have him again."

Donal Frederick was creating a small sensation of his own with young Emery and Frederick. "Maybe you know Latin, but I can talk Seminole! An' I'd like to see you kill an alligator by stickin' a pointed pole down its throat! An' I know Wildcat, I have his name, he gave it to me hisself, Coacoochee. I kin shoot a gun, an' use a bow an' arrow, an' find my way in forests and swamps, and you'd be lost in five minutes an' cryin' fer your mama!"

"Donal Frederick, that's enough. We all appreciate the things you know and the things you can do, but you will have to learn Latin too. And if Emery and Frederick had lived as you did, they'd no doubt be as good as you are at the things you know."

"Most assuredly they would," Emery said pompously. Looking at him, Cordelia had to stifle a giggle. He was definitely going to be a portly man in a few more years' time, and his hairline was receding. Not that any of those things mattered, but she could never, never have lived with him, with his overbearing ways. If Donal ever acted like that, she'd bring him down a peg so fast he wouldn't know what had hit him.

The next afternoon, Cordelia sat in Miss Virginia Baker's private parlor at the Academy for Young Ladies, drinking Virginia's excellent tea.

"Cordelia, I have had the most incredible letter from Señor DeHerrera. He wished me to travel to Solopi Heni, to spend at least a year with him and his bride, Rebecca, to polish her rough edges, so to speak, and to fill in the gaps in her education."

To travel, to board a coastal schooner, to live in Florida at that fabulous plantation, Solopi Heni! To have this opportunity to take a remarkable young woman in hand and fashion her into a legendary mistress for a legendary plantation! And more, to have the opportunity to learn about Florida, about plantation life, about the Seminoles, firsthand!

"You're going to do it, of course?" Cordelia asked. "You'll love it at Solopi Heni, there's no way I could describe it to you as it really is, and Carlos and Becky are wonderful people."

"Yes, I have made up my mind to accept the offer. Such an opportunity would never come again. I am no longer a young woman, and I'll be glad to turn this academy over to someone else. I would have wanted to retire very soon in any case. I'm afraid that I don't have the patience with empty-headed young geese that I used to have. So few of my young ladies want to think of anything except fashions and young gentlemen! You were an exception I will always

Heaven's Horizon

appreciate, my dear. It was a joy to teach you, and I expect that it will be just as much of a joy to teach Rebecca DeHerrera."

Cordelia placed her hand over Virginia's. "And after you have stayed at Solopi Heni for as long as you wish, you must visit us in England so that we can show you at first hand all those historical places you drummed into our heads when I was young. After you've spent months and months with us you can have your choice of staying in England or returning to Solopi Heni, or of coming back here to Boston. Unless"— and her eyes twinkled —"you decide to settle in Italy or the south of France or sunny Spain! Carlos will compensate you for your services so generously that I have no doubt ywu'll be able to afford to live wherever you wish. You must accept whatever he offers you, because I assure you he can afford it, and Donal and I owe you more than we can ever repay."

Virginia's head reeled. To see the Tower of London, to see Covent Gardens, to walk through Westminster Cathedral! Windsor Castle, London Bridge, Cheapside, Stratford-upon-Avon! The Haymarket, quaint country inns and cottages with thatched roofs, the changing of the guard!

All this, as well as the opportunity to make her remaining years useful, to fill a need! The color drained from Virginia's face as she remembered how she had hesitated over interfering in Cordelia's life, how she had trembled at the consequences if she had been found out! She didn't deserve all this, but she was going to take it, and savor it, and thank God every day that she had found the courage of her convictions, so that all this had subsequently come to pass.

Cordelia and Donal and Donal Frederick sailed three days' later. Lucy and Frederick, Nadine and Emery, as well as Virginia, saw them off. Nadine's tears were genuine as she kissed Cordelia good-bye, Lucy and Frederick's good wishes just as genuine. There was no fortune in the world as great as having good friends, Cordelia thought, her own throat tight with unshed tears.

She stood at the ship's rail as it sailed out of the harbor, her face turned forward now, toward the future, after her heartache at leaving everything she had ever known behind her. Donal's arm was around her, holding her close to his side, and Donal Frederick, standing at her other side, was so filled with excitement at the propect of the long sea voyage on a sailing ship that his face was flushed and his eyes were filled with eager anticipation.

Her husband, and her son, together, never to be separated again! And England ahead of her, filled with more than she could dream of. Cordelia would never forget the past. She would never forget the istihapo, and Weleka and Wacassa, Hilolo and Sam Brent and Stillipika and Little Acorn. She would never forget Carlos, or Becky, any more than she would forget Peter Breckenridge.

Donal had no idea that the amused smile on her face came from the fact that Carlos had written that Peter was seriously interested in another girl, that he was courting her, and that Cordelia's amusement stemmed from the fact that she had actually experienced a small pang of jealousy at learning about it! Was she so conceited, then, so self-centered, that she had to have the love of another man other than her Donal, just because Peter had loved her once? But the jealousy had lasted for only a moment, and then shame had filled her because of it, and a gladness that Peter was going to find his own happiness.

"Are you happy, darling? Are you as happy as I am?" Donal wanted to know.

Unashamed, uncaring about the gasps of shock from the other passengers who were lining the rail, Cordelia kissed him, full on the mouth, clinging to him with what amounted to pure wantonness. Let the other ladies blanch with horror, what did they know about grief and heartache and separation, what did they know of the joy of being complete and entirely happy after years of such storm that walking into the sunshine again had seemed an impossibility?

And then she turned her face toward England, as filled with eagerness as her son's.

Virginia Baker entered her academy, and called all of her young ladies together. She stood looking at them, and her back was very straight.

"Young ladies, it has not escaped my notice that at least a few of you greet each new day with eyes still heavy with sleep, with lagging steps and a deplorable lack of enthusiasm for what the day will bring. Wake up, wake up, and run to meet the day, because the world lies before you, filled with wonders as yet untold!''

Epilogue

Osceola was removed from Fort Marion in Florida to Fort Moultrie on Sullivan's Island, the most important harbor defense of Charleston, South Carolina.

He was afforded spacious and comfortable quarters, and allowed to move freely around the fort. Both of his wives were with him, to nurse him in the illness that was finally to cost him his life, and to bring him comfort in his declining health, when he spent, at the last, most of his time lying in front of the fireplace, his body bathed with perspiration as his fever worsened.

The artist George Catlin painted Osceola's portrait in prison shortly before Osceola died. Dressed as became the great leader he was, now a full chief, Osceola wore three silver gorgets around his neck, as well as a short string of beads and two long strings. His turban held a large black and white plume, and the shoulder band of his tunic was decorated with embroidered leaves and diamond-shaped designs. Catlin was greatly impressed with his dignity and regal bearing, and held himself fortunate to be considered as Osceola's friend.

Lydia Lancaster

When Osceola realized that he was about to die, he asked his wives to help him to dress in full regalia. He painted one side of his face and throat vermilion, and wore his hunting knife. Officers and their men alike at Fort Moultrie wept when he died. He was given a full military funeral, and buried near the main entrance of the fort. Mr. Patton, a gentleman from Charleston, donated a marble slab, inscribed as follows:

> OSCEOLA
> Patriot and Warrior
> Died at Fort Moultrie
> January 30, 1838

Coacoochee had learned well from the white men. As his followers dwindled, as hope was lost, again and again he promised that he would come in with his people and surrender. But his people were scattered, he said, and they were hungry. They needed supplies in order to regain their strength to make the journey to surrender.

Again and again, the supplies were granted, supplies that vanished along with Coacoochee and his followers as they used the goods to regain their strength, not to surrender but to carry on their fight against the white men who sought to exile them from their homeland.

But even a spirit as fierce as Coacoochee's could not go on fighting forever against odds so great. He surrendered at last to Colonel William J. Worth, in November of 1841.

Even in exile his spirit was far from broken. When he had trouble with the Creeks in Arkansas, he took his following of people and removed himself to Mexico, to set up a separate nation. This grandiose plan fell through, and eventually he returned to his reservation.

Little has been written of Coacoochee, but all those who knew him, all those who still remember his exploits, know one thing. Red or white, friend or enemy, Wildcat was a man.

Exciting Reading from *Valerie Sherwood*

___WILD WILLFUL LOVE (D30-368, $3.95)
This is the fiery sequel to RASH RECKLESS LOVE. She was once THE BUCCANEER'S LADY...but when beautiful, willful Imogene was tricked aboard ship bound for England, she vowed to forget Captain van Ryker, the dark-haired pirate who had filled her life and heart—only to banish her so cruelly. Somehow he would come to her again, and together they would soar to the heights of passion they first knew on the golden sands of a distant isle.

___BOLD BREATHLESS LOVE (D30-849, $3.95)
(In Canada 30-838, $4.95)

The surging saga of Imogene, a goddess of grace with riotous golden curls—and Verholst Van Rappard, her elegant idolator. They marry and he carries her of to America—not knowing that Imogene pines for a copper-haired Englishman who made her his on a distant isle and promised to return to her on the wings of love.

___RASH RECKLESS LOVE (D30-701, $3.95)
(In Canada 30-839, $4.95)

Valerie Sherwood's latest, the thrilling sequel to the million-copy bestseller BOLD BREATHLESS LOVE. Georgianna, the only daughter of Imogene, whom no man could gaze upon without yearning, was Fate's plaything...scorned when people thought her only a bondswoman's niece, courted as if she was a princess when Fortune made her a potential heiress.

___RICH RADIANT LOVE (A30-555, $3.95)
(In Canada A30-893, $4.95)

The thrilling conclusion to the saga that started with BOLD BREATHLESS LOVE, this book takes up the story of the glorious Georgiana, who must now learn her true identity and leave her husband, the swashbuckling Brett Danforth. Her adventures take her from an elegant Hudson River estate to the lush, danger-laden hills of her native Bermuda to the arms of a devil-may-care rogue.

Don't Miss These Other Fantastic Books By HELEN VAN SLYKE!

__ALWAYS IS NOT FOREVER
(A31-009, $3.50)
(In Canada A31-022, $4.50)

Lovely young Susan Langdon thought she knew what she was doing when she married world-famous concert pianist Richard Antonini. She knew about his many women conquests, about his celebrated close-knit family, his jet-paced world of dazzling glamor and glittering sophistication, and about his dedication to his career. Here is an unforgettably moving novel of a woman who took on more than she ever counted on when she surrendered to love.

__THE BEST PEOPLE
(A31-010, $3.50)
(In Canada A31-027, $4.50)

The best people are determined to keep their Park Avenue cooperative exclusive as ambitious young advertising executive Jim Cromwell finds when he tries to help his millionaire client get an apartment. In this struggle against prejudice, the arrogant facade of the beautiful people is ripped away to expose the corruption at its core.

__THE BEST PLACE TO BE
(A31-011, $3.50)
(In Canada A31-021, $4.50)

A NOVEL FOR EVERY WOMAN WHO HAS EVER LOVED. Sheila Callahan was still beautiful, still desirable, still loving and needing love—when suddenly, shockingly, she found herself alone. Her handsome husband had died, her grown children were living their separate and troubled lives, her married friends made her feel apart from them, and the men she met demanded the kind of woman she never wanted to be. Somehow Sheila had to start anew.

__THE HEART LISTENS
(A31-012, $3.50)
(In Canada A31-025, $4.50)

Scenes from a woman's life—the rich, sweeping saga of a gallant and glamorous woman, whose joys, sorrows and crises you will soon be sharing—the magnificent tale ranging from Boston of the roaring twenties through the deco-glamour of thirties' Manhattan to the glittering California of the seventies—spanning decades of personal triumph and tragedy, crisis and ecstasy.

__THE MIXED BLESSING
(A31-013, $3.50)
(In Canada A31-023, $4.50)

The sequel to THE HEART LISTENS, this is the story of beautiful young Toni Jenkins, the remarkable granddaughter of Elizabeth Quigley, the heroine of the first book, torn between her passion for the one man she desperately loved and loyalty to her family. Here is a novel that asks the most agonizing question that any woman will ever be called upon to answer.

Thrilling Reading from WARNER BOOKS

___**TO THOSE WHO DARE**
by Lydia Lancaster (D90-579, $2.95)
A saga of three women who flaunted the rules of protocol to obey the unwritten law of love. In a growing town on the Erie Canal, they dared to follow their dreams and choose love instead of prestige, passion instead of pride.

___**LOVE'S TENDER FURY** (D30-528, $3.95)
by Jennifer Wilde (In Canada 30-767, $4.95)
The turbulent story of an English beauty—sold at auction like a slave—who scandalized the New World by enslaving her masters. She would conquer them all—only if she could subdue the hot unruly passions of the heart.

___**DARE TO LOVE** (D30-590, $3.95)
by Jennifer Wilde (In Canada 30-753, $4.95)
Who dared to love Elena Lopez? She was the Queen of desire and the slave of passion, traveling the world—London, Paris, San Francisco— and taking love where she found it! Elena Lopez—the tantalizing, beautiful moth—dancing out of the shadows, warmed, lured and consumed by the heart's devouring flame.

The *BEST* of Romance from WARNER BOOKS

__NO GENTLE LOVE
by Rebecca Brandewyne (D30-619, $3.95)

She was a beauty, besieged by passion, sailing from Regency, England to mysterious Macao on an uncharted voyage to love. She was also unready to accept the love in her heart for the domineering, demanding man whose desire for her was jealous, violent, engulfing, but enduring.

__FOREVER MY LOVE
by Rebecca Brandewyne (D90-981, $2.95)

They were born to hatred, but destined to love. Echoing across the stormy waters of Loch Ness came a gypsy's haunting curse, foretelling a forbidden passion that would drench the Scottish crags with blood. And from the first moment that Mary Carmichael lifted her violet eyes to those of Hunter MacBeth, the prophecy began to come true. Theirs is a legend of struggle against relentless hate, of two wild hearts who pledged defiantly, FOREVER MY LOVE.

To order, use the coupon below. If you prefer to use your own stationery, please include complete title as well as book number and price. Allow 4 weeks for delivery.

WARNER BOOKS
P.O. Box 690
New York, N.Y. 10019

Please send me the books I have checked. I enclose a check or money order (not cash), plus 50¢ per order and 50¢ per copy to cover postage and handling.*

_____ Please send me your free mail order catalog. (If ordering only the catalog, include a large self-addressed, stamped envelope.)

Name _____

Address _____

City _____

State _____ Zip _____

*N Y State and California residents add applicable sales tax